Lancelot clamped a hand...

over Gwenhwyfar's mouth and pulled her back through the trees, holding her against him. "Don't scream. It's Lancelot. We're going home."

Wildly, she twisted to look at him. Her eyes were blank and he saw no recognition there. She began to struggle.

He gave her a little shake. "Gwen. Come to your senses. It's Lance. Arthur is waiting. We're leaving the land of Faerie."

Her eyes widened a little, but there was still fear.

"We've got to go. You have to come with me. You'll be safe."

She moved her head negatively and tried to pull away.

He spun her around quickly and kissed her before she had time to scream. She did not respond; nearly desperate, he cradled her head and prodded her mouth open with his thumbs, thrusting his tongue inside, letting her taste him. His arms moved around her and his hands kneaded her back. *Mother, Goddess, don't let me be too late. Not after all of this.* Then suddenly she was kissing him back, clinging to him, sobbing in the back of her throat. He leaned back a little, watching her.

"Lancelot!" She was crying now, her arms wound tightly around his neck. "It is you? I'm not living another illusion?"

"No, my love. But we must hurry." Already the sounds of fury behind them had begun to diminish. Lancelot took her hand and they began to run.

Fate of Camelot

Cynthia Breeding

Highland Press Publishing
Florida

Fate of Camelot

For information, please contact
Highland Press Publishing,
PO Box 2292, High Springs, FL 32655.
www.highlandpress.org

ISBN: 978-0-9815573-8-0

HIGHLAND PRESS PUBLISHING

Excalibur

ACKNOWLEDGEMENTS

Although this book is a work of fiction, it would have been impossible to lend any air of authenticity to the historic period without the facts I gleaned from the following non-fictional works.

I have not met any of these writers, but I owe each of them a heartfelt "thank you" for lending me insight of life in post-Roman Britain in the Sixth Century.

Barber, Chris & Pykitt, David:	Journey to Avalon
Baigent, Michael, Leigh, Richard, Lincoln, Henry:	Holy Blood, Holy Grail
Barber, Richard:	King Arthur: Hero and Legend
Berresford Ellis, Peter:	The Druids
Castleden, Rodney:	King Arthur: The Truth Behind the Legend
Dunning, R.W.:	Arthur: The King in the West
Gardner, Laurence:	Bloodline of the Holy Grail
Goodrich, Norma Lorre:	King Arthur, Guinevere
Karr, Phyllis Ann:	The Arthurian Companion
Markale, Jean:	King of the Celts
Snyder, Christopher:	King Arthur
Strobie, Denise:	Exploring King Arthur's Britain
Turner, P.F.J.:	The Real King Arthur: Volumes 1 & 2
Wood, Michael:	In Search of England

Arthur's Britain
Alclud
Dalriada
Lothian
Wall of Antoine
Joyous Garde
Wall of Hadrian
Luguvalium
Carbonek
Rheged
Cameliard
Diera
Eboracum
Deva
Lindum
Lleyn
Gwynedd
Powys
Demetia
Siluria
Gwent
Caerleon
Glevum
Aquae Sulis
Londinium
Ynys Wydryn
Camelot
Ambreshyrig
Calleva
Astolat
Durovernum
Lindinis
Venta
Tintagel
The Weald
Isca
Portus Adurni
Clausentum
Ictis Insula
Kernow
Armorica
Benoic

~ Prologue ~

The gloaming had settled early on the eve of All Hallows Day. The nave of the church at Glastonbury Abbey was dark and somber as the newly appointed bishop, Dubricius, emerged from the gloom of the chancel. He was about to step out the side door when the music stopped him. From where it was coming he didn't know, but it was more hauntingly beautiful than any choir he'd ever heard. The melody rose softly, a light sound of whispering and sighing on the wind. Even as he strained to hear, he caught the scent of apple blossoms.

A softly wavering light began to glow from the vestibule. As he watched, the flame grew stronger and he realized someone—no, two boys—were holding large candlesticks. A man walked in front of them carrying a spear, and an auburn-haired girl bearing a platter followed him. Weapons weren't allowed in the church and the young bishop started to call out and then stopped, his mouth dropping in amazement.

The golden-haired maiden at the end of the procession bore a chalice. He had a glimpse of silver and gold and then the cup began to glimmer with an unearthly glow until all was brilliant around it. The maiden became a silhouette as the beacon blazed with brightness illuminating the whole church. The bishop whimpered and covered his face, for the luminescence blinded him.

Then suddenly, the radiance was gone. When he lowered his hands, the nave was deserted; only one cool silver moonbeam slanted its way across the floor.

The story is old; I am older still. It is I who carries the chalice in the eternal procession toward Enlightenment. My name is Astrala, and I am the maiden sworn to protect what the Christians call the Holy Grail.

I find it strange that the Christians so readily accept the gifts of the Goddess, yet shun Her ways. On Samhain, that night just after Dubricius had been made a bishop, we scared him when all we meant was to make peace. But then, when the Romans took over the Church, much of the Christos' intent was stripped away. They made even the Procession false.

They mistook the spear of Lugh, the Shining One, for the spear of the Roman, Longinus, who pierced the Christos' side. The platter didn't catch blood from the spear as they say; it wasn't a platter at all, but the flat stone of destiny called the *Lia Fail.* That stone would set the Wheel of Fate spinning for Camelot. The blessings of Belanos gave the candles that great fiery blaze; the fire of which would forge the sword of Nuada, known to our Lady, Nimue, as Caladvwlch and to Arthur as Excalibur.

As for the Grail, the Dagda brought it to us after he'd successfully escaped from Arawen, god of the Otherworld. It is truly a cup of abundance; those who are worthy will realize their hearts' desires.

And that is where this tale begins. The Goddess, the Great Mother, lent the cup to the carpenter's son when he completed his druidic training on the Isle of the Mighty. Ah...but that is another story.

Joseph of Arimathea brought the cup back to the Isle after the Christos was so brutally murdered. As a foil, he let it be rumored that the Magdalen took it with her when she fled to Gaul. Joseph meant to give the chalice back to the Ladies of Avalon, but his son, Josephe, didn't trust the priestesses. Even then, so shortly after Jesu's death, His message was being twisted.

Josephe gave the Grail to his father's friend, Nascien, who took the cup north. For certes, the Great Mother could have stopped him, but his was a goodly soul so she thought to leave the chalice in the world a while longer.

Destiny is an interesting thing. As the generations passed and the centuries drifted by, Joseph's daughter's descendants eventually begat Pelles of Carbonek, father of a scheming young woman named Elaine. Tragically, Pelles misused the Grail and I removed it from the world. Meanwhile, Joseph's son's lineage bore King Lancelot I, grandfather to the man who would marry Elaine, albeit not by his choice, and beget Galahad.

Galahad—bless the child and pity him—struggled through childhood. Separated from his father as a baby, his mother filled his head with vicious stories of Lancelot's desertion and devotion to Queen Gwenhwyfar. Galahad's was an old soul and the vision of the Grail came to him early, filling him with peace and contentment while his mother raved. When Galahad was eight, he finally met his father and was terrified of the tall warrior who was Arthur's right-hand man. Only the feeling of peace from his visions sustained him through the rigorous soldiers' training he never wanted, but had to endure.

Galahad's cousin, also from the line of Nascien, dreamed of the Grail as well. Peredur was raised in as much innocence as Galahad was in turmoil. Our own Woman of the Forest taught him to be true to his nature. If he, as he so often does, blunders along blithely expecting goodness...were we wrong? Many believe him to be foolish and naïve, but he wanted everyone to experience the good will the Grail vision brings. Our Lady didn't argue the point. It was then that I returned the Grail to mankind.

There are quests of a different sort than Galahad and Peredur set out on. Quests of love, where one would risk his life to be with his soul's mate. One man would have to venture into the land of Faerie, where even the priestesses of Avalon do not go, and withstand the tempting illusions of Morgan le Fey, Queen of Faerie. That man would have to challenge Cernunnos, the demi-god of the Wild Hunt, and that man would break a life-long friendship. But...love drives a man.

And so, this quest begins with Lancelot, pagan prince of the Lady of the Black Lake of Brocéliande.

~ Chapter 1—Aftermath ~

Lancelot brushed his dark hair off his forehead with a tired hand. His weary group plodded steadily along, the litter swaying between the two horses, the night after the great battle at Cam's Landing. Their bodies ached and their feet grew heavier with every step along the rough path. But they had no time to stop.

Arthur was dying.

The first rays of dawn were breaking on the horizon when they finally reached the Lake. The barge stood waiting, the hooded poleman in place.

"Bedwyr?" Arthur gestured weakly, for his blood loss was great. "I name Custennin my successor. You must help him keep the concept of Camelot alive. Send Galahad and Peredur for the Grail."

"Hush, Arthur." Nimue ran her hand over his sun-bleached hair. "Save your strength. You will need it."

Arthur drew a ragged breath. "The Grail...the cup of forgiveness. If we can get the Saxons to sit down with us..." He moaned softly against the pain of his wound. "There need be no more war." He beckoned Lancelot and Gwenhwyfar to come to him. Bending low, they could barely hear his whisper. "She is yours now, Lance."

Lancelot covered Arthur's hand with his. "My friend. We'll go to Joyous Garde and raise my daughter together."

"The child she always wanted." Arthur attempted a smile.

Tears welled up in Gwenhwyfar's green eyes and she no longer held them back.

Arthur turned his head and reached up feebly to stroke her long auburn hair. "You cry. Do you love me then?"

"I have never stopped loving you," she sobbed uncontrollably. "My curse has always been to love both you and Lancelot."

Nimue touched Gwenhwyfar's arm. "Do you remember when I told you, long ago, that you would have to make a choice? That Arthur's life would depend on it?"

Gwenhwyfar stared at the Lady of the Lake. "Yes."

"This is the time. You must come with us. The day you and I consecrated Arthur's and my daughter by the circle of stones, we both accepted responsibility for the marriage of the king to his land. Once more, we must combine our life forces to save the king." Nimue paused, glancing at Lancelot and then back to Gwenhwyfar. "You must come with us through the land of Faerie to Avalon."

Lancelot started. *Had Nimue gone mad? Had he? This wasn't supposed to be happening. Gwen was his now. Arthur had released her.*

"Gwen will not be able to return. She lacks the fey blood."

"Is that true?" Gwenhwyfar asked, her face paling.

"Mayhap," the Lady answered. "Those of us who have the Old Blood can merge with the land of Faerie for a short time to pass through the portal. It's true no human has ever passed through twice. Arthur's birth was wrought by Myrddin's wiles so he will be able to bring Arthur back. I will do what I can."

"Myrddin?" Gwenhwyfar sounded confused now. "He's been dead for years!"

"Not dead. Asleep in Avalon." Nimue gestured to the hooded figure on the barge. "Look."

Slowly, Gwenhwyfar turned, as did Lancelot. Even before the arch-druid threw back the hood to reveal the tawny hair, his golden eyes were trained on Gwenhwyfar. Beside him, a shimmer of light grew steadily stronger and a female form took shape. She floated above the water, her gossamer gown and long brown hair fluttering about her in the effervescence of faerie light.

Lancelot shook his head. Even though his mother was a priestess and he'd been born of the Great Rite, which meant he had some fey blood, he'd never seen a faerie.

"Faeries don't exist," Gwenhwyfar whispered.

The apparent apparition gave them an amused look. "But we do, I assure you. I am Morgan le Fey, Queen of Faerie. It is through my lands that you must pass." She winked at Lancelot and then gestured for a nearly unconscious Arthur to be placed on the barge. "You are a handsome one," she crooned as she held his head in her lap. "You must not die."

Gwenhwyfar turned back to Nimue. "What will happen to me if I can't return?"

"I cannot say," Nimue answered, "but Avalon is a peaceful place."

"You are asking her to give up her life!" Lancelot felt his temper rising. "I will not let her go!"

"If she stays, Arthur will die. Camelot will fade away. His work will have been for naught," Nimue said simply. "I can't do this alone. I need her." She looked worriedly at Morgan and Arthur and turned back to Gwenhwyfar. "We have not much time, Gwenhwyfar. Make your choice."

Don't leave me, Gwen. Not now when we've a second chance at happiness. You've done your duty. It was all Arthur would expect of you.

As though she'd heard his thoughts, Gwenhwyfar turned to him. "My heart belongs to you, Lancelot. It always has. If I could turn back Time..." She looked into his smoke-colored eyes and drew a deep breath. "I love you, but I cannot let everything Arthur has done be lost. He must be healed. Britain's future is more important than us." She kissed him and quickly stepped onto the barge.

"Gwen, don't go!" Lancelot pleaded as Myrddin poled away. He heard the sound of tinkling faerie laughter. Morgan. Apparently, she'd created an illusion he thought was real. Gwenhwyfar should be standing on the bank with him. In his head, she'd agreed to marry him. Yet here he stood alone, his beloved carried off to the Land of Faerie. The Land of No Return.

The ever-present fog wrapped its tentacles around the barge, shrouding it in a thick, grey blanket, as it made its way to the Isle. Once, before they were lost to the mists, Gwenhwyfar turned back.

"You have fey blood, Lancelot! Find a way for me to return!"

I won't let you be lost to me. Lancelot made sure his voice carried across the water as he raised his fist. "I will find a way, Gwen. You have my oath, my geis."

Three moons had passed since that fateful day. Lancelot was restless. Seated at the Round Table at Camelot he listened to yet another argument. *By Mithras, how had Arthur ever been able to get this group of arrogant, self-centered warlords to agree on anything?* Lancelot watched as Custennin slammed down his wine cup in frustration, sending droplets of the rich, red liquid spraying across the vellum in front of him.

"I tell you, it's only a matter of time before Cerdic will march. He just waits to see if Arthur is really dead."

The men seated in the council room stilled. All eyes turned to Custennin, but it was Bedwyr who spoke quietly. "He lives."

The other men exchanged glances. Many of them were young, the sons of the Cymbry who'd fought with Arthur at Cam's Landing. Lancelot was glad Bedwyr had spoken. Mayhap they would believe Gwenhwyfar's brother. No one seemed to believe Lancelot when he insisted Arthur had been taken to the Holy Isle of Avalon. He knew the men thought him half-mad these days, talking about Gwenhwyfar having gone to the land of Faerie. Everyone told him it was common for queens to quietly fade away to a nunnery when their lords were killed. He knew differently.

"Why has no one had word then?" Cai's son, Ryons, asked.

"The Lady hasn't been seen either," the prince of Gwynedd broke in. "My father says it's time for us to look to defend our own lands, especially since no one knows where Medraut and Morgana fled to."

"Your father always has been the one to look after himself first," the powerful king of Powys interjected.

The young prince's face turned red, but before he could speak, Custennin interrupted, his brown eyes flashing. "This is not the time to argue. Soon it will be spring. We must plan our strategy to keep the Saxons in check, with or without Arthur." He glanced at the northern warlords seated at the table. "Even if Cerdic waits, we still have the young hotbloods—Aesc's son, Eormenric, Aelle's son, Cissa—if the south is overrun..."

"We've got the barbarians in the north, too," Keidyaw, whose kingdom was past the Wall near Lancelot's Joyous Garde, stated. "Defending our borders is just as important as yours, Custennin."

Lancelot sighed and brushed his dark hair from his forehead. These northern kings hadn't rallied until it was too late. He knew Custennin could depend on the men of southwestern Kernow; he'd been leading them since Marc relinquished the command to spend more time with his young wife, Iseult. Too bad Tristan wasn't here to help. He had the gift of diplomacy that Custennin lacked. But Tristan and Iseult had been madly in love. Marc had nearly killed him and now he lived in exile across the sea in Léon.

"I didn't mean to imply otherwise." Custennin sounded tired. "I am well aware of Ida's Saxon ambitions north of the Wall. But, at the moment, Cerdic poses the greater threat. He did not lose men at Cam's Landing."

Bedwyr nodded. "He left the fight to the firebloods and took advantage of Cam's Landing to move toward Londinium, but he's always been willing to parley."

"That's because Arthur kept his son, Cynric, as hostage," one of the young lords shot back. "My da says the king should never have released him."

Lancelot leaned forward. "Cynric saved the queen's life."

"And yours, if I remember the story right," Keidyaw said dourly.

Lancelot straightened. *By Mithras, does he want to fight?* "What's that supposed to mean?"

Custennin interceded again. "Sirs, let's leave the past. Our numbers are low; we cannot afford to fight amongst ourselves. In the event Arthur doesn't return,"—he held up his hand as Lancelot started to protest—"we need to be prepared."

"Why hasn't anyone heard anything?" Gwalchmai's son, Guinglain, repeated the former question. "Nimue could tell us whether Arthur lives." He turned to Lancelot. "The Lady is your cousin; can you not contact her?"

Lancelot slumped back and gave the boy a lopsided smile. "I've tried; believe me, I've tried."

If only they knew how hard I've tried.

The hour was late and Lancelot pulled his boots off wearily and lay back on his cot in the officers' quarters. They'd spent the day arguing and were no closer to agreement.

He closed his dark eyes. *Gwenhwyfar. Gloriously wild, brown-gold hair framing a striking face, with high cheekbones and beguiling green eyes, the color of a forest in shadow.* He pictured her in her favorite outfit of soft doeskin boots, trews and a man's oversized linen shirt, ready to gallop wildly across the fields with him. Something they'd done countless times. In his mind, he reached to put his arms around her, to feel her soft, pliable lips under his. For a moment, he thought he felt her response, demanding more than just his mouth.

His eyes flew open and he sat up. It had been so real; he could have sworn she was here. He shook his head. *Mayhap I am going mad.* He looked around the room; nothing had changed. His sword, in its smooth leather scabbard, stood propped against the table by his bed, his dagger under the pillow.

He pulled on his boots, picked up the dagger, and went outside. All was quiet, the guards walking silently along the battlements. He climbed the ladder and leaned on the embrasure, remembering the first time he'd brought Gwenhwyfar up here. It had been the night of Arthur's Kingmaking, when Arthur and Myrddin had gone to the circle of stones so he might perform the Great Rite of marriage to the land with Nimue, who was a maiden priestess then. Gwenhwyfar had been newly wedded and upset. They'd talked. *She is always so easy to talk to, even in those early days when I went to Cameliard to escort her back to Camelot.* And they'd kissed that night. They hadn't meant to and it was just a small kiss, but enough for him to know he had to leave.

How many times did I leave, thinking I could forget her? He'd crossed the narrow sea to deliver horses, traveled through Saxon country to avenge her near rape, then moved on to Joyous Garde, tucked safely away north of the Wall, all to no avail. When he'd see her again, his heart gladdened. Arthur had known, nearly from the start, more than twenty-five years ago. It was a mark of greatness in the man that he never blamed either of them for their love. Even at the end, before he lost consciousness, Arthur had given her to him.

He banged his fist against the merlon. Now, she was in Avalon, that place between the worlds, with Nimue and Arthur. He should have been able to make contact. He'd gone to the Lake and argued with Barinthus, the poleman, to take him across the water to the Isle of Avallach. The man would not budge until the mists carried the whispered message from the priestess, Argante. *"Let him come."*

Argante met him on the shore. She was the daughter of Nimue and Arthur, petite and silver-haired like her mother, but her steady, grey eyes were her father's. Already, her reputation for power and healing surpassed Nimue's. Silently, she beckoned him to follow as she wound her way up the labyrinth to the top of the Tor.

A circle of stones stood like silent sentinels on the summit. She gestured. "The portal to Avalon is in the circle. I cannot open it; you must find it for yourself."

He started to step inside when her hand stopped him. "Leave your weapons here. Do not go in anger, Lancelot. The Goddess will decide whether to allow you passage."

He stayed inside the circle until sunset, praying to the Great Mother. Throughout the long hours that he sweated and cried and pleaded, nothing stirred. Argante finally came for him.

"The time is not yet, Lancelot. Mayhap my mother and the queen are using all their energy to heal the king."

He looked up at her from where he knelt by the altar stone. "Have you not had a Sighting or even a message?"

She shook her head. "Avalon is surrounded by Faerie. Time moves differently there. A message might take a long time to travel."

"Or it might never arrive." Lancelot stood and took a deep breath to still his trembling.

The priestess only inclined her head in reply.

"Are you all right, sir?" The sentry's question brought Lancelot back to the present.

"Yes," he answered and looked at the rising moon. *Mother Goddess, let me find a way to help Gwen return."*

"Why don't you come with us, Father?" Galahad asked for the second time as he finished folding his clothes into the satchel several days later.

Lancelot glanced at the gold cross hanging from his seven and ten-year-old son's neck. "Seeking the Grail is not my quest." He looked into his son's eyes, blue like his mother's. "If it exists."

"The Christos used it at his last meal," Galahad answered adamantly and stuck his chin out.

Bel's fires! Are we going to argue again? "Hmm. Your Christos was a poor man, wasn't he? A son of a carpenter? Do you think this cup has value?"

"It has power." Stubbornly, Galahad brushed the wayward strand of dark hair off his forehead.

Lancelot quirked an eyebrow. "I thought you didn't believe in magic."

"Not magic, Father. Peace. Contentment. The Grail is a cup of forgiveness; if enemies drink from it, they will fight no longer. No more blood need be shed!"

"Forgiveness?" Lancelot asked bitterly. "We lost over three thousand men at Cam's Landing—Gwalchmai, Cai—Arthur's most trusted captains. All because that bastard, Medraut, stirred up the Saxons. They don't deserve forgiveness."

"God will have all men to be saved, and to come unto the knowledge of the Truth," Galahad quoted stiffly from the Bible.

Lancelot stifled a retort. *How could I have sired such a pious son?*

Peredur looked up from his packing, his brown eyes serious. "I am pagan, as you, my lord, but in my dream I have felt the joy I want to share with the whole world." He shrugged. "The cup is ancient. If the Christos used it, mayhap he forgave the traitor in his midst."

Galahad looked surprised. "Judas. I didn't know you knew scripture, Peredur."

"Queen Gwenhwyfar told me the story." Peredur turned back to Lancelot. "It's true. In my dream of the Grail, the maiden who hands the vessel to me is full of love."

Lancelot lifted the corner of his mouth slightly. "Love, Peredur? Then search for the right woman and marry her."

Peredur colored. "I hope I might find that lady—one day."

"For certes, I am never going to marry!" Galahad's voice had a steely edge. "It seems there is much unhappiness when a man is bound to a woman."

Lancelot nearly laughed. "You're young, Son. Wait."

Galahad raised his chin. "You and my mother hated each other! The queen was forced to return to Arthur and she didn't want to. Where's the happiness in that?"

The half-smile left Lancelot's face and he stepped closer to his son, his eyes growing darker. "Say no more."

Galahad swallowed hard, but didn't look away.

Lancelot glared at him and then his face softened. He picked up his cloak and walked to the door. "I refuse to be angry with you on the eve of your departure. I hope you find some tolerance along the way."

"You think I'm foolish to go on this quest instead of staying home to fight." He took a deep breath. "I think we can live in peace with the Saxons. When we find the Grail, we'll share it with them. Britain will have peace."

Lancelot studied his son. *I believed that once; I shared Arthur's dream. Do I have the right to thwart Galahad's?*

"I pray you're right," Lancelot said as he left the room.

"I guess you could say I'm on a quest, too." Bedwyr's hazel eyes were somber as he finished breaking his fast the next morning.

Lancelot handed him the dagger he'd been sharpening. "Finding Medraut is a quest I wouldn't mind going on."

"You've got to parley with Cynric," Bedwyr reminded him.

Lancelot grimaced. "I'm not the diplomat you are."

"You have a bond that I don't have. Cynric will listen to you."

A bond. *How long ago was it that Medraut had nearly raped Gwenhwyfar? Eight years?* No one had realized how far Medraut had sunk into madness over his infatuation with the queen. Thank the gods for Cynric's quick thinking.

"I remember the day we captured him wenching in Venta while Arthur caught up with Cerdic after the battle of Nettley Marsh." Lancelot grinned. "Holding him hostage halted his father's raids, but it didn't stop Cynric from finding his way into our serving girls' beds."

Bedwyr laughed. "Arthur wasn't even upset. He said it was the beginning of a new era, half-Saxon, half-Briton; we'd have to live in peace."

"Do you think we might actually achieve peace?" Lancelot asked.

Bedwyr stood and strapped his swordbelt on. "Mayhap. The Saxons lost as many men as we did at Cam's Landing. They'll need time to lick their wounds. Except for Cerdic, who kept his army intact, which is why you need to talk to Cynric."

"I never trusted Cynric, yet he's the one who convinced Medraut not to rape Gwen." Lancelot paused, thinking he'd probably be dead also. Cynric had been able to persuade Medraut to wait for Arthur to return that fateful night Lancelot had gone to Gwenhwyfar's bedchamber and they'd thrown caution to the winds. "Where will you start your search for Medraut?"

"The seaports. Clausentum. Portus Adurni, Isca Dumnoniorum," Bedwyr answered. "If he hasn't taken a ship, he's somewhere in Britain. I will search every inch of ground until I find him."

"You don't think Eormenric is giving him refuge? The Saxons of Durovernum have always been our greatest enemy." Lancelot leaned his arms on the table where he was sitting.

"True. But they're weak right now. They must know we'll come looking for the traitorous bastard. Wherever he's found, it will be annihilation for the people. The Saxons know it."

"His mother will be with him."

"Morgana." Bedwyr's voice went cold. "I'll kill her, too."

Lancelot nodded. "We had enough reason, many times: the poison she told Gwen would help her conceive, the gift of the cloak that would have disfigured her, then keeping me tied and drugged so Arthur would fight—he lost the scabbard and that almost cost him his life—giving Elaine the potion to seduce me." His voice turned harsh. "I wish I'd disobeyed Arthur at the last meeting before Cam's Landing. Morgana was an easy target with Medraut only at her side. By Mithras, I should have killed them both."

Bedwyr placed a hand on his shoulder. "Don't be so hard on yourself.

Arthur would have been furious. There's no honor in murder."

"No, I don't suppose there is." Lancelot stood. "May the gods bring you swiftly back. I don't know how long Custennin can keep our new leaders from each other's throats. Arthur will be displeased at that when he returns."

"When he returns," Bedwyr affirmed as they walked into the bailey.

As Lancelot and Bedwyr emerged from his quarters, Custennin came striding from the Great Hall. "Are you sure you don't want to take some troops along?" His sharp, brown eyes looked over the extra weapons Bedwyr was carrying. "If for no other reason than to let us know of your progress or if we have to send more men."

Bedwyr shook his head. "I'm faster and less noticed traveling alone, especially if I enter Saxon country. I don't want to start another war. I want to rid the world of Medraut and his mother."

Custennin nodded. "Well, if you're heading east, you'll be safe as far as Astolat."

Lancelot winced. Bernard's daughter, Elen, might still be alive if he'd never heard of the place. "I'm not sure they'll be happy to see anyone from Camelot," he said quietly.

Custennin raised an eyebrow. "It wasn't your fault that young girl was enamored with you, Lancelot. You affect women like that."

He scowled. "Elen was only five and ten. She had her whole life ahead of her."

"I doubt I'll be going there." Bedwyr ran a hand through his chestnut hair. "We've had no sightings of Medraut. I suspect he's across the sea."

"If the trail leads to Benoic, send for me," Lancelot replied. "I wouldn't have to honor Arthur's law there. My brother, Ector, will allow death to be slow."

Bedwyr began to reply, but stopped as Galahad and Peredur approached, leading their horses. "Do you mind if we ride with you?" Peredur asked.

"Suit yourself. I ride south."

Lancelot looked over his son's light mail. "Where are your hauberk and helmet? Your shield?"

Galahad mounted and looked down at his father. "I do not intend to fight. Remember Myrddin's prophecy? That a soldier who would not shed blood will help bring peace to Britain?"

"You're mad if you ride off unprotected. You need to defend yourself." Lancelot wondered if anything he'd taught his son had penetrated his brain.

Galahad shrugged. "My hauberk is on the pack animal. My shield is cracked; I will find one along the way."

Lancelot glanced over at the mule. Galahad's harp was slung on one side.

"Are you planning to practice being a bard?" Lancelot asked, a half-smile on his face now that he knew his son had his armor.

"The music is for me."

"Then, may your Jesu bless you, Galahad, and your search be successful. If you reach Joyous Garde, check on your sister for me. I've work to do here and I imagine she's giving her nurse a hard time."

Galahad nodded and smiled slightly. "Old Augusta spoils Elen and you know it."

His father sighed. Even though he cared nothing for the woman he'd been forced to marry, he was sorry Elaine had died in childbirth. His three-year-old daughter already displayed an ability to have her way. *Gwenhwyfar should be here, helping me raise her as she'd wanted to do, as Arthur had wanted*...abruptly, he refocused.

As Peredur mounted, Lancelot turned to him. "May the Mother watch over you as well."

Custennin shook his head as the three of them rode away. "I think the boys are fools to search for a cup, even if it's worth a treasure."

Lancelot looked at him. "The tale is ancient. The druids claim it's one of the three and ten treasures of Britain. Arthur requested Galahad and Peredur search for it, before he...left." He felt the brown eyes study him.

"You don't think Arthur's coming back?"

"I don't know anymore. There's been no word. I would have thought Nimue..." Lancelot straightened and looked into the distance. "We must keep this land united."

"Hmm." Custennin sounded thoughtful as they watched the riders disappear. "Mayhap, we need to build the story of the Grail to the other lords. Give them something to believe in."

"You always were shrewd; it's worth a try."

Custennin turned to leave. "Let's hope I'm smart enough to hold these men together."

Lancelot watched him walk away. *If we can just get the warlords to keep faith until Arthur returns. He must. Arthur will bring Gwen with him; he would never leave her behind.*

~ Chapter 2—Avalon ~

Gwenhwyfar swayed on her feet, nearly jolting Arthur's bier as the barge scraped against the hardened sand of Avalon's shore. How they had traveled here, she had no idea. The last thing she remembered was the dragon's damp breath of thick fog enfolding them as they approached the holy Isle of Avallach.

Nimue stepped off the barge and made obeisance to the tall, white-robed woman who awaited them. "I bring Arthur to you, Lady. Only the magic of this place can make him whole."

The high priestess, Rhiannon, stepped closer and laid her hand on the blood-soaked bandage, her fingertips touching the scabbard lying on Arthur's chest. "If not for this scabbard, he would already be in the Otherworld." She frowned slightly. "Sulis is our healer; even she will have work of it." She made a sign of blessing and then nodded imperceptibly.

From nowhere, a dozen small, dark manlike figures scampered to do her bidding. The creatures had large heads with curiously pointed ears, eyes that slanted upward, and sharp noses over wide mouths. Although their bodies were small, their arms were heavily muscled and their hands long and graceful. They gripped the litter on which the king lay and lifted it as though it contained nothing but air. Chattering to each other in their own joyful language, they carried him up the hill.

"Are they laughing?" Gwenhwyfar asked Nimue as she joined her on land and tried to secure unruly wisps of auburn hair. "I see no reason—"

"You must be the queen." Rhiannon's nearly black eyes bore through Gwenhwyfar. She clamped her mouth closed, forcing herself to meet the imposing gaze.

"The elfins," the priestess explained in a more gentle voice, "are a happy people. Your husband still breathes. Is that not cause for gladness?"

Chastened, Gwenhwyfar whispered, "Forgive me. If you can heal Arthur, I will do anything."

Rhiannon studied her awhile longer, then nodded. "You will have your work ahead." She gestured. "Come, let us follow the king."

They walked past a group of whitewashed buildings that were living quarters for the nine holy women of Avalon and the slope of the hill became steeper, leading to a small apple orchard. *This place reminds me of the Isle*, Gwenhwyfar thought as she listened to the lazy droning of bees and inhaled the sweet scent of the white blossoms on the newly leafed trees. *Strange. It was autumn in Camelot.*

They broke through the trees and ahead of them was a marble cliff; steps had been hewn into the shining stone. Gwenhwyfar glanced up and stopped in amazement. At the very summit, a great light shimmered and scattered rays of brightness in all directions. She shielded her eyes and looked again. Now, she saw it was sunlight reflecting off great panes of glass. She blinked. The entire structure was glass.

"This is our house of healing," Rhiannon explained as they climbed the stairs. "The solarium provides both warmth and light from Bel as well as the Mother."

Inside, the air was mild and moist, reminding Gwenhwyfar of the breezes that blew along the coast of Lyonesse. The stringent scent of eucalyptus drifted toward her from a far corner. Herbal beds were neatly laid out and they passed one enticingly spicy patch. Along the far side stood rosebushes, thorny stems hidden behind hundreds of huge blooms, sweet fragrance floating on the air. Toward the center of the solarium, a ring of lavender grew, the aroma blending with the roses. Inside that ring, on a raised altar stone well padded with a straw mattress and down cover, lay Arthur.

A small, brown-haired priestess was removing his bandage. She didn't look up as Rhiannon, Nimue, and Gwenhwyfar entered. Beside her, an identical-looking woman added herbs to a large bowl of steaming water on the table. Arthur groaned as the bandage was gently pried from the wound edges where dried blood had formed a paste.

"Isis, your hand," Sulis said, but the other had already read her twin's mind and touched Arthur's forehead. He quieted instantly. "Did Brighid go for her harp?"

Even as she spoke, a young, red-haired woman slipped silently past Gwenhwyfar. She sank to the floor gracefully and plucked a string, then another and a third. A hauntingly beautiful melody, rich and mellow, Gwenhwyfar had never heard a bard play so well. *I wonder how many others...*

"There are nine of us in Avalon," Rhiannon answered her unspoken question. "Each of us has a special gift. The music is very soothing, is it not? He will hear it."

"It is," Gwenhwyfar felt herself physically relaxing, the first time since she'd found Arthur. *When was the last time I slept? Odd, I don't feel tired.*

"Are all of you healers?' she asked tentatively.

"No," Nimue replied. "Each of the nine has special responsibilities. Arianrhod spins the Wheel of Life for those about to incarnate. Morrigan recovers the soldier's souls that were given in battle..."

Gwenhwyfar felt a chill sweep over her. "Morrigan. Is she old? Yet her face is ageless?"

"Yes." Nimue looked thoughtful. "Did you see her at Cam's Landing?"

Cam's Landing. Gwenhwyfar closed her eyes. She didn't want to remember, nonetheless the memory invaded her mind.

As they rounded the bend at the river's ford, they came upon an old crone, bent over, washing clothes in the river. Much of it was blood soaked, but there were no wounded or dead bodies about.

"Why is your clothing so bloody?" Gwenhwyfar called out.

The old woman straightened and turned. Gwenhwyfar inhaled sharply. The face was unlined, although the hair was white. The eyes were as black as raven feathers.

"I wash the clothes of those who are dead. The battle is done."

"What battle?" Gwenhwyfar asked. "We seek King Arthur. Has he passed this way? Have you seen him?"

The strange eyes turned on her, flickering indigo as the sunlight flitted over her face. She pointed up the river. "The battle joined there. I have not seen the king this day."

Moments later, Gwenhwyfar discovered Arthur, nearly dead.

She breathed deeply and opened her eyes. "I saw her."

"We were both busy that day," Rhiannon said sadly. "So many sacrifices."

Gwenhwyfar turned to her, nearly afraid to ask. Finally, she whispered, "What is your gift?"

"I am the escort to the Otherworld. Arawen is my Consort." She paused, then added softly, "Arthur's name had been given me that day."

Arthur lay in a trance for many days. Myrddin sat beside him, talking softly in the Old Tongue. Gwenhwyfar watched as the arch-druid softly stroked the king's sun-bleached hair; she'd never seen any gentleness in him before. Even his golden eyes had lost their penetrating, hawkish look.

"Arthur has been his son as much as he was Ector's or Uther's," Nimue explained. "He tutored him as a child."

Myrddin stood as they approached and moved aside, his eyes not leaving Arthur's face. Nimue did not speak and Gwenhwyfar knew she was gathering the energy she would need. She'd taught Gwenhwyfar the healing ritual and everyday at dawn and dusk, the in-between-time when the barrier to the spirit world was less resistant, they performed it together. Gwenhwyfar centered herself quickly so the mind-link could be established. Determinedly, she steadied the yearning restlessness for Lancelot that she'd been feeling the past few days.

Gwenhwyfar stood at Arthur's head, holding the vial of rue and myrrh oil as Nimue cast her circle of protection widdershins. She watched the priestess call the quarters, moving from west to south to east and finishing at the northern censer. The fragrance of frankincense filled the air.

Nimue nodded to Gwenhwyfar. "Anoint him."

She placed a drop of the precious oil on Arthur's forehead and moved around to his wrist, the soles of his feet, and the other wrist. Nimue opened his shirt and carefully folded it back over the bandage. Gwenhwyfar placed the last drop over his heart and set the vial aside.

They held their hands in the air over the wound and closed their eyes. Nimue began the chant in the Old Tongue and as Gwenhwyfar listened, she lost herself to the melodious intonation. She swayed on her feet and felt heat leaving her hands and entering Arthur's body. In her mind, she saw the skin respond, closing itself, interweaving the tiny threads that formed the muscle and tendon and ligament. How long they stayed in that position, she never knew. Only at the end of it, twice a day, she was too weak to stand.

Arthur slumbered through all of it; Myrddin at his side. Sulis would rouse the king long enough to eat, then put him gently to sleep again.

"Better that he not move," she explained. "The wound is deep; even with your ritual, I'm having trouble keeping the skin laced together."

Gently, Nimue touched the skin. "The wound is deeper than you know. He grieves for the men he lost and for his shattered dream."

"He'll rebuild his dream," Gwenhwyfar said as she prepared a poultice. "Camelot's not dead!"

Sulis glanced at Nimue and then at Gwenhwyfar. "He'll need to remain here for quite some time. Things may be changed when he returns."

"How long?"

The healer shrugged. "I cannot say. Many moons. Mayhap, years."

"Years?" Gwenhwyfar echoed. "He must go back sooner. The Saxons will march; Medraut needs to be found. I have promised to raise Elen..." she stopped, aware of Myrddin's hawk eyes studying her. Nimue's words came back to her. *No human has ever passed through the portal twice.* "We will be able to go back?" she asked Myrddin.

He nodded. "I will get Arthur through."

She breathed a sigh of relief, then the implication struck. She stared at Myrddin; for once, his face was full of sympathy, the golden eyes glowing softly. She turned to Nimue and found the same expression of concern. She covered her face with her hands and sank to the floor.

"I won't be able to return, will I?"

Arthur stirred restively in his sleep. The Grail Maiden had been talking to him for some time. Her voice, pleasantly melodic, rose and fell softly in tune with music he couldn't quite hear. But it was there—the music—light and airy, yet somehow vibrant.

When the maiden moved, a fragrance sweeter than apple blossoms filled the air. The scent carried a piquant aroma as well, like the headiness of sandalwood mixed with the tangy smell of the sea. The delicate odors drifted around him in a soothing blanket of air.

"Behold!" she said now, her voice strong.

He struggled through the pleasant fog of dream, then grimaced, turning away. "No. I don't want to see."

"But you must," she gently insisted, "so you will never want to kill again."

Although she didn't touch him, he felt himself inexplicably being turned. Against his will, his eyes opened.

Cam's Landing. So much blood, so many dead. The cries of the wounded and the screams of dying horses filled his ears. "Stop!" he pleaded. "The battle was not begun by me!"

"No." The images disappeared. "Your son was responsible. Medraut still lives. You must forgive him." Her eyes, the palest blue beneath the golden hair, implored him.

"Forgive him? The product of incest and a thorn in my side always? I cannot."

The sounds of battle came to him and the place stank of men's entrails and defecation. He groaned and closed his eyes. "Please. Let me hear the music and smell the perfume again."

"You must forgive," the maiden said kindly.

"How can I?"

"Look at me, Arthur." The voice was majestic now.

Slowly, he opened his eyes, then put his hand across them for protection from the light. The room was ablaze in golden white radiance, warm as the sun. Once again, music and fragrance filled the air. Carefully, he lowered his hands and squinted.

Astrala raised a hand and the light settled and drew itself in toward her. She held something in her hands.

A wine goblet. The silver of its simple, graceful line was etched with ancient runes, the mouth rimmed in gold. The glow that accompanied it was not a reflection of the metal. The light emanated from the cup itself, raising and lowering itself like a flame, pulsating with its own rhythm.

She held the cup out to him. Tentatively, he accepted it and gazed into its liquid content.

"Drink of the cup of forgiveness and be healed of your hatred of Medraut."

He stared at her, but she simply smiled in a way that was alluring, compelling and comforting, all at the same time. His vision blurred and she became three: the maiden still, but also the mother and the crone. He blinked and she was back in her maiden form, clothed in silver-white.

He took a long draught. The nectar was sweet and full-bodied, yet more delicate than the finest imported wines. Suddenly, a sharp pain pierced his chest, then it was gone. He heard the thrashing of large wings and saw a shadow slip to the window. A most joyful feeling of grace filled him. He looked at the girl wonderingly.

She nodded to his unspoken question. "You are through with hate." She took the cup serenely from his hands. "The Grail will grant peace to any who drink from it. There can be no war if opposing leaders share the cup."

"May I take it with me? Britain has much need of it, I fear." Arthur held out his hand.

"No. I have been the Grail's protector from time beyond Time. Once, I lent it to a carpenter's son, who'd been blessed to bring a great message of peace and love to his people." She stopped and closed her eyes, as if listening to a greater voice. "Ah," she said at last.

"What is it?" Arthur whispered.

"Two men in your land have seen this vision also. Even now, they search for this cup." She opened her starlit eyes. "They seek, but they aren't ready to attain. I will place the cup in the world again when each has found his own soul."

She smiled and her image began to fade. "When you return, try to avoid bloodshed. The mighty king you once were will serve as the example for peace."

"Wait," he cried, but she was gone and the room was cold.

Gwenhwyfar began staying at Arthur's side day and night, dozing sometimes in her chair. She and Myrddin had declared a silent truce, as though healing Arthur had defined a bond between them. Nimue had urged her to discover the pleasures of Avalon, but she refused to leave the solarium, except to attend the baths. In her cell, she became too despondent for rational thought. She could not abide being alone. Her husband was going to leave her and she would never see Lancelot again. *Lancelot, my dear love, do you search for me?* The thoughts were too painful. Much better that she keep busy.

She'd just finished bathing one evening and slipped a loose tunic on to return to Arthur's side when a priestess with long blonde hair approached. Her face was unlined, but the blue eyes held an ancient wisdom.

"I am Hetaira," she said in a surprisingly seductive voice. "Come. Walk with me."

Gwenhwyfar started to refuse, but felt an irresistible pull moving her forward. "Where are we going?" she asked as they started down the hill toward the small forest that lay across the meadow at the bottom.

"Not far," the priestess answered. "Have patience."

Just inside the forest, the air was cool, with a refreshingly clean smell. The oaks leaves rustled and the ash trees swayed lightly in the wind, as though dancing to silent music. The birches' silvery trunks sent the last of the sunlit sparkles floating through the air. Below their feet, the moss was soft and thick as velvet.

Hetaira stopped before a natural spring. A round, concave space had been dug in the earth and lined with stones to catch the water and form a small pool. "Have you any practice with scrying?"

Gwenhwyfar nodded. "When I visited the Isle, Nimue showed me an image in the Sacred Pool." *The face had been Medraut's, as a child, before he became a madman. Mother of God, I wish I had never seen him.*

"Nimue and I had a talk this morning. You ache for another man."

Gwenhwyfar started. "No. I love Arthur; I came here to help him heal."

"And so you shall," Hetaira smiled. "But you love two men and they both love you. Am I not right?"

"God forgive me, yes," Gwenhwyfar whispered. "I have tried not to love..."

Hetaira placed a gentle hand on her arm. "Never try to deny love. It is a gift of the Goddess to be able to feel such emotion."

"Mayhap platonic love," Gwenhwyfar said shakily, "but I yearn to kiss him, touch him, feel him inside of me. My very soul cries to him, even though it is a mortal sin."

"Ah, sin." The priestess' voice was soft. "The new religion is governed by men who are afraid of woman's power. The Old Way sees no 'sin' in pleasure. Surely, this man has told you of thigh freedom."

Gwenhwyfar looked up at her, startled. "How did you know?"

She looked amused. "The Lady Niniane raised her son well."

Niniane. Certes. Lancelot's mother was a priestess, too. Gwenhwyfar looked at Hetaira hopefully. "Can you bring him here? He has the fey blood."

She shook her head. "I cannot summon him. Only the Goddess can decide to open the portal. He has tried to come to you, but has been denied."

Gwenhwyfar hung her head. "You see? This is my punishment. I should be thinking only of Arthur. He would not betray me, yet I..."

She felt a firm hand under her chin, forcing her to look up.

"Gwenhwyfar. Mayhap you are in need of healing, too. How long have you struggled with this guilt? You are aware that Nimue cares for Arthur as you do for Lancelot?"

"Yes, I know that." Gwenhwyfar swallowed. "But each of them is strong enough to deny lust."

Hetaira lifted an eyebrow, looking amused again. "Well. That is not the reason we are here. Look." She swept her hand over the water.

The water shimmied, then was still. Gwenhwyfar gasped.

Lancelot entered his quarters at Camelot, exhausted from a day of arguing with the young warlords. She watched as he tossed his dark hair back from his forehead, pulled his boots off and lay back on his cot. She saw him form an image of her. It lingered in the air above his head, transparent, yet totally alive.

She felt herself merging with the image, then he wrapped his arms around her and pulled her close, his lips soft and gentle in that first exploratory, teasing kiss.

Fire blazed deep within her, surging upward. She pressed herself against him, her tongue finding his, eager for the taste of him, her hands roaming his back...

The spell broke abruptly as his eyes flew open and he sat up.

"No! Don't go!" Gwenhwyfar was on her knees by the pool, hugging herself. "Come back, Lancelot! Please..."

"There will be other times, Gwenhwyfar," Hetaira said.

She looked up. "What happened?"

"You made contact on the spirit plane. He just didn't realize what was happening. He will learn."

"I can do this again? Anytime I want?" Gwenhwyfar smiled for the first time in days. She turned to the pool again, noticing a pale glimmer begin to emerge from a patch of primroses beside the water. The light glittered and shimmered as it rose. A woman's form began to take shape, transparent as the image Lancelot had formed. Sparkles glistened around the form, making translucent rays of the most delicate pinks and blues and greens.

Her voice was as sultry and husky as a woman warm from coupling. "You might want to ask permission next time. This is my pool."

Hetaira inclined her head. "I've been expecting you. Come forth."

There was a girlish giggle and the form materialized into a petite woman. Her long, chestnut hair framed an ageless face, the green eyes slanting upward. Her nose was pert, her mouth full. Her gown tied above her shoulders, exposing delicate arms. It floated away from her in layers of fragile samite in palest shades as she gracefully glided forward. She smiled impishly at Gwenhwyfar and made the smallest of reverences to Hetaira.

The priestess raised a hand. "Well-come, Morgan le Fey, Queen of Faerie."

"Faerie?" Gwenhwyfar leapt to her feet. "I am in the land of Faerie?'

Morgan laughed, a light, soft sound like a small silver bell. "Not quite. The land of Faerie surrounds Avalon." She pouted a little. "This is my pool."

"It's a wonderful pool." Gwenhwyfar forgot her fear for a moment. "May I use it again?"

A sly look came over the faerie's face. "If you'll introduce me to that handsome man I just saw."

"Morgan..." Hetaira warned.

"What?" she asked innocently, eyes wide. "I don't get much opportunity to play with mortal men and this one was most comely. Wasn't he with you at the Lake?"

"You...you were there? With Myrddin?" Gwenhwyfar tried to remember. *Everything is so hazy. I left Lancelot, Arthur was nearly dead, time felt distorted, but yes, a lady had emerged floating above the water.*

"You could not travel through Faerie without me." Morgan slanted a glance sideways at Gwenhwyfar. "What's his name?"

"Lancelot," Gwenhwyfar stammered, unable to stop herself.

"Morgan," Hetaira said again. "If you wish to seduce Lady Niniane's son, you may well find your queendom shrunk."

The faerie's eyes widened at Niniane's name. "I have heard of Lancelot, Champion to the queen." She tilted her head, her green eyes appraising Gwenhwyfar. "Or was it Consort?" She seemed pleased with herself when Gwenhywfar's face heated. "So that is how it is."

"No." Gwenhwyfar felt the flush deepen. "No. I am married to Arthur."

Morgan shrugged. "And I have a Consort also. That won't stop me from enjoying Lancelot or any other man..." She giggled suddenly. "Myrddin no longer lies in trance; mayhap, I will go find him. He found me quite attractive at one time."

Even as she watched, Gwenhwyfar saw Morgan's form begin to fade. Her laughing voice came from far away. "Use the pool whenever you wish. I shall look forward to sharing your visits!"

Gwenhwyfar turned to Hetaira. "I don't want to share my visions!"

The priestess lifted a shoulder. "Better to have Morgan your friend than your enemy."

Gwenhwyfar looked at the water. "Will I be able to see anyone else? My brother, Bedwyr? Lancelot's daughter?"

"Yes. With time, as you learn, you will be able to summon pictures, but only those with fey blood will be able to sense your presence and respond."

She looked up. "Did Lancelot actually know I was there? Was it real?"

"Real enough." Hetaira gestured past the spring toward the hawthorn bushes. "Do not go past this point, though, or you will enter the land of Faerie, full of illusion. Reality fades, time runs differently. Many mortals go mad. Few return. Now come, it's time to go to Arthur."

Gwenhwyfar passed her hand over the water. *Good night, my love. Dream of me.* The water stirred: At Camelot, Lancelot turned over in his sleep, a smile on his face.

"Nimue?" Arthur's voice was weak and his hand groped along the bedside.

Gwenhwyfar pushed the candle closer and leaned over him. "Do you want me to get her?"

She heard him gasp. “Gwenhwyfar? Is it you? Where am I?” He struggled to sit, but she pushed him firmly back.

“Lie still. You’ll open the wound again.” She leaned over and fluffed his pillow. “You’re in Avalon. Nimue and Myrddin brought you here.”

“The place between the worlds.” Arthur caught her hand and brought it to his chest. “How come you’re here then? Lancelot was supposed to take care of you.”

Gwenhwyfar forced herself to smile. “My energy had to merge with Nimue’s in order for you to heal, and it had to be where the solarium is.”

Arthur’s grey eyes, nearly black in the near darkness, studied her face. “You left Lancelot to come with me?” His voice shook, whether from fatigue or emotion, she couldn’t tell.

“Yes. Now, get some rest. We can talk in the morning.”

He gave her hand a squeeze before he released it. “I love you.”

After that, Arthur made slow, but steady progress. When he mentioned his dream, Gwenhwyfar smiled slightly. “I may not be able to forgive Medraut, Arthur, but I am glad you can.”

“Nimue says it was a true vision,” Arthur added, thinking of the radiant light and feeling of total acceptance. “The Grail Maiden will allow the cup to be found; Galahad and Peredur will be successful.”

“I hope they are,” Gwenhwyfar said softly.

The day finally arrived when he was able to leave the solarium and walk outside. The leaves had turned to brilliant oranges, reds and golds; the air contained a hint of crispness although the sun blazed brightly in a cloudless, azure sky.

“It’s still autumn.” Arthur turned to Myrddin.

“Here, not at Camelot,” Myrddin answered. “When we arrived, it was spring on Avalon.”

“Avalon is in the heart of the land of Faerie,” Nimue said. “Even the protective circles cannot entirely keep us synchronized with Earth.”

“How long have I been here.” Arthur began shaking and Myrddin steadied him. “I must get back. The Saxons...”

“So far, are still at peace,” Myrddin answered. “You must gain more strength before you leave.”

Nimue agreed. “You aren’t nearly ready.”

“Come, Arthur,” Gwenhwyfar said suddenly as he began to pace. “I can put your mind at ease. Let’s ask Lancelot.”

Arthur stopped raking his hand through his hair and stared at her. “Lancelot is here?”

She glanced at Nimue. “No, but I’ve been taught how to find him.”

They walked slowly down the hill to the forest line and Gwenhwyfar sank into the lush grass beside the spring. “Sit beside me,” she said as she swept her hand over the water. “Look.”

He stared into the pool of water. Lancelot smiled back, his smoky eyes warm.

“*Hello, Arthur. I’m glad to see you again.*”

Arthur heard the words, although no one had spoken. He took Gwenhwyfar’s arm. “How...?”

She shook her head. “We are on another plane. Just think your questions and he will answer."

Arthur had a thousand questions. All stumbled into one another, climbing over each other incoherently.

The image in the pool held up a hand. *"Peace, a moment! Slow yourself, my lord. Let me have a word with Gwen while you think."*

The conversation went still, although Arthur could still see the image. Gwenhwyfar remained motionless, but he could feel contentment radiating from her. Finally, she gave a small sigh and turned to him. "Go ahead and ask now."

He began with Custennin. *"Does the kingdom hold together?"*

Lancelot shook his head. "Barely. Custennin does not have your finesse. He doesn't ask for cooperation; he demands it."

"Custennin doesn't understand Camelot's concept then!" Gwenhwyfar interrupted and Arthur turned to her.

"You can hear us? I couldn't hear you..." His voice trailed off as she blushed slightly and turned away. He turned back to Lancelot. *"What of Cerdic?"*

For a long time, they talked. Finally, Arthur exhausted himself and Lancelot bid them both good night. His eyes turned smoke-colored when he looked at Gwenhwyfar and there was a moment of stillness in which Arthur was sure an intimate conversation was being shared, but then Lancelot grinned at him and was gone.

Suddenly, Gwenhwyfar knew Morgan was with them and had heard her conversation with Lancelot. She could feel the vibration in the air as the faerie took form. Morgan frequently peered over her shoulder when she visited Lancelot, an annoying habit that inhibited her and prevented intimacy.

Lancelot had given her his lopsided grin when she told him that on a rare visit before Morgan had found them.

"Ah, Gwen." He pulled her to him for a long, deep kiss, his hand easing open the front of her tunic. "You've never been inhibited! It's been too long for us."

She moaned, feeling the strong arms around her; her body ached for him. Slowly, they sank to the ground, their mouths hungry for each other, their hands pulling at each other's clothing.

"Oooh," Morgan breathed with a sigh of pleasure.

Gwenhwyfar froze.

"She's faerie," Lancelot murmured against her mouth. "Let her watch."

"I...I can't." Frustrated, Gwenhwyfar pulled her shirt together.

"Ignore her." Lancelot pushed the material aside and gently kneaded a breast. She closed her eyes in bliss.

"Oh yes..." Morgan's voice floated on the air. "Very nice."

Gwenhwyfar's eyes flew open and she pushed against him. "Lancelot, if you love me, stop."

With a groan, he gave her a final kiss and brought the shirt together. "You're still carrying that Christian guilt with you, my love, even there in Avalon." His smile didn't quite reach his eyes.

"I know," she said miserably, "but I just can't...what we do...she

wants me to share you."

Lancelot glared up at Morgan, but she just giggled and winked.

Abruptly, Gwenhwyfar returned to the present and slowly turned around.

Morgan stood beneath an ancient oak, dressed from head to toe in hues of green and brown, blending with the tree. Behind her, Gwenhwyfar could detect movement in traces of light that swiftly glided through the air; she thought she heard giggling as well, but Morgan was somber.

She moved forward fluidly, the filmy layers of her gown floating behind her like falling leaves. She curtsied low. "King Arthur. My people make you well come."

He stared at her. "Your people? Who are you?"

Green eyes glanced upward seductively through long lashes. "I am Morgan le Fey.

If you look behind me, you will see my people." She made a graceful gesture to her right and the woods came alive.

Among the hedges stood manikins, looking like happy, small children. Respectfully, they doffed their green caps, beady eyes bright. Beside them were groups of mature men, just two feet tall, dressed entirely in brown, tools of their trade laying at their feet. They, too, removed their pointed hats. Deeper in the forest, thin, grotesque black gnomes lurked behind trees. Elfins stood to one side, chattering and nodding toward Arthur. A single silver unicorn gazed at them shyly from the protection of a thicket. Gwenhwyfar stared; as a child, she'd believed in unicorns!

A soft flurry of color rose and came drifting from the left side of the forest. The colors twinkled and faded, returning even more brilliantly. Soft music, nearly inaudible, accompanied the cloud. Overshadowing the subtle colors, a darker shape followed. As they approached, the faeries slowly shaped themselves until, when they reached Arthur, three and ten beautiful maidens—fair, flame-colored, raven-haired—stood before him. Their beguiling eyes watched him. A second group of handsome males emerged.

Awestruck, Gwenhwyfar didn't notice the man who'd followed them. Suddenly, she felt an eerie, magnetic pull and turned slightly. A strange sensation washed over her as the man stepped from the shadows. Light hazel eyes stared at her penetratingly. His curly hair was a dusky umber, his skin bronzed. He had powerful arm and shoulder muscles, like those of a smith, and his brown tunic fit tightly over them. He moved with lithe, animal grace.

Morgan turned her face upward and he leaned over and kissed her lightly. "Cern," she said, "meet King Arthur of Camelot and his queen, Gwenhwyfar."

He bowed slightly. "Morgan says you had a grievous wound and spent a long time healing." His voice, deep and full-timbered, resonated through the trees.

Arthur fidgeted. "Aye, but I am almost ready to return."

Cern looked surprised. "Return? To Camelot? I hoped you would stay and hunt with me. We have interesting game in this forest."

"I'm afraid I have to refuse the invitation," Arthur replied. "I've

Saxons that must be kept in place. Time for me to go back."

The hazel eyes narrowed imperceptibly. "You are not fey; who will take you?"

"Myrddin, I guess," Arthur answered, "and Nimue. They brought us."

"Ah. The druid and the Lady." He looked thoughtful. "Was she not the one who performed the Great Rite with you?"

Obliquely, Arthur glanced at Gwenhwyfar. "Yes. A long time ago."

Cern shrugged. "Time. Of course. It moves differently here; it seems just recently to me." Then he turned to Gwenhwyfar. "Who will be escorting you, my lady?"

She bit her lip. "I...am not sure."

"What are you talking about, Gwenhwyfar?" Arthur asked. "You'll go back with me when I do, along with Myrddin and Nimue."

Morgan gave a disgusted look. "He hasn't been told."

"Told what?" Confused, Arthur looked about. "I won't leave without her."

"Then," Cern said quietly, "you might want to reconsider the hunt."

Arthur's face hardened and he turned to Gwenhwyfar. "What is this all about? Do you want to stay here?"

"No." She shook her head, tears threatening. "I want to go home, but I cannot. You will be going back to Camelot without me."

"What do you mean, she cannot go home?" Arthur nearly shouted at Myrddin.

They were seated in the pavilion near the apple orchard, Gwenhwyfar in tears, Nimue trying to provide comfort and yet answer Arthur.

"We will try," Myrddin said.

"Try?" Arthur stood. "Why should there be a problem?" He paced.

"Arthur." Nimue's soft voice was soothing and he stopped to look at her. "The idea was mine, let me explain. Please sit." She waited until he settled beside Gwenhwyfar. "Avalon sits far away from the world of men, protected by Faerie. Few mortals who wander into the land of Faerie ever return."

"Then how am I getting back?" Arthur looked from her to Myrddin. "Or do I stay also?"

"You go," Myrddin said steadily. "I will use my magic to see you safely returned."

"Then use your magic on Gwenhwyfar as well." Arthur turned back to Nimue. "You can summon it also, can you not?"

She took his hand in her two small ones. "The magic that Myrddin speaks of is love, Arthur. Only his strong, intense love for you will carry you back with him. Even so, he will need my help."

Gwenhwyfar said dully, "Because you love him, too."

Arthur looked quickly at her. "Gwenhwyfar, Nimue has never..."

"Please." Gwenhwyfar turned away. "You don't think I know? Or that you return the feeling? But it matters not."

For a moment, Arthur was nonplused, then he turned to Nimue. "Why can't my love take her through the portal?"

"It might, if you had the fey blood. But it's going to take both Myrddin and me to get *you* back."

Arthur raked a hand through his hair. "You knew this before you brought her here. How could you do it, Nimue? What possessed you to bring her?"

"She gave me a choice, Arthur," Gwenhwyfar interrupted.

He turned to stare at her, puzzled. "Why would you ever consent?"

"Because you would have died without her," Myrddin spoke flatly. "The energy of love is what healed you. From both of them."

Arthur slumped in his chair. "You cared that much, Gwenhwyfar? To imprison yourself here?" He turned slowly to Myrddin. "Then, I will stay also."

"No!" Gwenhwyfar's eyes blazed green fire. "I did my duty so Camelot would not die. Your goals of peace and unity were also mine. You cheat me if you don't return to hold it together."

"There is a possibility…" Nimue began and stopped. All eyes turned to her. "Some mortals do find their way out of the land of Faerie. If we could enlist Morgan's help…"

"How can you trust a faerie, Nimue? Their whole world is illusion and enchantment. Why, even today, when I met her consort, I had the feeling that I had known him before, that we had shared something…" Arthur shook his head. "It carries too much risk."

"Morgan le Fey's consort?" Nimue asked in a suddenly still voice. "What was his name?"

"Cern." Gwenhwyfar answered.

"What was your impression of him?" Nimue asked in a voice barely above a whisper.

"He had wise eyes and an animal alertness to him, like a great stag," Gwenhwyfar answered. "In fact, he asked Arthur to go hunting with him. He seemed pleasant enough."

"You got no other feeling?"

Gwenhwyfar squirmed a little and blushed. "There was an odd sensation…"

Arthur watched Gwenhwyfar's expression and turned to Nimue. "Do you know this man? Will he help us to get Gwenhwyfar out?"

"No. He will not help." She sighed slightly. "You are quite right that you have shared something with him. At the Kingmaking, you shared me."

"You aren't making sense, Nimue. There was no one in the circle of stones except us."

"Do you remember what I called you when I bid you enter the circle, Arthur?" Nimue asked.

In his mind, he traveled back twenty-seven years.

He stepped inside the circle of stones, wearing a mantle of deerskins. His chest and legs were bare, and only a leather loincloth covered him. His headpiece was a magnificent rack of antlers.

Nimue sent her golden aura to meet his. Arthur's eyes widened when he felt the slight crackle in the air, but he didn't move.

Nimue said softly, "I will call the Goddess. Well come, Cernunnos."

Arthur sat there, stunned. Finally, he said the name. "Cernunnos. The Horned God."

"He only appears to mortals when he wants them." Nimue looked at Gwenhwyfar thoughtfully. "He is impossible to resist." Then she turned to

Arthur. “He has offered you immortality, Arthur. No human rides the Wild Hunt across the night sky.”

~ Chapter 3—Flight ~

The ship's bow rose and fell in the troughs between the sea swells. Clutching to the rail and trying to remain upright, Medraut complained, "I don't know why we couldn't have gotten off this thing in Léon."

Beside him, Morgana stood, legs parted, knees relaxed, perfectly balanced to the ship's rhythm. She lifted her head and breathed in the tangy salt smell, adjusting to the pitch of the boat. "Too many people in Léon are loyal to Arthur. Would you actually want to pass through Benoic?"

"Benoic. Land of Lancelot. I hope the sorry bastard is dead," he said bitterly. "If it weren't for him—" He stopped abruptly.

Do you still lust after Gwenhwyfar, Son? A pity the maid tried on that cloak I made for Gwenhwyfar. She wouldn't be so pretty now. "He may be," Morgana answered mildly. "He never leaves Arthur's side in battle, but he was not there when you wounded your father."

"Killed him, you mean." Medraut smiled a little, then clutched the rail again as the ship heeled sharply starboard. "Damn ship."

"We'll hear soon enough, once we land in Gaul," Morgana replied. They'd caught the first ship leaving the battle after Cam's Landing.

"You don't think there's a chance he still lives?" The ship had taken a rolling action as they neared land and the swells decreased. "By the gods, will this motion ever stop?" He narrowed his grey eyes, so like his father's. "The wound was deep, he couldn't have crawled very far."

"Arthur's will is strong, Medraut. I have not sensed the death aura. I tried to mind-meld, as much as I hate the pain it leaves in my head." Morgana turned to admire the young, muscular dockhands preparing the lines on shore. Idly she wondered if any were virgins. That might be fun. "I can't even find Gwenhwyfar," she added absently.

"She's missing?" Medraut tried to sound calm and she knew it was only a ruse.

Gwenhwyfar, the foil to all my plans, the cause of my problems. Arthur wouldn't put the barren whore aside and he wouldn't acknowledge me as his true consort because of his wife, even though I gave him his only heir. I remember well the Beltane night Arthur took me, unaware we were brother and sister. And my son—besotted by that woman—enough to almost get both of us killed when he'd tried to take Camelot. If Gwenhwyfar were dead, all the better. But she hadn't been able to find her anywhere.

The captain, Chelric, appeared on deck. "You'll need to go below while the men work the lines."

Medraut glanced at him, then at his mother. He winked at her and grinned.

She sighed, hating to leave the sight of so many hard masculine bodies. She brushed her inky hair back and put her arm through the German mercenary's. "Do you think you could arrange a wagon for me? We need to get to Paris. I'd be most grateful."

The captain looked down at her slightly parted lips. "Everything has its price."

"Mayhap we could discuss it over a meal and some wine?" Her breast brushed against him as the ship gave a final lurch before thudding along the dock. She made no effort to move away.

Chelric grinned. "Mayhap, we could."

Medraut smirked as he turned away, but Morgana ignored his leer. The German had a solid body, not gone to fat. She wouldn't mind warming his bed for him. Not at all.

The Frankish king, Childebert, looked less than pleased with his guests. Morgana thought she knew why, for she'd researched places to go should Cam's Landing not turn in their favor. Paris was the best option, even though Childebert was already protecting young Judwal of Léon from its ruling Regent, Jean Marc. He didn't need trouble with the Britons right now, while he was having discord with the Burgundian king, Sigismund. But she thought they'd be safer here since Britain itself was unsettled, not knowing which way the land lay since the disappearance of Arthur.

She sighed as she looked at him from across the council table. She was having trouble getting him to believe her request for asylum; she rarely had trouble handling men.

"Cam's Landing should never have happened," Morgana said in a softly beguiling voice. "Medraut only asked for some lands in his name, which is his right as Arthur's only child. Arthur refused. Now, the heir to Britain has had to leave his homeland in fear of his life!"

"Why not seek exile in Armorica? Why come to Paris?"

"There are those in Armorica—especially Benoic—who wouldn't forgive me, nor believe my wish to live in peace," Medraut said.

"Hmm. You're fugitives. What makes you think you'll not be followed here? I have no need of war." Childebert sounded unconvinced.

"We escaped Britain with the German mercenaries before anyone could account for us. We wish to remain incognito. You will be safe from attack if no one knows we're here." Morgana smiled prettily at him. "I could be of use to you."

He raised a brow. "In what way?"

"I have much knowledge of herbal lore and healing. I can personally attend you." She tilted her head and gave him a wide-eyed look.

"I have no need of a witch, my lady. I am a Christian man."

Morgana could see he was having trouble forcing himself to sit still and not fidget beneath her subtly seductive gaze. "For certes." She looked down demurely. "Arthur—my brother—how it pains me to think him gone! Arthur bid us attend the Christian church as well."

Medraut glanced at his mother sideways. “Mayhap, I could also be of service.”

Childebert turned to him. “How?”

“I’ve trained with Arthur. His captains, Bedwyr and Lancelot, taught me everything. I know how the Cymbry thinks, their battle strategies, their weaponry training and how to build a cavalry. I would offer you those skills.”

“Why would I be interested in how the Cymbry thinks?” Childebert asked steadily.

Medraut leaned forward. “Because they were the best army in the world. Even stronger than the ancient Romans.” He sat back. “I think one day you’ll want to acquire the lands that right now only accept suzerainty.” Medraut’s gaze penetrated the Frankish king’s.

Childebert looked away. Morgana pressed the point home. “Every king needs an ever stronger army. Let Medraut build that for you. Use it as you like, or rest easy that you have the best defense. Either way, you gain.” She reached for his hand and brushed his fingers softly with her own. “Please. Don’t send my son away to be murdered. The Christos is a merciful god, is he not?”

Well aware of how she affected me, she knew her touch was like fire because he nearly jerked his hand away. The illusion of glamour she wore and the potions she used kept her looking more like Medraut’s sister than his mother. “You won’t be sorry,” she said.

Morgana presented herself the next morning in the black habit of a convent nun. *As much as I hated those years in that convent Uther condemned me to, at least I know how to act like a holy sister.* She curtsied to the king and queen as they were breaking their fast.

“I think you’ll find my dress and decorum fitting for a pious healer.” She held Childebert’s gaze a moment longer, then turned to his wife. “My name is Anna and my son is called Mordred.”

“Are you well-learned in the herbal arts?” the queen asked.

Morgana hid a smile. “I had a reputation in Britain. Is there something you need? An elixir to beget a child, mayhap?” *Or a potion to make the child stillborn? I can do both.*

The queen blushed and excused herself.

Childebert quickly changed the subject. “It’s clever of you to change your names and appearances. I want to talk to Medra...Mordred about purchasing horses for the cavalry.”

“Certes, I will send him to you.” Morgana looked into his eyes and allowed a slight smile. “I think you’re going to find us both very useful.”

Medraut scratched at the beard that had finally fully grown out. “I don’t much like this; it spoils my looks, I think.” He replaced the mirror on his mother’s dressing table.

Morgana, reclining on the chaise, raised an eyebrow. “Has it stopped you from getting whatever wench you want?”

He grinned. “Frankish women are more willing than the Britons; so far, I’ve not had the same wench twice. Have you found the same for the men?”

"I'm a nun, Medraut, remember?" Morgana looked at her son in mock seriousness.

"During the daytime, Mother." He went and sat beside her. "It seems to me I've heard talk of a new courtesan that makes an appearance at a certain hostelry at night. They say her hair is black and her skin as pale as yours."

Morgana remained unruffled. "Nuns go to bed at Vespers." *And Frankish men are definitely interesting in bed.* "The night belongs to me and I must say it's a useful way of extracting information. Did you know Arthur seems to have disappeared? No one has seen or heard from him, and his body hasn't been found."

Medraut sobered. "And Gwenhwyfar?"

His mother slanted a disgusted look at him. *Still obsessed, my son?*

"Some say she's taken refuge in a convent and wishes to remain unknown." Morgana smoothed her own habit and smiled hugely. "Ironic, isn't it? But she should be of no concern to you; our life is here now, at least for the present. One day you'll lead the Franks against Britain. Concentrate on making yourself invaluable to Childebert."

"You're already doing that, Mother." Medraut smirked and moved out of range from her talons. "Gwenhwyfar will always be my concern. I love her...and one day, I will have her."

Morgana stared at her son. *Mayhap, murdering Gwenhwyfar when I find her will be the only solution.*

Lancelot stopped the destrier at the gate of the Saxon holding near Clausentum. The guard's eyes widened when he saw the blue and silver banner and waved him through.

Cynric stood outside the Great Hall, giving orders to several soldiers, his arm casually draped around a young serving girl. Lancelot smiled as he dismounted. *Nothing much has changed here.*

"I'll take your horse, sir." A blond-headed boy of about eight looked at him earnestly, his eyes the same ice-blue as his father's.

"Ceawlin?"

"I'm his brother, Cutha." The child hesitated. "Are you Lancelot?"

"He is." Cynric approached and extended a hand. "Careful with that horse, Son." He watched as the boy led the animal away.

The girl at his side ducked her head, a strand of golden hair falling over her face. Slowly, she looked up at Lancelot, a smile playing on her lips.

Cynric gave her an affectionate swat on her rump. "Let the man shake the dust off his boots before you try to seduce him. Now, off with you, Frida." She dipped a quick curtsy and smiled openly at Lancelot before she turned and left, swinging her hips for effect.

"She's about to wear me out," Cynric said as they turned and walked to the hall.

Lancelot quirked an eyebrow at him, remembering the girls at Camelot who had swollen bellies while he was hostage there. "I didn't think that was possible."

He laughed. "Take her this evening, you'll see. She isn't afraid to try anything."

Lancelot was spared an answer by Cutha's return. They walked into the Great Hall where Cutha ran off to find his brother and Cynric led the way to a small room in the back. "Tell me what really happened to Arthur." He poured a cup of mead for Lancelot, then sat back, stretching his legs before the small fire in the brazier. "Have you talked to him?"

Lancelot nodded. "In a way. He is secluded."

"Where? My father has had men out searching all of Britain." Cynric's light eyes met Lancelot's dark ones and he grinned lazily. "You knew I would ask."

"Cerdic should send his men looking for Medraut; he's the real source of trouble."

"I agree. He deserves to die, but Custennin will have your men searching." He shrugged. "I think my father would welcome Arthur back. He doesn't think Custennin is strong enough to hold the Britons together."

"Wouldn't that be to his advantage?" Lancelot asked.

"Mayhap. But if your warlords break apart, they will begin to harangue the Saxon settlements. Peace treaties won't be honored. Time is needed to rebuild. Too many men died in both camps."

"There's truth in that," Lancelot replied grimly. "Do I have your oath that you will not fight?"

"For certes. I did not fight at Cam's Landing. I prefer the pleasures of life; I see no reason we cannot live together." Cynric leaned forward, his face serious for once. "I cannot speak for my father. If Arthur returns, I think he will hold fast."

Lancelot nodded. "He will return, but it will take time."

"I heard his wounds were deep; that Gwenhwyfar saved him by finding his scabbard."

Lancelot felt a flicker of pain. *Gwen, how can I bring you home?* "Peredur had it and forgot about it; he'd found it the day I killed Accolon. But yes, Gwenhwyfar took it to him. Just in time."

"Is she with him? There are wild rumors circulating about her and Nimue." Cynric casually poured a second cup of mead.

Lancelot pushed it back. "You wouldn't believe me if I told you. People think I'm half-mad."

"Try me." Cynric gave him a steady look. "I have always respected both the Lady and the queen. I would like to know."

Lancelot took a deep breath. "They are in Avalon, a place between the worlds, in the heart of Faerie."

"A spiritual place? We have Valhalla, the warriors' reward, and Asgard, which is like your Otherworld."

"Not the Otherworld. They are still mortal. I see...Gwenhwyfar can contact me sometimes."

"How?" Cynric's voice was low. "Do you dream of her?"

"For certes." Lancelot smiled a little. "How could I not? This is different. I am awake and suddenly she is there. I can see her and feel her and we talk, but I know also, that she is in my mind, only real. Does that make sense?"

"No." Cynric took a swallow of mead. "But I don't think you're mad either. The bond between you and Gwenhwyfar has always been strong, else neither of you would have risked angering Arthur."

Lancelot looked at him. "Besides Arthur, you might be the only person who understands that."

"Yes, well. I might have been tempted myself, if I'd thought I stood a chance against you." He set his cup down. "What about Nimue?"

"She is taking care of Arthur."

"I have always thought," Cynric ventured, "that had she not been a priestess..."

"That thought has occurred to all four of us," Lancelot's voice held a hint of irony. "For Nimue, the Goddess has spoken. She will uphold her vows and the remaining three of us will continue on."

"Mayhap that will change when they return."

Raw yearning lurched in Lancelot's stomach. "I will be happy with just looking at Gwen, if I could bring her back."

Cynric grinned at that, breaking the conversation's seriousness. "I suspect you'll do more than just look at her." He leaned his arms on the table. "Lancelot, take Frida. Let her give you release. I've had the things from my old hideaway brought here; there's a special room upstairs."

The hideaway. If Morgana hadn't kept me tied and drugged there, I would never have known it existed. Lancelot stood. "Thank you for the offer, but I doubt that even the courtesans my mother selected for my early training could bring me comfort from this."

"Courtesans?" Cynric's grin widened. "You never told me. Then teach Frida a thing or two and she can show me."

Lancelot shook his head. "If you don't mind, though, I'd like to see the room again."

"Last door on your left." Cynric drained his cup and walked to the door. "I'll see you in the morning then."

The room was just as he remembered it. The soft, thick rug, tapestries denoting various forms of lovemaking, even the polished tin on the ceiling. Lancelot shut the door and moved to the bed. He lay back and looked into the mirror.

"Gwenhwyfar?"

In a moment, her body formed in the ethers. "I'm here, Love."

"Come to me. I need to touch you."

"Morgan is with me, Lancelot."

He groaned. "Ask her to leave. For me. I must hold you or I will go mad."

A buzz of conversation followed that he could not hear and then Morgan appeared beside Gwenhwyfar. "I will not leave. I enjoy watching you. I have told Gwenhwyfar not to be so foolish."

"Please, Morgan. Don't you have someone of your own?" Lancelot pleaded.

"I do. And he is as handsome, strong and virile as you. But you would be new for me. Her need of you is great; she will break down and then all three of us will be happy." She giggled.

"I'm sorry, Lancelot," Gwenhwyfar's eyes were suspiciously bright. "Dream of me."

He got up and went to his own room, where he tossed and turned until finally falling into a fitful sleep well past the midnight hour. He dreamt first of Bedwyr.

Bedwyr had already been to several ports with no luck; two southern ports remained. "You're sure no one matching the descriptions took a ship from here?" he asked the harbormaster.

"A small, raven-haired woman with large breasts and the ability to bewitch a man?" The harbormaster laughed. "A young warrior with black hair and grey eyes I might not have noticed, but I always remember the women who pass through here." He shook his head. "They didn't take one of my ships."

"Dark eyes, nearly black, and pale skin," Bedwyr explained to the boatmen when he arrived at the port of Isca. "A provocative way of moving." He winked. "She makes you feel as though you were the only man she's ever been interested in."

"Aye," one of the captains grinned. "I know the type...and as faithful as a bitch-dog in heat."

An older seaman clamped him on the shoulder. "Find yourself another woman. There's plenty that's willing to be bedded."

Bedwyr looked down at the floor and played his trump card. "Mayhap. But this one owes me some money, as well."

"Well now, that puts a different light on it," another one said. "Any chance she might still be in these parts? We can keep a look out."

"Thank you. If you see her, send word to me at Camelot."

The captain who had spoken earlier raised an eyebrow. "You're one of Custennin's men?"

"Yes." He rose to leave. "The name's Bedwyr."

"Good luck," a young longshoreman said. "Take your money out of her hide when you find her."

The older seaman laughed. "A woman like that will probably like it."

Bedwyr smiled and turned away.

If only they knew, Lancelot thought in his dream.

His second dream was of Gwenhwyfar, and then suddenly she was beside him, her soft breasts pressed against him, her fingers working magic on him, and delighting him with her mouth as she took him.

He reached down for her shoulders. "Come here, Gwen, while I can still control myself. I want this to pleasure us both."

She did not reply, nor did she acquiesce, merely increasing the pressure of her mouth on his throbbing hardness, her hands expertly holding him in place.

"Gwen, I can't wait..." and then the world exploded into blinding light and total darkness as the release of the frustration of the six months since Cam's Landing came.

He shuddered and at last pulled her to him. She snuggled into the crook of his arm. "We will do this again, in a little while, Gwen. My turn." She stroked his chest and he sighed contentedly and drifted into sleep.

In the morning, she was gone. Bewildered, Lancelot sat up. *Had it been a dream, after all? No, it had been too real and there was physical evidence on the sheets.* He pushed his legs over the side of the bed, and then he saw several strands of blond hair left on the pillow. *Frida.* He smiled then and wondered if maybe he should send Galahad to Cynric's. Frida would be a good introduction to physical pleasure.

~ Chapter 4— The Quest Begins ~

Galahad laid another piece of kindling on the fire and held his hands near the flame. "How can it be so cold this late in the season? The Christos' resurrection is almost upon us."

Peredur turned the hare on the spit and poured himself a generous helping of wine. "This will keep you warm, if you'd only try it."

Galahad looked at the cup a bit contemptuously. "The Lord Jesu preached our bodies are temples. You know I have forsworn liquor."

"Aye, and everything else that is pleasurable as well," Peredur grumbled. "For certes, riding with you this past year has been a lesson."

"Mayhap if you'd keep your mind focused on our quest, we'd already have found the holy cup." Galahad shook his head obstinately. "I've seen you eyeing the wenches. A woman will control you if you let her get close."

Peredur's warm brown eyes held a smile. "I would never dishonor a woman, but I'd like to be wed and settle down, once this cup is found."

"You'll only find trouble and sorrow."

"How can you say that?" Peredur handed him a portion of the meat. "I know your father and mother cared not for each other, but look at the king and queen. He worshipped her."

"Most times he was miserable, knowing..." Galahad stopped.

"I never have believed those rumors," Peredur said quietly.

"Then you're a fool, Peredur! The rumors are true. Do you forget that I lived with my father and Gwenhwyfar at Joyous Garde? And with the queen and king at Camelot? I've seen what love can do."

"Be careful, Galahad. You speak close to treason here."

"No. I bear no ill will toward the queen. She was kind to me when I arrived at Joyous Garde, scared out of my wits at the sight of Lancelot. She encouraged me to read and play the harp, and on more than one occasion she eased my father's anger at me because I didn't want to be a warrior. "She was the only one who could ever persuade him to change his mind about anything. She has that power because he loves her. Because she is a woman. They nearly destroyed Camelot."

"She did the right thing, though, going with the king."

"For certes." Galahad sighed. "For all my father's talk about the queen being in the land of Faerie, he should accept the fact that Arthur died on the Isle and Nimue stays hidden. Gwenhwyfar is probably in a convent in Armorica."

"What?" Peredur stared through the smoke. "They're in Avalon. You placed him on the barge."

"I don't think Avalon exists. The Good Book has not spoken of it."

Peredur shook his head unbelievingly. "We spent time on the Isle of Avallach with the Lady, protected from the Saxons during the battle of Cam's Landing. How could you doubt after that?"

"I believe that God, the Holy Father, shielded us," Galahad answered confidently.

"On the ISLE? The home of the Goddess?" Peredur nearly laughed. "I have no reason to doubt your God, but the Great Mother protected us, and She will heal our king and return him to us."

"You know I don't accept the pagan ways," Galahad replied stiffly. "How can someone live in a place between the worlds? We either go to heaven or to hell. But I will pray that you see the Light."

"And I," Peredur said softly, "will pray that, in this lifetime, you find tolerance in your soul."

They rode silently the next morning. The sun had already dried the dew on the grass before Peredur spoke.

"Mayhap, we should part company. We have searched the south of Britain to no avail. If separate, we could cover twice the territory."

Galahad brushed his dark hair off his forehead, but looked straight ahead. "That may be best." Peredur never seemed to feel the anguish he did every time they searched a church, only to find nothing.

They rode easterly for several more miles over gently rolling hills that flattened onto a plain and then through a sparse forest. They stopped at a natural spring near the crossing of two roads. A willow tree stood close, bits of cloth hanging on the newly leafed branches. Peredur took the traveler's cup from its rock niche above the spring and poured an oblation before offering it to Galahad.

"Why are those rags tied to that tree?" Galahad asked as he dismounted.

"They're offerings to the spirit of this spring," Peredur answered. "Acknowledging her presence brings good luck."

"That sounds like more of your pagan superstitions," Galahad replied. "I'd better get going."

"Let us not part angry; we have been friends too long."

"That we have." Galahad paused, and then suddenly threw his arm around Peredur. "I will miss your companionship."

"Before you leave, might you keep an old man some company?"

Startled, they both turned. An ancient man, greatly stooped, regarded them from beneath his shaggy eyebrows, his white beard reaching his waist. He waved a scrawny arm behind him. "I have a good stew brewing. It is a cool day for spring."

They followed him a short distance to a small stone hut hidden from the road. He didn't speak again until he'd filled their bowls and they were seated at the table.

Galahad inhaled the spicy aroma appreciatively. Neither he nor Peredur had done much more than roast what game they could find and buy bread and cheese. Tasting the soup was even better than it smelled. "This is good. What's in it?"

The hermit's faded eyes twinkled. "Besides the usual, a few special herbs a lady long ago taught me to use. I grow them out back."

"Your wife?" Galahad asked politely.

"Ah, no!" he laughed. "This was a pretty young thing, hair black as a raven, skin like snow. She lived at a convent nearby and came into the village with her herbs a time or two." He winked. "I was a lot younger then and quite randy." He paused. "She brought me the stew one time. It fortified me well." He cackled at that.

Galahad looked away in disgust, but Peredur blurted naïvely, "If she could cook like this, you should have married her!"

The old man stopped laughing and looked into the distance. "I would have, son, for there was something about her that could bind a man. King Uther married her off to Uriens, one of his warlords, up north."

"Uther?" Galahad turned back to him. "Did you know him?"

"I might say I did," he responded. "I was the cooper when he kept his camp at Ambresbyrig. Now those were some rowdy days, I can tell you. Uther's men were a lusty lot, plenty of women always around."

Peredur looked at him, eyes wide. "Was King Arthur there, too?"

"Eh?" The ancient pulled himself back from the story he was about to launch. "Arthur? Oh, yes. He made quite a name for himself early on. Funny how nobody took him for Uther's son."

"Is it true he led the twelve battles that forced the Saxons back?"

"Well, I don't know about all of them; he was only five and ten when Uther took him in. But he developed a small band of strong men who were always with him. You boys may have heard of them—Cai, Gwalchmai, Bedwyr—they fought hard, but they could tear up the town at night. Especially Arthur. Women were attracted to him like a bee to the first rose of spring. We should have known he was Uther's son, by that alone." He cackled again.

"Which battle do you think was most important?" Galahad wanted to forestall the story about women.

The old man looked at him thoughtfully. "Hard to say. But, when he was about twenty-six, he was nearly killed chasing the Saxon, Colgrin, through Anglia. A lad barely old enough to fight saved him."

"How did he do that?" Peredur asked eagerly.

"Well, the story I heard was Arthur had asked the boy to ride beside him, as a favor to his father, King Ban of Benoic. A Saxon started to throw an ax at Arthur and the lad threw his lance and deflected the blow. The men called him Lancer after that."

Galahad started to interrupt, but Peredur encouraged the man. "I had not heard that story."

"After that, Lancer was always beside Arthur. Good-looking young man, too. Dark hair and eyes, a devil of a smile...the kind women find irresistible and men can't compete with. Arthur had met his match." He winked again. "Word was Lancer's mother had him trained by a dozen courtesans before she sent him here."

Galahad looked at him in horror. "That can't be true!"

"No?" The shaggy eyebrows wiggled. "A lot of women would have argued with you about that, son. There were a lot of broken hearts and weeping maidens when he became the queen's Champion."

"Why would his being the queen's Champion make a difference?" Peredur asked before Galahad could silence him.

"Ah. He fell in love with the one woman he couldn't have. Of course, we all heard the story of what happened, years later." The old man shook his head. "Love is a funny thing." He peered at them. "Either of you two been in love?"

Peredur shook his head and Galahad gave him a small lopsided smile and brushed his hair from his forehead. "No."

The old man's eyes widened a bit. "You looked just like Lancer, then. You practice that smile and you won't have any trouble with the ladies, either. Ah, to be young again..." The old man drifted off into his private world, eyes glazed.

They finished the stew in silence, the hermit lost in his own thoughts. When they stood to take their leave, he looked at them as though surprised they were still there. Then he put a bony hand on the table and pushed himself up. "Wait. I never asked your names."

"Peredur."

"Galahad."

The old man's eyebrows lifted at the name, but he made no reference. "Where are you bound to?"

"We are on a special quest looking for the lost cup of the Christos," Galahad said.

The man studied them, then nodded. "You are the ones. I have something for you." He hobbled to a shelf and pulled out a neatly folded piece of parchment. He handed it to Galahad. "The new Lady of the Lake left this for you."

"How would she know we'd come here?" Galahad asked suspiciously.

The hermit shrugged. "Why would I question her? She has the Sight. She only told me that I would recognize the two of you. This is the answer for what you seek."

The writing was in Latin, in Argante's fine hand:

To be immersed direct at None
To wander ever lone
To heed the call of one in few
And give the stone its due
The sound of heaven will be heard
As sweet the song of bird

"What can it mean?" Peredur asked.

Galahad shook his head. "I think the sound of heaven will happen when we find the Grail. I have no idea of the rest."

The hermit shook his head. "A riddle, boy. If the Lady wrote this, then these are trials that you will have to meet to be successful." His eyes began to glaze again. "Now you'd best be on your way; I always take a nap and dream of the lady who gave me the recipe." He winked. "I'm glad you liked it."

They parted ways, Peredur heading west, Galahad heading east.

An hour later, Galahad wiped sweat from his face. *Lord's mercy, but it's grown hot.* He shielded his eyes and slanted a look at the sun. Hidden partially behind a cloud, it had already taken a western path. *Strange, to be so warm on a cool day.*

He rode for another hour, aware that a restlessness had begun to stir within him. He wished he had someone to talk to. The horse's gait, usually so smooth, jarred him at every step. *Is something wrong with the horse? Thrown a shoe?* He turned off the road toward the trees. *I'll take a look and rest awhile.*

The coolness of the shade did nothing to relieve the heat radiating from him. He bent to check the horse's hooves. All were shod, the frogs clean of any stones. He straightened and felt his face flame. *I need some water.* He spotted a dim trail and led the horse farther into the wood in search of a stream.

He'd not gone far before he heard water gurgling over rock. The path turned sharply to the left and he followed it, stepping into a glade and then he stopped, dumbfounded.

The girl sat naked, her back to him, in the small pool that formed where beaver dams had stopped the flow. She was singing quietly as she splashed in the fresh water.

A succession of tingles, like tiny pricks of a needle, washed over him and his breathing became shallow. The girl's hair, pale as moonlight, created a halo of light. Sound became defused, at once acute, yet muted. He watched as she dipped one graceful arm and then the other. He prayed for her to turn around and then prayed she would not. His body was burning now and he wanted to leap onto his horse and gallop madly away, but he stood transfixed. Never in his life had he felt like this.

The stallion scented another horse and neighed. Startled, the girl turned, her blue eyes wide in terror. Galahad glimpsed the exposed, milky white breasts with the pink rosebuds, before she covered them with her arms. An instant throbbing occurred inside his trews.

"Get out of here!" The girl was furious. "This is my father's land; you have no business here."

Galahad tried to move or look away, but he couldn't. The throbbing had developed into an aching bulge and it took all his willpower not to clench himself. *In the Lord's name, what is happening?*

"Sir!" Her voice was cold now, like icicles breaking under the rise of a winter sun. "If there is any honor in you; you will allow me to get my clothes, unmolested."

Honor. The word broke through his dazed mind and loosened his limbs. The bulge diminished. Now he could see her clothing lying on the bank near to him. He walked over to the bank and picked up the thick, thirsty towel. The girl watched him silently, submerged to her neck, arms still crossed.

"Here." He turned around and held the towel out behind him. It seemed he waited an eternity before he heard the rippling of the water. For a brief moment her fingers touched his hand as she took the towel and heat flared through him again. He clenched his jaw and forced himself to stay turned away, yet the sounds of her clothes rustling drove him nearly mad.

"I'm dressed." Her voice came softly now.

He took a deep breath and pivoted. She was wearing a lady's riding habit, the short jacket accentuating her narrow waist. "I'm sorry if I scared you. What are you doing out here by yourself?"

A look of guilt passed fleetingly over her face. "I slipped away unnoticed. Everyone is preparing for the Easter feast and I was bored." She raised her head defiantly. "I'm old enough to do what I want."

He guessed she was only a year or two younger than himself. And spirited and beautiful. He clenched his fists to keep himself from touching her. "You could get into serious trouble unescorted."

She raised an eyebrow. "Do you think me defenseless?"

"You were when I saw you."

"Hmm. You're right, I suppose." She pulled a dagger so quickly from her boot that it appeared to be a silver streak of sunlight. "I should have kept this within arm's reach."

Galahad grinned lopsidedly. "Lady, that can easily be taken from you."

"Would you like to try?" she taunted him.

He moved without thought. Years of forced weaponry training with Lancelot had taught him well. He caught her wrist with one hand and spun her around with the other, her back against him. He applied just enough pressure with his thumb for her hand to go numb. The dagger dropped to the ground.

He released her and she turned, rubbing her wrist. "How did you do that? Will you show me?"

"It's an easy tactic." He picked up the dagger and handed it back to her. "I didn't hurt you, did I?"

"No, but my hand just wouldn't work." She sheathed the dagger. "Show me, mayhap, I could use it." She took his hand in hers. "Where do you press?"

Her touch inflamed him and he tried to withdraw his hand, but she held fast. Reluctantly, he placed her fingers over the pressure points. "There."

She seemed delighted when his hand suddenly relaxed. She massaged his wrist then, and looked up at him, smiling.

He stared at her, his body filled with an aching need he'd not known he possessed. He felt he could move earth and sea to get to her, to hold her; passion raged, barely confinable. *Is this how my father feels when he sees Gwenhwyfar?*

She stepped closer, and reached up to brush the dark hair back. "You're a handsome man and well-mannered, too."

Galahad squirmed and forced himself to keep his hands at his side. "You're a lady." *Holy Mary, Mother of God, pray for me...*

She frowned a little. "My father doesn't let me do anything that's fun. That's why I sneak off to swim here. Why don't you keep me company for a while?"

"I don't think that wise."

"Why not?" She looked up at him.

He stared over her head into the distance, not trusting himself to look at her. "I might do something unforgivable."

She took his hand. "My da won't let me be alone with a man. I've never even been kissed. Would it be so unforgivable to do that?" She smiled, her dimples showing.

Galahad wrapped his arms around her. Their mouths found each other, fumbling at first with tentative explorations, but at the probing of his tongue, her lips parted willingly. Galahad lost himself in her, crushing her to him, loving the taste of her, the feel of the softness beneath his hands, the outline of her curves. It was some time before they finally stopped, gasping for air. She leaned against him and he lay his head atop hers. They rocked gently. *I had not known it could be like this...so right.*

Finally, they stepped apart. He smiled apologetically. "I've never asked your name."

"Elen. I'm named for my aunt, rest her soul."

"My sister's name is Elen," Galahad answered. "Where do you live? I want to meet your father." He had no idea he would ever be able to feel this way about a woman.

She smiled happily and gave him a quick kiss. "My father's name is Tirre. We live at Astolat, less than a mile from here." She tilted her head and giggled. "And your name, kind sir?"

"Galahad. From Camelot." He smiled back, reaching for her hand, but she stepped away, a look of disbelief and anguish on her face.

"You're Lancelot's son?"

He frowned. "Yes. Why?"

"You don't know?" Tears welled in her eyes. "You will never be well come in my father's house! Your father was responsible for my aunt's death!" Turning, she ran to her horse.

"Elen! Wait!" Galahad ran to her, but she'd already mounted. "Please, don't go. Whatever happened has nothing to do with us! I love you!"

"That cannot be!" She wept openly. "Never." She spun the horse and gave him his head, leaving Galahad choking in the dust.

He stayed in the glade that night, with his horse for company. When he awoke in the morning, the effect of the aphrodisiac had worn off. With a clear head, he remembered Elen and what she'd said. It was ridiculous for her father to hold him accountable for his father's sins, whatever they had been, and he thought he knew. *I'll go and talk to Tirre myself.*

He rode into Astolat, but before he could dismount, man came walking toward him. "I'm Galahad," he said, "and I'd like to talk to Tirre."

The man's eyes were cold as he stared at him. "I am Tirre and even if Elen hadn't come home crying yesterday, I would know who you are. You look just like your father. You and I have nothing to talk about."

"I'm not anything like my father," Galahad protested. "I think I love Elen and I've come to ask your permission...I'd like to get to know her better."

Tirre raised an eyebrow. "I'm sure you would."

Galahad felt himself growing angry. "I would not dishonor her."

"Mayhap you wouldn't," her father answered. "Mayhap you would stay just long enough for her to give her heart, like my sister did, and then you'd leave. What mission were you on when you met my daughter?"

Galahad thought of the quest. It was true; he would traveling on. But surely, to stay a few weeks, to earn his keep... He felt Tirre watching him.

"I'm searching for a Grail, one I've seen in visions, much like Bishop Dubricius. It is to bring peace to Britain."

"You're a dreamer." Tirre snorted. "Just the kind of man that is beguiling enough to win an innocent girl's heart. Your search won't let you stay with her, though. So, no. You will never see my daughter again. Be gone."

"But..."

"I said go. Do I have to call the guards?"

Galahad looked at the men who were already assembling near the barn, hands on their sword hilts. He wished he'd never met Elen, then he wouldn't be feeling this pain as though something were tearing apart inside of him.

"I'll go," he replied, "and I'll be sure to give my father your best regards." He turned and spurred his horse to a canter.

He felt like a dog licking its wounds. By afternoon, he found himself back in the glade where he'd met Elen. He drifted numbly through the day and slept fitfully that night. Then, as he sat there well into the next morning, having no ambition to leave, the grief turned to anger. *I've been right all along. Allowing a woman to get too close is dangerous. I almost made the same mistake my father did and the king, too. Well, I won't be that stupid again. Women are the enemy.*

He didn't leave the glade the third day until the sun was high in the sky. On the road, people were traveling to church. *It is the day of the crucifixion!* He chided himself for nearly forgetting. *Just one more thing women do; they make a man forget what's important.* With a growing fear, he hoped he hadn't defiled himself and become unworthy of finding the Grail. *It was just a kiss*...and then he remembered the insatiable urge he'd felt. He hung his head in shame. *May the Lord forgive me; I will do penance.*

He stopped at the next town walked quietly inside its church. People had gathered to pray before the service. He sat in the back, intent on his own prayers. *Oh, merciful God, who gave his Son to die for us this day that we may be saved, help me. Make me worthy to accomplish the quest of the Holy Grail. Let me bring it back to our people so peace may be had. And give me strength to withstand the false lures of women.*

The service soothed his turmoil. When over, the small, rotund priest announced he would be performing Holy Baptism in the river outside town. Any who wished to be saved or to renew their vows to the Christos were well come.

Galahad followed the small group. His mother had made sure he was baptized, he knew, but with the sin he'd wanted to commit with Elen, it would not hurt to have the blessing again.

The last one, he entered the river and sank to his knees, the water just below his chin.

The priest intoned, "Repent and be baptized...in the name of Jesu Christos, you are made whole." Holding Galahad's shoulders, he immersed him in the water.

When he emerged, the bells from the distant church tolled the hour of Nones and he remembered the first line of Argante's riddle.

Peredur stopped at Camelot on his journey northwest. Lancelot met him in the bailey. "Galahad did not come with you?"

"We decided if we went separate ways, we could cover more ground," Peredur answered. "It is slow work, stopping at every church and shrine."

Lancelot studied him thoughtfully as they walked to the Great Hall. "You think a priest may be keeping the Grail? With all Bishop Dubricius' talks, I'd think a priest would have come forward if he had it."

"I believe the cup lies in pagan hands, well hidden, but Galahad feels otherwise." Peredur shook his head. "All I want to do is share the joy I feel when I dream of the cup. My endurance has been tried on many an occasion this past year."

"Oh? How so?" Lancelot nodded to the servant to bring wine as they sat in front of the unlit hearth, in the comfortable overstuffed chairs Gwenhwyfar had insisted on having. *Bel's Fires! Even the chairs remind me of Gwen!*

"We spent our days on the road, our nights sleeping outside, the food was plain and simple, what free time we had was spent in contemplation."

"Galahad's idea?" Lancelot asked dryly.

"He thinks to remain pure in heart requires sacrifice...abstinence from any pleasures."

"Ah." Lancelot waited for the wine to be poured. "Could it be wanting a woman that has separated the two of you?"

Peredur blushed and looked away. "I am well past twenty. I think it's time."

Lancelot quirked an eyebrow. "You'll get no argument from me."

"I had a strange thing happen three days ago." Peredur spoke softly, not looking at Lancelot. "We'd stopped at a hermit's cottage to share his stew and afterward—Galahad turned east and I west—I was alone and suddenly my body felt aflame and I itched and burned and couldn't sit my horse. I know I've never been a good horseman, but this was torture. Even my shirt rubbing against me was unbearable. Then, I went half-mad, thinking of every pretty girl I'd seen. I couldn't stop."

Lancelot grinned. "There must have been an aphrodisiac in the soup. Why, I don't know, unless the man had other plans before you two came along." He hesitated. "You've never felt lust before?"

Peredur kept his head down. "I was taught to honor and respect women; I have always treated them kindly. These thoughts weren't...I'm ashamed to say it, but I undressed girls in my mind."

"There's nothing wrong with undressing a woman who wants to be unrobed." Lancelot thought about the easy lovemaking and private games he and Gwenhwyfar played. A piercing blade knifed through him. *Gwen, I need you.*

Peredur looked up, wide-eyed. "But how do you know if that's what they want?"

Lancelot stared at him. *Can any boy over five and ten not know that*? He strove to keep his face serious. "Peredur, you may always take a kiss, if it's freely given. After that, the woman will let you know what she wants."

"But I would want to honor the lady; could I take a token from her? To show my love is pure?"

"Don't offer protests of love where none exists," Lancelot answered. "It's unfair to the lady."

"For certes, I would have to love her if I...I did any of those things I thought about." Peredur sounded shocked.

Lancelot hid a smile. *Is the man a total fool?* "Love and lust are two different things. You only felt the urge to do what comes naturally to both men and women."

"Women feel like this, too?" Peredur seemed unbelieving.

Lancelot no longer resisted a smile. "If they didn't, we men would be in a lot of pain...or we wouldn't be here at all."

Peredur blushed again and looked at the floor.

Lancelot leaned forward. "Go into the village to the tavern. A woman will find you. Choose an older one who can teach you about pleasure."

Peredur looked up suddenly, his eyes wide. "The hermit told us stories about Arthur and he mentioned you. Said a dozen courtesans trained you! Is that true?"

Lancelot sat back and frowned. "Who was this hermit?"

"He said he was the cooper while Uther was king. "Not only did he have stories about you and Arthur, he rattled on about himself as a young man and some black-haired girl with white skin and large breasts who lived in the convent nearby."

Morgana? Lancelot remembered Arthur explaining the woman who'd waylaid him on his return to the fort at Beltane so many years ago. Arthur hadn't known Uther had sent Morgana to the abbey or that she was his sister. Medraut had been conceived of that one-time incestuous union.

"Was it true?"

"What?" Lancelot asked, coming out of his thoughts.

"The courtesans? A dozen of them?"

"Only eight...and there was a reason." He looked seriously at Peredur. "Is that what you want? Custennin can send for one."

"No." Peredur stood. "I still think I will wait for love. Good night, Lancelot."

Lancelot nodded absently as he left. *Morgana. She must have seduced the cooper before she was sent north to marry Uriens. So, Morgana's herbs have worked once again.* He thought of how Elaine had tainted his drink the night she seduced him. Galahad had been the result.

Galahad. By Mithras! If my virgin son ate that stew, what had the reaction been? I would love to know.

Peredur continued westward. He'd not returned to his father's holdings in Dinas Emrys since he was a small boy. His mother had sent him away from Pellinore's court because she'd lost her other son, Lamorak, as hostage to Queen Margawse of Lothian. Dyonas, the Forest Woman, and cousin to Lady of the Lake had raised him in the Summer Country. Now, he was making his way slowly toward the rugged mountains of Gwynedd.

He stopped the first night in Aquae Sulis and enjoyed the old Roman baths. *Galahad would never approve of this.* He'd have to leave soon, for the baths would open to the ladies shortly. His mind drifted to the thought of a lady sitting in this very spot, enjoying the water. *No, I will wait for love.* Still, Lancelot had said if a kiss were freely given... He wondered how a woman's lips would feel against his. *What kind of a fool have I been never to have been kissed?*

A restless night's sleep did not erase the thought. Tired, he mounted his horse and set out on the road to Glevum. He held the reins loosely, letting the horse choose the pace. His mind drifted and after an hour on the road, he began to doze.

He wasn't prepared for the large stag that leaped across the road, barely a lance length from his horse. The animal reared in surprise, unseating him, and thundered down the road as the men who'd been pursuing the stag emerged from the wood.

"Is he alive?" Peredur faintly heard a man ask through his daze.

"He breathes," another answered, "but he must have hit his head. I suppose we'd better get him to our tents and have someone go after his horse."

The first man sighed. "I'd hoped for venison tonight."

Peredur felt himself being lifted, then he knew no more.

When he fully woke, night had fallen. Stars were scattered like rare diamonds against black velvet. Carefully, he sat up, rubbing his head gingerly. The last thing he remembered was he'd been lightly dreaming.

Looking around, he was in a clearing of the forest; several tents had been erected, but he lay on a pallet near a steadily burning fire. Nearby, he could hear the soft blowing and stamping of horses on a picket line.

The largest tent held a small light. Slowly, he got up and walked toward it.

The guard in front slumped against a tree, snoring softly. Peredur frowned. Arthur wouldn't have tolerated that. *Who are these men?*

He pushed aside the flap and entered. An oil lamp on the table cast a golden glow. A stuffed chair sat beside a table that held the remnants of the evening meal. Soft rugs covered the grass, and the bed toward the back was laden in rich furs. *For certes, the lord lavished himself well.* The hump in the bed told Peredur the man was probably asleep. He pondered whether to wake him. *I need to know what happened.*

He approached cautiously, his hand on his sword hilt. Gently, he touched the shoulder.

The bundle groaned and rolled over, spilling brown curls across the pillow.

Shocked, Peredur looked at the girl. She awoke and for a minute, sleep rendered her mute. Then she opened her mouth to scream.

"Shhh!" Peredur put his hand over her mouth. Her blue eyes widened in fright and she began to struggle. He leaned over, and put his other arm over her chest, holding her down. "Don't be afraid. I won't hurt you. I just have a question."

She fought harder, thrashing with her body, the covers sliding away in her effort. He half crawled on the bed, a leg over hers to keep her still. "Please, stop thrashing! I mean you no harm."

Eventually, since he made no other move than to stay in that position, she quieted, but he felt the wild beating of her heart. Then, he became aware of the softness of the breast beneath his hand. A throbbing began in his loins. Tentatively, he began kissing her awkwardly.

Her body went rigid, but she didn't fight him. *She is allowing me to kiss her,* he thought happily, remembering what Lancelot had said. *And she is not clothed; I don't need to worry about that!*

Clumsily, he began to explore her body, squeezing the breast gently and then moving along the curve of her body and down her hip. She did not move. *She is letting me do what I will. Lancelot said a woman will let me know...* He sat up quickly and removed his shirt. He was beginning to pull off his trews when he heard her whimper. Glancing at her, he realized she was crying.

"What is wrong, my lady?" he asked tenderly.

She stared at him and reached to cover herself.

He frowned. "Do you not want me to love you?"

She pulled her legs toward her and scuffled to a sitting position at the far side of the bed. "No. Please leave. Please. I won't tell anyone you were here if you do." The covers were under her chin now and her eyes pleaded with him.

He shook his head and slowly got up and moved to the chair by the table and sank down in it. "I have dishonored you." He reached for a piece of meat and chewed it numbly. *Mayhap I misunderstood Lancelot.*

"Who...who are you?" she finally asked.

"My name is Peredur. I have no idea of where I am or what happened. I saw your light. That is why I came in here."

She regarded him suspiciously. "You weren't going to rape me?"

"The Goddess forbid, no!" His voice shook. "I respect women."

"A strange way you have of showing it."

He hung his head. "I thought you were willing."

She didn't reply for several minutes. "My name is Blanchefleur. You fell and hit your head. My uncle, Gornemant, found you. We are on a hunting expedition."

"I am thankful for that. I was riding toward Glevum."

"Yes. We recovered your horse."

"Again, I am in your debt," Peredur murmured, "and to think how I frightened you. Let me make amends." He walked back to the bed and sat on the edge. "I am on a quest to seek an ancient chalice which may hold power. If you will give me some token, I will do this in your honor."

She studied him, the covers still pulled tight to her. "Have you no lady?"

"No." He hoped she couldn't see him blush in the dim light. "But if you will allow it, I will serve you."

She studied his face, then slowly held out her hand. "You may have this ring."

Slowly, he removed the golden ring with its single emerald and placed it on his little finger. "I will treasure this forever," he said fervently, "and I will remember your beauty and kindness, too." He bent to pick up his shirt. "I am sorry you didn't want my kiss. Please forgive me."

He felt the gentle pressure of her fingers on his shoulder. "Peredur," she said softly. "You may kiss me if you wish."

Peredur returned to his pallet well before dawn, the ring safely tucked away. He'd fallen in love with the one sweet kiss she'd given him. He played it over in his mind for hours.

Seeing him awake the next morning, Gornemant explained what had happened.

"You lost a fine stag because of me," Peredur said. "If you'd like, I could stay and help you hunt."

"You'd be most well come," Gornemant replied jovially. "Another spear will come in handy." He looked up as Blanchefleur approached with fresh oatcakes and soft cheese. "I doubt you've met my niece."

Peredur inhaled sharply. In the bright morning sunlight, she was even more beautiful. "I am honored, my lady."

She smiled shyly. "I hope you'll find this simple fare satisfactory."

"Blanchefleur is an excellent cook," her uncle bragged. "A pity we have nothing more to offer."

Peredur's eyes didn't leave her face. "I've been on the road a year with only my cooking to eat. I could wish for nothing better."

"Why have you been on the road?" Gornemant asked. "I took you for one of Custennin's men."

"I am, but King Arthur made a request..." He paused. "I'm searching for a Grail. The new religion claims the Christos used it at his last meal; the Lady of the Lake says it's always been in the hands of the Goddess from beyond Time."

"The Grail?" Gornemant asked. "The same one Bishop Dubricius claims to have seen?"

Peredur was surprised. "You've heard of it?"

"Aye. The good bishop thinks it is worth a ransom of treasure." He tilted his head and eyed Peredur. "Is it fortune you seek?"

"No. Arthur thinks the cup creates peace for those who share in drinking from it. I am honor-pledged to keep looking for it."

"Did you know Arthur well?" Gornemant's tone was light, but Peredur felt himself being evaluated and he squirmed a little.

"Well enough," Peredur said proudly. "I lived at Camelot for two years. The king himself practiced weaponry with me."

"You said your name was Peredur?" The older man was silent for a minute, and then a look of recognition came across his face. "I fought beside King Pellinore many years ago when I was a young soldier. He had a son with your name."

"He was my father."

"Well." Gornemant looked from him to his niece and back again. "He was a fine man. Why don't you plan to spend some time with us? Surely, the quest can wait a few weeks?"

Peredur carefully avoided looking at Blanchefleur and she studied the ground equally well. "I would like that, and would I have your permission to pay court to your niece as well?"

"If she is willing, I'll give my permission."

She looked up then, her face aglow. "I am willing."

Throughout the summer Peredur trained with Gornemant. He wanted to please Blanchefleur in every way and had a thousand questions for everyone who'd known her since she was a small child. Finally, Gornemant took him aside and told him not to ask so many questions.

Eventually, Peredur could wait no longer. It was mid-fall and if he were to get to Gwynedd before the snows made the passes difficult, he would have to leave.

The night before, he'd asked her uncle for Blanchefleur's hand in marriage and now that they were betrothed, he openly wore the ring she'd given him that first night.

They'd decided on a picnic for his last day, and sat beneath the beech trees that edged the bank of the River Usk, having finished the midday meal several hours before. The autumn day was unusually warm, the sky a brilliant blue. Blanchefleur gently traced a pattern on his arm with her fingers. "I wish you didn't have to go."

"I cannot delay any longer. "As soon as I find the cup, I will come back for you." He watched the lazily flowing river. "I cannot refuse Arthur's last request."

She sighed and tucked her hand inside his arm. "I suppose he's dead. It's been two years since Cam's Landing. For so long, we have thought he would return."

"The Lady of the Lake has not returned and the queen went with her," Peredur answered. "As long as they stay gone, he lives."

She looked at him wide-eyed. "You have that much faith in your Lady?"

"The Lady took him to Avalon, a place of great healing."

"Where is it?"

"It lies between the worlds, through the land of Faerie."

"The Christian priests say there is no such thing." She frowned. "I would feel better if you had the Christos' blessing on your quest."

"I am pagan. I will take your blessing, my lady, as representative to the Goddess." *Every good deed I do, I will do in your name.*

She hesitated and he stood, pulling her up with him. "Galahad has oft told me of this practice of the cleansing of the soul—Baptism—is that the word? The pagans also have rituals of purity. Come with me to the river; the Goddess will speak through you."

When they reached the river's edge, he stripped off his clothes, embarrassed a little to be standing before her naked. She averted her eyes; he gathered his courage and took her hands gently in his. "You must join me. I love you. Nothing can be more purifying than that."

Awkwardly, he undressed her, marveling at the perfection of her body, caressing her tenderly. Since that first night, she'd always been properly dressed when he saw her. Gently, he led her into the water, less cold than he would have thought it. He pressed her against him, bumping noses as they kissed and sank beneath the surface. When they emerged, he whispered huskily, "Your blessing, my lady; will you lay with me?"

She smiled and they waded to the bank and wrapped together in the blanket, their hands exploring each other hesitantly and a bit clumsily at first, then gasping at the pleasure spots they found, rejoicing in their closeness. As passion consumed them, Peredur was aware of his soul expanding and he felt himself loving the world, and everything in it, with unconditional surrender. Then came an explosion he hadn't known possible and the world went dim.

A vision floated through his mind. Far away, a bell was tolling Nones at a castellum of someone called the Fisher King.

~ Chapter 5— Arthur Returns ~

"You must go." They were sitting at the table in her bed-chamber.

"I cannot leave you here!" Arthur said angrily.

"We've already talked about this." Gwenhwyfar was resigned. "Myrddin told you they can only take one mortal at a time. They will come back for me."

"Nimue was more blunt," Arthur retorted. "She doesn't know if they'll have the strength to attempt it."

"What she said was they would need some time to build the energy before they tried." Gwenhwyfar took Arthur's hand. "You must go back. Lancelot said that Cerdic's troops are mobilizing."

Arthur sighed. "I had hoped Cynric would be able to persuade him to hold fast."

"He did, Husband. But you've been gone for two years and Custennin has not been able to rally the men. Even now, he's losing ground near Camelot. Lancelot says Cormant is gaining power and moving eastward."

Arthur nodded. "As second in command to Agricola, he is a strong warlord; that's why he was given leadership of Glevum. Mauron is still ruler in Corinium; I believe they understand the need to remain allies. Together, they're strong enough to oppose Cerdic."

"But you might be able to avoid bloodshed." Myrddin interrupted from the doorway, with Nimue and Rhiannon at his side. He gestured. "Come. It is time."

Arthur handed Excalibur to Rhiannon. "I must surrender this sword for I am no longer king."

"You will always be king," Rhiannon answered, "but you are correct that you will serve in another way. I will have use of Excalibur again."

Arthur gathered Gwenhwyfar to him for a long kiss. "Are you sure...?"

"Yes." She gave his hand a squeeze and stood. "I will watch for you in the pool." She looked at Nimue, avoiding Arthur's eyes. "Soon I will be with you again."

Nimue put a hand on Arthur's arm. "I will do everything I can to bring her back."

Gwenhwyfar forced a smile through trembling lips. She backed away from Arthur's hug. "This is not good-bye."

He dropped his hands helplessly. "I will see you again, Gwenhwyfar."

When Arthur awoke, the full moon was high, washing over him in cool white light. He lay on the grass atop the Tor inside the circle of stones. His joints felt stiff as he pushed himself to a sitting position. *How long have I been asleep?* He stretched and was surprised his shoulders hurt. Slowly, he stood and looked around.

Alone, in total silence. The wind was still and the air hung heavy with a damp chill. No ripples or lapping of waves appeared on the silver reflection of the Lake far below. Not even the night creatures stirred. The quiet was eerie.

When Nimue touched him, he jumped. *By Mithras, my nerves are on edge!* "I didn't hear you approach. We're back?"

"Yes."

Arthur peered at her. Even in the moonlight, her face was too pale, the delicate features set in sadness. "What is it? What's happened?"

She took his hands in hers. "Myrddin is dead. He gave his prana—his life-force—to you when you went through the portal."

Arthur sank to the ground, pulling Nimue with him. "I killed him?" he asked hoarsely.

"No." Nimue turned to him. "He gave it willingly. It was his gift."

"But why?" Arthur's voice choked.

She stroked his face. "Because you have no fey blood. Myrddin gave you his."

He buried his face in her hair and fought the tears. "He should not have done so."

"Self-sacrifice is the ultimate druid ritual, my dear." Nimue held Arthur close. "He is one with the gods now, and need never return to an earthly body unless he chooses. Take the precious gift and be wise in your remaining years." She rocked him gently until he no longer trembled. "There is something else you should know."

"What?" He sat up and rubbed his aching back.

"Myrddin's prana has aged you. At least in appearance."

Arthur held out his hands and realized for the first time the beginning of gnarliness to his knuckles. He put a hand to his face; it felt more lined. "I guess that explains the little aches and pains?"

"I have remedies for that, but your hair is grey now and your eyes have a silvery cast, although the eyes may be a gift from Cernunnos. You have an otherworldly look to you, Arthur." Nimue paused. "Rather attractive, I think."

He attempted a grin. "I won't scare Gwenhwyfar?"

Nimue was silent and the half-grin disappeared. "Gwenhwyfar! Oh, God," Arthur whispered. "If it cost Myrddin his life to bring me back, she will be imprisoned in Avalon forever."

The next morning, Arthur carried Myrddin down to the crystal cave inside the Tor that had served as a druidic training center since time beyond Time. Near the cave's mouth lay the splintered trunk of an oak.

"The break is fresh." Arthur examined the pale, moist broken ends.

"It fell last night," Nimue answered, "to serve as his coffin."

Together, they hollowed the inside of the trunk and laid the arch-druid inside, placing it far back in a small chamber that had been

Myrddin's private cell. Nimue found flint and candles on a small shelf and lit them. The light reflected off of thousands of tiny quartz crystals embedded in the rock. She chanted softly the Song of Passing.

As she finished she said, "Now all we have left is to seal the entrance to this chamber so no one will ever know where he lies. I may be blamed in the future for taking his life, but you, my lord king, will know the truth."

Arthur was puzzled. "He has mentored you and taught you much. Why would anyone blame you for his death?"

Nimue smiled sadly, a distant look in her eyes. "But they will, Arthur; they will."

Arthur halted his horse on the broad road that led up to Camelot. He studied the place he'd loved so well. The hillfort rose nearly five hundred feet and the stone curtain wall that surrounded the plateau was twelve feet thick. Along the hillside were four lines of bank and ditch defense, the first armed with a deadly palisade of wooden stakes. The cobblestone road wove back and forth toward the double-ended gatehouse, another precaution for enemies trying to storm the walls. He'd been spotted and the gates opened. He took a deep breath and nudged the horse forward.

"So, you are returned, healthy and whole." Custennin's sharp, brown eyes searched Arthur's face as they took their wine to the chairs in front of the hearth.

"I am," Arthur replied somewhat grimly, for Argante had told them of the warlords' unrest. "I don't much like the news I hear."

Custennin looked away. "So many of your Cymbry are dead. The new warlords have been difficult to control."

Arthur raised an eyebrow. "Do you think getting Lot and Uriens or Agricola to agree was easy?"

"No," Custennin answered, "but now that you're back, the young ones will rally to the Pendragon."

"I don't plan to raise the Pendragon banner."

"What?" A range of emotions flowed across his face: surprise, disbelief, a flash of anger, and a bit of relief. "You don't want your crown back?"

Arthur shook his head. "My goal has always been peace and unity. I think I can better serve that end by acting as an emissary between the Britons and the Saxons, rather than as a king."

"Before you talk to the Saxons, you might want to talk to Cormant," Custennin replied bitterly. "He is as hungry for land as Cerdic is. He's even hired Vandal warriors from the black continent."

Arthur shrugged. "I did the same with the Visigoths when we needed to raid Fergus Mor by sea. Cormant has not attended your councils?"

"Not after the first six months."

"He is an ally. Why did he stop coming?"

Custennin looked at him directly. "I have not your gift for diplomacy. The meetings usually ended in argument, with no decisions made."

"Did Bedwyr not help? He has always been good at mediating."

"Bedwyr has not been at Camelot. He still searches for Medraut."

"I did not mean to make that his life's quest!" For a moment, Arthur was nonplused. "What about Lancelot then?"

"Lancelot is at Joyous Garde. While he was here, he tried to establish agreement, but..." Custennin clamped his mouth shut.

"But what?" Arthur's silvery eyes watched him steadily.

He swallowed hard. "Some of the men say he's half-mad."

"Why?" Arthur asked in the same silky, conversational tone that was so dangerous to men who knew him.

"My lord, don't..." Custennin stopped, then continued. "He is frantic about Gwenhwyfar." He laughed nervously. "We all know it's common for a widowed queen to take the veil or even to go into hiding, but he says... He says she's lost in the land of Faerie. Like it exists!"

"He may be right," Arthur said sadly.

Custennin started. "Don't tell me, that is where you have been?"

Before Arthur could reply, the doors burst open and a rider, clearly exhausted and out of breath, stumbled into the room. He took no notice of Arthur, but spoke to Custennin in a barely audible voice.

"My lord, Cerdic has laid siege to Corinium!"

"Will you go with us?" Custennin asked after he'd given orders to ready his men and the bailey clamored with noise.

"For certes," Arthur answered. "I will parley with Cerdic; we've done it often."

When they arrived, however, Cerdic was firmly entrenched just beyond arrow range of the city walls. His forces were split, half trying to harry Mauron's men out, the other half preparing to defend the rear flank.

"I had no idea he'd gained so many soldiers," Arthur said as they crept up the ridge for their first glimpse of the warcamp.

"Aye." Custennin surveyed the field below them. "After Cam's Landing, when Cerdic took Londinium, he hired Frankish mercenaries for reinforcements. It didn't take long before more followed."

"There must be hundreds." Arthur scanned the hordes. "Does he not fear Frankish takeover from Childebert? That king is ambitious."

"He would rather take that risk, I think, than be overrun by independent Briton warlords who won't keep the treaties."

Arthur's face grew dark. "That has been happening?"

"So far there have been only skirmishes, but Gormant is ever mindful that Cerdic's territories now border his. If we lose Corinium, Cerdic will move swiftly to Glevum. Once that happens, Britain will be effectively divided north and south, with a wide band of Saxon in-between!"

"Where is Gormant, then?" Arthur asked irritably.

"He'll be here by morning, I'm sure," Custennin answered. "We may not like each other, but his men are fierce fighters. This tempest has been brewing for two years. The men are eager for battle."

Arthur shook his head. "Let me go talk to Cerdic." They slipped back down the hill and he went to his horse.

"Wait!" Custennin reached for the reins. "You aren't going to ride in there alone, are you? Let me send a guard with you."

"No." Arthur was firm as he mounted. "Cerdic knows me. I'll not be harmed."

He rode toward the tent that bore Cerdic's standard. As he expected, guards surrounded him within minutes, their axes raised.

"I come in peace. I wish to speak to Cerdic." Arthur eyed them calmly.

The men laughed. "Who do you think you are, that you can ride in here and think our lord will grant you time?" one said in the Briton tongue.

Arthur's eyes turned to flint. "Tell him King Arthur has returned."

Total silence fell. Some of the men lowered their weapons and backed away. Even the one who'd challenged him looked unsure.

"He's dead. No one has heard from him for two years."

"I believe I'm very much alive." Arthur looked around. "Then again, I may have returned from the Otherworld to claim your souls and you'll never experience Valhalla. Shall we see?"

At the mention of the warrior's final reward, trepidation appeared on their faces. One of the younger men turned and went to the tent. "My lord," he called in a somewhat shaky voice, "a man asks to speak with you. He claims he is the dead king."

The curtain parted and a tall, grey-headed warrior stepped out, indignation on his face. "What are you talking about, boy? Have you been into the mead and the sun not yet high?"

"No, my lord," the soldier pointed to Arthur astride his horse in the midst of the circle of guards.

Cerdic followed his direction. For a moment, he stood rigid, in total silence. Then a grin spread across his face. "I never thought I'd be glad to see you, Arthur." He waved the guards away and they quickly scattered. He gave a slightly ironic bow. "Won't you join me in my tent?"

Arthur dismounted and followed. Cerdic's attendant began to pour mead, but Cerdic took the skin from him. "I'll do it; you may go."

When alone, he sat back and studied Arthur. "So, what are your plans now that you're back?"

"I have come to parley. Custennin waits beyond the ridge; Gormant will join him soon. Give up this siege so we can live in peace."

Cerdic shook his head, a small smile on his lips. "I have held to the treaty these past two years. Your warlords have not."

"Let me talk with them. There's no need for more bloodshed."

"They're thirsty for it. They fight among themselves. How will you stop them?"

"I've only just returned. Let me try." Arthur took a deep breath. "What are your terms and conditions?"

Cerdic looked pensive. "Drought and famine run rampant in their homeland. All the Saxon want to do is survive." He leaned forward, his arms on the table. "Remember, I am half-Briton, Arthur, and I love this land. The Saxon people love it, too. Land is worth more than gold to them. I would not have married a Saxon woman otherwise."

So they talked and argued until a guard appeared at the entrance. "What is it?" Cerdic asked.

"Soldiers!" The young man swallowed hard. "Thousands of them. We are surrounded by the enemy."

Cerdic leapt to his feet and brushed past the man. The ridge was lined with cavalry, and infantry stood three deep on both sides of the city walls, extending to the slopes that led to the ridge.

He glanced at Arthur. "You were a diversion."

Arthur felt his eyes flash. "I told you they were coming. Let me speak with them and grant you safe passage to retreat."

"My lord," one of Cerdic's younger, brasher officers interrupted. "We have never been cowards. Let us take this king as hostage. They will be the ones who retreat."

Cerdic looked at the man long and hard, then he looked at Arthur. A small smile played on his lips and he turned back to the young officer.

"There is a word you need to learn the meaning of. If you, or those men out there, understood it, we would not be in this situation." He struck the man with his hand and the officer reeled backward. "That word is honor. Arthur came here in peace and he will leave in peace."

He turned to Arthur. "I cannot accept your offer to parley. We will fight."

Sadly, Arthur watched the battle engage. The infantry formed into the old Roman phalanx blocks of eight men, shields locked to form a wall, their spears extending outward as they advanced forward, giving the appearance of a steel hedgehog on the move. The spears kept the Saxon from wielding their fearsome axes, unless they wanted to throw them and be defenseless. The cavalry charged as soon as the infantry began to move and the archers came out from the city walls to get within range. Cerdic's army was literally surrounded and the net closed quickly, turning the churned-up earth crimson.

The Saxons fought hard, urged on by their berserkers, but when the battle was over, Cerdic limped home with fewer than half his men.

Arthur turned away. He prayed Galahad and Peredur would find the Grail and peace would at last prevail.

Several weeks later, Lancelot galloped into Camelot's bailey, sliding off his horse before it had stopped. "Is he here?" he asked the stableboy who came running for his mount. Without waiting for an answer, he ran up the steps to the Great Hall.

"Where is he?" he demanded as Custennin met him inside the door. "Where's Gwenhwyfar?" *By the gods, Gwen, it will be good to see you again. To touch...*

"Arthur's in the map room, trying to determine borders for Cerdic."

Lancelot walked swiftly to the back hall and the small room next to where the council held its meetings at the Round Table. He flung the door open.

Arthur looked up. His slightly annoyed expression changed to one of gladness instantly. "Lancelot!" They met in the middle of the room with a soldier's embrace and a bear hug. "Brother, I have never been so glad to see anyone! Come and sit. Boy!" Arthur called, but the servant had already gone for wine and victuals.

Glad as he was to see Arthur, as they exchanged pieces of news, Lancelot looked around for Gwenhwyfar. *In just a few minutes, once she finds out I'm here, she'll come through that door.* He willed himself to concentrate. "There's a new warlord in Anglia. A Saxon named Wehha. Has Custennin any plans for holding him in check?"

Arthur shook his head. "He hasn't mentioned it." He told Lancelot about the siege of Corinium. "It could have been stopped. Those lives didn't need to be wasted."

Lancelot scrutinized Arthur. The hair and eyes were different, but there was something else; he no longer wore the hard look of a warrior. "Avalon has changed you."

"Spending time in the House of Healing would change any man," Arthur replied, "for they truly work miracles. But I had a dream—a vision—Nimue said."

"What was it?" *And where is Gwen?*

The servant arrived and Arthur waited until they'd been served and were alone again. "I have spoken to no one of this, since my return." He hesitated, then plunged on. "Lancelot, I have seen the Holy Grail!"

Lancelot furrowed his brow. "The cup Galahad and Peredur are seeking?"

"Yes! I can't tell you the feeling of total contentment and fulfillment I had!"

"The Grail is in Avalon then?"

"No," Arthur answered, "but I saw it. A silver goblet rimmed in gold, with ancient runes traced into the metal. An ethereal maiden carries it and a radiance of some sort of light surrounds it."

"It sounds like a ceremonial cup, like the druids used. What does Myrddin make of it?"

At the mention of Myrddin's name, Arthur's smile vanished. "Myrddin has passed permanently to the Otherworld."

"What?" Lancelot set his wine down, stunned. "How can that be with his power? What happened?"

Arthur studied the floor for several minutes. Finally, he looked up, the silvery tone in his eyes bright. "He and Nimue thought they could bring us through the portal. Something went wrong. Myrddin transferred his life-force to me."

"The ultimate sacrifice," Lancelot said softly. "My mother used to tell me of the levels of initiation the druids strove to attain."

"Nimue said something like that, too," Arthur said.

"Nimue and Gwenhwyfar passed through unharmed?" Lancelot asked. *Any minute now...*

"Nimue is at the Isle." Arthur looked away. "Gwenhwyfar didn't come."

For a moment, Lancelot remained silent while he struggled to remain calm. His tone was deceptively flat when he spoke. "You left her there?"

"I didn't want to; I refused at first to go without her."

"You left her there?" Lancelot's smoky eyes turned darker.

"Nimue and Myrddin couldn't bring both of us through at the same time. They planned to go back for Gwenhwyfar."

"You left her."

"Will you stop saying that? I had to. I thought I could prevent further bloodshed; it was the Grail's message for me. Gwenhwyfar insisted I go."

"For certes, she would." Lancelot was on his feet and began to pace. "By the gods, I have tried to get to her, but the portal won't open for me and I have some fey blood. If it killed Myrddin to bring you back, how in

Bel's fires do you think she can pass through and return?"

"Nimue will bring her back," Arthur answered, somewhat shakily. "I have faith in her."

Lancelot turned on him. "While you were lying unconscious on the barge, Nimue told Gwenhwyfar she didn't know if she could return. I tried to stop Gwen, but she said healing you to save Britain was more important. She knew then, just like she knew when you left."

Arthur stared at him, white-faced and stricken. "That can't be true."

"I don't lie, Arthur."

"For certes, Lance. I did not mean..."

"You left her there." Lancelot shook his head and walked to the door. He turned just before he left. "I am going to see Nimue. I will spend the rest of my life striving to bring Gwenhwyfar back. She has my geis."

"And you have mine," Arthur whispered hoarsely.

"I release you from it," Lancelot's voice cut like steel. "I swear, until Gwenhwyfar returns, I can no longer honor our friendship." He turned on his heel and marched out, slamming the door behind him.

A moment later, Arthur heard his horse pounding out the gate. He brushed at his eyes with his hands. *Sweet Jesu, I have lost my wife, and my mentor and my best friend. I was not able to curb the bloodshed. Why was I allowed to come back? Why did I survive Cam's Landing?*

He put his head in his arms on the table. He'd never shed tears before Cam's Landing. Now, for the second time since his return, he wept.

~Chapter 6—Land of Faerie~

Gwenhwyfar watched from the pool as Lancelot stomped off. His anger had prevented contact. She wanted desperately to tell him to befriend Arthur. Her heart ached when Arthur wept and she put her hand into the liquid trying to reach him.

He gave no response and her tears mingled with the water.

She sensed the faerie presence. "They've gone, Morgan. The bond between the two men I love most in the world is shattered, because of me."

A strong bronze hand covered hers. Startled, she turned to face Cernunnos.

His luminous hazel eyes held her spell-bound. "Why do you weep, my lady? They are mortal men; they will make amends."

She shook her head. "Lancelot made an oath. He will keep it. I must find a way to return."

"That cannot be." He tilted her chin and lightly traced the tear streaks on her cheek. "I can make you forget the world of mortals. You will feel no grief, only pleasure. Come with me into the forest."

Gwenhwyfar felt physically drawn to him, though the demi-god hadn't moved. He still held her gaze and suddenly, she wanted his protection to make the pain go away. Her eyes widened and darkened as she tentatively stepped toward him.

Cernunnos smiled.

"Gwenhwyfar! I thought you might be here." Morgan stepped from the trees. "You are wanted in Avalon's hall."

Gwenhwyfar blinked, the spell broken. *Sweet Mary, what had just happened? The pull had been nearly irresistible.* She backed away.

Cernunnos sounded amused. "Was that really necessary, Morgan?"

Morgan turned to him. "I'm Queen of Faerie; you are my Consort. I will decide when I am tired of you."

The rack of antlers formed in the ether above Cernunnos' head. He leaned down. "And I'm the god of the forest and the Wild Hunt. I take what I want."

Morgan's eyes glittered green as fresh grass. "Do not think to trifle with me, Cern."

He waved his hand and a wind squall swept through the trees. "I never trifle with anything, my jealous queen. Or do you not remember last night?"

She raised her arms and the wind stilled. "I do," she purred, running one hand through his brown curls. "And you may beg my forgiveness by repeating that pleasure."

He grinned and lifted her easily, but before he carried her into the wood, he gave a long, thoughtful look at Gwenhwyfar. "Another time, my lady."

"No!" *Never*. Then Gwenhwyfar turned and ran for safety.

"I have helped with the harvest thrice," Gwenhwyfar said as she picked through the windfall and chose unbruised apples for her basket. "Have I been on Avalon three years? Time is so confusing here."

The priestess, Inanna, spoke gently. "The seasons turn; don't concern yourself with the passing of the Wheel. Be content."

Frustrated, Gwenhwyfar sank to the ground. "I don't belong here; I want to go home." *Where I belong. To see Lancelot...and Arthur...*

The priestess knelt beside her. "We would send you back if we could. You know that Lancelot prays daily. The portal remains sealed." She rocked back on her heels. "Does not the gift of the pool help you?"

Gwenhwyfar wiped at a tear. "Yes, but Arthur and Lancelot's friendship is severed. I can only observe Arthur and feel his sadness and can do nothing to help."

"You can talk to Lancelot."

"Ah. Yes. Talk. That is all we can do for Morgan is always present. I have begged Lancelot to forgive Arthur, but he refuses until I return." She frowned. "Am I doomed to live here for the rest of my days?"

"Are you so miserable here? Avalon is a place of beauty and abundance."

Gwenhwyfar sighed. The conversation always ended the same way. She had everything she needed: the solarium held warm baths, the air inside was always fragrant. The gardens produced bountifully of vegetables, as did the fields of grain. Game was plentiful and the food well seasoned with rare and delicate herbs. She wore fine silks and maidens saw to her every need. A horse had even been provided; she suspected Cernunnos' hand there, for the white mare had eyes as red as the eyes and ears of the hounds he kept. She had the freedom to go where she willed, except past the edge of the forest. She did not venture into the land of Faerie.

"I am not ungrateful. "Mayhap I will feel better if I go to the pool."

She walked slowly down the hill from the orchard. She hesitated when she got to the pool, feeling restless. *There is something I need to see,* she thought, *and not a pleasant experience either*. Slowly, she passed her hand over the water.

The woman was clothed in the black veil and vesture of a holy sister. To her right, sat a man in a finely woven woolen tunic of deep blue over doeskin leggings. A soft cloak of sable lay across his back, blending with his hair. Beneath the fine clothing, though, were the heavily muscled shoulders and arms of a man of war. To the nun's left, a younger man with long black hair and a bearded face leaned forward, intent on his conversation with the older man.

"Your army is ready. Sigismund isn't expecting attack. Why wait?"

The warrior king shook his head. "You've done an excellent job with the cavalry; the horses are as fleet of foot as you promised, even though costly. But my brother, Clotaire, wants my dead brother's land and I can't afford to let him have Orleans. If I move on Burgundia, I turn my back on the memory of Clodomir. He wanted me to have that land. I can't trust Clotaire."

The holy sister handed the king a cup. "Drink this. It'll soothe you," she spoke softly. "You are Regent for your nephews since Clodomir's death; has Clotaire forgotten that?"

He grimaced. "The oldest turns of age soon. He has not a wit of sense in how to run a kingdom and has no love for me. Like as not, Clotaire will persuade him to stand against me."

The younger man raised an eyebrow. "Then, mayhap he shouldn't reach the age of majority."

"Are you suggesting I murder my nephews?"

Grey eyes held the older man's gaze. "What do you suppose your brother will do once the Regency is no longer yours? Let the boy live?"

The king studied him, then said to the nun. "What do you think?"

The nun raised her face.

Gwenhwyfar gasped. It couldn't be! The habit covered everything but her face and she bore a striking resemblance to Morgana. It couldn't be; the sister was too young, her skin soft and unwrinkled.

The nun laid a hand on his arm. "As harsh as it sounds, if you wish to hold your power, you must expand your base beyond Paris. You must be in control of Soissons and Orleans, not your brother."

"I do not relish killing my kin, Anna." The king sounded unconvinced. "It is mortal sin."

The sister sighed and kept her voice pious. "Then let my son do it."

The king turned to him. "You would do this?" When he received a nod, he looked wary. "What would your payment be?"

The younger man grinned. Gwenhwyfar's hand flew to her mouth in shock. The grin was familiar and the eyes...Arthur's eyes.

Medraut. Alive...and Morgana as well. Where were they? Who was this king?

Suddenly, Medraut looked upward, as though sensing her presence. Quickly, she stirred the water, breaking the vision.

She sat for some moments, her head reeling. Arthur must be warned. She murmured a prayer and swept the water.

She found him at Camelot, talking to Custennin and Cormant. From the intensity of the gestures, the two men were angry and Arthur was trying to appease them. She sighed. This was often the scene when she observed Arthur. The Briton warlords were less and less likely to listen to reason. She cleared the images.

She could not communicate with him. Lancelot would have to break his silence.

"*Lancelot*?" The water remained calm. "*Where are you?*" Nothing. She took a deep breath. *I must center myself; it is the only way I can reach him.*

"Oh, good." Morgan settled beside her. "You're calling Lancelot."

Gwenhwyfar looked at her in annoyance. "Morgan, I have to talk to him about something private."

She looked hurt. "I'll be quiet. I just like looking at him."

"Does Cernunnos approve of your interest?" Gwenhwyfar asked tartly.

"Whether he does or doesn't, I will do what pleases me," replied the queen of Faerie, her tone slightly condescending.

The earth rumbled as the demi-god pushed through the bracken. Gwenhwyfar drew back, awed by the sheer bulk of solid muscle, yet had a compelling urge to move closer.

He reached down and lifted Morgan to her feet as lightly as though she were air itself. "We will leave the lady alone for once."

Morgan's image faded and she reappeared on the other side of Gwenhwyfar. "I plan to stay."

His eyes took on a hawk's predatory look. The water in the small pool began to churn, breaking upon itself in small, sharp waves.

"Please!" Gwenhwyfar cried, "I'll not be able to find him like this!"

The pool calmed and Cernunnos leaned over her and sained widdershins. Lancelot appeared on his knees through the watery image.

"Gwenhwyfar?" He stood, brushing off the dirt. "Is there a reason you knocked me down?"

"I didn't, love."

"Then who—" Lancelot stopped abruptly as Cernunnos' face appeared over Gwenhwyfar's shoulder. He narrowed his eyes. "What is the Horned One doing with you?"

"So you know me, Lancelot du Lac. I remember your mother, Niniane, well." Cernunnos inclined his head. "My lady, Morgan le Fey, is intrigued with you. I thought I should make your acquaintance."

Lancelot nodded stiffly. "I would appreciate it if you would take your lady away and leave Gwen with me."

Cernunnos laughed and the water rippled. Lancelot began to fade.

Annoyed, Morgan raised her hand and stilled the water. "Leave him be."

"You see?" Cernunnos asked. "The lady does not want to leave. What magic have you wrought with her?"

"Me?" Lancelot replied in exasperation. "All I want is to spend time alone with Gwenhwyfar. There are things...I worry about her."

Cernunnos let his gaze linger on Gwenhwyfar before he turned back to Lancelot. "I will take care of your woman."

Gwenhwyfar saw Lancelot's eyes turn smoky and she quickly interceded, "Lancelot. I have important news. Medraut lives. Morgana, too."

Instantly, he refocused. "Where?"

"I don't know. With a king, I think. He was richly dressed. I heard the names Clodomir and Clotaire."

"Childebert's brothers. They're in Gaul then. The bastard is shielding them."

"They have disguised themselves, Lance, no doubt with new names, as well. Mayhap the man doesn't know. Medraut wears a beard and Morgana is a nun."

Lancelot smiled. "Isn't there something in the new religion about mockery? I would think your God would strike her down for that."

"You must warn Arthur."

He sobered. "Arthur and I don't speak. You know that."

"Lance! Arthur must know about Medraut! Do this for me, please."

Lancelot was silent.

"Mayhap if you let him lay with you," Morgan whispered in her ear and looked over her shoulder to wink at Lancelot, "he would do your bidding."

Gwenhwyfar turned on her. "I would willingly go to him. I just don't want an audience. Will you leave, just this once?"

Morgan pouted. "It is my pool."

"Enough of this," Cernunnos pulled Morgan to his side. "Go to him, my lady."

Gwenhwyfar opened her eyes to the brilliance of a cloudless, cerulean sky. She lay on her back on a nest of sweet clover in an unfamiliar meadow, the earth warm from the sun. Peripherally, she saw a stag and his doe grazing at the forest's edge nearby. Bees droning and swarming over daffodils scattered in the field, played lazily in her ear. Gwenhwyfar stretched languidly.

"You're actually here." From behind her head, she heard Lancelot's whisper. Hands slid over her shoulders. His face loomed over her for an instant before he gave her an upside down kiss.

She stared up at him. "You are real. Am I back?"

He moved around and gathered her in his arms, burying his face in her hair. "We're not home, Gwenhwyfar," He nibbled her neck. "I think we're in the land of Faerie, but I care not. We're together."

Gwenhwyfar caressed his face. "And Morgan is not watching?"

Lancelot unfastened the bodice of her gown. "I don't see a shimmer like there usually is." He leaned over, his tongue encircling her nipple, teasing her.

She shuddered in delight. Their frantic kissing continued while they undressed each other, hands feverishly remembering all the pleasure spots. Then, as Lancelot filled her, Time suddenly stopped. As if in a dream, the rhythmic thrusting slowed into one long fluid motion, bringing both of them to a frenzied pitch, yet locked in stillness, only able to feel the experience go on, stretching into the unending future. Their bodies were no longer theirs to control, becoming receptacles of undulating pleasure. Sheer ecstasy and exquisite torture. *I can take no more; I am going mad!*

Time returned and Gwenhwyfar lay gasping, arms and legs wrapped tightly around Lancelot. She could feel his chest pressed against her breasts, heaving as he took in great gulps of air. Both of them too exhausted to speak.

At the edge of the meadow, the doe's eyes gleamed with a tainted green shadow as she watched them lying intertwined on the soft grass.

Cernunnos turned his antlered head toward her. "We will have to send them back, Morgan. He is not yours to keep."

She stamped a dainty hoof. "I noticed you didn't take your eyes off her."

"No need to be jealous, my queen; I will pleasure you any time you wish," he said solemnly, but the antlered head swung back to the woman beneath the man and the stag's luminous eyes began to glow.

"Did you hear something, Lancelot?" Gwenhwyfar whispered.

He raised his head to look around. "There's nothing here, save a pair of deer." Even as he said it, the animals disappeared into the forest. "Nothing, Gwen."

"What happened?" Gwenhwyfar looked up from the pool to where Cernunnos and Morgan stood. "Where is Lancelot? I don't remember..." She rubbed her eyes. "I'm so tired."

Cernunnos place a hand under her elbow and lifted her. "You were upset with him because he would not speak to Arthur."

Gwenhwyfar shook her head. "No. I was with him. I touched him, not on the spirit plane, but in the flesh. We kissed, then I don't know what happened."

"Mayhap you need some rest," Morgan suggested slyly.

"No. I want to know what happened." Gwenhwyfar glanced from one to the other. "I will not leave until someone tells me."

Cernunnos looked amused. "Are you sure you want to know?"

"For certes," she answered firmly, lifting her chin.

"You were in my land of Faerie," Morgan answered with a giggle.

Gwenhwyfar widened her eyes. "I thought mortals could not return from there."

"A human who enters of her own accord seldom returns," Cernunnos agreed, "but I sent you and I brought you back."

"Why?"

He swept his hand over the pool. "Look."

She stared at herself and Lancelot locked in wanton lovemaking, and memory flooded through her, followed by intense heat. She turned to run, but Cernunnos held her, forcing her to watch the scene play out.

"Did you not enjoy it?" The demi-god's voice was close to her ear.

"I...were you watching us?" Gwenhwyfar refused to look at him.

"Indeed," Morgan giggled again. "Your man is very skilled. So forceful and yet so gentle. I liked the way he..." She stopped and sighed. "I liked it all."

Gwenhwyfar groaned, covering her face with her hands.

Cernunnos took her hands. "There's no cause to be embarrassed."

"I don't know why you mind so much," Morgan frowned and then suggested, "We could arrange for you to see him again."

"Alone?"

"For certes not," she answered. "Watching you gave us great pleasure, too." Morgan thrust her lower lip out. "I suppose we could stay hidden."

Gwenhwyfar slowly sank to the ground and stared into the calm water, remembering now that prolonged, eternal moment of passion that only continued to build upon itself, growing in intensity until there were no bodies, only a melding into one thought, one being. *I want to feel that ravishing rapture again! It surpasses anything we've done before.*

When she looked up, she was alone. She stood and slowly walked up the hill, wondering if she had the courage to follow through.

Several days later she was summoned to the meeting room where the ritual councils were held. She was surprised to find it empty, save for the priestess Arianrhod. Of all nine priestesses, the one least seen, she spun the Wheel of Fate and wove the fabric of Life for souls wishing to return to earth in another incarnation.

"Sit down, Gwenhwyfar." The voice was soft, but distant. When she was seated, the priestess continued, "Samhain will be upon us in nine days. Normally, we perform our rituals secretly. This year, we have decided to include you."

Gwenhwyfar was startled. "Why? I have no magic."

Arianrhod spoke softly. "I know, but we are going to use an old druidic ritual to establish contact with Nimue. If the connection is strong enough, we may be able to send you home."

"Home?" Gwenhwyfar sat straighter. "Why haven't you tried before? It's been a year since Arthur and Nimue left."

"And it has been three years, in your time, since you arrived here. The number three has much power. If we anchor that to the cross-quarter of Samhain, when the door between the worlds opens, we may achieve what you want."

"What if I go to the Otherworld instead?"

Arianrhod nodded. "That is a risk you take. However, I do not believe your soul is ready."

Gwenhwyfar hesitated. "What must I do?"

"We have a purification ritual. You'll be isolated for nine days and maintain silence. You may not use the pool to scry. The maidens who prepare your bath each evening will not speak to you, nor will the one who delivers your food." She was silent as though thinking. "In the mornings, a cup of periwinkle tea will be delivered and in the afternoons, you'll be given a small serving of the sacred mushroom. These will enable you to meditate throughout the day. In the evenings, an ointment of monkshood will follow your bath, allowing for clarity in dreaming. You must make your choice now. I need to begin spinning the threads today."

"I cannot say goodbye to Morgan or Cernunnos?"

The priestess frowned. "It would not be wise. No thread should hold you to them. Cernunnos will ride the Wild Hunt on that night; Morgan will be plotting mischievous tricks. A good night, all in all, for you to leave." She paused. "With both of them busy, you should have no trouble passing through the land of Faerie on your return to your world."

Gwenhwyfar waited near midnight on Samhain for the priestesses to arrive. She felt light-headed and disoriented from the herbs and the fasting of the past twenty-four hours. Underneath her white woolen robe, she was sweating lightly, even though the evening had turned cool. *Let this soon be over*, she prayed, *that I may awake in Camelot. Let Nimue have the strength to bring me through the portal.*

Arianrhod knocked lightly on her door. She stepped outside and the other priestesses, also dressed in white, formed a silent circle around her. Each carried a blue glass bowl suspended in a web of leather, wrapped at the top to provide a handle for hanging. Inside each globe, a candle burned. They proceeded up the hill to the copse of oak trees behind the House of Healing. Making no sound, each priestess hung her candle on a branch to form a perfect circle of light. The moon had not yet risen and the blue flames reflecting off the white robes cast an eerie glow.

Gwenhwyfar was bid to sit in the middle. Arianrhod stood over her. They waited in silence and, as the rounded sphere slowly rose in the east, the priestesses began a gentle chanting, growing louder as the moon flooded them in silver light. Arianrhod lifted her voice to implore the Goddess. "Sacred Mother, allow your daughter to return to Mortality."

Her prayer went on in the Old Tongue. Gwenhwyfar heard her call sharply to Nimue.

Then Nimue stood in the midst of the circle of stones atop the Tor, skyclad, arms raised in supplication, the moonlight washing over her. The time was nearly here; the precise moment in-between-time when the ethers would allow for transformation.

She began her chant as the bells from the Christian abbey below the Tor began their midnight toll. Her voice rose and mingled with the tones from the ethers. She concentrated harder, and Gwenhwyfar could feel her reaching out toward Avalon.

"Send her to me; the portal is open."

Gwenhwyfar felt happy, floating on the wind, free as a leaf, leaving care and worry behind. Only freedom lay ahead.

But something isn't right. I should be in the circle by now. She dimly could hear Nimue call.

"Janus, keeper of the gate, guardian and escort to the Otherworld, turn Gwenhwyfar back; do not allow her passage. Her time is not yet."

The wind freshened and Gwenhwyfar felt a brutal chill to her skin. Then, riding a squall, the voice of Janus came from across Time, deep and hallow and resonant.

"She is not here."

Then she heard Nimue crying, "Gwenhwyfar, where are you?"

She tried to reach across Time, but Nimue's image faded.

"She can't just be gone." Arthur stared at Nimue unbelievingly.

She took his trembling hand. "I have not been able to find her. The past three days Argante has kept the priestesses in meditation, searching on the astral plane. I have scryed each night. Nothing."

Arthur sank in his chair at the empty Round Table in the council room and raked fingers through his silver hair. *By Mithras, Gwenhwyfar, where are you?* Nimue stood silently beside him, waiting. Finally, he spoke. "Have you tried the pool she uses to communicate?"

She nodded. "It remains still."

"I suppose the nine on Avalon have also tried to find her?"

"They have."

He rose and paced silently for several minutes before sitting again. He made a final attempt. "Could she be lost in the land of Faerie?"

Nimue frowned. "If she is, she is cloaked well."

"Have you asked the Faerie queen for help?" Arthur knew his voice had a desperate edge.

"Morgan le Fey cannot be trusted. She lies on a whim with no thought of the consequences. She is a creature of the moment in which she lives."

"Still," Arthur pursued doggedly, "have you asked?"

She sighed. "Yes. She said there is only one queen in her land. That could mean she's the only one there or she's not acknowledging Gwenhwyfar."

"What about Cernunnos?"

"I don't know. Morgan began to pout when I asked to see him." She rested her hand on his shoulder. "I'm sorry, Arthur. I'll keep trying."

His shoulders slumped. "She should never have come with me to Avalon. Lancelot should have forced her to stay with him."

"No." Nimue sat beside him. "You would have died. She knew that. She made the choice willingly."

Arthur looked at her, despair and desperation in his eyes. "I've killed Myrddin and now I've probably killed Gwenhwyfar, too. Why didn't I listen to Myrddin? She didn't even want to marry me, you know. "

"That was a long ago," Nimue said gently. "She grew to love you."

"I remember the first time I saw her as a woman. She'd been working in the stable—dirty, disheveled, hair loose from its braid—those green eyes flashing fire when Bedwyr told her not to come too close to my stallion." He smiled in remembrance. "At supper I deliberately goaded her, just to watch that temper fly. She didn't back down once. I knew life would never be boring with her. I wanted her; that was all that mattered to me."

Nimue touched his forearm. "She agreed to marry you."

Arthur shook his head. "I contracted for her hand without her permission. She was forced into marriage."

"You offered her the choice to back out."

He lifted Nimue's hand and held it. "She would not dishonor her father or bring shame to Bedwyr. I should have heeded Myrddin's warning. She would be alive and well with Lancelot now."

They both froze. *Lancelot.*

"He'll have to be told," Nimue finally said.

Arthur nodded sadly. "He will never speak to me again."

"My cousin is acting like a child. This isn't your fault."

"He has loved Gwenhwyfar since the day they met," Arthur replied simply. "He resisted acknowledging it for years, but he is helpless to fight that feeling, as I well know. I don't blame him for hating me."

"He doesn't understand, Arthur. You could do nothing to bring her back; had it been Lancelot, he wouldn't have done any better."

"He would have stayed with her." He took a deep breath. "Lancelot has sworn to spend his life trying to bring her back. On Avalon, you told me that the love you and Myrddin had for me would bring me through the portal. If you worked with Lancelot, added your power to this bond, do you think that she could be found?"

Nimue contemplated. "Lancelot inherited fey blood, but I've never seen his power exhibited on another plane. He is so purely physical."

Arthur raised an eyebrow. "Obviously."

"Lancelot has that sense of standing apart, being only partially accessible. Women are attracted to him because they can't have him." Nimue shrugged. "Gwenhwyfar was the only woman he couldn't have; and he gave himself to her, heart and soul." She paused. "Mayhap, working with him will help. It's worth trying. I will go to Joyous Garde."

Arthur stood and wrapped his arms around her, holding her close for a minute. His voice became ragged. "Tell Lancelot...tell him...that if he is successful in finding her, I will grant a divorce. He may marry her." He ended in a whisper. "I love her enough to let her go."

Gwen, gone! Lancelot, in his rage, had overturned tables and benches and swept heavy utensils from the serving board. He didn't see the six-year-old cringing in one of the massive chairs in front of the hearth in the Great Hall of Joyous Garde.

"How in Bel's fires could you have let this happen, Nimue? You are the Lady of the Lake; are your powers no longer strong?" Lancelot paced, slamming the fist of one hand into the palm of the other.

Nimue remained calm. "In truth, my power has lessened since we brought Arthur back. And many have fallen away from the Goddess, lured by the eternal salvation the Christian priests preach, but I don't think Avallach is ready to fade away."

"I don't need a lesson on my mother's religion!" Lancelot spun and stomped back, towering over her. "I want to know what went wrong."

From the chair came a slight whimper. Lancelot turned at the sound.

"You're frightening your daughter," Nimue said.

He fought to calm himself as he walked to the hearth. "Elen?"

The scared voice came back, haunting him. "Yes, Da."

He went around and knelt in front of the chair, studying the dark-haired child who looked so like him. Her eyes were wide with fear. Ashamed of himself, he gathered her in his arms, stroking her hair softly. "Everything is okay; don't be afraid of me."

The child clung to him, but didn't cry. "You will not hurt the Lady?"

"I have never hurt..." He stopped, remembering suddenly how brutal he'd been with Elaine when Elen was begotten. "No," he answered, standing and carrying her with him back to Nimue. "I will not harm her."

Nimue smiled at Elen. "I've known your father a long time, my child. I'll be safe with him."

Lancelot set his daughter down. "Why don't you find your nurse and practice your Latin? I need to talk to Nimue alone."

Elen looked skeptical and Nimue bent down. "When you're a little older, your father can bring you to visit me on Avallach and I'll show you some Latin scrolls I have. Would you like that?"

She laughed suddenly, her dimple showing. "Da, will you take me?"

"Yes, if your Latin improves. Now run along."

He turned back to Nimue. "By Mithras, why didn't you tell me? I had no idea she was there."

Nimue nodded. "You were in near battle frenzy."

Lancelot stared at her. "You could have been hurt then."

"My power isn't so weak that I could not have avoided you," Nimue smiled. "Now, if you'll listen, I'd like to give you Arthur's message."

When she finished, he was silent. "When Morgana accused Gwen of treason and Arthur let me rescue her—and bring her here—those were the two happiest years of my life." He paused. "The choice would be Gwen's."

Nimue laid a hand on his arm. "Gwenhwyfar's done her duty. It was all she ever promised him."

Lancelot looked at her in surprise. "Duty? She loved him; she carried the guilt of that for years. It's why she returned to him."

Nimue shook her head. "She wanted to prevent you from killing Bedwyr when we came to take her back to heal the land. It was her duty."

"I asked her, at the last tournament before Cam's Landing, if she were happy," Lancelot said quietly.

Nimue raised an eyebrow. "And?"

"She said her life was not her own. But Arthur treated her well."

"He accepted the love she could give him." Nimue looked thoughtful. "I don't think he ever resented you, Lancelot. He reconciled himself to what was. You've wounded him deeper than you know."

Lancelot's face hardened. "I cannot forgive him for leaving Gwenhwyfar behind on Avalon."

Nimue sighed. "You've become hardened. Mayhap if Galahad finds the Grail, it will work its magic on you."

"I don't even know where Galahad is." Lancelot returned to the subject. "I will only forgive Arthur when I can find Gwen. I have not been able to contact her since before Samhain."

"I saw her on Samhain. The portal was open; she was carried into the ethers. After that, nothing. We've tried everything I know to do."

"Did she have to pass through Faerie?"

"Yes. But that should not have been a problem. Morgan was busy that evening, doing what she likes to do. Spy on mortals and tweak their lives."

"And Cernunnos?" Lancelot asked, remembering the waking dream of the afternoon in the meadow. *I know it happened; I was still brushing the dirt from my trews when I returned.*

Nimue hesitated. "I have not been able to summon him. He should have ridden the Wild Hunt that night."

Lancelot snorted. "He almost lured Gwenhwyfar into the forest one day. Morgan intervened just in time."

Nimue's eyes widened. "A demi-god would be almost impossible to resist. Are you sure?"

"Nimue." He leaned toward her. "I know the look of hunger and desire. I saw it often enough on Medraut's face and felt it on my own. He wanted her."

"If you're right," Nimue replied softly, "she may be lost to us forever. Cernunnos is used to taking what he wants."

Lancelot straightened, his jaw set. "Then I must find a way to take her back."

"I cannot send you to the land of Faerie. The portal opens only on Samhain and when the Goddess wishes. You will have to wait."

He resumed pacing. "Waiting is not something I do well."

~ Chapter 7— The Quest Continues ~

Galahad was tired. In the two years since he'd left Peredur, he'd traveled throughout the southern lands and was no closer to achieving his goal. He stopped in every chapel, prostrating himself and praying for hours. No sign appeared. He'd spoken with priests and been shown many ancient relics, but none of them was the Grail. In despair, he kept trying to understand Argante's clues.

He stopped for the night at a village on the outskirts of the fens of Anglia and wandered into the tavern for food. It had turned chilly; the warmth of a fire and a good mutton stew filled his thoughts.

As his eyes adjusted to the dim light, he caught sight of a young serving wench squirming in the arms of a half-drunken soldier in a dark corner. *Eve tempting Adam again.* He sighed and wished he'd had a choice to eat elsewhere.

Two men at the makeshift bar nodded and moved over to make room. "I tell you Custennin cannot hold them," one of them said. "Since Wehha landed in Guinnion, he's brought more of his bloodthirsty Saxons over. They'll be moving westward soon enough." The soldier who spoke slammed his empty cup down on the plank.

"Aye," his companion nodded. "Arthur wastes his time in talk. He should be looking for that scoundrel son of his."

"Medraut's dead, more like. What worries me is Arthur supports that old seawolf, Cerdic."

The man snorted. "Cerdic lies in wait until Arthur fears him no more. Then, he'll make his move."

"You would criticize the king?" Galahad asked mildly.

"He didn't try to take his crown back. His brains are addled from Cam's Landing, I think," the second soldier answered. "Who could live peacefully with the Saxons? It's our land."

Galahad cleared his throat. "Peace would save lives."

The first soldier eyed him speculatively, noting the black stole and gold cross he wore over his light mail. "Are you priest or warrior?"

"Mayhap, a little of both," Galahad answered. "I see no reason for bloodshed except for defense."

The second man laughed. "You sound like a woman to me."

Galahad studied him with piercing blue eyes. "The Good Book says to turn the other cheek." *Why are soldiers so willing to die?*

"You would stand here and let someone hit you?" The first man wiped ale from his mouth and joined in the laughter.

Galahad's expression did not waver as the man's hand rested on his sword hilt. "I'm not looking to fight. The Saxons are starving in their homeland. What harm if they live in the Fens, where Britons have never settled? It's nearly all marsh."

The man's sword flashed, but Galahad's own weapon deflected the point and sent the other's flying from his hand. Before the second man could draw, Galahad had the tip at his throat.

"Yield. I have no wish to fight."

The sword clattered to the floor. "Who are you? I've not seen a man handle a sword like that since Arthur yielded Excalibur."

Galahad sheathed his sword. "I'm only a man on a quest to find the Holy Grail of the Christos' last supper. It will bring peace to the land."

The first soldier shook his head. "You've been trained to fight, and well. Who trained you?"

"It's not important. My path lies in a different direction."

Just then, the girl in the corner screamed. Turning, Galahad saw the man had torn her blouse nearly off. The frightened girl was trying to cover her exposed breast and fend off the soldier at the same time.

Galahad moved with catlike quickness. He caught the man's shoulder and spun him around. Before the surprised drunk could focus, he was sprawled on the ground.

"Thank you, sir," the girl whimpered between sobs, her arms crossed in front of her. "Who are you?"

"My name is Galahad," he replied and frowned. As upset as she was, mayhap she hadn't been encouraging the man. "Go now and get some decent clothes." He saw her glance fearfully at the tavern owner and Galahad stared him down.

The girl didn't linger, fleeing the room.

The tavern owner spoke. "I've heard of you! Galahad, the wanderer. Son of Lancelot."

Instinctively, the first soldier stepped back. "Lancelot?" Then, as Galahad maintained his silence, the man grew bolder. "If that's true, I suggest you ride to your father and tell him Wehha is amassing soldiers. We probably have until Spring." He stepped closer. "The men that once would have followed Arthur will follow his captain. Tell him to come."

Why he went, Galahad wasn't sure. He told himself he hadn't seen his sister since she was a toddler and she was seven now. He would see if she were doing well with his father.

Lancelot met him in the bailey. "This is a surprise. Have you come to your senses and quit the quest for the Grail?"

"No, Father. I won't rest until I achieve it." Galahad swung down from the saddle in a quick, fluid motion. "I just needed some time to decide where to go next and I thought to see Elen again."

"Come in then." Lancelot handed the reins to the stableboy who'd run over. "Tell me the news from the south."

He frowned as he listened to Galahad's tale from the tavern in the fens. "These soldiers, were they Custinnen's men?"

"I don't think so. Cormant's more likely."

"And they don't believe Arthur can keep peace?"

"They seemed thirsty for blood, to me. Warriors always do, when they haven't fought in a while." *One more reason why I have to succeed.* "Will you go?"

Lancelot shook his head. "Custinnin is still king. It's their battle, not mine."

"So it's true then," Galahad said quietly. "You're no longer loyal to Arthur."

"I won't fight for him." Lancelot contemplated a moment, then sighed. "But I won't fight against him either."

"This has to do with Gwenhwyfar's disappearance, doesn't it?" Lancelot had told him earlier of Nimue's attempt to bring Gwenhwyfar home from wherever she was. Had his father not been so deadly serious, Galahad would almost have smiled. How can anyone be suspended in Time? "You blame him?" Galahad tensed, waiting for his father to unleash his anger.

But Lancelot's voice was resigned. "You wouldn't understand. You've never loved a woman."

Galahad felt himself color. "But I have."

"What?" His father began to smile. "When did this happen? I'm so glad..."

"Don't be," Galahad replied coldly. "She brought me pain and nearly made me unworthy to seek the Grail. I'll never let a woman get that close to me again." *Never.*

The corner of Lancelot's mouth quirked up. "Don't condemn all women. If this one turned you down..."

"It wasn't that."

"What then?" When Galahad didn't answer, he asked warily, "Don't tell me you didn't enjoy..."

"I wouldn't know," Galahad said bitterly. "When she found out who I was, she ran away."

Lancelot looked at his son, a puzzled expression on his face. "Why would it matter who you are? You've nothing to be ashamed of."

"Apparently, you do."

"You'd better tell me what you mean by that, unless you want a good thrashing." Lancelot's voice was even, but his eyes were stormy.

For a moment, Galahad hesitated, feeling like the small, frightened boy he was when his mother had brought him to Joyous Garde. Then he lifted his chin.

"Her name was Elen of Astolat."

Lancelot stared at him. "I spent a year at Astolat, healing from a wound. Elen took care of me. She couldn't have had a daughter."

Galahad shook his head. "She is her niece. Her father, Tirre, hates you. When I followed her home, he threw me out. What did you do?"

"Nothing! I swear," Lancelot answered. "Elen was young and in love with the idea of Camelot. Mistakenly, she turned that affection on me. I didn't realize how besotted she was until too late."

"You didn't dishonor her?" he asked suspiciously.

"I did not. Once I knew how she felt, I left."

"What happened to make Tirre hate you?"

Lancelot paused then sighed. "Elen had been such a gentle soul, kind and caring. We'd walk in the evenings—chaperoned, of course," he added at Galahad's raised eyebrow. "She'd tell me her dreams. Then we held a small tournament; I should not have worn her favor. She got the wrong idea." He was silent for a moment. "She died because of a love I couldn't return, and they sent her body to Camelot."

Galahad stared in disbelief. "How can anyone feel that strongly?"

"I wish I could convince you of the depth of love," Lancelot answered.

"You feel that strongly about Gwenhwyfar?"

"Much more than that," his father replied. "More than life itself. One day, I will find her."

His son shook his head. "Pain. That's all I see. I will travel alone."

"Then I feel sorry for you." Lancelot hesitated. "You're in need of healing. Mayhap, you should postpone this quest awhile and visit your grandmother in Benoic. She may be able to convince you otherwise."

"I don't think I'd feel comfortable spending time with the high priestess of the old religion when I believe in the new. And, I've heard the rumors of how she trained you, bringing in harlots to teach you all forms of depravity."

Lancelot gripped the arms of his chair, his eyes nearly black. Galahad stepped back, realizing he may have pushed his father too far.

"Don't refer to them as harlots in my presence again." Lancelot clipped each word. "Those courtesans taught me how to provide pleasure for a woman and to respect her. If they were paid for that experience, it makes them worth no less than the wife who puts up with an oafish husband nightly."

"The Good Book says a wife has a duty to submit to her husband."

"Women have the right to choose." Lancelot eyed Galahad. "Mayhap, it's better you do travel alone. Doesn't your religion teach you not to judge? You need to find tolerance, my son."

As he rode away several days later, Galahad reflected on his father's philosophy. *The priests teach marriage is sacred; my father evidently doesn't fear for his mortal soul. Lusting for Gwenhwyfar is wrong; how did Father ever get so entangled with her?* Then he remembered the second line of Argante's riddle. He shook his head. *If I have to wander alone, so be it. Women are not worth the risk of eternal damnation.*

Peredur hadn't been successful. Briefly he'd gone home to Gwynedd, and his brother Dornar had a great feast prepared in his honor. He'd seen his sister, Dindrane, for the first time since a baby and had promised to bring Blanchefleur to Dinas Emrys once he found the Grail. He sent messages to her whenever he encountered one of Arthur's relay stations.

After leaving Dinas Emrys, Peredur trekked over the mountains of Powys southerly through Siluria. The Old Religion still was strong in the rugged terrain of the West and he conversed with the doires of the springs and shrines he came to, but none had the Grail. Yet, through their encouragement, he felt rejuvenated to continue.

He traveled to the lower lands of Demetia. Here, the Scotti had settled peacefully after Agricola's men had subdued them over ten years ago. Arthur's way had always been to seek alliance from his defeated enemies rather than kill them.

So Peredur was surprised when he came to the castellum of Cardigan to find a man chained to a stone at the foot of the moat bridge. He lay half in and half out of the fetid water. Nearby, three soldiers sat gaming.

One of them looked up as Peredur approached. "Halt and state your business."

"I'm looking for the sacred cup of the Goddess."

The man arched an eyebrow. "You'll not be finding anything like that here. Best you ride on."

Peredur did not budge. "Why is that man chained?"

All the men watched him now. "He refused to grant our lady's favor," one finally said. The other two guffawed at the remark.

"A lady's favor, provided it is honorable, should always be granted," Peredur answered.

The man grinned. "Mayhap, honor was not the intent."

Peredur's brow furrowed. "What then? If the man refused to do an unhonorable thing, why is he being punished?"

The soldier shook his head. "The man asked for lodging. Our lady took a liking to him. He refused to become her paramour." He pointed to the sodden man. "This is to remind him he could have enjoyed the comforts of a warm bed and a willing woman." All the men laughed.

A willing woman. Peredur thought back to his conversation with Lancelot. *Did that mean a man is obligated if the lady is willing?* He frowned, then had another thought. "Was he discourteous in his refusal?"

The men stared at him unbelievingly. Then, one pointed to the battlements. "She does not like being refused."

Peredur looked up. An old crone, her white hair blown by the wind away from her scrawny neck, leaned over the embrasure. She smiled gap-toothed at him.

"Would you like to come in?" she called in a shrill voice.

One of the men nudged him. "Seems she's taken a liking to you, boy. I warned you to ride on." He laid his hand on the hilt of his sword. "Unless you want to join the man you were so concerned about, you'd best go in and do as she bids you."

"What does she want with me? I'm a stranger."

"Are you a complete fool, too? She likes bedding of young men."

Peredur shuddered as the implication set in. The only woman he'd ever had was Blanchefleur. And that was holy, the goddess blessing his quest. He looked again at the ancient hag and swallowed hard, aware all three men now had their hands resting on their weapons. He glanced at the man chained to the stone. *Am I honor bound to do this?*

"If I do what you want, will you let him go?" He pointed to the man and shouted across the moat.

The woman cackled, a dry-sounding pitch that ended in a hacking cough, spittle drooling from her mouth. "For certes, Laddie."

The chained man struggled to sit up. "Make her loose me first."

Peredur nodded. "Will you undo his chains and set him free?"

He waited while the hag thought. Finally, she nodded her assent. One of the soldiers handed him a keyring.

He slipped from his horse and strode to the man, kneeling to undo the chain. “I’m Persides,” the man whispered, “Arthur’s man. I’d heard Queen Gwenhwyfar was being detained here against her will.” He glanced at the guards. “It wasn’t true. Can you hold off two of them with that sword? I’ll engage the third until I disarm him, then we’ll finish them off.”

“She expects me to go in,” Peredur muttered.

“Don’t be a fool. Are you mad? Why would you want to bed a shriveled, dried prune like that hag?”

“A man’s word is his honor.”

Persides snorted. “Honor is won in battle. You will be enslaved if you go in there. Believe me.”

Peredur shook his head as he undid the lock and stood. Swift as an adder’s strike, Persides pulled the sword from Peredur’s scabbard and rushed the unsuspecting soldiers. He cut to the left, slicing the nearest soldier’s hand clear as he pulled his sword. He kicked the sword toward Peredur. “Defend yourself; I’ve committed both of us.”

The soldier who’d warned him away now came at him, teeth bared. “You will pay for that. He was my brother.”

Peredur sidestepped his lunge and thrust. The man was in a rage and charged again and Peredur parried. Suddenly, he heard Arthur’s voice inside his head. *“Watch the eyes as well. Anticipate. Stay in control. A man’s anger leaves him vulnerable. Watch for it.”* Clear-headed, Peredur balanced lightly on the balls of his feet and feinted right, only to deliver a swift blow to the man’s right shoulder. He delivered a series of repostes as he met the soldier’s cuts. “Yield!” he cried. “I have no wish to kill you.”

“Then you’ll die,” the soldier snarled and lunged again.

Peredur spun away and Persides was beside him, returning the thrust, his sword finding the soft spot below the ribcage and ripping upward. A red, gaping hole appeared and the soldier grasped the loose edges of his skin, trying to hold the organs in. He fell to the ground, blood spurting from his mouth and nose.

Persides cleaned the bloody sword on the grass near the other two dead soldiers. “We’d better ride, before she sends out more men.”

Already, they could hear the gate cranking open. Peredur nodded sadly, wishing Persides had not killed the men.

Persides flung himself on one of the guard’s horses. “Come on, boy! What do you think they’ll do to you if you stay?”

Quickly he mounted and they galloped away, but he made a vow that he wouldn’t shed blood.

Peredur turned down the dirt road leading to Blanchefleur’s home, Beaurepaire. Three years had passed since the day of the picnic; how good it would be to see Blanchefleur again. Even though he hadn’t found the Grail, he dreamed of it often, joy filling his soul. He decided to ask her to ride with him on his search. He sighed contentedly, thinking of her brown hair and cream-colored skin, so soft to his touch. The aching inside his trews grew nearly unbearable. *I will marry her tomorrow.*

A new seneschal greeted him in the bailey. “Your name and business, sir?” he inquired as a groomsman appeared behind him.

“Peredur.” He swung down and handed the reins over to the groom.

"I am here to see the lady, Blanchefleur."

"I am Engygeron," the new seneschal replied. "What would your business with the lady be?"

Peredur grinned happily as they walked to the Great Hall. "I'm here to marry her. Anon."

The seneschal stopped abruptly. "Really?"

"Where's her uncle, Gornemant?" Peredur asked as he looked around for a familiar face. He didn't see anyone he remembered.

"He's at home in Gohort."

"Who's protecting Blanchefleur then? Her father is dead."

"Clamadeu protects her." Engygeron began to look amused.

"Who?"

"Her husband, Fool, whoever you are. She's married and has a child."

Peredur blanched, an icy fist clenched at his insides. "That cannot be. She said she would wait for me."

The other man narrowed his eyes. "She didn't. I suggest you turn around and go back to where you came from before her rightful husband comes home."

"I must see her." Peredur stood rooted to the ground. Indeed, he felt as though he were made of lead. "Please. I must hear this from her."

"I've told you..." He was interrupted from the steps of the Great Hall.

"Peredur?"

Peredur stepped around the man to see Blanchefleur walking toward him, carrying a toddler. She set the boy down shakily and gazed up at him. "I didn't think I'd ever see you again."

He stared at her, noting the fine lines on her face. Her eyes had lost their sparkle and she looked resigned. "It's true then? You married someone else?"

She looked at the seneschal who stood there. "Let's go inside where we can talk." Turning to Engygeron, she dismissed him. "Return to your duties. I'll not need you for assistance."

Unwilling to leave them, but not having a choice, he bowed stiffly. "I will send a maid with food and drink."

Numbly, Peredur followed Blanchefleur inside, the toddler faltering awkwardly beside him. Absently, she reached for the child and sat him on the horsehair lounge. She smoothed his hair and beckoned Peredur to sit beside her. "The child is yours. His name is Lohengrin."

Peredur looked at her, dumbfounded, then at the child whose brown eyes studied him seriously. "How can that be? We were together only one time, when I asked the Goddess' blessing."

She smiled wanly. "He is your blessing, then."

He took her hands in his. "How did this marriage come to be? Didn't you get my letters? I sent one every time I reached one of Arthur's relay stations."

"I got one. If you sent more, they were intercepted." She shrugged. "Clamadeu of the Isles asked my father for my hand when I was but ten years. My father refused him, saying the decision would be mine when I became of age." Lohengrin climbed onto her lap. "My father died a year before I met you. When we returned from Gohort, after you left, Clamadeu laid siege to Beaurepaire. We weren't prepared. My soldiers sallied, but were far outnumbered. Clamadeu let my uncle live, in return for my marrying him."

"I will challenge him." Peredur stood and began pacing. "A fight to the death. You and I have a son; we belong together. The Goddess will protect me."

"Ah, Peredur," Blanchefleur smiled gently. "Everything is so simple for you and it's what I love about you. But you cannot challenge him. He knows who you are if he has the letters. You will die. I won't have your blood on my head."

He stopped abruptly. "Have you no trust in my skills? I'm better with a sword than I am with a horse. King Arthur, himself, practiced with me."

"I know." She placed Lohengrin on the ground and came to stand beside Peredur. "Clamadeu is a skilled warrior, practiced in the art of killing. What is worse, he enjoys it. He fought against Arthur with Fergus Mor; he always thought the king was a fool for letting them both live." She touched his face softly. "Even if you were to win, the soldiers here are his; you would not stay alive long."

"Then come away with me. We will go to Camelot." Peredur held her close in desperation, his face buried in her hair. *Lohengrin is my son! You were betrothed to me!*

She disengaged before someone discovered them. "I cannot. Our child is too young to travel. The terrain is rugged. How far do you think we'd get? You would be killed and I would be beaten...or worse."

"He beats you?"

She shook her head. "No, but he's described what he would've done to Queen Gwenhwyfar had he been Arthur and found her in bed with Lancelot. Clamadeu's an arrogant man; he wouldn't let me go unpunished. He'd humiliate me and make me pay. Please, Peredur, you must go and forget me. Continue searching for your Grail. It will put joy back into your heart."

He looked at her sorrowfully. "I cannot forget you, but I cannot put you at risk, either. I will wander alone. For now. But I will come back for you. We belong together." He looked at the emerald ring on his little finger and then at the toddler. "I'm going to send Lohengrin a chain of gold to wear. Tell him he must never take it off...and tell him about me. Tell him, one day, to be ready. I will return."

He dared not look back as he rode away.

~ Chapter 8—Lost Souls ~

The baying of the hounds grew gradually louder. Suddenly, it seemed Gwenhwyfar was in the midst of them. Then she became aware of the rocking motion of the horse's canter, but the hooves were pounding only air.

Powerful arms encircled her, holding her in place in front of the rider. Above, the full moon glittered like a single jewel, darkening the stars; below, the pale light–shadowed fields and homes, stretched to the horizon.

"I hope you'll enjoy the Hunt, my lady." Cernunnos' breath puffed warmly against her ear.

"What am I doing here? I should be on Avallach." Gwenhwyfar tried to turn, but the demi-god pressed his cheek against hers and she heard his rumbling chuckle.

"Yes, I saw you trying to leave," he answered. "I thought you might enjoy a night ride first. Tonight I look for the unwary to join me."

"Am I to be one of the souls you take?" Gwenhwyfar knew her voice had an edge.

He pulled her closer. "Ah, no. Your soul you can keep. It is you that I want."

"No. Let me go." She tried to wiggle loose, then grabbed Cernunnos' arm as she started to slide from the slippery withers.

"That's better." He pressed her against him. "Relax, and see what Samhain is all about." He laughed, spurring the horse on.

The animal plunged downward at a full gallop and Gwenhwyfar gasped as the wind whipped her hair and stung her face. The earth was rising to meet them and her blurred eyes could see a lone man walking along a deserted road. He carried a bow, a sack slung over his shoulder.

As they touched the ground, the noise of the horse's clatter and the dogs' barking suddenly began. The man turned, startled, then a look of terror crossed his face. He started to run, but the phantom horse was already beside him, the hounds closing.

"Say farewell." Cernunnos swept his arm down and touched him. The man fell to the ground and was still.

The horse and hounds rose again, streaming through the sky toward a field of needfire. "Do you kill everyone you find tonight?" Gwenhwyfar asked shakily.

"No. That man was a poacher; those that honor the Old Ways are left unharmed." He pointed toward the fires. "We'll take a look at those."

As they slowed and hovered, she could see the smaller fires were laid out in a circle surrounding a much larger, central fire. A man and woman capered, dancing in ritualistic form, mystically moving in and out of smoke. Both were naked, save for a set of prong antlers secured to the man's head.

Cernunnos set the horse down quietly and slipped off, reaching up for Gwenhwyfar. "If you're thinking about screaming, they won't hear us." He pulled her closer to the blaze. "We're here in spirit, as always happens when someone honors me. Would you like to experience it?"

Gwenhwyfar drew back and he laughed. "I was there when your husband coupled with Nimue at his Kingmaking, my lady, and before, when Lancelot's mother begat him in the Great Rite with King Ban. I think you'll find the sensations enjoyable through someone else's eyes."

Then she was inside that ring of light, feeling the heat on her bare skin, the softness of the grass beneath her feet. The man had stepped closer and put his hands on her hips, moving her slowly around the circle to the rhythm of subliminal music. His touch burned into her flesh, sending a searing flame of desire throughout her body. Cernunnos' luminescent eyes shone through the man's face and he nodded slightly, the ethereal antlers growing majestically from the small, physical rack on the mortal man's head.

The unheard music played faster and drew her closer to the man until their bodies were pressed together and they moved as one, spinning around the fire until everything blurred and there were no more separate fires surrounding them, only one force, uniting everything.

They fell to the ground, the man inserting himself savagely, ruthlessly, but the woman only screamed with pleasure and clung tightly to him, the wrapped thighs locking him to his position. Outside the flames, others coupled on the grasses.

Suddenly, the air was chill and Gwenhwyfar found herself leaning against the horse unsteadily. Beside her, Cernunnos stood benignly. "Well? Was it as I said?"

She smoothed her woolen robe, not sure if it had ever come off. "Was it real? Did I...?"

A shimmer of effervescence emanated from his eyes. "Did you want it to be?"

Gwenhwyfar looked down at the ground. "I want to go home."

He touched her shoulder, and again she felt that brief burst of irresistible craving. "You don't have to be afraid of me, my lady."

She shrugged his hand off and looked up, green eyes fervent in the brightness of the illumination. "I have asked to go home. Take me to Avallach."

Cernunnos looked surprised, then he sighed softly. "Home. As you wish." He reached for her, but she stepped back quickly. "I'm only going to lift you onto the horse," he said wryly, "or would you rather try straddling it with what you're wearing?"

When she was seated sideways, he leapt on behind her and the horse and hounds rose again, beating a silent cadence into the wind. She watched the landscape sweep along beneath her, wondering where they were and how far to Avallach. Then she saw the familiar fog lying low on the ground, writhing like...dragon's breath, Myrddin used to say. She nearly laughed, thinking she would be pleased even to see him again.

The mists rose to greet them, enveloping them like a warm, soft blanket. The horse sank silently through until his hooves touched solid ground.

She slipped from the stallion and looked around. She couldn't see the Isle, the fog was so dense, but she could hear water lapping at a nearby shore. She looked up to Cernunnos. "Which way? Will you show me?"

"I still have work to do this night." He pointed. "Walk just a few feet and the path will be clear."

His horse spun and was gone.

Gwenhwyfar inhaled deeply. *How good the earth felt again.* Never had she thought she'd be glad to be on the Isle. Tomorrow, she'd see Arthur...and Lancelot. *My love! I'm home!*

Nearly giddy with anticipation, she walked in the direction Cernunnos had indicated. The mists dissolved quickly, leaving the path leading to the trees clear. *This is not the usual direction I've entered from before; we must have arrived on the other side of the Isle.*

She passed an oak and an ash tree, standing together; on the other side of the path, a single hawthorn grew. She continued on until the trees opened unto a glade. Suddenly, *déjà vu* struck. *This is the same meadow in which Lancelot and I made love that day Cernunnos sent us into the land of Faerie.* Gwenhwyfar stopped sharply, a hand to her mouth. *It can't be...*

Then she heard a giggle and slowly turned, knowing who she'd find.

"Well come back, Gwenhwyfar," Morgan le Fey said.

"Very good, Elen," Lancelot gave his daughter a hug as she finished practicing with her wooden sword. "That last parry I didn't expect."

She smiled up at him, taking the compliment as her due. "I want to be as good as Gwenhwyfar."

He gazed into space, a deep hunger inside, then he hugged Elen again. "I don't know how good she was at your age."

The eight-year-old shrugged. "She must have been good. You said she fought beside you."

"That she did," he answered, "when that bi...when her wicked sister-in-law and Maelgwyn tried to abduct the queen."

"Tell me the story again," she begged and settled on the bench.

Lancelot sat beside her. "I'd just brought back Arthur's new horses from across the channel. Arthur had gone to squelch a rebellion in Llongborth. Gwenhwyfar and I were up late, talking, when we heard a noise in the back hallway."

"Was it Morgana?" Elen asked.

"Yes, but I didn't know it because all four intruders were hooded. I cornered two of them in the hallway, but the other two made it around the front and were trying to carry Gwenhwyfar off."

"But you stopped them."

"We stopped them," he corrected, "fighting back to back. The queen held her own."

"Didn't she kick one of them in the face?"

"Yes." He looked past his daughter, remembering those two Saxon mercenaries. *They tried to rape Gwen at a later time, and I managed to stop them then, too, but the incident also forced me to acknowledge to Arthur that I loved Gwenhwyfar.*

"Then what happened?" she persisted.

Lancelot refocused and grinned at his daughter. "You know what happened. You've heard the story before. When Arthur got back, he decided the queen needed someone to protect her when he was not there. That's how I became her champion."

Elen gave him a satisfied smile. "You're going to bring her back, aren't you?"

He closed his eyes, then opened them again. "I'm going to try, child. It's been four years, but Samhain is close by. The portal may open for me this year."

She touched his hand. "I heard the Lady say once that nothing could keep you and the queen apart. That you were des...dest...meant to be."

"When did she say that?" Lancelot asked quickly. *Ah, Gwen, were we as transparent as that?*

"When I was little. You took me to the tournament. I met the queen that time. She was nice."

Surprised, he said, "You remember that? You were barely three years old."

"I remember the king, too," she answered smugly. "He was laughing and talking to the Lady. They seemed to like each other a lot."

"They've been friends for as long as the queen and I have."

"Aren't you and the king friends?"

Lancelot hesitated and the old pain flowed through him. He missed Arthur, for they had been closer than brothers. Yet, it was because of the closeness that he couldn't understand how Arthur could have left Gwenhwyfar in Avalon.

"We were."

"What happened?"

"You're too young to understand. Mayhap, some day when Gwenhwyfar returns, we'll see each other again." He stood and pulled her up beside him. "Now, why don't you practice your Latin so you can read to Nimue when she comes?"

Elen wrinkled her nose. "Latin is boring. I'd rather hear a story about a magical circle of stones on Avallach."

"You can ask Nimue about that, too," Lancelot answered with a smile, "but not until you can read your Latin."

With a sigh, she turned and walked away.

Lancelot watched her. He could teach her to defend herself and to ride, and force the reading lessons, but she was getting close to the age when she would need a woman to confide in. *Gwen, we need you. Please, Great Mother, let the portal open this year.*

When Nimue arrived a fortnight later, she brought bad news. "You must go to Brocéliande. Your mother is dying."

Lancelot stared at her. "What's wrong with her? She's not that old!"

Nimue smiled gently. "The years have gone by, Lancelot. She's near eighty."

"She is high priestess! Can she not heal herself?"

"Mayhap, she has no wish to," Nimue replied. "When Vivian was ready to cross to the Otherworld, I begged and pleaded with her and with Myrddin. He said we must let the Goddess take her back."

"But who will take her place? The last time I visited, the school for maidens was closed."

"Yes," Nimue said sadly, "she is the last of the Old Ones. Even the enchanted forest is giving way to landholders. Since Clovis converted, the new religion has swept Gaul and extends into Armorica. When your father and uncle died fighting him, there was no one left to resist the Christians. His son, Childebert, is also Christian and he is ever hungry for more land. That is why you must go. Your mother needs you."

"Can I wait until Samhain? To see if the portal opens?"

Nimue shook her head. "If it did, you would not be there for your mother. I believe she will leave us on that night. The Morrigan will escort her and Janus will be waiting."

"This has come to you in the Sight," Lancelot said, not making it into a question. "Have you any other news?"

Nimue shook her head. "The pool remains still; not even Morgan appears. You will have to wait until next year. I'm sorry."

He sighed. "Bors will be waiting at the pier?"

She nodded. "He was preparing the boat at Portus Adurni as I left. Will you be taking Elen with you? She'd have a chance to meet her grandmother."

"On a ship? Unchaperoned?" Lancelot looked incredulous. "Augusta is too old to travel..."

"Elen is a strong, healthy child." Nimue smiled. "I doubt any harm will come her way, but if it would help, I could send Argante with you. She and Niniane have always liked each other."

Lancelot looked relieved. "If you'll tell Elen, I'll go and get a tongue lashing from Augusta. She won't be pleased with me."

"She'll understand. She's loved you as her son, too." Nimue turned to go find Elen.

The passage was smooth, the winds light and seas near calm. Lancelot wondered if Argante had anything to do with it, for she spent most of her time in the bow, looking across the water. Elen took to her immediately; Lancelot found them often deep in conversation. Once he'd heard something about a circle of stones and smiled, thinking of the active imagination his daughter had.

Now, they approached the small, secluded valley near the dark lake deep within the forest. The sun, breaking through the clouds, cast moving patterns across the still water. Lancelot paused, taking in the stillness. Even the birds were quiet, as if in mourning. Faintly, he could detect the high whirring pitch of the windsingers, perched high in the trees.

He reached for the knob on the old oak tree. Within seconds, he felt the slight swish of air that indicated the tree dryads were on their way to give his mother the message of his presence.

He nodded to Argante. "Follow me."

They walked past the old pilings and climbed over a jumble of rocks. Behind them, a great stone had been rolled away, indicating the entrance to the cave below the lake. Lancelot lit the torch and proceeded down the carved stone steps, the fire flashing and reflecting from thousands of crystals made the whole tunnel appear to dance. When they reached the bottom, he extinguished the torch and opened the door to the lavishly furnished, vast cavern room. A strange scent filled his nostrils.

Argante lifted her head and sniffed. "Death is not far away." She reached for Elen's hand and motioned for Lancelot to lead.

Niniane lay on a bed of furs wrapped in her priestess robe of dark blue silk, interwoven with silver threads. She'd shriveled to almost nothing since he'd last seen her.

"Madame?"

The hazel-grey eyes, a lighter shade than his, turned to him. She smiled and held out her hand. "Galahad. You've come."

Elen looked surprised. "His birth name," Argante whispered.

He sat beside his mother. "What is it, Madame, that you cannot be healed?"

She shook her head. "My time has come. Do not feel sorrow. It is enough that you have come." She looked past him. "Argante. You will be our hope. The Old Religion is gone here, but in Britain, it will live on."

Argante came forward with Elen. "This is your granddaughter, Lady."

Elen made obeisance and Niniane studied her. For some moments, no one spoke and Lancelot wondered if his mother were fading away before his eyes. Finally, she reached for Elen with her other hand.

"Yes, I believe you are," she said aloud to an unspoken question and looked at Argante. "Do you agree?"

The younger priestess nodded. "It is still soon to say."

Niniane smiled. "The Goddess will decide." She turned back to her son. "I would like a private word with you."

She waited until Argante and Elen left. "Do you still search for Gwenhwyfar?"

Lancelot started. "How...?"

"Many years ago when you were a child and Myrddin sent you back here, I knew the bond that would be between you and Gwenhwyfar." Niniane's voice sounded surprisingly firm. "Yet he and I had both hoped, somehow, to keep you apart, for Arthur's sake." She looked into the past. "Arthur did what no other king has done; he brought the Britain warlords together and drove the Saxons back. You saved his life. He needs you now, yet you refuse to go to him."

"Madame—" Lancelot stopped, then continued. "When I met Arthur, I near worshipped him, for he already was a leader in Uther's army. When I came to know him, I respected him and believed in his dream as much as he did. He has been my brother; more times than I can count, we have saved each other." He paused again. "But Gwenhwyfar is my soul. For years, I tried to deny it, then came the two years at Joyous Garde...the happiest I've ever been." He looked at the floor.

His mother kept silent, waiting for him to finish.

When he looked up, his eyes glittered darkly. "I don't understand how Arthur could leave her in Avalon, to forfeit the rest of her life. I'd have stayed with her."

"Camelot would have faded away. Two lives would have been forfeit for naught. Arthur has to try to keep peace and unity."

"But he left her, his own wife."

"Arthur is king first. His marriage to the land overrides his human one."

"Madame, I cannot agree."

"You are not a king, Galahad. You could have been, had you stayed here. Gwenhwyfar is a queen. She understand, regardless of her personal love for you, the matter of Britain comes first. Did she not tell you that?"

He hung his head then, remembering her words as she stepped on the barge to Avalon.

"That should be her legacy, Son, that she was willing to give up her earthly life so Britain would survive. If only history will dwell on that, instead of her being the downfall of Camelot. She was a great queen."

Lancelot looked up, "Was? She is not dead, is she?" *Dear Goddess Mother, that can't be true.* His voice was barely above a whisper. "Is that why I haven't been able to contact her? That she is in the Otherworld?"

"She still lives. I meant merely that her life as a queen is over."

"I must find a way to go to her, then."

Niniane shook her head. "Do not abandon your daughter. Be patient. Let the Goddess work."

"Patience is not a virtue of mine."

"Nor is forgiveness," she answered, "and you must do both. Be patient and forgive."

"Forgive Arthur?"

"Yes. The choice was Gwenhwyfar's."

Suddenly, Lancelot knew she was right. Part of the guilt Gwenhwyfar carried was over how her actions hurt Arthur's dream. He remembered many conversations they'd had over that. And Arthur would be struggling with his guilt over abandoning Gwen. *I've been no help, only made the pain worse. I must go to him.*

"I will try, Madame. I will try."

The next morning, Argante found Niniane permanently asleep, a peaceful expression on her face. She prepared the body and together with Lancelot, placed the high priestess in a long, bronze box that had been made many years ago, when she first became Lady. The horses pulled it to the raft tied to the pilings. They spent some time, laying the rocks inside the box, surrounding the body. Only when the raft began to sink did they pole out to the middle of the lake. Gently, chanting in the Old Tongue, Argante and Lancelot eased the heavy, sealed casket into the water, where it quickly sank to the bottom.

Then they began their journey home to Camelot and to Arthur.

Time had come for forgiveness.

The guard at Camelot's gate tower sounded the gong. "Rider coming!"

Custennin and Arthur both looked up from the horse they were inspecting in the paddock. "Alone? What banner?" Custennin shouted.

"Alone," the guard called back. "I see no banner, but he rides like a warrior."

Arthur handed the horse over to a groom and followed Custennin to the gate. The horseman was approaching at a slow canter, looking to his right and left as though admiring the countryside.

"He seems relaxed enough, whoever he is," Custennin remarked. "No bad news, I hope."

Arthur squinted. The late afternoon sun was behind casting the rider in silhouette. "Do you recognize his armor?"

"No, I don't think so. Wait..." Custennin's eyes widened. "Bedwyr! When he rode out, he wore plain armor instead of the crest of Cameliard. He finally returns!"

The rider was near the gate when he reined his horse to a stop and asked admittance. Arthur ran out to greet him.

Bedwyr stared at him, and Arthur knew he was taking in the grey hair and silvery eyes.

"Is it really you, Arthur?" Then he was off the horse, in a bear hug grip with Arthur.

"I'd not known you either," Arthur joked, "with the beard and the hair not cut."

They made their way into the Great Hall and proceeded to the council room. "So, why didn't you come home after we sent word Medraut had been discovered?" Arthur poured Bedwyr a cup of wine. "I thought you as upset with me about Gwenhwyfar as Lancelot is."

Bedwyr grimaced. "What happened in Avalon wasn't your fault. If he's still angry with you, I'll seek him out now that I'm home." He ran his hand along the back of the chair that had Lancelot's name emblazoned on it. "To answer your question, I'd planned to go to Paris and see Medraut for myself, but the turn of events in Leon these past two years has kept me there."

Arthur leaned forward, frowning. "What's the trouble?"

"After King Derock died fighting Clovis, his son, Jonas, took the title in Leon. While you were in Avalon, Derock's mother remarried...a neighbor, the Count of Poher, Jean-Marc. Jonas died shortly after."

"What was the cause?"

"He was found murdered in his bed."

"By whom?"

"By his wife. She went nearly mad and accused the count."

"Why?"

Bedwyr shrugged. "Apparently, the count wanted to unite the two properties and, since he was elder, to run them."

Arthur raised an eyebrow. "Make himself king? What did he expect Jonas to do?"

"Jonas' mother tried to persuade Jonas to accept but he replied that he was a married man with a son and would not descend."

"How old is the boy?" Custennin asked.

"Six and ten. The count named himself Regent as soon as Jonas was killed."

"Is the boy being fostered somewhere?" Arthur remembered his own childhood at Ector's in Bonmaison. Myrddin had been afraid that someone would try to kill him if they knew Uther had an heir.

"You might say that." Bedwyr smiled a little. "He should have gone to his cousin, Samson, and stayed at the Abbey of Dol, but his mother wanted him farther away. He's in Paris, under Childebert's protection. Whether as fosterling or hostage, I cannot say."

"Hostage?" Custennin asked and looked at Arthur, then back at Bedwyr. "Why would the Frankish king need a hostage? Are there threats of war?"

"Not yet," Bedwyr answered, "But if Medraut and Morgana are there, I would not be too trusting."

"Umm," Arthur replied. "Not many months ago, Cynric went to Gaul; he mentioned he'd seen the buildup of cavalry south of Paris. Mayhap, I should go myself. The last thing we need is a Frankish offensive. And with Medraut there, the boy might not be safe."

"Aye," Custennin said bitterly, "while you were across the sea, helping Hoel, Medraut planned his ambush well. He might be persuading Childebert to attack. But how do you think Britain's soldiers will be received?"

Arthur shook his head, "I won't be going as king nor will I need soldiers."

"I know you want to mediate peace, but you can't travel alone! They could take you hostage, as well!" Custennin said.

Arthur thought awhile. "Childebert has never met me. I'll take a derivative of my name...Arthmael...and I'll go to Benoic first. Lancelot's brother, Ector, holds it; he can tell me how his neighbor, the count, fares. From there, I'll travel to Gaul...mayhap as a hermit...the hair is grey enough now. I'll let it grow...and a beard, too."

"This is madness," Bedwyr said earnestly, leaning forward on the table. "Let me go back with you. I've learned the lay of the land."

"No," Arthur replied and laid a hand on his friend's shoulder. "You have Cameliard to care for. Gwenhwyfar is not returning...and even if she did, I have sworn to...well, I have nothing to lose by going. And, I may be able to do some good." He grinned suddenly, feeling an old spark of adventure come to life. "Childebert is a Christian king; he'll grant an old man of God a place to stay. I can find what the rumors are and how it lies with the boy. What's his name?"

"Judwal," Bedwyr replied. "If you're coming from Benoic, Armel would be the better name. But what if Medraut or Morgana recognizes you? I think you're playing with fire."

Arthur leveled his gaze on him. "We will have to meet one day and this will give me the advantage. I can find them before they find me, since they don't know I'm coming."

Bedwyr studied him. "It's like planning a war campaign."

Arthur gave a slight nod. "Only I hope this campaign will be less deadly."

Gwenhwyfar sat with her back against an ancient oak and idly stroked the satin skin of the unicorn resting beside her. His soft muzzle nudged her hand gently. The day was pleasantly warm, as all the days were in the land of Faerie, the sun burnishing the leaves to a vivid, glossy green against an azure sky. A kestrel soared lazily in the air high above and, nearby, a meadowlark called to its mate. She gave an empty sigh.

"What ails you, my lady?" the blonde Faerie maiden, Sadi, asked. "It is a perfect day!"

"All of them are," Gwenhwyfar answered. "I don't even know how many of them have passed. Everything blends together."

The Faerie tilted her head. "Why are you so concerned with time? It matters not to us here. We eat when we're hungry, we play until we're tired, our men pleasure us when we will..."

A chorus of giggles accompanied the last remark and Gwenhwyfar saw several of the other females emerge from the wood. Branda, the red-headed one, called to them. "We're going for a swim. Come along!"

Sadi jumped to her feet, clapping her hands delightedly. "Will Ganus be there?"

"If you are, he will," Edan, one of the dark-haired Faeries, laughed. "Since you have charmed him, he takes no notice of the rest of us!"

"Come with us, my lady! Put away your cares for once," Sadi said. "Our men can provide quite a diversion, I promise!"

"What she says is true," Morgan came walking through the trees. "I believe I'll go to watch. Come along, Gwenhwyfar."

She rested her hand on the white withers of the unicorn. "I'd rather stay here."

Morgan shrugged and turned to the giggling girls. "A game. The first one in the water gets her choice of partners...even Ganus," she added with a sideways look at Sadi.

With swift, fleet-footed turns, the Faeries were gone, leaving only the sound of their laughter's residue in the air. Gwenhwyfar leaned back and closed her eyes.

"You should have gone with them, my lady."

She opened her eyes slowly. Cernunnos stood close, looking down at her. She'd become used to his appearing at odd times. Now, with svelte, animal grace, he lowered himself to sit beside her, causing the mystical horse to raise itself and trot away. "I am bothered by your brooding."

"How long have I been here, Cernunnos?"

He shrugged. "We keep no track of time. It moves differently here."

"I know that," Gwenhwyfar said in frustration. "How long have I been here?"

His brow furrowed. "I rode the Wild Hunt again not long ago."

"Samhain? I've been in Faerie a year?" When he didn't reply, she added, "I should be home. Why did you bring me here?"

Cernunnos smiled. "You know why. I want you."

Gwenhwyfar raised her chin and felt her eyes flash. "I've told you no."

He grinned. "I can wait." He slipped closer, not quite touching her. "Mayhap, in your time, I should do something about that."

She shifted away from him, resisting the alluring urge not to move at all. "I assume that even here in the land of Faerie, there is honor enough among you not to commit rape."

The demi-god's eyes narrowed. "I do only what brings pleasure."

"For you?" she asked, refusing to look at him.

A static charge filled the air then quickly disappeared. "I don't think you'd be disappointed." He touched her shoulder briefly, his fingers trailing down her arm.

She hugged herself, not daring to meet his hypnotic gaze. "Please don't do this."

The hand lingered, then he dropped it. "Not many women have refused me." She did not reply. "You still want that mortal...Lancelot."

Gwenhwyfar looked up quickly. "Always. Will you let me go?"

"No." Cernunnos shrugged. "Even I cannot open the portal. I was only able to prevent you from leaving through it."

Tears welled up as she said dejectedly, "I can't even find the pool anymore."

"The pool is on a ley line between us and Avalon." Cernunnos' eyes darkened. "You cannot leave Faerie on your own, but I could take you there."

Gwenhwyfar's face brightened. "You would do that? Let me talk to Lancelot again?"

"For a price."

A chill swept over her. She took a deep, ragged breath. "Name it."

He leaned forward and tilted her chin toward him. "You already know."

For a moment, she hesitated. Then, at last, she nodded. "I will think about it."

They stepped out of the wood and Gwenhwyfar felt the change...the air seemed heavier, the day not as bright.

"The land of Faerie is an easier place to live," Cernunnos gestured to the pool. "Call your man."

Gwenhwyfar sank to her knees, her hands shaking as she stretched them over the water. *It has been so long...Lancelot, do you hear me? Come.*

The water slowly stirred, an image forming. Then, a tentative voice. *"Gwen?"*

"Yes, Lancelot," she tried not to cry. "Where are you?"

"Bedded down for the night with Argante and Elen on the road to Camelot. I need to forgive Arthur," Lancelot's voice cracked. "By the Goddess, is this why I can see you now? Because I will make peace with Arthur? Can you come to me?"

She shook her head. "Cernunnos is with me. He brought me to the pool."

Lancelot's smile wavered. "Why is he with you?"

Cernunnos leaned over her shoulder. "She lives with me now, in the land of Faerie."

"You cannot hold her prisoner!"

The demi-god's eyebrows raised. "Do you wish to argue with me, Lancelot du Lac, or to enjoy Gwenhwyfar's company?"

"Please, Lance, don't spoil our time together," Gwenhwyfar begged.

Lancelot clenched and unclenched his fists. "Ah, Gwen, there is so much I want to say..."

She tried to reach him on the spirit plane, to touch and hold him, but something blocked her. They had to content themselves, spending the next hours whispering endearments between bits of news from the world. Finally, Cernunnos signaled it was time to go.

"Nimue will keep trying to open the portal," Lancelot said. "Do not give up hope. But now that I can see you again, life is tolerable."

Gwenhwyfar forced a smile, fearing what the price would be for each visit. "I will always love you, Lance." She made a last effort to kiss him and felt a transcendent rendering of current around her. Then she was tasting him, their kisses salty with tears of gladness, arms wrapped tightly about each other, crushing one another, not wanting to let go.

"You broke through," Lancelot said, nuzzling her neck, his hands exploring her.

Just as suddenly, she was back on the ground at the pool. Lancelot's image began to fade. She looked up at Cernunnos. "Why did you bring me back just then? It's been so long..."

He lifted her with one hand. "That wasn't supposed to have happened. The visit was to be talk only. How did you break the barrier?"

She stared at him, dumbfounded. "You created a barrier? Why? Morgan always encouraged the touching."

"Morgan wanted Lancelot, not you." He smiled. "And I'm a covetous man; I don't like to share." He cupped her face in his hands. "I believe you have a bargain to keep."

Gwenhwyfar took a deep breath and closed her eyes, steeling herself for his kiss. The hands holding her in place were warm and gentle. *Mayhap, he'll realize this isn't what I want*...the hands dropped suddenly and she opened her eyes.

He stood a few feet away, studying her. She forced herself to meet his limpid gaze. He said nothing, but held out his hand. Gwenhwyfar felt an irresistible tug propelling her forward. As she moved closer, she could feel heat radiating from him. It pricked her skin, stinging like a thousand little needles, yet tickling too, making her flesh tingle, while a deeper pulsation penetrated her muscles. She shimmied a little, lured on as if mesmerized and then stopped, inches from him.

His lips came down to her neck and she reached up pulling him still closer to her. Her body sank into him and she felt his heat.

When Cernunnos reached to undo the shoulder ties that held her flimsy, silken gown in place, she felt herself blush and quickly pushed away from him. She couldn't let this happen.

He stepped close once again and wrapped his arms around her. "Did I disappoint you, my lady?" he whispered against her ear.

"You know you didn't," she said as she stood quietly inside his embrace, "but how much of this is enchantment?"

"Does it matter?"

"It does to me. I...just want to know. The night of Samhain, when you took me inside that woman's mind...I was not really there...so much is confusion in Faerie."

He sounded amused. "Why don't you ask Lancelot?"

"What do you mean by that?"

"He never left."

"What?" She suddenly felt as though ice had frozen the blood in her veins.

"See for yourself." Cernunnos carried her to the edge of the pool. Lancelot's horrified face looked back.

"NO! No...Lancelot..." Gwenhwyfar crumbled to a heap on the ground. "Oh, my love. forgive me..."

Cernunnos looked at Lancelot, a small smile on his face. "I always win."

"You bastard! Let me come to you."

"And you'll do what? Challenge the Horned One? You can hardly deny the lady enjoyed it."

Lancelot paused, anger, jealousy, and grief warring on his face. He looked at Gwenhwyfar. "How long has he been trying to take you? I can't blame you...Gwen...Bel's Fires, why? And why did you make me watch...? Damnation, Gwen. WHY?"

Tears streamed down her face. "I didn't know...Oh, Lance...I thought I could do this so I could visit you."

He was suddenly quiet. "What do you mean?"

"It was the payment I requested to bring her to the pool," Cernunnos said affably, "And I'll repeat my offer if you want to continue to see her. We will all get what we want. No harm done."

For a moment, Lancelot stared at him. Then, for the first time, Gwenhwyfar saw what Arthur had warned her about. The other side of Lancelot; the battle-frenzied warrior. With a berserker's scream, he faded from the pool and the water lay still.

Cernunnos grinned and lifted Gwenhwyfar. "Mayhap, one day we will meet, Lancelot du Lac."

Cynric stood in the doorway to the tavern in Clausentum, letting his eyes acclimate to the dim light. The tender at the keg gestured toward the far corner of the room.

Tables had been overturned and only one man sat slumped on a wooden chair, boots out in front of him, staring sullenly into the fire burning feebly on the hearth. No one had the courage to replenish it until the man moved away.

The noon meal had just passed and the few patrons huddled on the room's opposite side. Cynric moved his head slightly and, like a working ant bed, they quickly scuttled out. Even the tender followed. Cynric searched the room and stairs for hidden stragglers, but all was empty. He removed his swordbelt and put his dagger on the table near the door. Then he approached.

"Lancelot."

The figure didn't move nor appear to hear. Cynric stepped closer.

"That's far enough."

Cynric halted. "What happened?" Silence. He waited, not moving.

Finally, Lancelot spoke. "She's gone. I've lost her."

"Gwenhwyfar's been gone...been away...for over five years. Have you lost the contact you told me about?"

"Worse. I've given her to him."

Cynric frowned. "To Arthur?"

"NO!" Lancelot howled. "To Cernunnos...the Horned One!"

"The demi-god? I don't understand..."

Lancelot whirled in his chair, dagger in hand, a crazed, anguished expression on his face.

"I'm not armed, Lancelot. Put the knife down." Cynric dared not move; Lancelot was ready to spring. "I want to know what happened to Gwenhwyfar. I care about her, too."

Lancelot looked at him blankly, then down at his hand. For some minutes he studied the dagger, asininely fascinated with it. Suddenly, he sheathed it inside his boot. When he looked up, his eyes had lost their maniacal look and his voice was rational.

"I'm not insane. I'd had no contact in a year, I was afraid she'd gone over to the Otherworld. Then, last night, she was suddenly there. I'd never been so happy."

Cynric retrieved an overturned chair and sat. "Tell me the rest."

"We talked. When it was time to leave, something held me in place and I saw...what happened." He was quiet for so long Cynric was tempted to speak, but didn't. "He wants her. And what he wants, he gets."

"Against her will? Did he...?"

"No." The pain in his voice was wrenching to hear. "In the end...she... wanted him, but broke away." Lancelot clenched his fist and banged his hand on the table.

"This may sound cold," Cynric paused, "but don't you think she ever wanted...Arthur?"

"For certes. Gwenhwyfar has always been a passionate, feeling woman. But Arthur was...is...her husband. It was her right."

"Then what's the difference, Lancelot? She's been stuck in that place...between the worlds...for a long time. Mayhap, she only did what men do all the time. Enjoyed the moment."

He shook his head. "She is being held in the land of Faerie because he desires her. He told me that...he said he always wins...and that if I...if I want to see her again, he will make it happen."

Cynric leaned forward. "Think a moment. If he's saying she has to couple with him if she wants to see you...that doesn't sound like lust on Gwenhwyfar's part."

Lancelot hit the table again. "He mesmerizes her...all he did was hold out his hand and she moved to him, as though she had no thought of her own. And once he touched her...his will was hers."

"I've never known Gwenhwyfar to let anyone own her."

"I challenged him...I told him to bring me there. He laughed. I can't compete with someone who is only half-human. He'll continue to seduce her until she...she gives in...forgets the human world."

Cynric stood. "I think Gwenhwyfar is stronger than that. Why don't you come home with me? Yule approaches...and the boys could use a good horseman. Or is there someplace you need to be?"

Lancelot shook his head. "I told Argante to take my daughter to Avallach. Lupin can take care of Joyous Garde. I was on my way to Camelot, but I can't face Arthur now...I can't tell him." He stood, too.

"Good," Cynric said as he picked up his weapons and they walked out the door. *Mayhap, Frida will be able to divert his thoughts.*

Lancelot swung up into the saddle and followed Cynric out of town, muttering to himself. "The only hope I have is to never contact Gwenhwyfar again."

~ Chapter 9—The Lineage of the Fisher Kings ~

Peredur looked away from the hermit with whom he'd spent the last year trying to come to terms with Blanchfleur's marriage. "I don't know that I'm ready to leave."

"The time of mourning is past," Ulfin said kindly as he gathered up the supper dishes. "You must journey on."

"Where will I go?" Peredur asked. "The Grail has eluded me; I haven't had the dream in a year. Can I not live in peace here?"

The hermit shook his head. "You're wallowing in pity. You mustn't waste your life."

"It's mine to do with as I choose," he returned. "I'll find another place where I may live alone."

"Before you do, why don't you visit your uncle Pelles? He's suffered more pain than you'll ever know; he lost his wife, his daughter, and his grandchildren, yet he does not dwell in self-pity, even though he is in physical pain from the wound that won't heal." The sage smiled gently. "Mayhap some good will come of it. Carbonek is not far from here."

Two days later, Peredur had ridden from the fertile green farmlands through forest that grew ever thinner until only dry, brown grass covered the earth. Now, he approached the small holding and stared up the barren hill. He remembered Pelles was also Galahad's grandfather and he nudged his horse forward, wondering if Galahad had visited him recently. He suddenly had the feeling he should try to find Galahad.

The bailey was deserted and an elderly groom came for his horse. "Where are your soldiers?" Peredur asked.

The old man smiled. "We have little need of many soldiers here. Carbonek has been a wasteland for many years. No one bothers us. Please, go inside. The king will be glad to see you."

The door opened as he approached and a thin woman of middle years smiled at him. "Come in, young man. Well come to the home of the Fisher King."

"Fisher King?" Peredur was puzzled as he followed the housekeeper inside. "Why is he called that?"

"Ah," the housekeeper answered as she plumped pillows for him on the lounge in the receiving room and signaled a maid to bring wine. "Before he was wounded, he had fleets of boats and supplied Arthur's army with the gifts of the sea."

Peredur started to ask how he'd been injured, for rumors ran rampant about the mystery of the unhealed leg, but he hesitated, remembering Gornemant's advice not to ask so many questions.

"My name is Yanna," the woman told him. "It's nice to have a visitor. May I tell the king why you're here?"

"I've been on a quest to find the sacred Grail that will bring peace to the land. Or I was. I've been looking for five years; I don't know any longer if it even exists."

She studied him. "I think," she said at last, "the king will be very glad to see you. He has waited for your coming." With that, she turned away, leaving him to ponder what she meant.

Evening meal was a banquet. The serving board groaned with roast boar and mutton, quail in pomegranate sauce, sweetmeats, bannocks, oatcakes, honey and cheese. A rich plum pudding followed the meal. Peredur wondered where all the food had come from; Carbonek didn't look like it could support this bounty.

As if in answer to his thought, Pelles said, "My neighbors keep me well-supplied. They're afraid if they don't, their land will become cursed also."

"Cursed?" Peredur asked.

"It's a long story," Pelles answered and changed the subject. "Yanna tells me you're looking for a holy relic?"

Chastened, Peredur remembered again about asking questions. "A cup. The one the Christians say Jesu used at his last meal. Our Lady says it came to him from the Goddess beyond Time."

Pelles leaned forward, his elbows on the table, fingertips pressed together, making a point below his chin. "What do you want with it?"

"Arthur thinks it will bring peace and understanding between any two parties who drink from it."

"Ah, so the quest is for Arthur." He sat back and shifted his weight, obviously relieving the pressure on his leg. "A pity he won't take the crown back. Custinnin and Cormant bicker between themselves and forget the Saxon presence grows ever stronger."

"The Grail could put a stop to that," Peredur answered dejectedly. "If only I could find it."

The fisher king did not reply. Then he gestured toward his seneschal. "Bring me the sword."

The man came back a short time later and carefully unrolled the soft leather in which a sword lay. Pelles held it up to catch the firelight on its shank and turned it, extending the gold overlaid pommel to Peredur. "This sword was made by a master smith named Trebuchet. He crafted only three; the other two have disappeared. It is the Sword of Truth. Mayhap, it will help you find what you seek."

Peredur took the sword and stood. The sword was incredibly light, as though the metal were woven of some mystical fabric. The balance was perfect and Peredur found it easy to move fluidly and gracefully with it. He felt the energy pulsating from it to him. "This gift has renewed my faith," he finally said as he sat down. "I will continue the quest for however long it takes."

Pelles nodded and stretched his injured leg, grimacing. "If you're pure in heart, you'll find what you seek. I've been told that such a man may heal me."

"I don't know how I can heal you, but I swear to always be true to myself," Peredur answered and noticed, in his peripheral vision, a man enter the hall by the front door and proceed to a hallway at the far side of the room. He carried a spear and was followed by two young boys carrying candlesticks. A girl with neatly braided auburn hair carried something flat that looked like a platter. Behind them walked a maiden with pale, golden hair, dressed in white samite. A scent of apple blossoms drifted across the room. Peredur turned his head to see more clearly, but the procession had disappeared. He blinked, not even sure of what he'd seen. *Mayhap, they are going to the chapel next to this building*. He turned back to admiring the sword.

Pelles sighed and rose stiffly. "I'll take my leave now, for I'm tired and need to rest."

Peredur rose also. "I thank you for all you've given me this night. I will strive to remain pure of heart, so I may return to you, successful."

"Yes," Pelles answered, but his voice seemed distant. "I'll wait for that."

When Peredur arrived in the dining hall the next morning, it was empty. He wondered if he should wait for the king to appear or at least, a servant. Then, spying newly baked bannocks and soft cheese on the serving board, along with fresh goat's milk, he decided to help himself.

The place was utterly silent. He remembered yesterday the old groom had said they had no need of many soldiers, but how odd no one was about. He ate slowly, waiting for someone to appear. Finally, he went to the front door. His horse was saddled, waiting for him, but no servant was in sight. He wanted to thank Pelles again, but reluctantly mounted and turned toward the open gate. He shook his head. Unfortified and isolated as Carbonek was, the gate still should have been closed.

He rode out and cantered down the hill. At the bottom, he stopped and looked back. The gate had closed. Suddenly, he felt he'd somehow made a big mistake, but he didn't know what it was.

Peredur was still pondering the thought when he stopped at a spring several miles farther to water his horse. He tied a bit of cloth to the tree beside it, giving thanks to the spirit-keeper and knelt to drink.

When he looked up, a tall, slender woman with long chestnut hair stood before him. She smiled gently. "I'm the doire of this spring. The Goddess thanks you for your offering, but I think, mayhap, you're troubled."

Peredur sat back on his haunches and told her the story. When he finished, she nodded. "You didn't ask the question the Fisher King needed to hear."

"What was I supposed to ask?" Peredur replied. "Gornemant told me to squelch my curiosity and not ask so many questions about everything."

"You must follow your own heart, Peredur. To be curious is to be alive, to learn, to feel...from your own spiritual depth."

"Should I go back?"

She shook her head. "The opportunity is gone. Pelles will not see you until you have found your soul. The Lady Argante gave you a riddle to solve, did she not?"

"Yes!" Peredur was surprised. "How did you know?"

The doire smiled. "I was told to wait for you. Avallach's workers are becoming few in number, but I'm one of them. You're to heed the call of one in few. My advice is to find Galahad. The two of you must work together, as you did when you first searched. You're both of the Sang Real."

"The Sang Real?"

"The Blood Royal." The doire smiled. "Descendants of Joseph of Arimathea, you through his daughter, Anna, and Galahad through his son, Galaad. Jesu would have been an uncle."

"What?" Peredur was thoroughly confused. "The Christos?"

"He was only called the Christos after the Romans used his teachings as religion." The doire watched him intently. "Jesu trained as a druid, didn't you know?"

He was still bewildered. *If Galahad knew...his religion and mine originated from the same man!*

The lady smiled again. "Proceed to Lleyn to the Abbey of King Mordrains. Galahad will come, for he's destined to make a discovery there." She made the sign of blessing and turned away.

Peredur sat for some time, staring after her, thinking that, mayhap, the quest was just beginning. He would find himself.

After leaving Lancelot that autumn, Galahad journeyed south and west toward the Marches. He'd heard of the White Abbey where Nascien, ancient prophet and friend of Joseph of Arimathea, lay buried. Might the Grail also be there? *Dear Lord, make it so! At last, let me find what I've sought!*

He arrived just after Vespers had started. Even as he approached, he could hear the monks chanting, their voices rising and falling in melodious cadence. A comforting sound, he longed to join them, but he was shown into the priory to wait.

He introduced himself only as a soul who was on a quest and begged time for contemplation. Once he explained his mission, the abbot smiled.

"I'm Abbot John. Join us in our prayers and service, my son. Your quest is a holy one; mayhap here you'll find the answer to where the Grail lies." The portly man's eyes shone with religious fervor. "The cup was here once."

"Was?" Galahad felt the heavy blanket of defeat smother him. He'd been so sure he'd been led here.

The abbot watched with tender eyes. "Come, I'll show you the burial tomb of Nascien."

Galahad followed him across the yard to the chapel. Behind the altar, the priest unlocked the heavy bolt of a solid door that opened to an anteroom. The room had no windows, but was lit with hundreds of sweet-scented beeswax candles. Heavily embroidered tapestries depicting religious scenes covered three of the walls. On the fourth hung a white shield, with a simple red cross for its insignia.

The abbot stepped back and motioned for Galahad to enter. The tomb itself was made of marble and sat on a raised dais. Galahad knelt in front of it.

"You said the Grail was here? Did Nascien bring it?"

"Yes. After Joseph died, his son, Josephe, felt it was no longer safe at Ynys Gutrin. The pagan women dwelling on Avallach were trying to claim the cup as belonging to their goddess. Imagine such sacrilege! Nascien brought it with him when he established White Abbey. He had no idea at the time of the miracles it could work."

Galahad was puzzled. "Why not?"

"Joseph brought the cup to remember his brother, Jesu, nothing more. A fiend from Perilous Rock tried to tempt it from Nascien, and in resisting, he received a near fatal wound to his leg that wouldn't heal. One day, as he celebrated the Eucharist, a drop of wine spilled onto his leg. The pain ceased immediately and the next day, the wound was healed." The monk paused, obviously reliving the tale in his head. "After that, he was convinced the cup should serve the people. He shared Holy Communion then with all who wished it."

"What happened to it? Was it stolen?"

"Oh, no. After Nascien passed, his son, Celidoine, took the cup with him when he traveled farther north. But the Picts murdered him ten years later, along with his wife. His son was too young to remember where the cup may have gone." The priest spread his hands. "For the past four centuries, no one has found it, although sometimes it appears in a vision or dream."

Galahad stared at him. "I have seen it when I play my harp."

The abbot inhaled sharply. "Truly? Then you are indeed blessed I thought only Bishop Dubricius had the vision."

"A third person has seen it, as well," Galahad answered. "A pagan by the name of Peredur."

The older man raised his eyebrows. "Do the pagans still think it is theirs?"

Galahad shrugged. "The Lady of the Lake claims it was lent to the Christos because he was a druid."

The priest reached for the edge of the tomb to steady himself, his face whiter than the marble. "What blasphemy is this? How come you by such knowledge? I thought you followed the Christos."

"I do!" Galahad stood and held out his cross. "I would not wear this elsewise. But Nimue—the Lady—is King Arthur's advisor and his friend. I spent several years living at Camelot."

Clear eyes appraised him now. "You knew Arthur well?"

"Well enough," Galahad answered, somewhat uneasily. "I was trained as a soldier there, although I would have preferred the priesthood."

"Mayhap I should ask who you are." The abbot's voice had gone flat.

Galahad took a deep breath; he usually found a way of eluding the question, but not this time. "I am Galahad, son of Lancelot of Benoic and my mother was Elaine, daughter of Pelles of Carbonek."

The monk gasped. "Do you know your sacred lineage?"

"Sacred?" Galahad smiled. "I don't think anyone would ever accuse my father of being holy."

The abbot walked to a small niche in the wall. Carefully, he withdrew an old leather book. Slowly, he turned the soft vellum pages. "Here," he said as he pointed, "your father's great-grandfather was the bard, Taliesin, descended from Mary Magdalin."

"Wasn't she a harlot?" Galahad asked, thinking that, given his father's reputation, that could be a possibility.

The monk pursed his lips primly. "She was a saint. The Old Records even say she was married to Jesu."

Galahad stopped smiling. "That's sacrilege!"

The man shook his head. "Holy Church does not sanction the theory, so we don't preach it." He returned to the book. "Your mother is descended from Joseph of Arimathea, which make you twice blessed." The abbot's eyes turned toward the shield on the wall. "That shield was used by Nascien's brother, Mordrains. Their uncle, Saint Peter the Fisherman, blessed it. Warriors have tried to take it, over the years, only to return it after being sorely maimed." He turned to Galahad. "Josephe blessed it again when he died, saying only someone who was true to God could use it. It is the Shield of Wisdom."

Galahad walked over to it and put a hand out tentatively. "Is it magic then?"

"No," the priest said firmly, "the power is spiritual, from God. Take it, Galahad, and go to the abbey of Mordrains. There is an old pagan spell on the place that the monks cannot break; a man lies frozen in Time. This will be a test for you and for the shield to let the Light prevail."

Galahad pulled his heavy woolen cloak closer about him and bent his head to protect his face from the icy pellets of rain that stung him. He loosened the reins and let his horse's head hang low to avoid the sleet. Traveling through Gwynedd to reach Lleyn in late fall was foolhardy, but soon the passes would be blocked with snow and he hadn't wanted to wait until the spring thaws to reach Mordrains' abbey. For the first time in years, he had a definable goal.

Night was falling fast when he reached the outer gates of the abbey. He pulled the bell cord and waited. The gate slowly opened a few inches and a hooded face peered out.

"I'm a lone traveler, asking for shelter and food." Galahad stomped his feet to keep them warm. "Will you let me enter?"

The gate swung wider and he led his horse through. The hooded figure gestured toward a small enclosure that served as a stable for a cow, several goats, a swaybacked horse and several dogs. It wasn't much, but it had a roof and the wattle walls would keep the wind out. He unsaddled his horse quickly and saw to its hay and water. He turned to follow the figure that had waited for him.

The warmth of the priory's hall nearly overwhelmed him; he held his hands over the flame in the hearth. "This feels wonderful," he said and turned to the boy who'd led him in. He recoiled in shock.

A girl threw back the hood and removed her cloak. She was short and delicately built, her shiny black hair glinted indigo by the firelight, her eyes a deep brown. Beneath the cloak, she wore a simple gown of pale blue. "I'm Branwyn. Well come to the abbey of Mordrains," she said in a dulcet, soft voice. "Let me get you something to eat. Please sit."

He remained standing. "I would like to see the abbot, please."

The girl smiled. "We're a house of women."

Galahad's stomach muscles tightened; he hadn't expected this. *What are women doing here?* "The abbess, then."

She smiled, showing amazingly white teeth. "What's your mission, so I may tell our lady?"

Best to get this over with and be gone from here. Mayhap, it won't take more than a day. "I'm here to break the pagan spell that holds this place, so you may worship the Christos in peace."

"Indeed?" Branwyn raised an eyebrow. "She'll be interested to hear that." She gestured to the table and chair by the hearth. "Be comfortable."

Reluctantly, he sat and looked around. The room was exceptionally clean, the walls freshly limewashed and the rushes on the floor still crisp. A delicious aroma of meat stew wafted about, mixed with the heady scent of a fragrance he'd smelled before, but couldn't place.

A servant brought him a steaming bowl of soup along with still warm, soft bread. He realized he was nearly famished and tried not to wolf everything down. He'd finished a second bowl when the abbess appeared.

She was also dressed in light blue, but with an over-tunic of white and a white mantle covering her head. She, too, was petite with the same dark coloring as the younger girl. Galahad stood when she entered and she inclined her head slightly.

"Please be seated." Her voice had a slight lilt to it, pleasantly soothing. "My name is Drem; I'm the abbess here."

"I'm Galahad," he said and waited for her to be seated. "Abbot John from White Abbey sent me to rid this place of a pagan spell. I didn't expect to find Holy Sisters here."

"We've been here for quite some time," she answered. "I'm surprised he didn't know."

"No matter. The abbot told me a man lies frozen in Time and must be released."

The abbess frowned slightly. "Brother John must be confused. We harbor no men here, alive or otherwise...other than you, of course." She tilted her head. "Mayhap he's thinking of Arthur's druid, who supposedly came back to rescue the king at Cam's Landing?"

Galahad started. *Myrddin had been at Cam's Landing. Nimue had insisted that he'd been suspended in Time on Avalon. Was this what Abbot John meant? But that was pagan thinking and this was a convent of holy women.* "No, I don't think so," he said doubtfully. "Is there something here that haunts you? I brought Nascien's shield; it is blessed with spiritual power."

Her eyes widened. "I'm aware of its power. If you carry it, then you must be the Grail seeker."

"How did you know about that?" he asked in amazement. As isolated as this convent was, near the sea, the abbess was well-informed.

She shrugged delicately. "The legend of that shield goes back before the time the cup left for...before it became missing, that is. We would be most honored to receive the Grail back."

"Back?" Galahad asked. "I seek it for King Arthur, who wishes to use it to ensure peace for Britain."

"For certes," the Abbess replied, "it can do that, but it needs to be protected."

Galahad slumped in his chair. "First, I have to find it. You don't know how often I've thought of giving up." *My father may have been right, after all.*

"You must never do that. The Grail will appear when you are ready, Seeker." She leaned forward. "Stay with us for a time. Look for your frozen man. Let me hear how you plan to search. Mayhap we can help you."

"I thank you, but I cannot stay in a house of women," Galahad answered. "If you don't mind, I'll search tomorrow to seek out anything that may be of danger to you, then I'll be on my way."

Her eyes glowed like coals. "As you wish. We'd be appreciative of your protection." A corner of her mouth quirked slightly as she gracefully stood. "The guest quarters are small since we don't have many visitors. They're down that hall." She pointed to a door on the other side of the room. "I'll see you in the morning and show you our other buildings."

He thanked her and retired to a small room someone had prepared for him. The fire had been lit, candles placed beside the bed, a water basin and pitcher on the dresser. He felt the pitcher; the water was warm. Quickly, he stripped off his shirt and washed, finding the bar soap soft and smelling of herbs, unlike the lye soap the army used. He sank into a bed of feather down, as fine as anything he'd ever seen Gwenhwyfar own, and wondered at the luxury the holy sisters allowed themselves. *Mayhap, it's only the guest quarters that are so well provided for*...and he drifted off to dreamless sleep.

Galahad awakened the next morning to a pre-seasonal blizzard. By the mid-day meal, the roads were impassable and the snow kept falling. He turned back to the fire to find Branwyn watching him.

"I guess you'll be our guest for a while," she said.

"Only for a day or two, until this melts. I'll try not to inconvenience you."

"Longer than that, I think," she replied. "Once these snows start, we're pretty much sequestered for the winter."

"What? I can't possibly stay here; you're all women!"

"You noticed?" A twinkle lit her eyes.

He felt like a dolt. These were holy sisters; for certes, they wouldn't be acting like the common wenches who tried to wheedle their way into his bed at many of his stops.

"Mayhap it will be good to have a man around." She grinned again and was gone, leaving him to stand staring after her.

The abbess appeared and took him to the buildings surrounding the abbey, even though the swirling snow nearly blinded them. He caught glimpses of several of the sisters, all small and dark, darting around corners, or silently and swiftly down hallways and through doors.

Galahad was surprised to find the main chapel empty. The interior was cold and damp; no candles sat on the bare altar and the crucifix lay on the floor. "This place has not been used in some time."

We are so few here, we use the Lady Chapel. It is much easier to keep warm." She tilted her head at his uneasiness. "Would you like to see it?"

The room was definitely smaller and well lit. A fire burned cheerfully in a brazier and the altar stone was covered in red silk. Behind it, a tapestry of the Virgin and her Son hung. Galahad studied it for some time. Mary was dressed in a sleeveless gown of white, fastened at the shoulders with narrow strips of cloth, and wore a laurel wreath upon her head with necklaces of flowers around her neck. The Christos lay on the ground beside her, wearing a tunic of green over brown leggings. A pool of blood surrounded him, seeming to flow and blend with the red silk of the altar. *A strange portrait of the Virgin and her Son.*

Drem moved to the door. "This completes everything I have to show you."

Galahad followed her, his eyes still on the tapestry. "Will I be permitted to join you in your services? I find comfort in Christian prayer."

The Abbess lifted an eyebrow. "I fear that would be disruptive. Several of the sisters were brought here as children. The presence of a man would be unsettling."

"I assure you, I will leave your women alone." Galahad felt affronted. *So that's why they've all been darting away so quickly, except for Branwen.* "I only wish to worship. How could that be a distraction?"

"I don't think you realize the effect you have on women." She smiled. "You remind me of someone..."

He drew himself up. "My lady, my actions and speech have been courteous, nothing more. I have done naught..."

"I know. Mayhap, that is what makes you so interesting."

"Branwyn is the only one I've spoken to!"

"Aye. And Branwyn has a lively imagination."

"Then I'll remind her of her vows," Galahad answered stiffly. "I'll not be guilty of leading a holy sister astray."

She eyed him thoughtfully. "Do you hold all women in such reverence?"

"Reverence?" He shrugged. "There is no honor in wenching and I have vowed never to marry."

"You are young to make such a decision."

Galahad looked away. "I've seen what loving a woman can do. I'll not risk my soul."

Her voice was gentle. "Do you think, then, that women are evil?"

He hesitated, then said, "The Good Book says Adam was seduced by Eve to eat the apple. She's the one who brought evil into this world." He continued when the abbess said nothing. "I know what seduction can do; my own father loved another man's wife."

The abbess looked at him intently. "Did she love him back?"

"Yes. And it nearly destroyed Britain." He stopped abruptly. "No, I didn't mean that. Only that...uh, her husband was a mighty warlord. There might have been war."

She raised her hand. "Do not lie, Galahad. Did not King Arthur, himself, ask your father to rescue Gwenhwyfar?"

He stared at her, dumbfounded. "How do you know that? How do you know who I am?"

"That news spread like wildfire, even here. And, apart from your eyes being blue, you look like your father."

Galahad frowned. "You know him?"

"In a way," she answered. "On his way north with the queen, he was followed. He left a token for us to, um, pray for his protection."

He looked at her incredulously. "My father asked a Christian to pray for him? He's pagan!"

"Is there harm in asking for help from another's god?"

"Arthur says there isn't," Galahad admitted, "but my father has sinned grievously, many times and all because of a woman."

"You judge him for his love of Gwenhwyfar?"

"I judge him for committing adultery with the queen!" he answered hotly.

The abbess smiled. "You have your father's passion."

He recoiled. "I do not wish to be anything like him. I will remain pure of heart!"

"A pure heart reflects love and forgiveness." She touched his arm gently and he felt a warmth sear through him. "Mayhap you are the man frozen in Time until you learn to be tolerant. Have you never thought of the pain your father carries? It is not for you to know what is in his heart."

Galahad stood speechless. Then, suddenly, he remembered a conversation with his father when he was young.

They'd been practicing weaponry. Father had driven him hard and determined not to show weakness, he'd angrily lunged and made contact with his sword before his father could step away. Surprised, his father had given him a rare compliment.

"I'm glad to please you, Father." His face had brightened.

"It should please you to learn these skills. You don't want to go to Arthur unprepared."

The smile disappeared. He didn't want to go to Arthur at all. He wanted to stay at Joyous Garde with his mother and the queen, who was always nice to him. Funny, he thought, she was the only one who didn't seem to be afraid of his father. But then, his father acted differently around her. He was more relaxed and approachable.

"What are you thinking about?" Father asked him.

"I was thinking about the queen."

"Gwenhwyfar? What about her?"

Galahad felt a flush creep up his neck and looked down. "You're different around her. Not so...hard." He fully expected his father to be angry at his boldness. He forced himself to look up. To his surprise, his father's face softened.

"Do you think me cruel?"

"I...Mother says you are." He looked away.

"Have you seen me hurt your mother?" he asked.

Galahad shook his head. "No. But she stays away from you."

His father sighed. "Your mother and I simply do not like each other, but I would not hurt her."

The child blurted, "Why don't you like her? Why don't you treat her like you do the queen?" He closed his eyes, shocked by his own impertinence, and braced himself for the blow.

It didn't come. He opened his eyes slowly to find his father watching him, a strange expression on his face.

"You will not understand why for some years yet. The queen and I have been friends since we met, five and ten years ago. That is nearly twice your age. A long time. Gwenhwyfar and I understand each other in a way that is very rare."

"Why did the king send her away?"

"Someone who didn't like the queen made accusations. Her life was in danger. Arthur asked me to bring her here and protect her."

"He must trust you then."

His father inhaled sharply and looked away.

The Abbess was still lightly touching his arm. He looked at her in shock. "I never realized. The pain—how hard it must have been—and then, to have to let her go."

She removed her hand and he sank to the floor, his head in his hands. "I've been so arrogant." Then an even more poignant thought came to him. *The abbess is right; my insolence has made me the frozen man, unable to feel love.*

Drem glided from the room silently, leaving Galahad leaning against the altar stone. He'd been given the opportunity to redeem himself, had been one of few to be called and knew what he needed to do. He would go to see his father.

A break in the weather occurred several weeks later and Galahad was determined to take advantage of the unusual thaw. He was carrying in a last load of firewood for the sisters when he heard the jingle of a horse's harness. Quickly, he dumped the wood and drew his sword.

The man who rode through the gates was wrapped in woolens and furs so that only his eyes were visible. *Fool, to ride alone, unable to draw a weapon quickly.* Galahad watched as the rider pulled the horse to a stop and dismounted none too gracefully, landing with a thud on both feet.

He approached the bundled figure with his sword still drawn. Clumsily, the man turned. "Galahad! It is I, Peredur. Put the sword away!"

Sheathing the sword, Galahad shook his head. "I should have known. Only you would trust the road to be safe. What brings you this far west?" he asked as they walked toward the main house.

Peredur unwrapped several layers of clothing before he spoke. "I was told by a doire to find you. That our journey would continue together."

They walked quickly inside and Branwyn brought wine for Peredur and a warm milk and honey drink for Galahad. She moved quietly, not looking directly at either of them. Unusual, Galahad thought and then noticed Peredur watching her as she left.

"If you're interested in her, she is one of the holy sisters."

Peredur started to say something, then stopped and sighed.

"I have vowed to never marry and I will not dishonor a woman. You have no need to worry."

Galahad raised an eyebrow. "Why the change of heart? I thought you were betrothed to Blanchefleur."

"She married someone else."

"Ah. She didn't want to wait." Galahad surprised himself that he wasn't cynical. Yesterday, he would have called her fickle.

"No." Peredur explained what had happened. "She only married to spare her uncle's life."

"Another incident of forced marriage, then." Galahad felt a twinge of pity for the girl. Why can't the right people meet at the right time?

"Another?" Peredur looked puzzled.

"Umm." Galahad answered. "My father was forced to marry my mother and Gwenhwyfar was duty-bound to stay with the king."

"You no longer sound bitter about that. Have you finally forgiven your father for loving the queen?"

Galahad felt heat flood to his face. "I had a conversation with the abbess in the Lady Chapel one day and somehow, I was able to understand how my father felt."

Just then, Drem came through the door. Peredur stared at her and she stopped suddenly, as if uncertain to proceed.

"Mother Abbess," Galahad inclined his head. "Allow me to present Peredur, my friend from Camelot. We'll be seeking the Grail together again when I leave."

Her black eyes studied the newcomer and a small smile turned up the corner of her mouth. "Yes, the Grail would be safe in your hands." Then, as quickly as she'd entered, she turned and left, leaving Galahad puzzled.

"I wonder what she meant by that?"

"Why did you call her Mother Abbess?" Peredur asked.

"She is the head of this convent," Galahad answered. "Why wouldn't I?"

Peredur gave him a strange look. "Will you take me to the Lady Chapel?"

"Certes." Galahad gestured for him to follow. They crossed the yard and he opened the door of the chapel and they stepped through. As Peredur looked around, Galahad said, "I find it strange there's no crucifix in here, but they do honor the Christos with the tapestry, even though it's an unusual one."

Peredur was quiet for some moments. Finally, he turned to Galahad. "These women are not followers of the Christos."

"What? For certes, they are. They keep the offices of Holy Church: Prime and Terce and Vespers...Matins..."

"Have you attended their services?"

Galahad paused. "Not exactly. The Abbess feared I'd be a distraction. I worship by myself in the larger chapel. Why do you ask?"

Peredur gestured to the wall hanging. "This is a picture of the Lady and the Oak King."

"What?" Galahad asked again, unbelievingly.

"Before the Romans, when the Goddess was worshipped throughout Britain, the Lady would take a consort on Beltane, who would rule as king for one year. Everything he could want would be his."

"What happened at the end of the year?"

Peredur inhaled deeply. "He would be sacrificed by the druids. Hung on a tree, his genitals slivered, the blood dripping into the land to ensure fertility."

Galahad stared at him in horror. "The man knew this beforehand?"

"Yes. In the ancient times, self-sacrifice was considered the highest honor."

"What kind of religion kills a man like that?" Galahad demanded harshly.

"Is it so different from your own?" The voice at the door was Drem's. She entered now and walked to them. "Did your people not sacrifice your Christos upon the cross?"

"But that is different! He died to save our immortal souls!"

"And he did this willingly?" she asked.

"Yes. To save us from sacrifices such as this."

She studied him. "A noble thing. Well, we no longer kill our kings, even when the Great Rite is used, as it was with King Arthur and Nimue."

He'd heard of this pagan ritual. The king would couple with a priestess...he stopped. Argante was Arthur's daughter, which meant the king had been unfaithful to Gwenhwyfar too. *Mayhap my father wasn't the only one to blame.*

"Who are you?" He was confused. "Are you a priestess like Nimue?"

She shook her head. "I am Sidhe. A descendant of the Old Ones who were here before the druids came. We are sworn to protect Britain always." She turned to Peredur. "Now that you have come, I can release Galahad. You will find the Grail together."

Galahad stood silently for some time after she left. "I thought she was a Christian," he said numbly. "I believed her to be good."

"She is," Peredur answered. "The Sidhe are known to protect those who will not harm. Think me a fool, but mayhap, you have learned a lesson today."

Galahad remembered his last conversation with Lancelot. *"You need to find tolerance, my son."* He turned to Peredur. "Mayhap, I have. Will you ride with me to Joyous Garde?"

Since it was on the way, they decided to stop at Dinas Emrys first. "I want you to meet my family," Peredur told Galahad. "We can celebrate Yule with them."

Dornar met them in the bailey, obviously glad to see his brother again. They spent the afternoon in the council room engrossed in what had taken place in southern Britain since Peredur had spent his last year with the hermit.

"Cerdic has taken Ynys Wyth," Dornar told them with a note of disgust.

"Custinnin made no move to stop him?" Galahad asked.

"No." He hesitated, then went on. "Arthur got Cerdic to agree to no further advancement north beyond Londinium in exchange for the isle off Clausentum."

"I've never understood why Arthur would trust that Saxon," Galahad answered.

"He's half-Briton, remember," Peredur answered, "and if Arthur got his oath...Cerdic controls Clausentum and Portus Adurni anyway; a small isle off the coast is not such a price to pay."

Dornar looked at his brother benevolently. "Is everything always so simple for you, Peredur?" He looked at Galahad. "Cerdic married a Saxon and his son, Cynric, will follow him. No doubt, he will allow more barbarians to land on Britain's soil."

Galahad smiled. "My father always said that Cynric is more interested in women than fighting."

Dornar raised an eyebrow. "Did he not bring his army to Camelot to defeat Medraut when Nimue was held hostage?"

Galahad shrugged. "I was a child at the time, still at Carbonek. I do know he didn't join the Saxons at Cam's Landing."

"He has that in his favor then," Dornar admitted reluctantly, "but I think Arthur gives too much away. He's no longer willing to fight."

"Must fighting always be the answer, Brother?" The voice belonged to a female standing in the doorway.

Galahad turned and drew in his breath sharply. The girl who entered the room could have been Gwenhwyfar, twenty years younger. Her auburn hair was loose about her face and she was dressed in a man's linen shirt and trews, such as the queen preferred to wear.

"Dindrane." Peredur went to hug his sister. "I want you to meet Galahad."

Her green eyes looked levelly at him and he felt as though a sword had been run through his stomach, pinning him to a wall. She held out her hand, not as a lady would for him to kiss, but rather as a man did in greeting. He felt unable to move and saw the subtle shift of emotion in her eyes; they were smiling at him now, even though her face was somber. *Is she laughing at me?*

He forced himself to extend his hand. Her grip was warm and surprisingly firm. He felt heat soar through him that he'd felt only once before. "A pleasure." He quickly dropped his hand.

She appeared not to notice. Turning back to Dornar, she continued, "Arthur is right. The time for peace is now. Why shed more blood when he can treaty with the Saxons? War is not always the answer."

"You're a woman. You're expected to feel that way," Dornar answered. "Have you informed the cook we have special guests tonight?"

Dindrane bristled, eyes flashing green fire. Galahad almost grinned. *Just like Gwenhwyfar's did when she was angry with Arthur.*

"Yes, I do have some manners! I was on my way out to work the colt you bought." She glanced at Galahad. "Are you good with horses?"

"Good?" Peredur interrupted. "For certes; he's the son of the best horseman Arthur ever had."

"You would be Lancelot's son?" she asked matter-of-factly. "Then come along. I can use your help." She didn't wait for him, but turned and walked out.

Dornar shook his head. "I'll never get her properly married before she becomes too old. Who will put up with that temper and independence?" He turned to Galahad. "You don't have to go; once she starts working with the horse, she won't even notice you stayed behind."

But Galahad was already near the door. "I don't mind. I haven't worked a green horse in a while."

He found her already in the paddock, starting to lunge the colt. It had the same beautiful carriage as the stallions Arthur and his father had ridden before Cam's Landing. The delicate, slightly dish-faced head, the large, intelligent eyes, small ears. The animal arched his neck gracefully, his tail lifting and flowing majestically behind him as he broke from the trot to a canter.

Expertly, Dindrane slowed the horse, until he stopped, snorting and pawing the ground fretfully.

"You really shouldn't let him do that," Galahad said.

"Why not?" she asked a bit sharply. "He means no harm with it."

Galahad vaulted the fence and joined her. "No, but he should. A good war-horse uses his hooves to help his rider fight."

"How do you know I'm training him for war?" She stroked the satiny sorrel coat.

Galahad grinned lopsidedly. "I doubt Dornar would let you make a palfrey of him. These horses from Mecca are good for light cavalry."

Dindrane smiled, erasing the look of annoyance that had passed over her face. "Mayhap you could show me how to make him stop then?"

He held out his hand for the rope and her fingers grazed his as she passed it. Again, that flicker of intense heat soared through him. He forced himself to ignore it and took the whip in the other hand. The colt shied at first, sensing a new hand on the lead, but then obediently began to trot. Each time Galahad stopped the horse, just as it began to stamp a hoof, the whip played over it, hissing, but not touching the skin. Within minutes, the colt was standing quietly after each gait.

Dindrane took the lead back from him, her eyes on the horse as she lunged him. "My father used to tell us stories of your father fighting beside Arthur, even saving the king's life; that he was afraid of nothing. Are you like him?"

"No, I'm nothing like him." Her eyes widened slightly as she glanced at him and then back to the horse. "I wanted to become a priest. My father forced me to learn weaponry; I was too afraid of him not to."

"Why would you be afraid of your father?"

"I...I didn't meet him until I was eight. I lived with my mother at Carbonek and when we moved to Joyous Garde, he wouldn't have anything to do with her. He hated my mother."

Dindrane stopped the horse and looked up at him. "I've heard those stories, too," she said softly. "Was he ever cruel to you?"

Briefly, Galahad wondered why he was telling her his life's history when he'd just met her. She seemed so easy to talk to. "Not cruel. He demanded a lot of me and expected even more. I always felt I disappointed him."

Dindrane said nothing as she closed the lead and walked to the horse. Silently, Galahad followed them into the barn. She handed him a brush and he began grooming one side of the horse.

"My da explained something once about Arthur's Cymbry." She continued the conversation as she brushed the other side. "Arthur depended on four men: his brother, Cai; Gwenhwyfar's brother, Bedwyr; his nephew, Gwalchmai; and your father, Lancelot. Of the four, Lancelot was hardest on his men, but they were also the strongest company in Arthur's cohort." She looked over the colt's withers. "Mayhap, it's just his way with everyone."

Galahad gave a short laugh. "Not everyone, Dindrane."

"You're speaking of Gwenhwyfar," she said bluntly.

"Yes. She lived at Joyous Garde for a while. He was different with her."

"What was she like?"

He thought. "Independent. She cared nothing for sewing and weaving or any of the things women are trained to do. She let the seneschals run the households. She preferred working with horses or discussing war strategy. She was opinionated and headstrong; she and Arthur argued a lot. I think he enjoyed goading her, just to see her temper fly."

Dindrane smiled. "Like Dornar does with me? Did she love the king though?"

"In her way," Galahad answered. "They were like opposites attracting each other. You would have needed to see them together."

"Did you like her?"

"Yes, I did," he answered. "When I first arrived, my father seemed so huge to me. He towered over my mother and I could feel something was not right, but I was too young then to know how they despised each other. They started arguing and Gwenhwyfar stopped them. Then she sat down beside me and asked me what I liked to do. When I told her I was learning to read and play the harp she didn't laugh at me." He paused, thinking some more. "She even stood up to Lancelot for me on more than one occasion. I used to wonder how she could be so brave."

"Your father was gentle with her?"

"Yes. He never lost his temper with her. If they were in the same room, they were always close. Now that I think back, they touched a lot. His face softened when he looked at her." He shook his head. "It's a wonder Arthur put up with it."

"Did he have a choice?" Dindrane asked cryptically.

Galahad looked at her, puzzled. "He was the king. He could have kept them separated. Even forbidden them in the same room together."

"What good would that have done? He needed Lancelot. Gwenhwyfar would not have loved Arthur more."

"Still, what happened eventually might not have," Galahad insisted.

"I don't know." Dindrane moved to combing the mane. "I think if two people truly love each other, no one or nothing can stop them."

"Are you speaking from personal experience?" he asked, almost afraid to hear the answer and then wondering why he cared.

She colored a little and concentrated on the comb. "No. What about you?"

He hesitated, thinking of Elen. "I thought I was in love once. I barely knew the girl." *How many penances have I done for misleading the maiden?*

Dindrane gazed steadily into his eyes. "Did you lay with her and make a promise you could not keep?"

Galahad knew he should feel indignant at the insinuation, but he didn't. In fact, he was surprised at how naturally the conversation was flowing. "The answer to both of your questions is no." He was suddenly glad he hadn't done more than kiss Elen. He grinned. "Is there anything else you'd like to know?"

She smiled back, unruffled. "Mayhap. I'll let you know."

By the time he and Peredur rode on for Joyous Garde, a fortnight later, he felt as though he'd known Dindrane forever. She was his friend; the first woman he was willing to trust.

~ *Chapter 10—Armel* ~

Galahad and Peredur rode in the gates of Joyous Garde a week later. Only Lupin, the seneschal, greeted them.

"I don't rightly know where your father is." Lupin looked embarrassed as they sat on one of the benches in the Great Hall. "Your grandmother was dying and Lancelot went to Brocéliande; he was supposed to go to Camelot when he returned, but he didn't get there."

"Has he been injured? Have search parties been out?" Peredur asked.

Lupin shook his head. "The Lady Argante sent word she'd taken Elen to Avallach and said Captain Lancelot needed some time alone. Undertandable, I guess, since he lost his mother."

Galahad looked dubious. "How long ago was this?"

"They left before Samhain. Yule is past, Imbolc approaches. Nearly four moons."

"Candlemas," Galahad corrected, using the Christian holiday automatically. "That long and no one has heard?"

Old Augusta shuffled in, beaming at Galahad. "Well come home, child...ach, forgive an old servant, you're a grown man now, I can see."

Galahad felt himself blush, but she didn't seem to notice. "Mayhap you can talk some sense into Lupin here. Your father has been gone too long without a word. The last time this happened—"

"Be still, woman," Lupin admonished.

"I won't. And you don't have rank over me, having raised Elen and been loyal to Captain Lancelot as long as you." Her wrinkled face creased into even more lines.

"What happened the last time?" Galahad asked sharply.

"Tell him," she demanded.

Lupin sighed. "A body of a young woman, Elen of Astolat, was brought to Camelot. Lancelot blamed himself for her death. She'd taken care of him when he was wounded and fell in love with him. He went half-mad, wandered the countryside, looking for fights." He glared at Augusta. "But not this time. There have been no rumors of that, anywhere."

"Tell him the rest."

"Woman, enough!"

"Finish it," Galahad said quietly. *My father told me of Elen, but he didn't mention what happened after. He actually felt something for her.*

Lupin gave him a long look. "Morgana and her lover, Accolon, followed him and finally waylaid him somehow. They kept him captive..."

Galahad stared at him. "Why?"

The seneschal grimaced. "She kept him tied and drugged, then Morgana sent a messenger to Arthur to either make her his consort and acknowledge Medraut as his heir, or to accept Accolon's challenge to fight for your father's release."

"Arthur fought?"

"Yes, but Lancelot broke free in time to reach Arthur. And he killed Accolon."

Peredur's face was white. "I remember that. I was there."

"What?" Lupin looked at him incredulously.

"The scabbard...that was the day the king lost it. Morgana made the switch with an identical one while they were fighting. I found it later."

"And you didn't return it?" The older man's voice was hard.

Peredur blushed shamefully. "I took it home; I was only a child. My foster mother put it away."

"Never mind," Galahad interrupted. "You remembered in time to save the king at Cam's Landing." He looked at Augusta. "You think my father is in trouble?"

"I don't know, but I think you should go to Camelot and ask for King Arthur's help." She stared defiantly at Lupin.

"I didn't think my father and Arthur were on speaking terms."

"Ach!" She raised a knarled fist. "That needs to end. The king will help you. Go to him."

The passage to Armorica had been rough, but Arthur enjoyed the challenge of helping Bors with the sails. He finished securing the lines at the pier and changed his clothes to a simple monk's robe with cowl and sandals. He left his sword with Bors who clearly told him he was insane to travel alone with only a dagger strapped to his leg and his eating knife.

Arthur tapped his stout oaken staff on the ground. "Myrddin could always defend himself only with this." He winked at Bors. "And I'm just a poor Christian man of God, remember. Who would harm me?"

"You may look the part, Sire, but how are you going to convince clergy—real clergy—that you know anything about their Good Book?"

"Ah. That may surprise you," Arthur replied. "I was raised as a Christian in Cai's household. Myrddin designed it that way. That I would have both upbringings—Pagan and Christian. And," he added, "I don't see a conflict. The new religion has adopted a lot of the old. The festivals are still celebrated; they just honor their saints. Even the Goddess remains as the Holy Virgin."

"And what of their Christos?" Bors asked. "Does he relate to the Oak King of the Old Ways?"

Arthur nodded. "Symbolically. But Jesu was a druid, trained on our Isle, Myrddin said. He made the ultimate sacrifice as is necessary for the seventh initiation..." He stopped, for Bors looked confused. "Well. Be that as it will. All gods are one."

Bors nodded, as the bony mule that Arthur would be using was led off the ship. "Good luck, then, my lord."

Arthur hesitated a moment before he took the reins. Then he mounted and turned. "Not your lord any longer, Bors. Only Armel."

"There's a Christian hermit at the gate, asking to see King Ector." Arthur could hear the guard laughing behind the partially open gate as he delivered the message. "I told him he'd be lucky to get table scraps, let alone see our lord!"

The seneschal frowned. "The king never refuses anyone a hot meal. Bring him in and set him in the kitchen."

A short time later, Arthur sat in the warmth of the hearth, enjoying a hearty stew. "My compliments to you," he said to the plump, young cook. "I haven't had such a good meal in a moon's worth of Sundays."

She turned pink. "Oh, be off with you. 'Tis only a common soup I fix."

"I suppose your king eats more finely than this?"

"On a time, not usually." She ladled more stew into his bowl. "He oft eats right in here, sittin' where you are."

"Do you think he will tonight?"

"Hard to say. Why?"

"I must speak with him, but I think the guards will oust me once I'm through eating."

"Tsk!" she hissed. "Some people think too much of themselves. If you want to see King Ector, so you shall, if you don't mind helpin' me with some chores. They can't well throw you out if you're workin'."

Arthur grinned and brought his bowl to her. "You've a good head on your shoulders."

She colored slightly and brushed at an imaginary crumb on the table. "The ax for wood choppin' is in that corner."

Ector and Lionel rode in an hour later, but Arthur kept his back turned. "Who's the monk?" Arthur heard Ector ask the seneschal as he dismounted and handed the reins to the stableboy who'd run up.

"Just a wanderer, a hermit. He's working off his free meal."

He knew they watched him as he swung the ax easily, splitting the wood evenly with one stroke. "He looks more like a warrior," Ector said. "Did you get his name?"

"No," the seneschal replied, "but come to think of it, the guard said he asked for you. Probably wants a coin or two."

"He asked by name?"

"I think so," the man answered, and Arthur heard Ector walking his way.

Arthur split the last piece of wood and turned around. "How are you, Ector?"

Lancelot's brother stood transfixed, then he rushed forward. He was nearly as tall as Arthur and his hand grasp was firm. "Is it really you, my lord? Your looks are much changed. Why is a king chopping wood?"

Arthur leaned on his ax. "I'm no longer king; I didn't wish to take the crown again. I'm here for more diplomatic reasons."

Ector looked troubled. "Still, you are a guest. Who told you to chop wood?"

Arthur laughed. "Mayhap, more kings should do it to remind themselves of the work their servants do. Your sassy cook came up with the idea to keep me here until you came home."

"Marie? Why did you need something to keep you here? You're always well come to Benoic."

Arthur gave him a strange look. "I wasn't sure; you know Lancelot hasn't..."

Ector held up a hand. "He'll eventually come to his senses."

Arthur grinned and tugged at his grey hair. "Anyway, I doubt your men recognized me."

"I'll change that." Ector started to call to the guard, but Arthur stopped him. "No. I prefer this. I've taken the name Armel and I'll explain why..." They turned and walked into the house.

Much later, when they were behind the closed doors of the council room and Arthur had finished, Ector sat quietly in thought. "There have been rumors Childebert has been reinforcing his cavalry. I hadn't thought Medraut might be with him. But you're right to be concerned about the count, Jean Marc. He's as hungry for land as Cerdic ever was. His own headquarters, Cairhaix, lies not far south of here and Léon borders the other side."

Arthur leaned forward. "When Vortigern brought Horsa and Hengist over and the traitorous bastards massacred our unarmed kings, my father and uncle had to flee. It was to Armorica that they came. I have roots here as well as in Britain. We must keep this land free for the Bretons." Arthur sat back. "You think Jean Marc may attack Benoic?"

"Not until he's sure of himself in Léon," Ector answered. "He can't afford to split his army."

"Have you sent word to Lancelot? He should know."

Ector shook his head. "I'm in charge of Benoic. Lionel and I train with my men every day. We will be ready if he advances."

"Send word anyhow. Lancelot's men are in the far north. Mobilization will take time. Ships, horses—"

"If I ask him to come here, who will defend the north from Ida? He sits practically on my brother's back door now."

"You're right." Arthur sighed and raked a hand through his hair. "Judwal's the last of the bloodline and he's young. Do you think he could rule?"

"Someone will have to back him, but yes, there's a lot of his grandfather in him. The people followed Derock, much like ours followed my father. And Jean Marc is a tyrant and cruel. Even his wife fears him."

"So Jean Marc could be overthrown?" Arthur frowned in thought.

"For certes." A corner of Ector's mouth quirked up and the resemblance to Lancelot was striking. "Judwal would have to return with an army though."

"Benoic would stand with him?"

"We will."

Arthur was silent for a while. Finally, he stood. "I'm going to spend some time in Léon, then I'll move on to Paris. Would you send word to Camelot to muster troops; have a cohort on standby. If we need them, tell Custennin to put Lancelot in charge. He can leave his own men at Joyous Garde. Benoic is his home. And it's time we meet again."

"You haven't seen my father, either?" Galahad and Peredur arrived at Camelot just after Imbolc.

Bedwyr shook his head as he led them to the small map room behind the dining hall. "Argante said he was in near battle frenzy when she left him. It's best to leave him alone when he gets like that."

I know. Galahad had always tried to avoid Lancelot when he was merely angry. "What could have caused it, though? They didn't have trouble on the sea. Was someone following them?"

"I don't think so. They'd returned from Benoic before Yule and were camped out on the way here to Camelot. She said she heard him scream like a berserker in his sleep and by the time she got to him, he was wild. Something about the Horned God and Gwenhwyfar. He just kept telling her to take Elen and go to Avallach."

"Bedwyr," Galahad spoke hesitantly, "you know my father better than I do. What aren't you telling me?"

He hesitated. "I don't know if I even believe it."

"Tell me."

"Well, only because Arthur swears it's true. When they were in Avalon, there was a pool, used for scrying. Somehow Gwenhwyfar could establish a link with Lancelot and they could talk."

More pagan magic. "Arthur believes this?"

Bedwyr nodded. "He says he talked with Lancelot the same way."

Galahad took a deep breath. "So Gwenhwyfar is the cause for his disappearance?"

"I don't know. But, if something has happened to her, something he can't fix..." Bedwyr sighed helplessly. "I love my sister and I know Arthur does, too, but with Lancelot, it goes beyond that."

Galahad nodded. "I saw it time and again when I lived with them. I used to hate him for it."

Bedwyr slanted a sideways glance at him. "Used to? And you don't now?"

Galahad looked down. "No, a wise woman finally made me understand."

"I thought you'd sworn off of women," Bedwyr smiled.

"She was Sidhe." Peredur spoke for the first time.

Bedwyr raised an eyebrow at that. "You took advice from an Old One?"

"It made sense," Galahad answered defensively.

"Well, I think your father will be glad to hear it, Galahad. He always thought you were too dogmatic. I wish Arthur were here; he'd be pleased as well."

"He's gone? We came to ask his help," Peredur said.

"He left for Benoic just before the first snows. Bors said they had confused seas."

"What was he going for? Is there trouble?" Galahad asked.

"Mayhap. He wants to see how matters lie in Léon; then, he's going on to Paris to talk to young Judwal and determine whether he's ready to assume leadership." Bedwyr hesitated. "Mainly, though, he's interested to see if Childebert is amassing an army. And if Medraut is there."

"He went alone?"

"Yes. I disagreed with him on that." Bedwyr grimaced and stood. "But the glint of the Arthur I knew was in his eye and there was no stopping him." He dropped a hand to Galahad's shoulder. "I wouldn't worry about

Lancelot. He's disappeared before and he's still every bit the fighter he was. He'll show himself when he's ready."

"I wouldn't even know where to look," Galahad admitted. "I'm not sure I'm good at finding anything; I've been looking for the Grail for five years."

"Why don't you rest from your Grail search, both of you? I think you are too intense on this thing," Bedwyr said. "Why not go to Gaul? I'd feel better knowing Arthur had some support. Wait quietly for him in Paris; see what you can find behind the scenes."

"Won't he be angry if he wanted to go alone?" Peredur questioned.

Bedwyr shrugged. "How angry can he be? Especially if you have helpful information. You might be able to access the might of Childebert's forces."

"What shall we say is our business?" Galahad asked. "I don't think the king of the Franks is going to welcome two Britons into his quarters for no reason."

"There is a theory that the Magdalin took the Grail with her when she fled to Gaul. Clovis converted his family to Christianity. Tell Childebert the truth. You search for the Holy Grail."

Anna/Morgana studied Childebert overtly from her side vision. He ran a hand across his face, pressing his eyelids shut. Taking a deep breath, he straightened in his seat. He looked at the closed door of the private meeting room and back to Mordred.

"Choltaire is dead?"

Mordred nodded nonchalantly. "I found it easier to do than kill the three boys. More efficient."

Childebert looked away.

The nun seated beside him stirred. "Your brother would have done the same to you. He wouldn't have been the wise ruler you will be. Soissons and Orleans are yours, as is Paris. Soon Burgundia will be also."

"That's only the beginning," Mordred added, "then we move on Armorica: Benoic, Léon...and after that, Britain itself."

"You have plans as ambitious as my own," Childebert said mildly.

Morgana glanced sharply at her son. *Ah, Medraut. Sense the danger in that tone.*

Apparently he did, for he said quickly, "The only payment I asked for was to be given the kingdom of Benoic. The rest is yours alone."

"Yes. Judwal is already here; I can train him to be my puppet in Léon."

"He has not been very responsive, so far," Mordred said softly. "Mayhap, he could be misfortunate enough to be killed in battle."

"No." The king's voice was cold. "I'll not sanction more murder."

A knock sounded on the door and all three of them jumped. "Enter!" Childebert called out.

The servant apologized. "Two men—Britons—are at the gate, requesting permission regarding a religious matter. They say they're from Camelot."

"Camelot? Custennin's men?"

"I believe so. Their names are Peredur and Galahad."

The sister raised an eyebrow. Mordred frowned.

"Do you know them?" Childebert asked, watching their reactions.

Anna shrugged. "I've heard of Galahad; he's the son of Lancelot."

"Will he recognize you?"

"They've never seen either of us. I was long gone from court before either of them arrived."

Childebert looked at Mordred, then at Anna. "I can't afford to insult them. I want no trouble from Britain now." Childebert nodded to the servant. "Show them in, then. We'll find out what they want."

"Thank you for granting us an audience, my lord," Galahad said formally once they were received and had been seated.

"I'm always honored to receive guests from Camelot. Our countries both seek peace. Allow me to introduce my companions. Sister Anna is my spiritual advisor."

Galahad inclined his head. "Greetings, Sister. When I was younger, I wished to become a priest."

Morgana choked. *Sweet Mary, but this is good. The son of that carnal-minded, pagan...a priest! He looks just like Lancelot.* Regaining control, she looked up and smiled demurely. "God's will be done."

"Thank you." He turned as Childebert introduced Mordred.

"My master of horse, Mordred."

The steady grey eyes bore into Galahad's and for a moment, he appeared disconcerted. Morgana glared at her hostile son until Medraut nodded stiffly in acknowledgment.

"I'm no horseman," Peredur was saying with a smile, "but Galahad is and his father was the best King Arthur had!"

"King Arthur?" Anna said. "A good man, rest his soul."

"But he's not dead." Peredur stopped at a look from Galahad.

Anna pretended not to notice and Mordred studied a fingernail. "Not dead?" she asked lightly. "How can such a miracle be?"

"He's talking about the rumor that still circulates in Britain," Galahad said quickly, "that King Arthur lies in seclusion, still healing from grievous wounds."

"After nearly six years?" Mordred asked disdainfully.

Galahad gave them a lopsided smile and Morgana involuntarily caught her breath. "The people near worshipped him. They don't want to let go."

"I can see how that could be," Childebert broke in. "My father respected him, even though they were on opposing sides at the last. So what brings you here?"

"We've come to ask your permission to search for a holy relic—the cup that the Christos used at his last supper. We think it may have been brought to Gaul."

Childebert frowned. "There is a legend of my ancestors, the Merovingian kings, guarding holy treasures from Jerusalem at Rennes-le-Château. But such treasures have long since disappeared. Lost, they say, when the Visigoths raided the area."

"We've been searching Britain for many years," Galahad answered. "Perhaps it's here. We'd like to visit the surrounding towns."

Morgana perked up. *What are they really here for?*

"I would like to pay honor to it as well," Childebert replied. "You would bring it to me first, if it is found here?"

Morgana nearly laughed, knowing that greed, not religion, was behind his remarks. *Still, if he were to take the relic to Pope John II himself...the backing of the church never hurt in war. And war was coming. Benoic would be Medraut's.*

Peredur and Galahad exchanged glances. "If we find the Grail in Gaul, we will bring it to you."

"And if you don't find it lying around here somewhere, why not try Burgundia? It will be on your way to Rennes," Mordred said cryptically.

Childebert inclined his head. "You have my permission. The Grail is of importance to me, as well. In fact, you may stay in the soldiers' quarters if you wish. "

They thanked him as the servant re-entered to escort them to the barracks. Silence followed in their wake. Morgana waited until the door was securely closed then asked, "Do you suppose Arthur may not be dead?" She made the sign of the cross.

"You can stop pretending, Mother. They're gone." Medraut snorted. "I killed Arthur, but where's his queen?"

Morgana held the urge to slap her son. "Have you not gotten over your obsession with Gwenhwyfar by now?" She watched as his face turned an angry red, but before he could reply, Childebert held up a hand.

The king turned to Mordred. "I don't know if the Britons are telling the truth, but I think it best if you're gone from here for a while. Return to Britain. Either Ida or Wehha can grant you refuge; they are my allies. Find out if Arthur lives. If he does, I must know. Burgundia is waiting, but I won't risk war if Arthur survived."

A month later, a holy man stood in the midst of the crowd waiting to gain entrance to the castle. Once a year, on Pentecost, the Frankish king spent the day hearing petitions.

The grey-haired monk shuffled along with the rest. The bell for Sext had struck before he approached the king. "I've been sent by the bishop of Llanildut in Léon to inquire about the wellbeing of our young prince, Judwal." Arthur saw the look of surprise and wondered if he'd been too direct.

"I don't get many inquiries about my charge." Childebert drew himself up to his full height, but Arthur was still taller. "What is your name?"

"Armel," the monk replied. "I would like to speak with him so I can report back to the bishop."

"How do I know Jean Marc didn't send you? You have the build of a warrior, not a priest."

"I am no priest," he answered, "only a man who seeks to make peace. Mayhap, if I could have a moment privately, I could tell you more."

"*Oui.* The time for the noon meal is already past. Why don't you join me, monk?" He nodded to a soldier standing nearby. "You don't object to being searched, do you?"

Arthur held out his arms. "A king must protect himself."

Once they were seated inside the cool dining chamber, Childebert leaned back. "Now, tell me what your real business is. You are no monk either."

Arthur shrugged. "I have taken no vows yet, it's true. But the reason I am here is no lie. The people of Léon are afraid of the ruling regent. They wish for me to bring Judwal back, so they may overthrow Jean Marc and establish him."

"They?"

"I cannot tell you their names, but I have been used as an emissary before. Judwal has a cousin, Samson of Dol, who will verify what I say. Send to him."

"Samson brought the boy here." Childebert smiled. "You don't really expect me to let the boy go with you?"

Arthur lifted his hands, palms up. "Let me go with an armed escort. They will quickly assess the situation. If Jean Marc isn't brought down now, he stands to take Léon and Benoic and from there Montagnes Noires or even Ille Et-Vilance. Ever closer to your own border."

"You think he has the power to attack Gaul?" the king asked cautiously.

"Not yet." Arthur paused. "Wouldn't it be better to prevent it with a prince who's been fostered in your own court?"

Childebert looked thoughtful. "I will send for Samson. If he confirms your story, I will consider your request. Before then, I want you quartered here, where you can be watched. Just precautionary, I assure you."

Arthur bowed and smiled. "As you wish, my lord."

They found each other at the evening meal.

"What are you two doing here?" Arthur asked incredulously as he sat down on the bench next to Galahad in the soldier's mess hall.

"Bedwyr thought you might be able to use us," Peredur answered. "We've been prowling around and watching—"

"What excuse did you give for being here? Spying is a death-by-torture offense!"

"No disrespect, my lord, but isn't that what you're doing?" Galahad asked directly.

He sounds like his father. Arthur nearly smiled. "I also have a legitimate cause for being here. To take Judwal back. Now, again, what are you doing here?"

"We've asked permission to search for the Grail."

"And he granted it?"

"Oh, yes," Peredur said, "he even wants to pay due honor to it if we find it. He offered us his hospitality. He seems to be a good king."

"He wants to watch you," Arthur warned, "and it's greed, not honor, that makes him want that cup. You need to be careful."

"He is ambitious," Galahad agreed. "Outside Paris, we've seen many holdings of fine horses and more able-bodied men in the villages than is usual."

"You think it a cavalry build-up?" Arthur asked.

Galahad nodded. "You taught us how to assess villages when we pass through them. There's been a lot of activity right here in Paris as well. The troops practice longer and harder each day."

"Any mention of the direction this army may take?"

"There's been talk about King Sigismund."

Arthur grew pensive. "So he moves southward first, to Burgundia."

Peredur turned to Galahad. "Didn't that man, Mordred, mention something about Burgundia when we first arrived?"

"He suggested we go there," Galahad said with a grim smile. "I'm glad we haven't seen him lately; he was so sour."

"Mordred," Arthur mused, "sounds like Medraut. That's the other reason I'm here. They may be working with Childebert."

"We haven't heard the name or Morgana's either," Galahad answered.

"Hmm. Well, have you seen a small woman with raven black hair, nearly the same color eyes, and white skin?"

"That sounds like the nun," Peredur answered.

"Nun?" Arthur laughed. "No, Morgana always has a come-hither look and she's well endowed. She'd be hard to miss."

Galahad stared at him. "This woman did look at me strangely, like she recognized me, but I knew I hadn't seen her before."

Arthur stopped laughing. "What did the man—Mordred—look like?"

"Warrior build. Black hair, beard, grey eyes..." Galahad stopped. "The eyes. I thought they looked familiar. Now I know why. They looked like yours."

"Do you know where I can find him?"

"They left. Childebert saw them off the afternoon we arrived with a lot of luggage. I wondered why a nun would have so much clothing."

Arthur sighed and sat back. "So the search will have to begin again."

"Arthur?" Ida's large belly shook as he laughed. "Aye, he returned from the dead, they say." He slid a cup of mead across the dining table to Morgana.

She smiled and laid a hand on his arm. "Have you seen him?"

"Me?" The Bernician warlord glanced at her hand and shook his head. "But Wehha swears Arthur parleyed with Cerdic at Corinium and urged him to surrender."

Medraut snorted. "Ever the talker, the king was. Peace, peace, peace. Meanwhile, Cerdic holds lands from Clausentum to Londinium and took them without much bloodshed."

Ida nodded. "He's a crafty one. But Wehha holds his border in Anglia. Cerdic won't advance there."

Morgana redirected the conversation again. "But Arthur, where is he?"

"Was," Ida petted the soft, smooth hand still resting seductively on his arm. "He was at Camelot with Custennin. He's disappeared again. Wouldn't take the crown back, they said."

Medraut lifted an eyebrow. "Why not? Custennin was only appointed. I should be...I would think..." His voice trailed off as Morgana frowned.

The Saxon gave him a curious look. "Custennin is no Arthur. It is only a matter of time before Wehha moves west."

"And you?" Medraut's level grey eyes were penetrating. "Would you move south then, through Lancelot's lands?"

Ida grimaced. “If it weren’t for that Roman-trained battle machine that is kept at Joyous Garde, I would already be past the Wall.”

“How many men does Lancelot keep?” Morgana asked softly.

“Two full cohorts, mostly cavalry.”

“That’s only a thousand men.” Medraut looked surprised. “Don’t your people outnumber him?”

“Mayhap, but he can gather more troops by collecting levies.”

“Villagers?” Medraut laughed derisively. “With their picks and hoes? They should be easy to subdue.”

“They may be villagers,” Ida answered, “but that Breton devil has been training them for twenty years. They all bear arms.” He shook his head. “If Lancelot hadn’t gone to assist at Cam’s Landing, I would not have been able to establish a stronghold here at all.”

“Cam’s Landing was seven years ago.” Morgana forced herself to look concerned. “How is it that you stayed alive when he returned?”

Ida rolled his eyes. “By the mad gods, I guess. He’s been preoccupied with the queen’s disappearance. I offered a peace treaty, not to advance past what I had. He accepted it.”

Medraut tensed. “Gwenhwyfar. Did she not return as well?”

Morgana shot a look at her son, which he refused to acknowledge. *Gwenhwyfar, always Gwenhwyfar, Medraut? Why? There may only be one way to make you forget her.*

“Nah,” the Saxon answered. “More like, she sought sanctuary at some convent. Isn’t that what widowed queens are supposed to do?” He leaned forward with a slight leer. “I heard tales she was more than a handful.”

“She was beautiful,” Medraut said simply. “No other woman—”

“Is Lancelot here, then?” Morgana interrupted, glaring at Medraut.

“No,”—Ida looked doubtful for a moment—“I usually have a scout or two tracking him. He left months ago for Brocéliande.”

“If he hasn’t been here for that long, why don’t you move?” Medraut asked. “Joyous Garde could be yours.”

“I told you. We have a peace treaty; I’ll wait until Wehha makes his move and mayhap, Childebert too, once Burgundia and Armorica are his. If Lancelot thinks I’m content, he’ll move south to help Custennin fight.”

“Well,” Morgana sighed with a helpless look. “We won’t be able to return to Paris until we know where Arthur is.”

“How do you plan to do that? You and your son are still wanted by the Britons.”

She slanted a look at him. “I have taken a liking to a religious order.”

“You?” Ida grinned, toying with her fingers.

Morgana shrugged gracefully. “Medraut will wear the turban and robe of a Saracen. My habit grants protection and allows me to move freely, unrecognized.” She gave him a sly smile. “I don’t wear it at night.”

His grin broadened. “My lady, you and your son are well come to stay on my lands for as long as need be.”

“Thank you,” she said and tucked her arm under his. “I feel at home already.”

Medraut smiled slightly at the act he was long familiar with. Morgana glanced at him. *Yes, Son. I still know how to use my feminine wiles. And I will find Arthur. And be rid of Gwenhwyfar, once and for all.*

~Chapter 11— The Path to Light ~

Recovered by his stay with Cynric, and with renewed determination, Lancelot reined in by the Lake's shoreline one early May morning. Barinthus was waiting and Lancelot stepped unto the barge. "She knew I was coming?"

The bargeman nodded. "She always knows when someone is on the path." He poled across, the fog curling its tendrils around them softly, like a blanket that muffled all sound save for a gentle lap of water at the bow.

Ceridwen waited for him on Avallach's shore. Since she'd taken vows of silence, Lancelot followed her quietly up the hill. She led him to the Lady's chambers and gestured for him to sit.

Nimue arrived a few minutes later. "I wanted to talk with you before I send for Elen." She sat beside him. "What caused you to go half-mad on the way to Camelot?"

When he finished, she looked troubled. "I fear you're right, Cousin. Cernunnos has great power; I called him at Arthur's Kingmaking."

"He was there with you?" Lancelot asked in surprise. "Arthur never mentioned that. Did he know?"

"Probably not. A skill of demi-gods and faeries is the ability to merge with another's mind, to step inside the body and experience what is taking place."

"So that's why Morgan was always watching when I talked to Gwen." *Mon Dieu*, can there be no privacy?"

"Yes, but there is a way to shield yourself. Faeries..." Nimue stopped and squinted her eyes thoughtfully at Lancelot. "Morgan is fickle, but she's fiercely jealous of her consort. She won't take kindly to his seducing Gwenhwyfar."

"Will she harm her?" Lancelot grew edgy again and began pacing.

"I think not. She's a master of illusion; she'll ply him with small tortures until she brings him to heel. But I'd wager she'd like Gwenhwyfar gone."

Lancelot halted mid-step. "Do you think she'd help us? Can she?"

Nimue stood. "I don't know, but we can ask. If nothing else, she'll keep Cernunnos away from Gwenhwyfar. Tonight, I'll have Argante meet us at the Sacred Pool. With the power of three, we may be able to make contact."

Lancelot stared at the moon's reflection in the water. On his left, Argante's arms were raised in supplication as she went through the ritual of drawing down the moon. To his right, Nimue's hand wove intricate designs over the pool. They waited, a slight breeze rising, causing the water to ruffle.

"You've summoned me?" Morgan le Fey's face lay below the surface. As she saw Lancelot, her whole body formed. She smiled coyly at him. "Did you wish to see me?"

"Morgan," Nimue said firmly, "we need your help."

The faerie did not take her eyes from Lancelot. "I might be willing to listen if he'll let me touch him." She gave him an impish smile and twirled a strand of hair around her finger.

"Morgan," Lancelot answered with as much patience as he could muster, "you have your consort. It's not me you need to touch."

She pouted. "But it is. Only I can't come to you. You have to ask." She began to fade away.

"Wait." Argante's voice rang like struck steel.

The faerie turned, surprise on her face. "You either have great power or lack of sense to order me."

Argante turned to Lancelot. "Reach out for her. Bring her here. Let her see for herself what Nimue can show her through the pool."

Lancelot forced a smile. "Forgive me, Morgan. If you wish to come to me, you may do so."

She tossed her head and looked at him through lowered lashes and a fall of hair. A little smile played on her lips. "Ask me."

He sighed. "Come stand beside me. Please." She giggled and then he felt her arms around his neck, her body pressing against him as she materialized. He glared at Nimue over her head.

An amused look flickered over Nimue's face for a brief instant. Then she reached out and took Morgan's arm. "Look," she said, gesturing to the water.

Reluctantly, the faerie disengaged from Lancelot and turned. Instantly, her face turned tempestuous and the wind began to gust.

"Careful," Nimue said, raising her hand to still the force. "Don't destroy the connection until you see it through."

Gwenhwyfar stood at the edge of the fragrant meadow just past the tree line, looking at the moon. Her lips moved as if in prayer. Cernunnos stepped from the shadows to stand beside her.

"This night is made for lovers," he whispered and drew her close to him. "There is a place I want to show you."

She gave a small moan, whether as protest or acquiescence was hard to tell.

He tilted her chin and leaned down. "I haven't kissed your lips yet. I can make you forget..."

"NO!" Morgan screamed in a rage and the picture in the water froze. She turned furiously to Nimue. "I will make him pay for that. I must go back."

Nimue nodded. "Will you help us get Gwenhwyfar out of the land of Faerie?"

Morgan's eyes flashed green bolts of fire. "For certes, I want her gone.

But I have not the power to open the portal."

"We will keep working on that," Nimue replied. "Just be ready...and keep Gwenhwyfar safe."

Morgan nodded. "I'll be watching her. Send me back while I can still put a stop to this." She didn't even glance at Lancelot as she stepped into the pool and was gone, leaving furious ripples in her wake.

The moonlight washed the meadow in silver shadows, the black trees looming skyward. Gwenhwyfar sighed. *Is the moon rising at Camelot*?

"I can make you forget." Cernunnos' hazel eyes held Gwenhwyfar spellbound as he put an arm around her waist and dipped his head, his lips only a whisper from hers.

"I don't want to forget." She struggled to free herself, but the arm was like iron. "I don't want to stay here and I don't want you."

His eyebrows lifted. "And you did not want me kissing you the last time? Do you deny it?"

She glared at him, resisting the magnetic urge to throw her arms around him. "That was magic and you're using it again now."

"I assure you I'm not, my lady." His voice sounded amused as a finger traced the curve of her cheek and the slope of her throat and stopped just short of her breast. She gave a small involuntary gasp and he grinned. "You're a passionate, carnal woman, Gwenhwyfar. I've seen it with your mortal and I've felt it with me. Why do you fight that? Give in and let me show you—"

"You're Morgan's consort."

"Yes." Cernunnos looked puzzled. "Consort. Not husband. She does not own me. I take what I want."

"Please," Gwenhwyfar pleaded as he untied the one shoulder strap and reached for the other. "I love Lancelot," she said, holding the silky gown to her breast.

In the dim light, his eyes began to glitter dangerously. "You exasperate me, Gwenhwyfar. I am tired of hearing about Lancelot."

She started to push against him, but her gown slipped and she caught it, realizing she would have to stand still. "You can't change how I feel."

"No?" His hand cradled the back of her head, forcing her mouth to meet his. She felt the pressure of his lips and then he yelped in pain as she bit him. From within the depths of the forest came howls of affinity. Around them, the high grass began to rustle noisily, as though some night creature slithered through it.

Cernunnos sucked the blood from his lip and turned a feral face toward Gwenhwyfar, the antlers glowing in the ether above him. "So you want to play rough, my lady. I have no quarrel with that."

She turned and bolted, tripping on the slipping gown. She hit the ground hard, Cernunnos rolled with her, pinning her beneath him, locking her arms overhead. His mouth clamped onto her breast and she cried out in fear as he spread her legs with his knee.

Suddenly, Cernunnos lay still, on top of her, as if in suspended animation.

Slowly, she opened her eyes. Morgan le Fey glared down at her. Gwenhwyfar wrestled herself from under Cernunnos and sat up. "I'm glad you came." She slipped her gown on quickly.

"Not quickly enough." Morgan's voice loomed large in the utter stillness that had descended.

Total silence surrounded them as though they stood in a deep canyon. She looked down at the inert figure on the ground. "Is he dead?"

Morgan laughed, the sound hollow. "No. I stopped Time; that's why nothing is moving. I can't kill him; he is only half-man." She glanced sideways at Gwenhwyfar. "What did you do to enrage him so?"

"I bit him when he tried to kiss me."

"You objected to that?" Morgan asked suspiciously.

"He told me he would make me forget Lancelot."

Morgan's voice softened. "Yes. A kiss has the power to do that in Faerie."

Gwenhwyfar turned to her. "Then you must help me, Morgan. Find a place for me to hide, away from him. Work your own magic."

"I intend to." Morgan smirked. "Now go. When I finish with him, he will be too exhausted to be able to try to do anything to you for a long time. And time is long here."

Lancelot took a deep breath after Morgan suddenly disappeared and Cernunnos appeared with Gwenhwyfar in the meadow. "I didn't need to see that." He turned and started back up the Processional Way.

"Wait!" Argante cried.

He turned. Nimue had sunk to her knees and was staring into the pool. Quickly, he went and knelt down. He started to ask what was wrong, but Argante gestured him to silence.

"Nimue is having the Sight."

He could see nothing. They waited.

Then, Nimue shook her head and looked up. "You must make a trip, Lancelot, to Carbonek to see your father-in-law."

"Pelles? Why?"

"I never question the Sight." She frowned at him. "I saw you and Elen at her grandfather's. There was a feeling of great peace and acceptance there."

Lancelot grimaced. "Pelles and I have never been on good terms. He's not forgiven me for not wanting Elaine nor for taking her again, even though she drugged me. I caused her to die in childbirth."

"And you've withheld Elen from him!" Nimue rose unsteadily and he reached out a hand to hold her. "Lancelot, this is about forgiveness. I think the portal remains closed because you have too much hardness in your heart. Even your love for Gwenhwyfar cannot overcome that."

Argante placed a hand on his other arm. "My mother is right. Go to Carbonek. You may find an answer awaits you."

Lancelot stopped the horse as he approached the turnoff to Carbonek.

"That was your mother's home," he said to Elen.

She petted her pony's neck and looked up the small hill where an old fort stood. The gate was open, but no soldiers manned the battlements.

"Shouldn't there be guards posted?"

"There should," Lancelot answered as he nudged his horse forward.

"But your grandfather has always maintained that since his land has gone to waste, no one will bother him." For miles the land laid barren, nothing but dried, brown grass and trees that only partially leafed out. The streams were but trickles. They hadn't seen wildlife in a day.

His daughter must have been thinking the same thought for she suddenly asked, "What does he do for food?"

Lancelot remembered the only time he'd come to Carbonek. After Elaine's death, he'd come to get Elen. Food had been plentiful, even though Pelles ate little and talked even less. Lancelot had stayed only two days, long enough to convince the wet nurse to go back with him.

"Many years ago Pelles suffered a thigh wound that never healed. Folks are superstitious. The people in the neighboring holdings bring him food to appease whatever gods are angry."

"How did he get hurt?"

"Pelles supplied seafood to Uther's army. The Pendragon had two soldiers who were twins, Balan and Balin—rowdy men, always looking for a fight. Pelles had a banquet here—the place was green and fertile at one time—Balin insulted Pelles and was challenged. His sword broke and, half-drunk, I suppose, he ran off with Pelles in pursuit." Lancelot frowned, trying to remember the tale. "Somewhere along the way, a spear was hanging on the wall—an old one, with a rusty tip—Balin grabbed it and turned to defend himself. He didn't want to kill Pelles, so he ran it through his leg in order to escape..." He stopped at the bored look on Elen's face.

"Galahad grew up here?" she asked, definitely changing the subject. Lancelot laughed.

"Until he was eight. Gwenhwyfar asked the king to send him to me."

She wrinkled her nose. "I don't think I would like living here."

"Well, don't tell your grandfather that." Lancelot straightened in the saddle. "We'll both need to be on our best behavior."

As Lancelot had predicted, the evening meal was plentiful. After, they retired to a sitting room still bearing touches of Elaine's handiwork. He sat uneasily on a brocaded chair and watched Pelles and Elen.

She asked questions. Too many, Lancelot realized too late. "Why did Galahad and my mother live here and not with Da?"

Pelles raised an eyebrow and glanced at Lancelot. "Your father preferred to be at Camelot."

Lancelot's eyes darkened, but he remained silent.

After a moment, Pelles went on. "The king needed him there. The Saxons were restless in those days."

"The Lady Nimue told me how my father saved the king's life and always fought by the king's side and once he saved the queen—"

"I think you're tiring your grandfather out, Elen. Time for you to go to bed," Lancelot interrupted. *I'm going to have a talk with Nimue...*

"But I'm not—"

"Elen," Lancelot said more sharply than he intended.

"Yes, Da." Reluctantly she got up and left, her lower lip stuck out.

Pelles' eyes followed her as she went. "She needs a mother."

"She has Augusta," Lancelot answered. "I do what I can. She obeys me."

"Does she fear you, like Galahad did?"

"Galahad did because Elaine..." Lancelot stopped. "I'm sorry. I came here to have you meet Elen, and to say I wish I'd done things differently."

The old man shifted in his chair and stretched his leg. "Would you have been a decent husband to my daughter?"

Lancelot felt a small stab of guilt. He'd never been attracted to Elaine. "Did you know I asked her for an annulment? The marriage should never have happened."

"It wouldn't have if you hadn't been willing to commit adultery with the queen," the old king said. "If you remember, you thought it was her you were going to."

Lancelot winced. "I deserve that, I suppose."

Pelles looked at him through narrowed eyes. "What would you have done differently?"

"I should have insisted on a divorce. She would have been free to find someone who loved her, and she might even be alive today."

The Fisher King was quiet for some minutes. "Elen wouldn't be here then. I suppose some good came of it. But she needs a mother. Why don't you remarry?"

"I haven't been interested."

"So it's still Gwenhwyfar." He leaned forward. "She disappeared six years ago, right after Cam's Landing. Probably in a convent somewhere."

If she only were... "Mayhap. Could we talk about something else? I didn't come here to argue."

Pelles sat back. "As you wish. How's Galahad these days?"

Lancelot told him of Galahad and Peredur's quest. When he finished, the old man had tears in his eyes.

"Peredur stopped by to visit me well over a year ago. I had no idea Galahad was searching also. If they're still no closer to finding it, they haven't learned its lesson."

"Lesson? I think it time they come to their senses, both of them. I'm not even sure the Grail exists." Lancelot yawned.

"I think it's time for bed." Pelles got stiffly to his feet and shuffled to the door. He stopped and turned. "Let them search. The Grail exists."

Lancelot awoke to find the room warmly lit with a soft glow. Beyond the glimmer, in the shadowed recesses of the chamber, a man carried a spear carefully. Lancelot reached for his sword then stopped, for the man was transparent. He blinked, but the image remained. He started to get out of bed, but found he was transfixed, the shimmer of light surrounding him and holding him in bondage. He noticed a girl—by Mithras, she looked like Elaine—carrying something flat like a platter, behind the man. He strained to see past the illumination. Suddenly, more light appeared from the dim shadows; candlesticks were being carried, but he could not tell who held them. Then, SHE was there.

He shrank back, for the light had become swirling colors of the palest pastels. A golden-haired maiden, in gossamer white, stood in the midst of the colors; now came the sweet aroma of blossoms and spices, floating lightly on the air surrounding her.

"Who...who are you?" he whispered.

"I am Astrala, sworn keeper for that which your son seeks."

A Grail Maiden? He wanted to go and kneel before her, receive her blessing, for he knew she was love and innocence and perfection. If I can just reach you...this inner pain will be gone...

She faded slightly.

"No! Stay. I want to be healed," he pleaded.

The maiden held up her hand and a blinding light stole his vision. He covered his eyes.

"Behold!" Her voice vibrated like a slowly plucked harp string, echoing and vibrating from the walls.

He opened his eyes slowly, squinted into the blazing fierceness. He could see an outline of a goblet, silver with a gold rim, then it was gone, although the maiden remained.

"Find Arthur. Make your peace. Only then will you be reunited with Gwenhwyfar."

The room went blindingly dark and it took a moment for Lancelot to regain his bearings. He stood shakily and walked to the window, seeing the moon at crescent.

The Grail. I've just had a glimpse of the Grail, and now I know what I must do.

Lancelot and Elen stopped at Cameliard on their way back from Corbenek and found Bedwyr had taken charge.

"How is Leodegrance?" Lancelot asked as they walked up the cobblestone path to the villa.

"Not well," Bedwyr answered. "He stays in bed most days. It's why I've returned instead of going with Arthur to Léon."

"Léon? Is there trouble?"

"Mayhap. I will tell you later, after supper."

They proceeded to Leodegrance's bedchamber. A pleasant-looking young woman with the flaming red hair and the pale skin of the Scotti was fixing his covers. She ducked her head shyly at Lancelot and gave Bedwyr a big smile.

"He sleeps."

"I'm awake." The voice was not loud, but surprisingly strong. "Who's there? Open the curtains! I want some light!"

Obligingly, the woman moved to the window. Lancelot noticed Bedwyr's eyes following her. "Thank you, Aidin." Bedwyr was rewarded with another of those flashing smiles.

Lancelot walked to the bed. "My lord, it's Lancelot."

Leodegrance stared at him, "Lancelot? Did you bring Gwenhwyfar?"

Startled, Lancelot looked over at Bedwyr who tapped his head. Lancelot turned back slowly. "No. She's at home in Camelot."

"Why doesn't she ever come to see me? Arthur was here just yesterday."

Again, Lancelot looked at Bedwyr who shook his head. "Arthur probably had to leave her home because he had business to attend to."

"Uh? What business? Do I have to go somewhere?"

"No, Father. I'll take care of it. Why don't you get some rest?" Bedwyr said gently as he came to the bedside.

"Rest," Leodegrance repeated. "What are the curtains doing open? How can someone sleep with this much light in here?"

Aidin glided quietly to close them again. Bedwyr sighed and motioned them out.

"How long has he been like this?" Lancelot asked when they were seated downstairs and wine had been poured.

"Aidin says over a year. I didn't know. I would have come home sooner." Bedwyr looked guilty.

"Don't blame yourself," Lancelot said. "He seems to be in good hands."

Bedwyr nodded. "Aidin never complains; she jokes with him when he's lucid. She's a saint."

Lancelot quirked an eyebrow. "Those smiles didn't seem too saintly." Bedwyr colored and Lancelot grinned. "So that's how it is."

"I found her—literally, alone and nearly chilled to death—on my way back from Cam's Landing. Her family had been killed in the raids. I brought her here and then I left, looking for Medraut." He paused and then added softly, "I'm going to ask her to marry me, if she'll have me."

"I'm happy for you, Brother. And," he added, grinning, "it's about time."

Bedwyr looked at him. "Don't you think you'd be happier if you found a woman to take to wife?"

Lancelot schooled his face not to show pain. "There's only one woman for me."

"And if she returns, she's still Arthur's wife."

Lancelot was silent. Finally, he spoke. "I need to find Arthur. I have to apologize. It's long overdue. We'll work something out about Gwen."

Bedwyr shook his head. "I never have understood the relationship among the three of you, but then, it's none of my business, is it? I wish all of you the best, whatever happens."

"That means a lot."

Bedwyr changed the subject. "How long can you stay?"

"Not long. I'll stop by Camelot before I go to Léon to see if there's been any word," Lancelot answered. "I need to take Elen home first."

"Why not leave her here with us? Aidin loves children and Elen could probably help her with some things."

"That's a good idea, Pelles said she was in need of a mother and I won't be able to provide one; at least, until Gwenhwyfar is found." He paused. "I think there's one more stop I need to make before I go to Camelot."

Bedwyr raised a brow. "Where would that be?"

"Astolat," Lancelot replied. "I have one more bridge to mend."

Lancelot dreaded it. He'd meant to return years ago, after Elen's body was sent to Camelot. Then he'd been captured and drugged by Morgana.

A girl stood near the stables, her back to him. *Slight of build, with the same long, blonde hair. Does she look like her aunt, too?*

She turned and he inhaled sharply. The same blue eyes looked across at him above the pert nose and full mouth. *She could be a reincarnation of the Elen who'd taken care of him. No wonder Galahad was attracted to her, aphrodisiac or not.*

She walked across the bailey, eyeing him curiously. "Can we help you?" Her smile was her aunt's, too.

"I've come to see your father," Lancelot said, but before she could reply Tirre had come out of the Great Hall and was walking his way. Lancelot sat tall in his saddle and waited. His horse tossed his head and he relaxed the tension on the reins.

Tirre stopped beside Elen. "I didn't think to see you again. Why are you here?"

"Papa!" Elen cried. "You're being rude!"

"It's all right," Lancelot said to her then looked at Tirre. "I had to come. It's many years too late, but I'm sorry for what happened."

Tirre frowned. "Would that she'd not gone riding that day. She wouldn't have found you at all."

"And I'd probably be dead. I should have left as soon as I was well." When the other man remained silent, Lancelot continued, "If I hadn't accepted the favor she made, she wouldn't have gotten the wrong idea. Over the years, I've thought she'd be alive if I'd just refused that."

Tirre's face softened a little. "Elen always was the romantic. She had all these ideas about Camelot and no idea of who you really were."

Lancelot nodded. "I never meant to delude any of you. I just wanted a place where I wouldn't be found by anyone who came looking." *How can I explain trying to deny my love for Gwenhwyfar by disappearing?*

"What are you talking about?" Elen looked from him to her father and back to Lancelot. "Who was looking for you? Are you a criminal?"

"No," her father interrupted. "He came from Camelot and it was the king—or more likely the queen—who sent out messengers inquiring."

"But why?" Elen was clearly puzzled.

"Because this man was the queen's champion." Tirre's voice held a trace of bitterness.

Elen's eyes widened. "You're Lancelot? I—"

"Yes. I believe you've met my son, Galahad."

"She came home crying after that incident," Tirre said grimly.

Without taking her eyes off Lancelot, Elen asked in a small voice, "Has he married? Is he well?"

"He's not married." Lancelot stopped at the look of hope that sprang into her eyes. *Bel's fires! I feel like I'm walking on boggy ground. Had my son really been in love with this girl, or did he lead her on by mistake, not knowing how vulnerable...* "He's on a quest for a religious cup." He turned back to Tirre. "That's the other reason I came. Should Galahad ride this way again, I'd ask that you don't hold him responsible for what happened between your sister and me. Arthur is in Léon and I'm leaving to join him there. I don't know when I'll return, but I wanted to make peace with you before I left. By the way, I named my daughter after Elen."

Warring emotions played over Tirre's face and Elen laid her hand on his arm. "Papa, if you hadn't told me you hated Lancelot, I would have brought Galahad home. He asked to meet you. I liked him; I believe he was sincere." She looked away.

Her father looked stricken. "Is that why you've refused the suitors who've asked for your hand?"

Lancelot felt like his horse had just kicked him. Unwittingly, Galahad had committed the same sin he had. He leaned down. "Elen, listen to me. I cared about your aunt. By the Goddess, if I'd not known Gwenhwyfar, I would have married Elen. But I couldn't, and she deserved more. So do you. I will tell Galahad that I've seen you, but until he finds this Grail he's looking for, there's no room in his life for anyone."

She looked up at him with tearful blue eyes. "I understand."

Tirre put an arm around Elen. "I think we have some talking to do." He looked at Lancelot. "If your son should pass this way, I'll not interfere."

"Thank you," Lancelot answered and hoped he hadn't brought more misery to this household as he cantered away.

Lancelot stopped briefly at Camelot before traveling on to Armorica. Custennin gave him the latest message that had come.

"Samson and Arthur went to Childebert's court and convinced him to let Judwal return to rule the kingdom. One hundred Frankish soldiers will be riding with them and Arthur wants a cohort from Camelot to meet him at Benoic as a show of strength so the Franks don't get greedy."

Lancelot grinned. "He doesn't trust the Franks to not try to take Léon themselves?"

Custennin nodded. "Five hundred of our men should persuade them to return to Paris once Judwal is accepted as king."

"Armorica has always resented Frankish interference. Certes, we won't welcome it now. Let me take the cohort," Lancelot offered.

Custennin looked relieved. "That was Arthur's intention, but we had not been able to find you."

"Arthur asked for me?"

"He did." Custennin hesitated. "By Mithras, it will be good for the two of you to fight together again."

Lancelot nodded. "I've held a grudge for something that wasn't his fault."

"Yes. Well." Custennin changed the subject. "The men can be ready in forty-eight hours. Give Tristan my best; I miss my cousin. Did you know he'd taken a wife?"

Lancelot was surprised. "I hadn't heard."

Custennin looked at him long and hard. "Mayhap he'll be able to help Arthur...and you."

Lancelot thought about Tristan four days later as he watched the unloading of the horses from the ships that had just put into the Armorican port. He hadn't seen him in more than five and ten years. Tristan and Iseult had stolen away, waiting to board a ship to Armorica when Arthur caught up with them; Marc had renewed his pledge of alliance after that. Lancelot shook his head, remembering the day he and Gwenhwyfar had left them at the hidden cottage tucked behind the hill where the circle of stones sat. Mayhap, there would be time to reminisce. *I wonder why he took a wife? I always thought his love for Iseult was as strong as mine for Gwen.*

His reverie was broken when one of the captains approached.

"All the horses are off the ships. Do you want to muster and ride or make camp for the night?"

He was tempted to make camp and put off facing Arthur one more day. Then he shook his head. "We ride; the king will be waiting."

They arrived at Benoic the next morning. Lionel rode out to meet him.

"I'm glad Custennin found you. We're about to move on Jean Marc."

Lancelot glanced up at the battlements. Guards stood at attention every ten feet. He turned to his cousin. "You stand battle-ready here? Is there more trouble?"

Lionel shrugged. "Probably not, but I don't trust the Franks. Tristan arrived several days ago; he told us Jean Marc knows Judwal is here."

"Then he'll be prepared for us." He was still scanning the soldiers as they rode through the gate into the bailey and saw Galahad and Peredur waiting for them.

"It's good to see you again, Father," Galahad said as he dismounted.

Lancelot studied him. "Usually you're not..."

Galahad colored slightly, but continued to look at him. "I've misjudged you; I ask that you allow me to make it up to you."

"So you've learned tolerance." His face softened and he added quietly, "I have amends to make myself."

Galahad nodded. "He's waiting for you inside."

Lancelot took a deep breath, climbed the stairs to his old home and went straight through the dining hall to the living area. Arthur stood with his back to the door, contemplating something outside the window.

"Hello, Arthur."

He turned then, the strangely silvery eyes penetrating. For some moments, neither said a word. Finally Arthur spoke. "Did Custennin order you to bring the cohort?"

"I offered to come."

Arthur's shoulders relaxed somewhat. "Thank you for that. I—"

Lancelot shook his head. "Stop. I also came because I needed to apologize. I know you would have brought Gwen back if you could."

"I'd exchange my life for hers if I could."

"As would I."

They stared at each other for a minute, both of them remembering the eternal tug between them. Then Arthur smiled slightly. "The choice will be hers if she returns."

"She'll return," Lancelot answered with a bravado he did not feel. *I cannot tell him she is lost to Cernunnos.* "Will you accept my apology? I've been an ass."

Arthur grinned then and gripped his shoulder. "For certes, you have. By Mithras, it will be good to have you fighting beside me again!"

Lancelot felt the blanket of stillness in his soul that had settled over him in his vision. *I've made peace with my son, with Arthur, but how do I make peace with myself without Gwen?*

"Jean Marc will have every village between here and Cairhaix fortified," Tristan said the next day as they settled down to council.

"How many men?" Arthur asked, looking around the table at

Lancelot, Ector, Lionel, Judwal and the Frankish leader, Theuderic. Galahad and Peredur were seated at the far end of the table, along with the captains of the cohort.

Tristan shrugged. "His army numbers three thousand, but they're spread thin to cover Léon as well. He'll have the bulk at his headquarters."

Theuderic leaned forward. "We only brought a hundred men as an escort. This was supposed to be a *coup du premier,* not a war!"

Lancelot watched the warlord covertly. *A big man, not young in years, a cousin of Childebert's. Seasoned well as a warrior, not afraid to fight, but did he want Judwal to succeed?* He looked over to where the young man sat, quietly composed. *A boy, really. Six and ten is young to shoulder a king's responsibility. Does he know who his friends are? Who will watch his back?*

As if knowing Lancelot's thoughts, the boy turned his dark head toward him, the brown eyes not yielding. The long, slender fingers of one hand tapped lightly on the table.

"*Monsieurs,*" he said softly, but the voice was firm. "If I am to be accepted as king, the people of Armorica will have to fight for me."

Ector nodded. "Benoic stands with you." He glanced at Lancelot who nodded imperceptibly. "We have well over four thousand men."

"And Kehydius, my brother-in-law, has another thousand," Tristan added.

Lancelot looked at him and wondered who the new wife was, that she could make Tristan forget Iseult. They would have to talk later.

"And from Camelot?" Arthur asked mildly, for they'd agreed he'd continue to be known only as Armel to the Franks. "Is the king willing to send more men, if needed?"

Lancelot nodded. "Custennin still has a second cohort in readiness and he can proclaim a levy from the lesser kings. As things stand, Cerdic maintains the treaty, my men hold Ida in the north, and Cormant stays Wehha of Anglia."

Arthur leaned back and looked at Ector. "What's your plan of action?"

"We'll use half the infantry from Benoic for they are Roman-trained, and half from Kerlouan." He nodded toward Tristan and then looked at his brother. "Camelot's men are yours, Lance. What will you do?"

"Three companies of Camelot's cohort will provide the right, left and rear flanks," Lancelot answered. "One will stay to defend Benoic in case Jean Marc creates a diversion and somehow slips through."

"He doesn't have men to spend for that, I think," Tristan said. "He's had to post men throughout all of Léon."

"And I'm expecting the other half of your men—Kehydius' men—to harry those troops, so they don't march and surprise us from behind." Lancelot turned back to Ector. "Custennin's last company will precede us and circle around to wait. I want there to be no escape for Jean Marc if he doesn't surrender and turn over the throne."

"What is our position?" Theuderic's voice held a twinge of sarcasm. "Do you expect us to sit here spinning with the women?"

Lancelot gave him a dour look. "Your job has been accomplished, I think. You've escorted Judwal. Better that you return home and let the people of Armorica take care of their own."

"I was sent to see Judwal established," Theuderic replied coldly. "We will not leave until that happens. Even then, we should stay to protect him from usurpers."

Arthur shook his head. "The Bishop Aurelian has granted me permission to watch over the young king." He nodded to a surprised Lancelot. "I was thinking of asking Custennin if I could keep a company from Camelot here for a time."

"For certes," Lancelot replied slowly, thinking. "You know the king has always respected your emissary skills, Armel."

Theuderic looked at Arthur suspiciously. "Are you Custennin's man then and not Armorican?"

Arthur's eyes turned pewter-colored. "I was trained in Britain, it's true; but I fought with Hoel here and Hoel was Derock's brother. I have an obligation to Judwal."

The Frank turned back to Lancelot. "We're not leaving. My men will ride with yours."

Lancelot shrugged. "Suit yourself, but I'll be the only commander."

"I command my own men," he returned angrily.

"Command them, but take orders from me."

"No."

"I'll not have men die because of confusion in the ranks." Lancelot tapped the hilt of his sword. "Would you like to take this outside?"

Peredur glanced uneasily at Galahad, who was watching the Frank, a slightly amused look on his face. "Your father will kill him," he whispered.

"That might not be a bad thing," Galahad answered softly.

"It'll mean war with Childebert," Peredur responded swiftly. "His brother is powerful."

Arthur glanced down the table and frowned, quieting both of them. He turned to Lancelot. "Save your sword for battle; there's no reason for the gauntlet to be thrown." He turned to Theuderic. "Lancelot stands as Regent for Custennin and he is prince here in his own right, just as you are in Orleans. If those of us present here agree for Lancelot to command, will you accept those conditions?"

Theuderic's face darkened. "I'm outnumbered." He glanced around and sighed. "As you wish, Prince." His voice held a trace of sarcasm.

Lancelot took a deep breath. "Your men will ride in front of the rear flank. He nodded toward the captains. "Ryons will lead it. Guinglain will command the left, like his father, Gwalchmai did. I will take the right. Galahad, I'm assigning you and Peredur to the right, as well." He gestured to Tristan and Lionel. "Yours is the infantry; have you still the old Roman rectangular shields?"

Lionel nodded. "You plan to use the tortoise?"

"If we have to lay siege to Cairhaix, it offers the best protection to get to the walls." Lancelot turned to Arthur. "I will be in need of your emissary skill, Armel. Will you ride with me?"

Arthur inclined his head. "As you wish, Prince."

"Much of the cohort is green," Lancelot said to Arthur as he raised up in the stirrups to watch Guinglain muster his troops. "They're eager to taste blood, I think."

Arthur watched Ryons on the other side. "You trained Cai's and Gwalchmai's sons yourself, Lance. They'll hold them in." He turned to the men behind, a smattering of Cam's Landing veterans among the group. They'd taken care not to recognize him in front of the Franks, but they were grinning now, happy to see their king once more.

"I'd like to keep this group when it's time for the rest of you to leave," Arthur said to Lancelot.

"You feel you must stay? Lionel can watch over him or Tristan. Britain needs you back."

He shook his head, smiling. "While I'm there, I weaken Custennin's hold, even though I don't want the crown."

Lancelot watched Galahad and Peredur making their way over to him. "You think there will be trouble with Childebert, don't you?"

"Eventually. Another reason to stay in Benoic. Now that I know Morgana and Medraut have been there, I suspect they will return."

A muscle in Lancelot's jaw twitched. "Will you kill them?"

Arthur sighed. "No. I must forgive them."

Lancelot jerked his head around, astounded. "Don't be a fool, Arthur. They deserve to die."

"Be that as it may," Arthur answered, "the Grail Maiden told me I must forgive. I can't explain."

For a moment, Lancelot stared at him. Finally, he took a deep breath. "You don't have to. She came to me, too." *There is no denying her.*

For all their anticipation, not much blood was shed. The village fortifications were easily overcome through sheer numbers alone and once the siege was in place, Armel offered amnesty to any who surrendered. As the days wore on into weeks, and the great double-armed ballistae hurdled rocks at the curtain wall, crumbling it slowly but surely, more and more of Jean Marc's men slipped out into the night to renounce him.

Lancelot's cohort was preparing the final phase of taking the walls when the white flag appeared over the gatehouse.

"We yield! Jean Marc is dead. We do not wish to fight!"

"Suicide?" Lancelot glanced at Arthur.

"More likely, assassination," Arthur replied, "if the stories the soldiers have told are true." He leaned back in his saddle, looking relieved. "Now I can attend to making Judwal into a real leader, as Myrddin did with me."

Within a moon, the people of Cairhaix and Dirinon had acknowledged Judwal as king. The Franks withdrew and Lancelot sent four of the cohorts' companies home. His right flank would stay to support Arthur's regency of Judwal.

"The people are declaring you a saint for keeping the bloodshed to a minimum," Ector told Arthur one night, several weeks after the successful overthrow.

Arthur laughed. "Lancelot can tell you I'm no saint."

Lancelot smiled and thought of Arthur's willingness to forgive Medraut and his offer to give Gwenhwyfar a choice. "You may be more of a saint than you think, Arthur."

Tristan came to see Lancelot as Kehydius' men were planning to return. "How is Iseult?" he asked.

Lancelot gave him a calculated look. "I haven't seen her. Marc rarely leaves his lands and she stays at Tintagel."

Tristan looked crestfallen. "I'd hope you could take a message."

"Why did you marry, Tris?"

He lifted his head. "A foolish mistake of mine."

"A mistake?"

"Yes. I was wounded in a fight aboard ship. It got infected. I was highly fevered when I got here; she tended me. I heard Iseult's name...in my delirium, I thought she'd come to me. The woman looked like her. When she was out of the room, I told Kehydius I was going to marry her, thinking it was Iseult. He told her."

Lancelot frowned. "Surely, after you healed, you could've told her you thought you heard the name..."

"I did hear the name," Tristan answered dismally, "for hers is the same."

"What?"

"Aye." He gave a short laugh that sounded like a bark. "Isolde La Blanche Mains. She saved my life; she fell in love. I was honor bound. And I had nowhere else to go."

Lancelot cringed inwardly. If he'd married Elen, what would the outcome have been? But he'd had some place to go; he'd been able to return to Gwenhwyfar. Tristan was banished from Britain.

"I've remained true to Iseult," Tristan said earnestly. "We made a pact before I left; I'd never couple with another woman. That was the message I wanted you to take. Tell Iseult I've never bedded my wife."

Silently, Lancelot remembered his own sorry wedding night and how he'd refused to take Elaine. Gwenhwyfar had been so happy when he told her. He put a hand on his friend's shoulder. "I'll see she gets the message."

"I should be getting back to Elen," Lancelot told Arthur one morning. "She's probably wearing out her well come at Bedwyr's."

Arthur smiled, a little sadly. "You're lucky to have two fine children, Lance."

He nodded. "I wish my mother had been able to know them better."

"I suspect the Lady Niniane knew more than you thought."

Lancelot laughed. "She always did. I think I'll visit the caves before I go. Galahad's never seen her place. Why don't you come along? The Black Lake is only a one day ride from here."

"Your mother's home?" Arthur asked. "Isn't that sealed off from the world now?"

He shook his head. "If you know where to look, there is a way in."

At the lake in Brocéliande, Lancelot reached for the familiar knob on the oak tree. A small, translucent cloud bore down from the upper regions of the trees, accompanied by the faint sound of a thousand whispers. Arthur stared while Galahad drew back. Peredur cocked his head better to listen.

"It's just the windsingers." Lancelot strained to make out any shapes in the floating fragile foam. "They used to let my mother know if someone approached. I'm surprised they're still here."

The humming grew louder, becoming an unfettered, strangely harmonious melody.

"Are they faerie?" Arthur asked, looking around curiously, apparently not ready to trust his eyes or ears.

"In a way," Lancelot answered. "Would that they could carry me there. Come." He led the way to the crevice between the rocks. "Watch your step; it will be dark."

Once below, with the candles lit and reflecting off the crystal, Galahad finally relaxed. "This is not so strange. My mother always said the Lady sacrificed—" He stopped.

Lancelot grimaced. "Elaine never met my mother. But this place has always been one of gentle power. No human or animal sacrifices have been made here from before Caesar's time."

Galahad looked skeptical and Lancelot sighed. "See for yourself what the temple was like." He moved toward a richly brocaded tapestry hanging at the far end of the cave room and drew it aside.

All four men entered slowly. The inner sanctum was only dimly lit from the torch Lancelot carried, but the rich murals painted on the walls seemed to glow softly on their own. On one side, a white hart stood majestically in the midst of a forest glade. On the other side, inside a circle of stones, a druid stood in his white robes, a golden sickle strapped to his belt, offering a spray of mistletoe toward the center panel.

Behind the white marble cromlech and encompassing the entire wall was a painting of the Goddess in her trinity: the Maiden, the Mother, the Crone.

"Do you feel the peace in this room?" Lancelot asked his son.

Galahad swiveled to look around. He studied the murals. "It is so pagan, yet it feels like a Christian chapel."

"Where good and sincere intentions are practiced, there is always peace," Arthur said quietly.

Lancelot approached the altar stone, knelt before it, and asked the blessing in the Old Tongue. He felt Arthur's hand on his shoulder and then Galahad's on the other. Peredur had moved behind him. He kept his head bent, not wanting to dissolve this one moment of complete acceptance. He knew, for one brief, shining moment all four of them were experiencing the same feeling of unconditional love. Knew and didn't know how he knew.

An incandescent, luminous light began to grow, softly radiating from the image on the wall. Its brilliance vibrated through the air, filling it with the rich, heady scent of apple blossoms and spices floating toward them, surrounding them while the illumination, like white velvet, wrapped itself around them, binding them together.

The voice, lighter than air, yet prolifically voluminous in its timbre and cadence, held them mesmerized. The maiden seemed to step from the wall, yet was still there. "A gift," she said, "because you forgave and have totally surrendered your will to Hers."

Light dazzled them, blinding in its pure radiance. Lancelot looked up, knowing the maiden once again held the Grail. He could feel its power reaching him, piercing, flowing through him to the others. He could have wept for sheer joy. *Gwenhwyfar, my love, if you could be here to experience this with us—to be one with us—Arthur and I and you. As one.*

The light began to fade as did the image of the maiden. Faintly, from far away, her voice carried through the vapors. “You have given the stone its due at this altar today. The Grail will become accessible. Search for it.”

The room grew cool as she slipped away, taking the fragrance with her. Lancelot felt himself being lifted and saw Arthur blink. Beside him, Peredur and Galahad stood, enraptured still. Arthur shook his head and looked down at Lancelot.

But there was only empty space where Lancelot had been kneeling.

~ *Chapter 12—The Rescue* ~

"What do you think has happened to him?" Galahad glanced around wildly then turned to Arthur.

Arthur became pensive. "I think he's finally with Gwenhwyfar."

"In the land of Faerie?" Galahad asked unbelievingly. "But, didn't you say a person can't come back from there?" His face turned white. "My father is gone; there's so much I should have said."

"Don't torture yourself," Arthur said kindly. "Your father was born of the Great Rite, he has a bit of fey blood. I believe he'll bring her back."

"How can he when you couldn't?"

"He'll find a way," Arthur said with more confidence than he felt, knowing it had cost Myrddin his life. "None of us can deny we've just witnessed a miracle. Let us pray for two."

Galahad turned back to stare at the mural in Niniane's temple room, even though the room now held only torchlight. "She is the woman of my harp vision."

"Yes," Peredur whispered, "and the one I saw in the Procession. We must continue on."

"What did she mean by paying the stone its due?" Arthur asked.

Galahad exchanged glances with Peredur. "Argante left us a riddle; we would find the Grail after we completed four tasks." He shook his head. "I had no idea it would be in a pagan place. I thought the cup belonged to the Christians."

Arthur put a hand on his shoulder. "I don't think the cup belongs to anyone. It is a holy relic meant to heal. Worship of the Mother is far older than the new religion that reveres the Father and the Son. Ah, Myrddin was wise," Arthur said, "to have Ector raise Cai and I Christian while he taught me the druid way."

"You're saying both religions—the old and the new—are right?"

"Something like that," Arthur answered. "Followers of the Goddess have an old adage, 'Do what ye will, with harm to none' and the Christos preached to treat your neighbor as yourself." He squeezed Galahad's shoulder. "I think you might find many such comparisons if you look."

"Nimue said the cup had been lent to the son of a carpenter once. Jesu was that," Peredur added.

Arthur nodded. "Aye. It united his men one last time as they all drank from it."

"Including the traitor," Galahad said softly.

"Man has free will," Peredur answered. "The Grail is only an opportunity to find peace within ourselves, I think."

Arthur smiled. "When men are at peace with themselves, they will not wish to fight. They will have tolerance for one another's beliefs."

Galahad grimaced. "Tolerance. My father always said it was a failing of mine."

"Not a failure," Arthur replied, "unless you refuse to learn the lesson."

"Another time Lancelot was right," Galahad sighed. "I used to wonder how you two could stay friends and comrades when you both—" He stopped abruptly. "I'm sorry."

"No need." Arthur's eyes were warm. "Fate works her will, even as the Goddess does. Myrddin warned me of the course my marriage to Gwenhwyfar would take."

"Yet you went ahead, knowing the pain would come." Galahad shook his head. "I don't think I'd have the strength; I still think women are dangerous."

Arthur laughed, lightening the conversation. "That they are, but so is the tip of your sword, yet you fear not to pick it up or to handle it." His eyes scanned the room. "Speaking of women, Nimue must be told what happened. I need you to return to Britain and tell her."

"You're staying?"

Arthur nodded. "I have given Judwal my oath to mentor him. Mayhap it's the reason I survived Cam's Landing, to keep Armorica free from Frankish rule. And," he added, "it must also remain free to help Britain."

He turned to Peredur. "You must go to Nimue. Tell her what's taken place. She can invoke Avalon's help in this matter. Tell her the portal has been opened."

Peredur nodded. "Do you have a personal message as well?"

"Just tell her I..." Arthur paused, inhaling deeply. "No. No message."

Lancelot stared into the pool, knowing it was the one Gwenhwyfar had used. Only now, he was looking into it from her side. He turned slowly to get his bearings.

He was standing midway up a steep hill, on a level earth bank. Within a few paces, the cool green shadows of forest began and below, an aquamarine lake rippled gently to shore, catching and throwing golden darts under the dazzling sun. In the other direction, up the hill to where the house of glass cast its beacon, just visible over the tops of the orchard trees, a tall blonde woman descended the path toward him.

"I am Hetaira. Well come to Avalon. The Goddess has smiled on you at last, Lancelot."

He dropped to his knees to receive the priestess' blessing. He had a thousand questions and yet only one question, but he dared not ask. *Gwen, I'm here.*

Hetaira motioned for him to follow. They didn't speak again until they were seated on one of the benches in the solarium. She handed him a honeyed drink that a maiden brought.

"The answer to your unspoken question is Gwenhwyfar isn't here."

"Cernunnos holds her hostage," Lancelot said simply.

A small furrow appeared above the priestess' clear blue eyes. "You know this?"

"He...allowed her a visit at the pool once," Lancelot answered.

The furrow deepened. "She told you she was hostage?"

"No." Lancelot thought back painfully to the price she'd paid. "But he wanted her and he told me he always won."

Silent for some minutes, she finally turned to him. "Cernunnos is powerful; her will may already be subjected to his. If it is, she will not leave him."

Lancelot shook his head. "Gwenhwyfar loves me."

Hetaira touched his shoulder sympathetically. "She may not remember you. The land of Faerie weaves its spells in ways we can't command. Even we priestesses do not go there."

"The Goddess would not be so cruel to allow me through the portal after all these years, only for naught," he answered stubbornly. "I will bring Gwen back. Is Morgan le Fey not as powerful as Cernunnos? She has promised to help me."

Hetaira smiled gently. "Morgan makes promises and forgets them just as easily. The Faerie nature is free and erratic."

"She wants Gwenhwyfar gone. She will help."

The priestess nodded. "We will pray she does. In any event, you must enter Faerie and for that, you must be prepared. We'll do a shielding ritual at the zero hour." She grew thoughtful. "Now I know why Rhiannon kept Excalibur. You will need it."

"Excalibur? It is a king's sword."

"And you are rescuing the queen."

"I'm not worthy..."

"Lancelot. The Grail Maiden wouldn't have appeared to you, nor would the portal have opened if you weren't. You became worthy when you let go of your resentment and forgave Arthur. Give back to him now the two things he held dear: his sword and his wife."

"Morgan le Fey!" Lancelot waited by the pool for several minutes. He was about ready to enter the forest on his own when she emerged.

Coyly, she tilted her head and slanted her eyes upward as she extended her hand. He bent over it dutifully, lips barely brushing her flesh. She looked disappointed.

"If you have need of my services, you might greet me more warmly."

"Forgive me." He gave his lopsided smile. "But I think you have need to have Gwenhwyfar gone as much as I have need to take her home. Does either of us have time to dally?"

She walked her fingers up his chest to his shoulders. "Time matters not in Faerie." Standing on tiptoe, she tried to kiss him.

He caught her hands and held them. "Morgan. Cernunnos is your consort. I have no wish to make him angrier than I have to."

Morgan pouted. "He's tried to lay with your woman; why can't I do the same?"

Lancelot winced at the reminder. "Even more so that I find her, before he subjects her completely to his will. Would you want Gwen falling in love with him?"

She narrowed her eyes. "No."

"Then help me. I'm asking you to escort me in your queendom and to bring us safely out." He kissed both her hands. "I know that few mortals get that chance."

She giggled. "Since you ask so nicely, I will help you."

They entered the forest and within the first few steps, Lancelot felt the distortion of time. He had no idea of how long they wandered, but it seemed the sun moved not at all. *Are we going in circles? Why can't I determine the path? Surely, I've been in this meadow before...*

"You have." Morgan breathed closely in his ear and suddenly he was aware of the muskiness of her scent. He knew he should tell her to hurry on, but the sun was so warm and the breeze gently brought a whiff of the sea. *Strange to have the tang of salt so deep within a forest.*

She moved a little closer, but did not touch him. "Mayhap, you would consider staying. Gwenhwyfar is already here. I would be content to share you. All four of us could be happy."

He felt a bubble of hysteria rising. *Will she not help us leave?* He took care not to offend her. "If I stay, Cernunnos would want to share Gwenhwyfar, too. I don't think that would suit you well, my lady."

Her face darkened momentarily, then she giggled. "It might be worth it to have the both of you."

Hysteria threatened Lancelot again; for a brief moment he wondered what life would have been like if he'd never met Gwen. "Please, Morgan. Help me."

Morgan studied him, then nodded. "Come. But prepare yourself. This will not be pleasant."

Gwenhwyfar sat dozing on a bench in the garden behind Morgan's small, elegant stone house. The morning sunshine peered over the trees, pleasantly warm on her face and arms. She let herself drift back to those wonderful days at Joyous Garde, when she'd lived with Lancelot. The memory kept her sane. *The feeling for him is strong this morning, almost as though he's near*. Lazily, she let herself sink deeper into the dream.

His touch was light on her arm, barely grazing the skin with his fingertips, his breath soft as he nibbled her ear and then nuzzled her neck. She moaned a little in pleasure and reached for him as he turned her in his arms.

"So you do like my touch."

Gwenhwyfar's eyes flew open and she gazed in shock at Cernunnos' face inches from hers. "How did you find me here?" She struggled to move away. "Morgan's supposed to protect me."

"Hmm. Morgan left earlier. She seemed to be in a hurry." He kissed her forehead lightly and then tried to brush his lips across hers.

"Don't...Please..."

"You can't deny me forever, Gwenhwyfar."

Cernunnos' eyes locked with hers and she felt herself weakening. She tried to look away, but could not. Damn this magic. She began to drown in the liquid amber depths that lured her closer.

"Kiss me, my lady."

"No. I will not," she protested, even as he brought her arms around his neck. She whimpered as he stroked her back.

"Yes." His eyes turned to molten gold, warm and glowing with a preternatural light. She tried to turn away, but his mouth swept hers and then his lips were pressing softly against hers, the pressure increasing as her resistance faded. His tongue tasted hers and she felt herself falling, far, far down...spinning...losing touch with the ground...floating.... drifting...the kiss went deeper until Gwenhwyfar knew no more.

Lancelot and Morgan stopped at the sound of voices from the garden.

"Gwenhwyfar," Cernunnos was saying, "Trust me. I can give you happiness. You'll have no regrets. Let me."

Lancelot gripped the hilt of Excalibur, but Morgan restrained his hand. "That's not the way. Let me lure him. Take Gwenhwyfar and meet me near the pool. The barrier force will not let you leave without me."

He hesitated, his hand still gripping the pommel tightly. "I can trust you? I'd rather fight him."

"You would lose, if not die." Morgan touched his lips briefly. "If sending you back means having Cern to myself again, I will do it."

He nodded once and she was gone, rounding the corner.

Gwenhwyfar's eyes were closed as she leaned against Cernunnos. His hands were cupping her breasts. Suddenly the bench was overturned and she was thrown to the ground as a mighty draft of wind blustered through the garden, bending the flowers flat.

Cernunnos rubbed his head and looked up at the faerie queen from where he'd sprawled. "There's no need to act childish, Morgan."

The wind velocity increased, howling now as the trees moaned and swayed. Cernunnos tried to stand, but a gust unfurled its wrath at him, knocking him down again.

"Enough!" he thundered and his hands made a wide sweep. The earth shuddered and Morgan sought to keep her balance.

The gale screeched now, picking up another bench and hurling it through the air. Gwenhwyfar rolled toward the trees as the earth convulsed once more.

Lightning bolted from a clear sky, striking dangerously close to the demi-god. Furious, he sent the missile back, causing a tree to split. Morgan pitched forward, landing near Cernunnos. In a moment, they were intertwined, the sounds of their fury giving way to passion.

Lancelot clamped a hand over Gwenhwyfar's mouth and pulled her back through the trees, holding her against him. "Don't scream. It's Lancelot. We're going home."

Wildly, she twisted to look at him. Her eyes were blank and he saw no recognition there. She began to struggle.

He gave her a little shake. "Gwen. Come to your senses. It's Lance. Arthur is waiting. We're leaving the land of Faerie."

Her eyes widened a little, but there was still fear.

"We've got to go. You have to come with me. You'll be safe."

She moved her head negatively and tried to pull away.

He spun her around quickly and kissed her before she had time to scream. She did not respond; nearly desperate, he cradled her head and prodded her mouth open with his thumbs, thrusting his tongue inside, letting her taste him. His arms moved around her and his hands kneaded her back. *Mother, Goddess, don't let me be too late. Not after all of this.*

Then suddenly she was kissing him back, clinging to him, sobbing in the back of her throat. He leaned back a little, watching her.

"Lancelot!" She was crying now, her arms wound tightly around his neck. "It is you? I'm not living another illusion?"

"No, my love. But we must hurry." Already the sounds behind them had begun to diminish. Lancelot took her hand and they began to run. *Lead me, Mother. Let me find the right path.*

Their sides were heaving when they finally reached the tree wall. "We have to wait for Morgan," Lancelot said between gulps of air. "I cannot get through on my own."

Gwenhwyfar slid to the ground, clutching her side, and looked at the lake below. "Fog," she said wonderingly. "I have not seen any since we left Avallach."

Lancelot glanced through the foliage. A bank of it lay heavy at the shoreline. He turned at the sound of feet running toward them.

Morgan burst from the path. "Quickly," she said, "Cernunnos follows. He will try to stop her."

Even as she spoke and they stepped through the barrier to the pool, the demi-god loomed large on the path. "Gwenhwyfar stays!" he bellowed and the creatures of the forest bayed their assent.

"She leaves to be with her people," Lancelot answered. "I'm taking her home."

Cernunnos raised his hand and Lancelot felt a mighty force pushing him back. He gained his footing and drew Excalibur in a single movement.

The shadow of antlers showed on Cernunnos' head. "You dare challenge me?"

"I do."

Astonished, Cernunnos nodded. "A sword," he roared and one of Morgan's black gnomes crept forward, carrying a scabbard. He drew the weapon and tested its balance and turned to Lancelot. "No quarter asked."

Lancelot nodded grimly. "No quarter given."

Cernunnos stepped outside the treeline as some faeries crowded closer to the barrier. Morgan silenced their twittering with a glance.

"A fair fight. Man to man." Cernunnos glanced briefly up the hill to where the priestesses gathered. "No magic. From either me or them."

Lancelot inclined his head, not taking his eyes from Cernunnos' face. They edged into position.

With a thrust, Lancelot lunged and Cernunnos quickly parried and reposted, only to be met by Lancelot's press on his blade. The two men held position, circling, then Lancelot stepped back for a quick disengage, placing his sword under Cernunnos' weapon and lunging again. Cernunnos feinted right, avoiding the hit. Lancelot maintained the offensive with a series of compound cuts meant to tire Cernunnos with the constant need to parry and counterattack.

But Cernunnos' arm seemed to be made of the very bronze that was the color of his skin. The two men watched each other warily, searching for weaknesses, looking for patterns, analyzing moves.

Excalibur felt like an extension of Lancelot's arm, but his legs were beginning to ache. *I'm near middle age, can I hold against a demi-god?* For the first time, in any battle, he began to doubt himself. With inner resolve, he gathered his strength. *I must win. Gwen is counting on me. I will not lose her again.*

In a final effort, Lancelot leaned forward over his knee and pushed off with his lead foot, propelling himself nearly horizontal to Cernunnos. It was a daring attack to make, but Excalibur struck home on the forte of the other blade, knocking the handle from the demi-god's stunned hand.

"Yield," Lancelot gasped as he held the point to Cernunnos' throat.

"You cannot kill me, Lancelot." The hazel eyes began to glow.

"You gave your word, as a man, the fight would be fair. It was. Yield." Lancelot was still breathing heavily, but Excalibur somehow felt light as a flower petal in his hand. It began to hum.

Cernunnos started to push the sword aside, but Excalibur was singing now. A thin slice of blood appeared on his hand. Surprised, he took a step backward.

"No magic, huh?"

"Not mine," Lancelot said. "This is Arthur's sword and it protects his queen."

"You have cheated me."

"I have won the right to take her home." Lancelot reached for Gwen's hand and pulled her to him.

Even as Cernunnos began his protest, the fogbank rolled upward from the lake below, shrouding the scene in trailing streams of vapor. It grew thicker, enveloping them in folds of grey mist. The demi-god's voice faded away gradually, until they were left in a blanket of opaque stillness.

Gwenhwyfar and Lancelot emerged from the copse, his arm draped protectively around her. Dazed, she looked around the glade, the sunlight momentarily blinding her.

"Where are we? Are we really back?"

"Yes, my love." Lancelot kissed the top of her head. "We're in Brocéliande, my mother's home. It was here that I saw the vision; the Grail brought me to you once I forgave Arthur."

She clung to him. "This must be a portal then, like the one at Avallach."

He nodded. "My mother said this was a place where the ley lines crossed, much like the Giant's Dance. Come, let me show you her realm."

They made their way down the stone stairs and Lancelot lit a candle. "The wax is warm and soft." He was puzzled. "I wonder if someone's been here or how long we've been gone."

Gwenhwyfar shook her head. "It could be a day or a year. You say I've been away seven."

"We have a lot of time to make up for." Lancelot nuzzled her neck slowly. "Or are you going to keep me waiting longer?"

Gwenhwyfar gave him a mischievous look as she reached for his trews and began working the laces. He grinned and pulled off his shirt. She knelt to remove his boots, then tugged his trews down. With a sigh of pleasure, she began a series of tiny kisses to his already throbbing phallus. Lancelot made a strangling sound and leaned down to lift her up.

"I'll never last if you begin there, Gwen. Have mercy on me." He reached over and pulled the ties on her shoulders and slipped the gown down, squeezing her buttocks and bringing her against his hardness. "For certes, it's easier getting you undressed from this than from the trews you usually wear."

Gwenhwyfar squealed as he picked her up and carried her to the bed. She pressed herself against the length of his body, her arms tightly around his neck, exploring his mouth with her tongue, loving the taste of him, fingering his hair, crushing her breasts to his chest. *Oh, it is good to be back!* She whispered, "I want you inside of me, Lancelot. Now."

Lancelot rolled her over on her back. "No, my lady. Let's linger over this. I've waited too long to have it finished so soon." He caught her hands and brought her arms up over her head and held them there with one hand as his other trailed down the inside of her arm.

"You aren't going to make me lie still, are you?" Gwenhwyfar tried to pull her hands away, but he just laughed. "Lancelot! You know what torture that is!"

"I know," he answered and nipped her neck gently. "And I know you like it." His hand merely brushed her breast and the nipple budded immediately. "See what I mean?" he asked.

"Oh, stop it, Lance!"

He feigned surprise. "You want me to stop what I'm doing?" His finger flicked the hardened nipple and she moaned. "Really?"

"No, don't stop. You know what I mean. Stop teasing me. Let me touch you."

"Later." He let his hand roam lightly across her ribcage and over her lower abdomen, up her stomach to her breasts and then down again, this time tickling the inside of her thighs. He repeated the pattern, his fingertips barely grazing the skin until Gwenhwyfar began to writhe, her body tingling from his stroking.

Lancelot rained kisses on her forehead and cheeks and tantalized her lips with the tip of his tongue before nuzzling her neck and moving to her breast. He released her arms then and gathered her breasts together, kneading them softly as he licked at the tips of them, moving from one to the other.

Gwenhwyfar groaned and ran a hand over his shoulders and hard back muscles, and then gasped as he took a breast in his mouth and suckled firmly. Her other hand found what she'd been seeking and he growled, low in his throat.

He nibbled his way down her stomach and between her thighs. His tongue, warm and pliant, slurped at her juice, causing her to nearly go into frenzy. Like soft velvet, he made swirls around her ultimate pleasure spot and Gwenhwyfar felt herself lose control. Her whole body went into the spasm of contraction and time seemed to stop.

The wave crested and then Lancelot was inside her, the strong, steady thrusting bringing on another undulation. The pitch increased and she rose on the swells and plunged in the troughs like a ship tossed on the high seas. She cried out when she peaked, and Lancelot held the moment for her and then she felt his release, flooding her and overflowing.

They lay together, wet and exhausted. Gwenhwyfar grabbed Lancelot's hand. "Can we just stay here? Forget about everything else. We could be happy..."

Lancelot wrapped his arms around her. "Ah, Gwen, I would like nothing better, but Arthur must be told you're back."

"He's in Camelot, a long way from here."

"No." He looked down at her. "Arthur is in Léon." Briefly, he told her what events had taken place. "I was leaving for Joyous Garde before I stopped here."

She clutched at his arm. "If Arthur means to stay in Armorica, I will have to stay with him. I can't bear the thought of your leaving, not now. It might be years before I see you again!"

"I have a home in Benoic." Lancelot stroked her hair. "I can always travel between the two."

Gwenhwyfar hung her head. "If you do, that Saxon whose lands border yours will take advantage. Arthur will expect you to stay in the north."

He sighed. "Well, we have the present. We'll spend the night here and tomorrow, begin the long walk to Benoic. We can rest there while I send word to Arthur that you've returned. Then we'll see what happens. Now hush," he said and ran a finger lightly over her lips.

Gwenhwyfar caught it with her teeth and he stopped, surprised. Slowly, she circled her tongue around the finger and then began to suckle, sliding it in and out of her mouth. Lancelot's eyes turned the color of peat and he grinned

"An invitation, my lady? So soon?"

She rolled on top of him and slid down his chest and belly. "My turn," she said.

The messenger entered the map room where Gwenhwyfar and Lancelot were studying the route from Léon. He handed a note to Lancelot. "Armel sends his greetings on your safe return. He will be here within the week." He bowed and retreated as Lancelot dismissed him.

For Arthur's sake, they had decided to keep Gwenhwyfar's identity hidden until they'd met Arthur. Lancelot watched the range of emotions play across Gwenhwyfar's face and moved closer to her.

"I can't handle this, Lancelot."

"You must." He gave her his lopsided smile. "Don't be intimidated. I'll be here."

She inhaled sharply. "You said something similar to me years ago when you first brought me to Camelot. Do you remember? I was so scared of the sheer hugeness of Camelot, and of Arthur. You told me you'd be there."

"Yes." His voice was almost a whisper. "Even then, I wondered how I would live without you."

Arthur had been shown to the private meeting room off Benoic's Great Hall. He interlocked his fingers, forcing himself to be still, waiting in anticipation, not quite daring himself to believe he'd see Gwenhwyfar again. *Am I going to be able to do this?* The servant opened the door; Gwenhwyfar stopped inside the doorway. Arthur studied her.

"I look so old and you so young, Gwenhwyfar."

She smiled, but didn't move. "Age becomes you, Husband."

He shook his head, knowing she must be shocked at his appearance. He rose and came to her, taking her hand and kissing it formally. "I'm glad to see you safely returned. Lancelot has succeeded where I failed." He brushed her cheek lightly with his lips. *I want so much to crush you to me and make you mine again. But then, I will not have the strength to do what I must do.*

She put her hand over his. "Arthur. You would have brought me back if you could. I never doubted that."

He nodded. "I know. And we tried, Nimue and I. Lancelot never gave up. I owe him a big debt. Where is he?" *Better to get this done.*

"Waiting outside."

Arthur walked to the door and opened it. "Come in, Lance. By Mithras, it's good to see you." Arthur hoped his voice wasn't shaky. He gestured to chairs. "Come sit. I want to hear how the rescue came about."

Lancelot looked uncomfortable, so Gwenhwyfar told the story.

"You fought the Horned God himself?" Arthur turned admiringly to Lancelot.

"He fought as a man," Lancelot answered, "and I had Excalibur." He drew the sword now and presented it to Arthur.

"Excalibur." Arthur held the sword as lovingly as a new babe. "I never thought to see it again. You have brought two treasures to me, it seems. You will not return to Joyous Garde empty-handed."

Lancelot's eyes turned smoky. "Yes, I suppose I must leave soon, before Ida decides to revolt."

"Surely, you can stay a few days yet, Lance," Gwenhwyfar pleaded.

Arthur looked from one to the other and then reached for Gwenhwyfar's hand. "You know I have vowed to help Judwal keep the Franks out of Armorica? I'm sure at some point Childebert will march westward, and we'll have to stand and fight. There's no need to put you in harm's way, when I am neither king here nor you, queen."

"What do you mean?"

"Simply this." Arthur took a deep breath and touched her face lightly. "I want you to return to Britain with Lancelot."

Lancelot stared at Arthur while Gwenhwyfar threw him a startled look. She turned back to Arthur. "I'm your wife. Don't I belong with you?"

Dear God, help me through this. "I am Armel now and officially, you have been declared dead." Arthur smiled weakly. "Marriage vows no longer bind you."

"But..."

Arthur held up his hand, silencing her. "You made the ultimate sacrifice once, to save my life after Cam's Landing. We almost didn't get you back. Only Lancelot's love and determination did that. I'll not ask for more than you've already done."

"But I love you, too, Arthur...I always have."

"I know, Gwenhwyfar, that you care; you feel duty bound to stay with me. But your heart loves Lancelot; it's not something you can help. Myrddin warned me, long ago."

Gwenhwyfar chewed her lip and stared at the floor, silent.

"I have a different mission now," Arthur said gently. "I believe I was saved at Cam's Landing to mentor young Judwal as Myrddin trained me.

He may be the last truly Breton leader Armorica has." He grinned suddenly. "Do you know the people think Armel is a holy man? A warrior turned hermit and wise? Bringing a wife into my life, especially you, Gwenhwyfar, who still look so young and beautiful...you would probably be recognized. Better that you return to Britain."

Her eyes held the depths of the forest's green shadows. "I am forever cursed to love the both of you. Can we not find a way for the three of us to be together?"

Arthur sighed. "Lancelot and I have competed for you for over thirty years. It's time for one of us to concede." Arthur drew a ragged breath and willed himself to say the final sentence, knowing it wasn't true. "Lancelot loves you more than I do."

He reached for Lancelot's hand, placing it over Gwenhwyfar's. "I did this once before, after Cam's Landing." He looked deeply into her eyes. "Don't refuse this a second time." He turned to Lancelot. "Take care of her, Brother."

He left them sitting in stunned muteness. Stoically, he maintained his dignity passing through the halls and bailey until he was inside his own quarters. Then, he sobbed as uncontrollably as a small child; now that she was finally home, he'd truly lost Gwenhwyfar forever.

~ Chapter 13—Home ~

The first person Gwenhwyfar saw when she and Lancelot stepped off the boat at Portus Adurni a fortnight later was Cynric. His sky blue eyes looked over her appreciatively.

"You're as beautiful as ever, my lady." He kissed her hand and held it for a moment, grinning indolently at Lancelot's slight frown. "The first time I admired her you cuffed me, if I remember correctly."

"You deserved it," Lancelot answered.

Gwenhwyfar smiled. "You were rather arrogant for a young man."

Cynric laughed. "I still am, only now I have to compete with Ceawlin." He signaled one of the dockworkers to take their belongings to the waiting wagon. "But come, we can talk as we ride."

"How's Cerdic?" Lancelot asked as they rode back to Cynric's holding.

Cynric was slow to answer. "My father died several months ago."

"I'm so sorry," Gwenhwyfar leaned over and put her hand on his arm. "I wish Arthur had been here." For all their near battles, Cerdic and Arthur respected each other.

Cynric glanced curiously at her. "Where is Arthur? Have you seen him since your return? He disappeared nearly two years ago."

"He's found a quest," she answered hesitantly, "but he wishes to remain unknown in its pursuit. I can say no more."

"You're not to be a part of that, my lady?" Cynric asked softly.

"No. Arthur thought it not wise."

She saw him glance over her head toward Lancelot. "So your champion has brought you back to Camelot."

She nodded. "You might as well know, Cynric. Arthur severed our bonds when I was declared dead. Lancelot and I were married in Benoic before we left." *It had been a short, private ceremony. Lancelot had insisted it was only fitting she be his wife. She could still see the sadness on Arthur's face when they broke the news to him. She'd gently asked him not to attend the vowmaking, but he'd replied that Lancelot had been forced to listen to theirs and she'd been forced to listen to Lancelot and Elaine's. He would not spare himself the pain. Then he'd added: 'This will make it final.'*

Cynric's eyes widened in surprise and Gwenhwyfar thought back to what a friend he'd turned out to be.

Lancelot grinned at Cynric. "I recommend the institution of marriage highly. You ought to try it."

Cynric smiled slightly. "If your wife has a twin, mayhap I will."

They stayed at Cynric's another day before moving on to Camelot.

"So Arthur decided to remain in Léon?" Custennin poured more wine for the small group seated at the round table. Peredur took a sip as Galahad declined the drink.

So my son still does not imbibe. Lancelot nodded. "Judwal is young; there's always the threat of assassination. Childebert will be aware of your men there, led by Guinglain and aided by your emissary, Armel."

Custennin looked thoughtful. "Childebert invaded Burgundia. Once he's established command, I wonder where his ambitions will lie?"

Peredur shifted in his chair. "Do you think he'll cross the channel to aid Wehha?"

"Wehha?" Lancelot looked at him sharply. "I've been gone too long. Is there trouble in Anglia?"

Custennin answered. "None yet. Our scouts say Wehha is amassing arms since Cerdic's death."

"He thinks he can take Cerdic's lands from Cynric?"

The king shrugged. "Cynric may prefer not to fight."

"He'll defend his lands!" Gwenhwyfar interrupted. "He's been ally to Camelot, even when his father was alive. Surely, you'll aid him and not let Wehha advance."

Custennin sighed deeply and Lancelot almost grinned. The new king *didn't think women should take part in men's discussions. He was probably wondering why she couldn't act like other women. Ah, Gwen. I love you for being you.*

"No, my lady. For certes, we prefer an ally to hold the land." He turned to Lancelot. "Now that you're back, I can pull my men from Joyous Garde and strengthen my own troops."

Lancelot raised an eyebrow. "Have your men been needed to supplement my own? Trouble lies there, too?"

"Ida's acquired a mercenary—a Saracen—a hardened warrior of great skill, I heard. His army is being trained with cavalry horses like you and Arthur favored. I thought a show of support from me might keep them from scheming too grandly."

"By Mithras! Do you know anything about this man? Who is he?"

Custennin shook his head. "I don't know his name. He dresses in traditional robes and headgear. I know ships have been seen docking with horses on board."

"Hmm." Lancelot frowned. "I'll find out when I get back. But I'll need your men there a short while longer. Gwen and I are going to visit Nimue and then get Elen from Cameliard before going to Joyous Garde."

Peredur turned to Gwenhwyfar. "Your home is here, in Camelot. Why are you going to Joyous Garde?"

She smiled happily. "My home is Joyous Garde now. Lancelot and I are married." Total silence encompassed that remark. She looked bewildered and turned to Lancelot. "You sent word ahead, didn't you?"

He stared at his son, whose handsome face had turned ashen. "I didn't think..."

Galahad sprang from his chair. "Have you no honor?" Without another word, he turned on his heel and strode out of the room, his mouth set in a tight, grim line.

Custennin glanced at Lancelot. "Does Arthur know about this?"

"He does." Lancelot was angry now and on his feet. "Galahad has no right to judge us nor do any of you. I'm going to—"

"No." Gwenhwyfar was on her feet, a hand on Lancelot's arm. "I plundered into this. Let me go talk to him."

"He deserves to be horse-whipped."

"Your temper will only convince him he's right."

Lancelot gripped the edge of his chair's back. "He's my son."

"And he lived with me at Camelot," she answered. "Let me try first. Please."

She looked at him and he felt a war of emotions. *I'm supposed to be the fearsome fighter whose name alone inspires young men, yet I can't refuse this woman.* He sighed, leaned, and kissed her. "Go."

"Galahad." Gwenhwyfar stepped into his room and walked over to sit on the edge of the bed. "I'm sorry the news was such a shock to you."

Stoic silence.

She tried again. "Surely, you know your father and I have loved each other for many years."

"You were Arthur's wife. The king's wife." Galahad turned a stony face to her. "I never wanted to believe the rumors; I knew of my father's reputation, but I always thought you virtuous." He turned away again. "Now I find out you're both traitors."

"That's a strong word, Galahad. One Arthur would not use."

"No?" He looked at her unbelievingly. "Don't tell me he knew my father was seducing his wife."

"Your father never seduced me." She reached for his hand, but he pulled it away. "I was only six and ten when my father gave me to Arthur. I didn't want to get married—to anyone—and I didn't know him. I was scared. Lancelot was sent to escort me; he befriended me and eased some of my fears. He was so easy for me to talk to. By the time we arrived at Camelot, I felt I had known your father all my life."

"If you were already in love with him, why did you marry Arthur?"

Gwenhwyfar sighed. "I was too young to recognize the feelings and I was duty-bound to marry. I would have shamed my brother and my father, to say nothing of the insult rendered to Arthur in front of his men."

"You never loved your husband then?"

"I did. I grew to love him. I shared his dreams of a united Britain, one of peace and prosperity. I envisioned myself helping him achieve his goals. To think of a world where blood isn't shed...you know the vision, Galahad. It's the reason why you seek the Grail."

"The Grail..." He paused. "It led my father to you, you know."

"Yes." She leaned forward. "Do you think we'd have been so blessed if our love was wrong?"

He looked unsettled. "But Arthur is alive. How can you be married to my father?"

"Do you remember the morning after Cam's Landing? Before Arthur was placed on the barge?"

"Yes."

"Arthur relinquished me to Lancelot. He told him to take care of me."

"The king thought he was dying."

"And I made the decision to go with Arthur to prevent that. It was the hardest thing I've ever done." Galahad did not respond and Gwenhwyfar was silent for some minutes. Then she said softly, "Arthur could not bring me back. I would not be here except for your father's love."

Galahad looked away. "I think I understand now why my father never cared for my mother, but why did he marry her?"

She touched the side of his face, only to find it wet. "Elaine had made arrangements to meet him, only he thought he'd be seeing me. I nearly had been maimed for life that day and he thought I needed him. They were discovered. He did the honorable thing. He married her." *No need to tell him Arthur had forced the marriage to avoid becoming a cuckolded king that men would not follow.* "Honor, Galahad. You insulted your father greatly today."

His voice shook when he asked, "How angry is he?"

"Enough to make most men cringe." She paused. "Why don't you stay in here until he's calmer?"

"I'm not a child. I'll face him." Galahad stood. "The standard punishment for insubordination among the ranks is flogging and Lancelot is still a captain in the king's army." He took a deep breath. "Will he do the whipping himself?"

She paled, recalling the public flogging Arthur had given his own son, so many years ago, when Medraut had wounded Lancelot. *Holy Mary, not again. That had turned Medraut against his father for all time.*

She lifted her head and squared her shoulders. "There will be no whipping."

While Gwenhwyfar was speaking to Galahad, Lancelot paced furiously, occasionally stopping to slam the table with his fist. Peredur squirmed in his chair, opened his mouth to speak then closed it

"What is it with you?" Custennin asked irritably. "Did some woman give you the pox?"

Peredur reddened. "No, Sire. I wanted to say something to Lancelot."

Lancelot stopped pacing. "What?"

He swallowed hard. "About Galahad. He didn't mean what he said."

"Oh? What makes you think that, Peredur?"

"After you disappeared from the chapel...he said there were so many things he'd never told you. He was afraid you were gone forever."

Lancelot regarded him silently.

"Arthur sent us back to inform Nimue what had happened."

"My son actually stepped foot on Avallach?"

"Yes. He's been there before." Peredur hurried on as Lancelot lifted an eyebrow. "Before Cam's Landing. The queen took us there for safety as the Saxons advanced. Anyway, he asked Nimue what he could do to help bring you back."

"Go on."

"She told him to keep you in his thoughts, to visualize your return. To pray to his Christos. To look for signs, and for both of us to continue our quest for the Grail. Then, a week ago, he started having recurring dreams of the procession I'd seen at my uncle's house."

"At Pelles'?" Lancelot's thoughts left Galahad as he remembered his own dream the night he'd spent there. "What kind of procession?"

"A man carrying a lance, a girl with a platter, boys with candlesticks, and another girl...carrying something...it's always unclear what, but I think it's the Grail."

Lancelot stared at him. He'd seen the procession, too. "The Grail. Do you think it's at Carbonek?"

"I don't know. My uncle told me only someone pure in heart would eventually be able to heal him. And Galahad has been praying ever harder since you left. Mayhap, somehow it's all tied together."

"Why haven't you left then? Why are you here?"

"That's what I wanted to say. When we got word you were returning, Galahad insisted on waiting. He wanted to ask your forgiveness."

"Instead, he insulted me...and Gwenhwyfar, too."

"Don't be too hard on him, Lancelot," Custennin intervened. "You surprised the hellfire out of me, as well."

"Are you going to pass judgment also?" Lancelot's eyes grew darker.

Custennin gave him a tight smile. "No. I'm saying no one expected Gwenhwyfar to ever return, let alone as your wife. You can't blame us for being shocked; Arthur probably was, too."

"Arthur condoned this," Lancelot started to say, but was interrupted as Gwenhwyfar and Galahad came through the door. He waited.

Galahad stepped up to him. "I apologize for insulting you, Father. I'm ready to accept the punishment for my actions." He stood at military attention, his eyes not wavering from his father's penetrating glare.

Lancelot regarded him. "The standard is flogging."

Galahad took a deep breath. "Yes, sire."

"No." Gwenhwyfar stepped forward. "This is my fault; I started the whole thing. If you strike him, Lancelot, you'll have to whip me as well."

"My lady, no! Don't say such things!" Galahad spun and sank to his knees, grabbing her hand. "I would take a thousand beatings than have my father harm you."

Something glinted deep within Lancelot's eyes and for a second, the corner of his mouth quirked up. "You're both mad if you think I'd hurt Gwenhwyfar."

She laid her free hand on his arm. "Remember Medraut, Lancelot. Mayhap, Cam's Landing wouldn't have happened if he hadn't hated Arthur so."

"He hated me more, Gwen. Arthur was right to do what he did." He brought her hand up to his lips as he saw the blaze beginning in her eyes. "Medraut tried to kill me, Galahad didn't. I won't flog him."

"Thank you!" Gwenhwyfar threw her arms around his neck and he held her close, his mouth against her ear.

"You are going to make up for this later, I assume?" he whispered.

For an answer, she pressed herself closer to him before stepping away and slanted a look up at him, a knowing smile playing on the corners of her mouth. "I promise."

Nimue took the news of the marriage more serenely. "Arthur knew."

Gwenhwyfar turned away from her study of the white hart tapestry hanging on the wall in the Lady's chambers. The few times she'd been in this room on the Isle she'd always been fascinated with the way the eyes followed her. "What do you mean?"

The priestess inclined her head. "That he would have to give you up. That Myrddin had been right. I think your being in the land of Faerie for so long made it bearable for him, in the end."

"Is that why he didn't pursue her like I did?" Lancelot asked. "Because he felt he'd lost either way?"

She shook her head. "You're wrong to think that, Lancelot. Arthur told me often enough, he'd have exchanged his life for hers."

Gwenhwyfar protested, "But he told me that his life's mission was different now; he no longer had need or want of a wife. I was to return to Britain."

"That doesn't mean his feelings for you changed."

Gwenhwyfar looked at Lancelot, stricken. "Why must my love for you always cause pain?"

Nimue laid her hand on Gwenhwyfar's. "You've caused Arthur much hurt over the years, but this time the cut was clean and swift. You're Lancelot's wife now, what you've both always wanted. Arthur will let you be. The kindest thing you can do now is stay out of his life, forever."

Gwenhwyfar bowed her head. "You're right. You told me long ago, I would have to choose."

"You chose rightly when you came with us to Avalon. Arthur returned that gift when he released your bonds. Appreciate it." She sat back. "I'll take care of Arthur. You said he does not wish to be known?"

"There he is Armel, an emissary of Custennin's. Even Lionel and the few older men of the cohort call him that," Lancelot answered.

"Is your mother's place vacant or has a priestess been appointed?"

"My mother trained no maidens. She was the last at the Black Lake." Lancelot studied her. "Are you thinking of going there?"

She glanced at Gwenhwyfar. "I don't want to see the old religion die."

Gwenhwyfar laughed a little shrilly. "And Arthur is a free man."

"Whether free or married to you has never been the issue," Nimue replied gently. "I chose to remain celibate."

"And now?" Gwenhwyfar asked with a slight tremor in her voice.

Nimue shrugged. "I'm growing older. I want no regrets. Argante is ready to become Lady. Mayhap, I should grant her the title."

Gwenhwyfar felt Lancelot's hand on her shoulder and sagged against him. "For too long, I've selfishly expected the love of both of you. Arthur deserves happiness." She drew a ragged breath. "Go to him, Nimue."

The news wasn't good at Cameliard when they arrived; Gwenhwyfar's father was dying.

"I'm glad you got here," Bedwyr said as he released her from a mighty hug. "He may not recognize you, but let's try."

Aidin had opened the curtains partially, allowing the afternoon sun to cast rays across the massive bed. She met them in the doorway.

"My wife." Bedwyr grinned. "I never thought I'd be a married man."

Gwenhwyfar gave her a huge smile. "I can see the improvements you've made in him already...and in Cameliard. The place is well run."

Aidin returned the smile. "My husband will be much happier now that you're back." She glanced curiously at Lancelot, but it was Bedwyr who asked the question.

"Arthur didn't come?"

"No." Lancelot gave him a direct look. "He released her, Bedwyr. Gwenhwyfar's my wife."

He stared at Lancelot. "So it came to that, after nearly thirty years."

"Be as happy for us as I am for you, Brother," Gwenhwyfar pleaded. "We've already had too many critics."

Bedwyr shook his head. "At least, you finally chose. May Arthur find strength."

"Nimue is going to him," Gwenhwyfar said wryly. "I doubt he'll be lonely for long."

Her brother raised an eyebrow, but before he could respond, Leodegrance interrupted. "Who's there?"

Gwenhwyfar went to the bed. "It's me, Da. Come home at last."

"Daughter?" His rheumy eyes peered through the dim light at her. The hand shook as he tried to raise it and she held it in both of hers. A terrific coughing spasm racked the skeletal body. "Where have you been?" His weak voice was quite lucid.

She hesitated. "I've been hostage, but Lancelot rescued me."

"Lancelot, eh? Why not your husband?" He looked around. "Where is Arthur?"

Gwenhwyfar exchanged glances with Lancelot, then turned back to her father. "In Armorica, Da, helping young Judwal to hold Léon."

Another fit of coughing overcame him and she heard the faint rattle of his lungs. "You know your brother's married?"

"Yes, Da. A fine girl."

"Who?"

"Aiden, Bedwyr's wife."

"Never met her. Who's that?" He tried to point at Lancelot. "Arthur! Well-come home, boy."

Lancelot approached resignedly. "Good to see you, sire."

Gwenhwyfar gave him a desperate look. "Mayhap you should get some rest, Da."

"I don't want to. I'm waiting for my daughter to come home."

"I'm home." Tears welled in her eyes, "Look, Da. It's Gwenhwyfar."

"Are you my new nurse? I need that window open," he said irritably as another seizure overtook him, spending his strength.

Gwenhwyfar felt a light touch on her arm. Turning, she saw Aidin's sympathetic face. She wasn't sure she wanted pity.

"I'll take care of him now. Bedwyr will explain."

Before she left, she leaned down and kissed him. "Rest well, Da."

"Guenhumara?" He was asking for his dead wife and tears welled in Gwenhwyfar's eyes. "Ah, my dear…I'm coming."

Bedwyr waited in the living quarters, a tall, dark-haired child beside him. They both turned at the sound of footsteps.

Elen smiled, her smoky eyes lighting up at the sight of her father. She ran to him and threw her arms around his waist. "Da! You've been gone too long." She looked at Gwenhwyfar curiously. "Who're you?"

Lancelot bent down to hug his daughter. "I'm glad to see you, too. Must you always be so direct?"

"She takes after you, Lance." Gwenhwyfar laughed and turned to the child. "You can only be Elen. I'm Gwenhwyfar."

Elen's eyes widened. "But...you're dead."

"Rumors," she said. "I was held hostage. Your father rescued me."

"And Da brought you here to live with your brother?"

"Gwenhwyfar is coming with us to Joyous Garde, Elen," Lancelot answered as he took a seat. "No more questions right now. Sit with us while we talk to Bedwyr."

She opened her mouth to speak, then closed it again at a glance from her father. She sat beside him, frowning slightly as Gwenhwyfar took her place on his other side.

"He seems to have gotten worse since I last saw him," Lancelot said.

Bedwyr nodded. "Most of the time he doesn't recognize anyone. But the cough came on suddenly. The medic says his lungs are filled with fluid. There's not much we can do."

"Aidin takes good care of him," Gwenhwyfar remarked.

"I help, too," Elen added. "I read to him."

"Has your Latin improved?" Lancelot asked. "Nimue promised you a visit on Avallach if it did."

"I'm ready," she replied confidently. "Uncle Bedwyr said he'd give me a real horse, instead of a pony, if I studied every day."

"You like to ride?" Gwenhwyfar asked with a smile.

"Yes. And I'm good." The ten-year-old regarded Gwenhwyfar somberly. "Do you ride?"

Lancelot leaned over. "She does, and she can teach you a thing or two."

Elen turned her dark gaze on her father. "You promised to teach me, Da."

"We'll both teach you," Lancelot answered and turned back to Bedwyr. "What are Leodegrance's chances of recovery?"

"Not good. A few days, a week, mayhap two."

"Then I'll stay here." Gwenhwyfar turned to Lancelot. "If you must see to matters with Ida, I can come later."

His eyes darkened and she caught the disappointment in them. "I'd rather we travel together," he said carefully.

Bedwyr was equally subtle in front of Elen. "You would be safer traveling with Lancelot and there's really no need to stay. Da's mind is elsewhere; he won't know if you're here or not."

"But he's dying! I want to be with him to the last." Gwenhwyfar was outraged her brother would suggest such a thing.

"So be it." Lancelot draped an arm around Gwenhwyfar's shoulder. "If you have the room, we'll all stay and see this through."

Elen looked astonished then narrowed her eyes slightly as she seemed to consider Gwenhwyfar in a new light.

Gwenhwyfar didn't notice, for she was smiling warmly at Lancelot. "Thank you, my... Thank you for understanding."

As it turned out, the wait was over in two days. Leodegrance was laid to rest beside the grave of his beloved wife on the hillside behind the villa. Lancelot's party was on their way the third day.

Lancelot watched now as Gwenhwyfar rode ahead of him with Elen. His daughter had been unusually quiet when he'd told her they were married. Even now, her answers were monosyllables and she made no effort to engage in conversation.

Her face brightened as they approached the gate and she saw Augusta standing on the steps to the Great Hall. She kicked her horse to a canter, obviously forgetting this was not her pony, and the big animal sprang forward, nearly unseating her. Gwenhwyfar caught up with her and grabbed the reins.

Embarrassed, Elen mumbled, "I'm all right."

"What in thunder did you think you were doing?" Lancelot brought his stallion alongside. "Always walk the horses through the gate."

She reddened. "Yes, Da."

Augusta had seen the near accident and hobbled as fast as she could toward them. "My child…" And then she stopped, gaping at Gwenhwyfar. "My Lady." She tried to curtsy, but Gwenhwyfar had already slipped from the saddle and stopped her. "I had no idea you were coming here. I'll have a room prepared at once."

"No need for that." Lancelot draped an arm around Gwenhwyfar's shoulders. "This time, she'll be sharing mine."

The old woman sputtered, "My lord, would that be wise in front of the child?" She looked around, but Elen was already walking her horse to the stables.

Lancelot grinned. "Don't you think it proper my wife share my bed?"

"My lord? Are you making fun of an old woman?" She pursed her mouth.

"Not at all." Lancelot gave the wrinkled cheek a quick kiss. "I've finally done the honorable thing and married her."

A sharp cough caused him to turn. He found Lupin staring at him. "You might as well tell the men," Lancelot said, much as he'd done the first time he brought Gwenhwyfar to Joyous Garde years ago. "Arthur consented to this. That's all they need to know for now."

Lupin's face remained immobile as he gave a quick nod. "Will you be having a feast of celebrations? I'll send out hunting parties this afternoon and tell the cooks—"

"Do that," Lancelot interrupted, "but prepare for tomorrow night. Gwenhwyfar and I will be dining in this evening." He took her hand and bowed over it formally, "Will my lady do me the honor of accompanying me to my quarters?"

He nearly laughed as he watched Gwenhwyfar trying hard to match his mock-seriousness. Finally, she managed. "If it pleases my lord."

A corner of his mouth quirked up. "I believe pleasing me will be easy to do."

Gwenhwyfar stopped just inside the door to Lancelot's bedroom. He'd gone to sit on the edge of the bed and now looked at her expectantly.

"Are you turning shy on me, Gwen?"

"No. I just wanted a moment to remember this room." Her eyes circled around, taking in the simple, sturdy furniture. A wardrobe and dresser along one wall, table and chairs by the window on the other side and the large four poster bed opposite her. The locked cabinet with its special toys. The tapestry—the one her mother had woven for her and she'd left with him—was still here. Its silver unicorn watched her from behind a tree. "It's as it was."

Lancelot came to stand behind her, arms encircling her waist, resting his head against hers. "I've not had need to change anything. I'll provide you with any creature comforts you want."

"A mirror might be nice."

"For you or for above the bed?"

Gwenhwyfar smiled wickedly. "I don't need to see my face."

"Ah, Gwen." He nuzzled her neck as one hand swept her abdomen, pressing her back against him. "Feel what you do to me."

She wiggled her hips appreciatively. He groaned and fondled a breast with his other hand, moving Gwenhwyfar closer to the bed.

"I'd like to wash the road dust off first." Reluctantly, she caught his hand. "The baths still work, don't they?"

"They do," he murmured, his hand going back to what it was doing. "But I'm not letting you out of my sight. I'll have the tub filled in the dressing room and do the honors of bathing you myself."

"Lancelot! You'll push Augusta to her grave. She'll be horrified."

"Things will be changing now that I have you here. They might as well get used to it." He stepped out to the hallway where the chamberlain waited. "Hot water for the tub and bring the lady's things to my room."

The man's eyes widened slightly. "Do you want me to send one of the maids?"

Lancelot grinned. "I think I can undress my own wife."

Gwenhwyfar noted the look of surprise the man tried to hide as he hurried away. Within minutes, hot buckets of water arrived. Lancelot bolted the door after the last servant exited and turned to Gwen. Steam rose from the tub, causing tiny ringlets to form on the wayward hair that had escaped from the mass piled atop Gwenhwyfar's head.

Lancelot brushed two of them off her forehead as he helped her into the fragrant water. He dribbled the soapy sponge across her back and shoulders then leaned over to encircle each breast. Gwenhwyfar closed her eyes and lay back on the side of the tub, enjoying the sensation.

"I'm going to have to join you if I'm going to do an adequate job of this." At the sound of clothing being removed, Gwenhwyfar opened an eye to watch him strip. His body was still magnificent, lean and firm.

"I don't think I'm going to get my bath with you in that condition." She giggled as he stepped in and splashed her.

"You'll get your bath. I always fulfill a promise." Lancelot moved the sponge across her stomach and then down one thigh. "It just may take a little longer." He began moving the sponge up the inside of the other leg. She gasped when his hand found its intended mark and then moaned in earnest as the soft, circling movements massaged her, the pressure gently increasing.

His lips were moist from the mist as he pulled her toward him for a deep kiss, easing himself into a sitting position beneath her, draping her legs over his hips, his hands pressing on her back, holding her close.

"From the moment I brought you back, I've dreamed of this time, when finally we'd be home, here in these very rooms, doing what we're doing." Lancelot tasted her mouth again. "Nothing will part us again."

Gwenhwyfar tightened her arms around his neck, spreading her fingers across his shoulders, feeling the hard muscles and the scar from the ax so many years ago. "Don't say that, Lance. It scares me. I'm afraid something will happen. I still don't believe this is real."

"We're home, Gwen. Here. I'm real." He grinned at her expression as he suddenly inserted himself. "Need I say more?"

In response, she ravaged his mouth, wanting more and more of him, urging him deeper inside as she wrapped her legs tightly around him and they lost themselves to the ancient ritual.

News of their return reached Ida within days. "Lancelot is back," he told Morgana and Medraut, "and he's brought a wife along."

"What?" Morgana asked unbelievingly. "Lancelot married? To whom?"

"That's the interesting part," Ida sat back, taking his time to answer. "The woman's name is Gwenhwyfar, same as the former queen's."

Medraut sat up straighter. "What does she look like?"

"I haven't seen her. The reports are she's a looker, even though she's not young. Wild, reddish hair."

It is she. Morgana watched as Medraut schooled his features to remain calm. She knew his blood was probably on fire. Somehow, Lancelot had found Gwenhwyfar. *Damn that whore.*

"That sounds like the queen." Medraut's eyes held a strange glint.

Ida waved his hands expansively. "Lancelot was gone a long time. Mayhap, he searched the convents until he found her."

"If it's Gwenhwyfar, then Arthur must be dead; Lancelot probably killed him," Medraut said.

Morgana narrowed her eyes thoughtfully. "I don't think Lancelot is capable of that. Their bonds—all three of them—were too strong."

"My father was willing to kill me for wanting her," Medraut replied.

"Arthur never loved you, Medraut. He loves both Gwenhwyfar and Lancelot." Morgana was bitter.

"For certes, my father would not simply give her to Lancelot!" Medraut looked at his mother incredulously.

"Don't be too sure of that, Son," Morgana reminded him. "He arranged for Lancelot to rescue her from the trial that I forced and he let her stay at Joyous Garde for two years."

"Only to save his precious Fellowship of the Round Table," Medraut responded heatedly. "A lot of his own men who felt like I did."

"Still,"—Morgana remained unruffled by her son's mounting temper—"if Arthur has hidden himself away somewhere, this may be a ploy. He wants us to think him dead."

Medraut stared at her. "If I were married to Gwenhwyfar, I wouldn't let her live with another man and definitely not that fey bastard who was courtesan-trained!"

"Fey and courtesan trained?" Ida interrupted. "Are you making him a legend?"

"It's true," Medraut answered hotly. "He's the bastard son of the Lady of the Black Lake...a high priestess. Gwalchmai was forever comparing his prowess against Lancelot's, claiming the ladies didn't find him lacking, even though he had not the benefit of courtesan-training."

"It's hard to see where Arthur's men had energy for fighting," Ida said mildly, grinning.

"Regardless of who this woman is," Morgana interrupted, "she may keep Lancelot busy enough not to notice our gathering forces. Now that Cerdic is dead and Childebert has taken Burgundia, the net draws closer to move. Wehha is probably thinking the same thing."

"I suppose, as a good neighbor, I could express my congratulations on his marriage," Ida said, "and reassure him I intend to honor the treaty."

Morgana smiled sweetly. "How wise of you. And, if the woman is Gwenhwyfar, mayhap you can let something slip about Arthur." *And tonight, when I lay with you, I'll mind-meld, painful as it is, and extract your thoughts.*

He smiled back benevolently. "I think I can do that."

She started to caress Ida's cheek when the sharp pain nearly blinded her. Then, she was inside Medraut's head. *"If this is Gwenhwyfar, I'll find a way to get to her. And when I do, I'll show her what pleasure she could have had. And when Lancelot tries to rescue her, I'll kill him. She'll finally belong to me."*

Horrified, she stared at her son. His eyes had glazed and the lewd smile held a hint of the old madness. *Not again. Gwenhwyfar will have to be dealt with. Once and for all time.*

~ Chapter 14— The End of the Quest ~

"There's a new Lady inhabiting the cave at Black Lake." Judwal looked up from the message he'd just received at the high table after the noon meal. "Do you suppose she's a true mystic or an impostor?"

Armel frowned. Lancelot had told him no maidens had been trained to take his mother's position. "Do you know where she comes from?"

"No. According to this, people who've seen her say she's neither young nor old." He pushed back his dinner plate and speculated. "Do you suppose she's a witch?"

"I doubt the powers the cave holds would allow a witch to stay there." Armel smiled at Judwal's shocked face. "Even though Christianity has a strong hold here, the Old Ways still linger. You must be tolerant."

He narrowed his brown eyes. "Sometimes, tolerance can be seen as weakness."

"That's why Custennin's cohort is backing you," Armel answered. "The sword is still mighty to those who are unwilling to accept peace."

"Did Arthur hold back the Saxons with the sword or with talk?"

"Arthur had to fight, many times over." Armel looked away for a moment then turned back to Judwal. "But he spared lives and offered peace to any who would pledge fidelity to him."

The young duke was silent for some moments. "Will I ever be that wise?"

"You're not quite twenty. Wisdom takes awhile. I'm not sure I've attained it."

"You?" Judwal looked surprised. "All of Armorica thinks you a holy man. A warrior, for certes, but a saint as well, for keeping the Franks away. You've even been compared to Saint Germanus."

Arthur was amused. "I assure you I'm no saint." He became serious. "I'm only repaying the service a wise man once gave me. Let's return to the subject at hand. Mayhap, this new Lady was sent from Avallach..." He froze suddenly. *Nimue*. Her image floated through his mind as clearly as Judwal in front of him. *Is it you?* "Mayhap, I should travel to Black Lake."

"You aren't afraid of her powers? I've heard those ancient priestesses could bewitch a Christian with a magic look."

If only you knew how easily she could enthrall me. Aloud he said, "Man has free will; only those who are willing to submit, will do so."

Judwal nodded. "Go with God, then, and return safely."

She was waiting for him in the glade. Throughout his ride, her image had become stronger and stronger until he no longer had any doubts.

Yet, when he saw her, the sunlight radiating from the pale, shimmering hair, the white gossamer gown floating around her small, slight frame, he was struck dumb. He pulled the charger to a halt and sat still in the saddle, staring.

Nimue smiled. “You came sooner than I thought.”

Her words released Arthur. Sliding from the horse, he reached her side in three strides, lifting and holding her tightly to him. He pressed his face into her hair. “It’s been nearly three years, Nimue. When did you get here? Why didn’t you send for me?” With a small sigh, he placed her on the ground, but kept his hands around her waist.

“I’ve not been here long. I didn’t wish to arouse suspicions; I knew word would get to you soon enough.”

“Do I dare hope you’re planning to live here, at Niniane’s cave?” His grey eyes searched her face intently. *Tell me yes, Nimue. Tell me yes.*

Nimue smiled. “If the Goddess wills, I’ll seek maidens to train so the Old Religion lives on and does not die.”

“Is that the only reason?” His hands brought her closer.

She traced his jaw hesitantly with her fingertips. “Not the only reason.”

Arthur inclined his head, hardly daring to ask. “You came for me?”

“I-I don’t want to grow old without knowing what it is to be a woman.”

“As I recall, I’ve already made you a woman.” He grinned boyishly. “I’ll be happy to remind you.”

Nimue blushed. “Your Kingmaking was a ritual.” She looked deeply into his eyes and he felt he was drowning in an aquamarine sea. “This time I want to pleasure you, too. You’re the only man I’ve ever cared about.”

His strong fingers gently traced the curve of her cheek. “You please me with your presence, Nimue. Now more than ever.” Arthur ran a finger lightly over her lips and tentatively, her mouth closed over it. He paused, enjoying the sensation. “Mayhap we should go inside before I lose my wits and take you here in the open.”

They walked arm in arm into the cave. When they got to the antechamber, Arthur lifted Nimue in his arms and carried her to the bed. Even though his hair was nearly white and the lines in his face had deepened, the muscular arms retained their strength. She watched him undo his shirt, admiring the still-taut belly, but when he slid his trews off and she saw the erectness there, she looked quickly away.

Arthur lay down beside her. “Are you afraid?”

“A little,” she answered, still not looking directly at him.

He gathered her to him like a small child. “I won’t hurt you; we’ll take this slowly.” He gave her a series of small kisses across the forehead and cheeks and felt some of the tension disappear. His lips brushed hers once, twice...then he kissed her, softly at first until she began to respond, and then with eagerness he hadn’t known in years.

Instinctively, Nimue pressed her body closer to his and he kneaded her buttocks, then slid his hands upward, stroking her back. "I think you've got too many clothes on," he murmured against her mouth. "Let me take care of that."

He took his time undressing her, reveling in her soft skin, allowing his fingers to discover which areas made her shudder in delight. She gasped as he suckled her breasts and dug her short nails into his shoulders, causing him to increase the pressure. Eventually, he probed the warm softness between her thighs, pleasantly surprised to find it wet.

Timidly, Nimue reached to touch him, then snatched her hand back quickly as the tip of him jutted sharply against her.

Arthur laughed. "It does that when it likes someone."

She delicately traced the length, smiling now, as the phallus grew larger. He moaned and she stopped. "Am I hurting you?"

"No." He smiled and placed her hand where it had been. "Just the opposite. It brings me much pleasure."

She fondled him harder then. "What else can I do for you?"

Arthur rolled over with her. "You can claim me as your man, now and forever."

"How do I do that?" Nimue's eyes were huge in her pale face.

Arthur made a growling sound, low in his throat. "Let me show you, my lady."

They lost themselves then in their passion until they lay exhausted in each other's arms. Arthur held her curled into the crook of his arm as she drifted off to sleep. *I think I understand now, Gwenhwyfar's passion for Lancelot.* He leaned over and whispered in her ear. "I love you, Nimue." *I've sought this fulfillment and never knew it; my quest is over.*

Galahad drew a shaky breath as he reined in his horse and looked up the hill at Carbonek. The dreams had become more vivid each night as they drew nearer. The Grail had to be here. He turned to Peredur.

"If it's not here, I don't know what else we can do."

Peredur nodded. "Are we just going to ask him if he has it?"

Galahad frowned. "I don't know that he knows he has it. Wouldn't he have said something to one of us since he knew we were looking for it?"

Peredur shrugged. "He's my uncle and your grandfather, but neither of us is close to him."

"I lived here until I was eight," Galahad answered, "but he stayed in his rooms so much of the time, always in pain."

"I wonder why his wound never healed?"

"My mother would never talk about it." Galahad urged his horse to a trot and Peredur's followed naturally. He looked toward the Great Hall. "Mayhap, this visit will be more successful."

Peredur was relieved to see his uncle was in no worse shape as they were ushered into his upstairs quarters. Pelles was reclining on a couch in his upstairs' quarters, his leg extended along its length.

"So you're both back. Come and sit. Tell me where your adventures have taken you the last three years."

When Galahad had finished, Pelles said softly, "So your father finally got what he's desired for over thirty years. Your poor mother never stood a chance."

Galahad looked away. "No. Neither did the king."

Pelles repositioned his leg with a slight moan. "She's bewitched them both, it seems."

"No, Sire!" Peredur was startled. "The queen has no magic about her; she's just naturally strong and spirited, not afraid to speak her mind."

"Most men prefer their women docile," Pelles remarked wryly. "Even more evidence she dabbles in some mysteries."

"I don't think so," Galahad answered. "She professes to be Christian."

The old man sounded sharp. "So you defend her, too?"

Galahad set his jaw. "Not exactly. Both my father and the king let their guard down around her. I've always thought women dangerous."

"You've spoken well enough of my sister." Peredur smiled.

"Dindrane is different. She doesn't give me simpering looks or expect compliments. She talks about things a man understands. I felt as comfortable with her as I do with you."

Peredur was silent, remembering how easy it had been to talk to Blanchefleur. *Would that I could see her again!* His reverie was broken by the appearance of a blonde maiden bearing a platter of food. She looked familiar, but he didn't think she'd been there on his last visit.

"Thank you," Pelles said as she set down the platter. She smiled and glided away gracefully. He gave her a strange look. "She must be new."

As they ate, their conversation turned to matters of the Grail. Galahad finally asked, "Grandfather, if the Grail can heal the land, would it be able to heal your leg?"

Pelles sighed. "I don't know. I received this wound because of the great sin of pride. I bragged at a banquet I gave that I had the Christos' cup that would provide whatever dish a guest desired, just as our Lord had prepared the feast of loaves and fishes." The Fisher King shook his head regretfully. "I guarded the Grail jealously and one of my guests, Balin, accused me of not having it at all because I wouldn't show it. I was afraid someone might try to steal it. I forgot to have faith in God. One thing led to another. Balin and I fought..." Pelles paused, remembering. "I did another foolish thing then."

"You don't have to explain, Grandfather."

"I've kept the secret for so many years, it's time I unburden myself." Pelles adjusted his leg. "Some months later, Balin returned to apologize, but I wouldn't accept it. He offered to be my champion, since I couldn't fight; he'd even brought a blank shield, saying he would earn the right to put devices on it."

"You turned him away?" Galahad looked puzzled. "That's not such a sin."

"No. I didn't turn him away." He became silent. "His twin, Balan, was staying with my neighbor, having just come from Meliot where he slew a Scotti warlord named Goholt. He'd brought back the man's charger and armor and was boasting that with the new horse and thicker lance, he could beat anyone in the joust."

"Even Lancelot?" Peredur asked.

"Lancelot had not yet come to Britain. Arthur knew nothing of this challenge. I told Balin he would have to prove himself. He would have to fight the man who was so full of conceit. I did not tell him it was his brother."

"Who won?" Peredur prodded.

"Neither." Pelles took a deep breath. "They killed each other, not ever knowing whom they fought." He straightened himself on the couch. "That is why the wound will not heal; I caused their deaths because of my pride. I was not worthy to be the Grail-keeper any longer."

They were all quiet for some time. Galahad finally said, "So the Grail is not here."

Pelles sighed. "No. The morning after the deaths, I went to the chapel to take it from its secret place. The niche was empty."

Galahad stared at him. "That can't be true! It must be here! The dream I keep having of the Procession...the same one Peredur saw when he visited!"

The old man turned to Peredur. "You saw this yet made no mention?"

Peredur felt himself flush. "I thought they were going to the chapel. Gornemant taught me not to ask so many questions."

"The maiden," Galahad interrupted, "carried the Grail."

Pelles did not answer and Peredur leaned forward. "This time I will ask a question. We've been searching for years, in hope this cup will keep peace in Britain. I say it would be a gift from the Old Ones; Galahad insists it's a Christian relic. Whom does the Grail serve?"

Pelles stared at Peredur. "What...what did you say?" he whispered.

"I asked whom does the Grail serve?"

The blonde maiden entered the room again. This time there was no question of whom she was. Soft light radiated from her and the ethereal shimmer made her almost transparent. She held out her hands and the light seemed to gather itself between them, glowing more intensely until the brilliance nearly blinded them. Peredur shielded his eyes and Galahad stared, dumbstruck. Neither could have moved, even if they'd wanted to.

Soft music surrounded them: vibrant, muted, slowly falling like a soft sigh. They were the music; it was them. And the air! Fragrant with the scent of apple blossoms!

A cup began to form from the essence of raw energy in the maiden's hands. Smooth silver etched itself in runes; a ribbon of gold wound itself around the lip. Pure power emanated from it and washed over them, flooding their souls with a love so vast, so unconditional, so understanding that Peredur wept for pure joy. Galahad and Pelles swiped at tears.

"The Grail serves those who would serve." The voice was molten gold, soft and full, vibrating from the walls.

As suddenly as the force had swept through them, it receded. In front of them now, the maiden held a silver chalice. She smiled at them. "My name is Astrala. I have been waiting for you."

She turned and held the cup out to Pelles.

He looked at her in wonderment and shakily stretched out a hand. "I may touch it again? After my great sin of pride?"

She nodded. "Just this one time. You have earned your freedom from pain."

Pelles clutched the chalice in both hands and held it to his heart. The old man closed his eyes and a smile played across his face. He took several deep breaths before looking at Peredur and Galahad. He slowly stood and took a step.

"Grandfather!" Galahad was on his feet, reaching out to steady him.

Peredur was on his other side, but Pelles motioned them away. "I've been forgiven." He walked to the window and looked down at the bailey where people were going about their daily business. He turned back to Astrala. "How can I thank God?"

She smiled gently and her form began to fade. "Serve your people."

Galahad and Peredur left Carbonek two days later, Pelles completely healed. They stopped at Dinas Emrys on their way south to Camelot. Now, Galahad carefully unwrapped the package in front of Dindrane and set it on the table.

"This is the Grail?" she asked as she looked at the silver cup with its gold rim. "Can I touch it?" She wiped her hands on her breeches.

"Certes," Galahad picked it up and handed it to her. "The cup must needs be handled if it is to bring peace between adversaries."

"The metal feels warm," she said, "but isn't it supposed to glow or something?"

"It can," Galahad said, remembering its first appearance. "I think the Grail has a dual purpose. The cup is material; it is solid and meant to be used. But I think the other purpose is spiritual; the holiness of the relic, from wherever it came, touches the soul. Our personal quest is to become a better person."

"Are you going to take it to Custennin?" Dindrane asked as she reluctantly gave the Grail back.

Galahad tried to ignore the streak of heat that leapt through his arm as their hands touched. "We've been searching for years to do just that. With Ida and Wehha both raising troops, Custennin may want to treaty with them."

"I don't know," Dindrane said as she began pacing, her boots tapping a quick beat. "I think the cup safer in your possession. Custennin may abuse the power."

"You're advising soldiers now?" Dornar asked from the doorway.

Her green eyes flashed fire. "I believe my advice is as solid as yours, Brother!"

"For certes, for what it's worth." Dornar stepped into the room. "I'm sure the king will be willing to listen to a twit of a girl."

She stomped up to him, hands on her hips. "I'm a grown woman and I'm literate. Why should my opinion not count?"

For an answer, he just grinned and pulled lightly on the strand of hair that had escaped the braid. "You'd have to be a bit more ladylike to be accepted at court, I think."

She tossed her head and the braid came undone, framing her face in an auburn cloud of loose curls.

Galahad had the strange urge to reach out and brush her hair back or run his fingers through it. *I wonder if it's as soft as it looks*? He gave himself a shake and inhaled sharply at her next words.

"I think I'll go to court just to prove you wrong. Peredur and Galahad can take me with them." She flashed a defiant glance at Dornar before looking at Peredur. "When are you leaving?"

Peredur stared at her; beside him, Galahad stood as though carved from stone. "Dindrane. I doubt it would be proper for you to travel alone with two men."

"Why not? You're my brother and Galahad would protect me, too. I'd be safe."

Although he was still as a block of marble, Galahad's mind was a spinning whirlwind. *Travel with Dindrane? This is a problem. When last I visited, I felt comfortable around her; now I feel unsettled...confused and like a fire is coursing through my veins.* He realized, suddenly, that she was addressing him.

"Galahad? Have you any objections?"

He smiled weakly, at a loss for words.

"I won't be any trouble. I'll take care of my horse and I won't need a tent; I'll sleep in the open with you."

He prayed his face wasn't turning scarlet. *I know she didn't mean it that way...and why am I so warm? There's no fire in the hearth.* He tugged at the collar of his shirt. She'd taken a step closer to him and he found himself looking into the limpid depths of a green sea.

"I'd be safe with you."

I'm not so sure you would. What in God's name is wrong with me? I've not felt like this since I met Elen, and that was the work of the herbs. He was embarrassed to feel movement beginning inside his trews and he turned quickly toward Dornar, who was watching him strangely.

"There may be bandits along the way; we'd need more men," Galahad managed to choke out. *People, lots of people around. Anything, to protect me...to protect her.*

"And a lady servant as well, to attend your needs," Peredur added.

"I don't need a servant! I can take care of myself." Exasperated, she turned back to Galahad. "Did the queen travel with women?"

More and more, she reminds me of Gwenhwyfar: the independence, the spirit...how can I say no? Is this what Arthur went through? Or my father? Deliver me, Lord!

"Did she?" Dindrane asked again.

"Not often." He was afraid his voice would squeak and cleared his throat. "Like you, she preferred wearing practical trews and shirt to the fancy gowns with all those back fasteners."

"And did King Arthur mind?"

"No, I don't think so." Galahad grasped the new direction for this conversation. "I wish we were taking the Grail to him instead of Custennin. I would know it was in safe hands."

"But he's in Léon," Peredur answered.

"Even more reason for me to go with you." Dindrane's eyes gleamed triumphantly. "I can help protect the Grail."

"Little Sister," Dornar spoke firmly, "there's no need for you to go to Camelot. Let the men make the decisions on the Grail."

"Mayhap if a woman had been its keeper, it wouldn't have been out of sight for so long! Peredur and Galahad have spent years searching; they should rightfully guard it." She shrugged. "Now I know they can't tell a king that. They're his soldiers. But I'm not, and I'm a niece to the old fisher king. I can at least try."

Galahad wondered what his father would think of Dindrane as he watched her lift her chin determinedly and realized they'd lost the argument.

"You're not my mother; I don't have to do what you tell me." Elen shoved the book off the table and folded her arms, scowling.

"I only suggested you spend a little more time on your studies." Gwenhwyfar reached down and retrieved the book. "Women should be literate."

"Why? I hate Latin! I'm going to go for a ride."

"Your father told you no riding until the lesson is finished." Gwenhwyfar opened the book and placed it in front of Elen. "Try the sentence again."

"No. You can't make me." Elen rose from her chair and started to the door, only to find Lancelot blocking it.

"You will apologize to Gwenhwyfar." His voice was flinty.

His daughter turned and ran to the large chair by the hearth and flung herself into it. Lancelot was beside her in three strides. "Do not walk away from me."

Elen curled herself deeper into the chair, her hair covering her face.

"Look at me, young lady, when I'm speaking."

Her chin jutted out as she threw her head up defiantly and met his glare.

"You will apologize for your rudeness and disrespect."

Across the room, Gwenhwyfar sighed. She'd been afraid it would come to this. For six months, Elen had been resistant to her overtures and Gwenhwyfar had ignored the slight barbs and insinuations, knowing Elen was only jealous, since she'd always had Lancelot to herself.

"I'm waiting." Lancelot was clearly running out of patience.

Elen held his gaze a moment, her eyes turning the same smoky color as his. Then her bravado cracked. "I'm sorry," she mumbled.

"You don't sound like it." Lancelot's voice remained harsh.

A small sob began in Elen's throat and Gwenhwyfar watched her fight for control, remembering how hard she'd always resisted breaking down. She felt a twinge of pity.

"Well?" Lancelot asked.

"What do you want me to do, Da?" Elen's voice rose shrilly. "I don't want her here. I've heard the men talk in the stables when they didn't know I was there. She's the reason you hated my mother!"

For a moment, there was dead silence and Gwenhwyfar held her breath. "What else did they say?" Lancelot's voice was soft, much like Arthur's at his most dangerous.

Elen didn't notice. "That when you brought her here, the first time... and my mother came...you wouldn't go near my mother because of her." She continued to rant. "They called her the great whore of Britain, whatever that means."

Gwenhwyfar gasped and Lancelot's face turned cold and hard as marble. "That's enough, Elen. I will take care of this. You will never repeat those words again."

Gwenhwyfar felt the blood drain from her face and was aware of Elen watching her. A sly look crossed the child's face. "Is it a bad thing, that word? They laughed about it."

"Enough!" Lancelot thundered. "Tell me who these men are."

"I don't know who..."

"Do not lie to me, Elen. Ever."

She hung her head. "I can't tell you."

"Give me their names or you'll not set foot in the stables again. Ever."

Elen remained silent, though her shoulders began to shake.

"Very well. You're confined to your room. Meals included."

Gwenhwyfar came and stood beside Lancelot. "Elen," she said gently, "your father cannot keep men who are disloyal. Their conversations were gossip that is many years old. Give yourself a chance to know me."

"I don't want to know you!" Elen jumped up and stomped to the door. "Even if I have to stay in my room forever!" She fled before Lancelot could react.

"I'm so sorry, Lancelot." Gwenhwyfar turned to him. "I never meant to come between you and your daughter."

He put his arm around her shoulders and held her to him, but his voice was grim. "She's strong-willed and I've let her have her way too often. I had no idea she wouldn't learn to love you like Galahad did."

"Galahad was scared of you, remember? Elen isn't. She's never had to share you with anyone. She's twelve—not a child, but not a woman. I'm competition to her. In time..."

"Mayhap," Lancelot answered, "but I think a visit to Avallach is long overdue. Nimue can make her understand. She's been with all of us throughout the years. Arthur, Elaine, you and me."

"If she hasn't already gone to Arthur." Gwenhwyfar said softly.

Lancelot glanced down at her. "Argante then. They seemed to get along. I think Elen would be better away from here until I can ferret out the men whose tongues have been wagging and get rid of them."

"What do you plan to do?"

"As your husband, I'd like to kill them." Lancelot sighed. "As a captain in Britain's army, I will have to follow the Code, although I think a flogging and being turned out is much too easy."

"They'll leave in disgrace. They'll not be able to fight in Custennin's army, anywhere. And what women will want them penniless?" Gwenhwyfar lifted her face and smiled.

"Umm." Lancelot gave her a lingering kiss. "That would be ironic justice." He kissed her again then released her. "I'd best see to it."

She forced herself to smile brightly, but she was troubled as she watched him leave.

It took Lancelot and Lupin less than a day to discover the culprits. Gant and Ywaine had joined them the year before. They left before the evening meal, armorless, walking in sandals and carrying their shirts, to avoid the bloody welts on their backs from sticking to the clothing.

Gwenhwyfar stood beside Lancelot at the front window and watched them stagger painfully down the road. "Did you give them provisions?"

"Two days bread and water, and coin from their wages."

She nestled against him. "Thank you."

His hand massaged her back. "I'll be leaving with Elen in a day or two. I hate having you stay here."

"They won't return, Lancelot. And Lupin will keep a sharp watch."

"True. But I don't like the build-up of Ida's troops."

"Mayhap he won't even know you're gone. It shouldn't take you much more than a fortnight, should it?"

"Probably not. Still, my scouts tell me Ida keeps the Saracen mercenary and the men are training well. I wish I knew who he was."

She leaned back to look up at him. "Have any of your men been able to get a close look?"

Lancelot shook his head. "He dresses traditionally with the head covered. His beard is black like all Saracens. He goes by the name Moham; that's all I know."

Gwenhwyfar ran her fingers through Lancelot's hair at the back of his neck. "At least you don't need to worry about him. He's never been seen off Ida's lands."

Lancelot moved in back of Gwenhwyfar and encircled her waist with his arms. He leaned his head contentedly on top of hers. "I wish I didn't have to leave, but I'll be back as soon as I can. Stay out of trouble while I'm gone?"

She laughed, settling her arms on his. "I promise. No trouble."

Morgana was pleased with the appearance of Ywaine and Gant at Ida's holdings.

Having been dismissed from Lancelot's company and thereby from Custennin's army, they planned on selling their knowledge to Ida.

She watched shrewdly as they told their tale of false accusations. She didn't trust men who could so easily be turned; yet inside information would be helpful in the future, especially if it concerned Gwenhwyfar.

"When did this happen?" Ida asked. "My scout tells me Lancelot is away."

Ywaine answered, "We were turned out a week ago. Lancelot was there then."

"Aye. We have the scars to prove it." Gant said.

Ywaine obviously wanted to impress the man who might grant them asylum. "I did hear him tell the seneschal he was taking his daughter away where she wouldn't be exposed to such rumors."

"Although no one knows who started them," Gant added quickly.

Medraut leaned forward. "Did Gwenhwyfar go with them?"

Ywaine shrugged. "The child did not much care for the lady."

Morgana gave him a scathing look and Medraut leaned back. "So Gwenhwyfar stayed home," he said.

"Well," Ida said to the two, "we'll see how good your skills are. Moham will work with you. If he thinks you'll do, you have a home here." He turned to Medraut. "Why don't you show them their quarters and explain the rules?"

"Certes," he answered pleasantly.

Morgana recognized the glint in his eye and wondered if he'd try a little torture on the new recruits. He always said the threshold of pain was a good thing to measure. But, judging from his disposition, she thought he had another purpose planned. No doubt it involved Britain's great whore.

Within a week, Lancelot arrived at Avallach. Barinthus looked at Elen curiously as he poled Lancelot and her across the Lake.

Argante awaited them at the shore. "Well come, Elen. I hope you'll stay with us awhile."

"I don't have much choice," Elen answered and Argante raised an eyebrow as Lancelot clamped a hand on Elen's shoulder. She retreated into sullen silence.

Lancelot sighed. "It was good of you to meet us. Nimue isn't here?"

"My mother is trying to restore the Old Ways in Brocéliande," she answered as they walked up the hill to the whitewashed buildings. One of the younger priestesses met them at the top.

"Please escort Elen to the House of Maidens," Argante instructed and then smiled at the dark-eyed girl who'd suddenly become very subdued. "I'll visit with you later. Don't be afraid. Remember our talks on the boat? No one here will hurt you." She turned to Lancelot. "Come with me."

He hugged Elen and watched her leave before he turned to follow Argante. Once they were seated in her chambers, the white hart looking from the tapestry at them, Lancelot found it hard to begin.

"She needs to be made to understand, Argante. I love my daughter, but Gwenhwyfar is my life."

She nodded. "I remember when I was small, visiting Camelot. The king had shown me my new pony and we were on our way back to the Great Hall. You were in there, with her..."

Lancelot smiled. "That was the day I told Gwen you had the blood of the Isle for so bluntly telling me we belonged together." He paused, then said softly, "It was the first time she told me she loved me."

The priestess nodded. "I was too young to know what love was, but I felt the pull between you."

"So you understand?" Lancelot asked.

Argante lifted a shoulder. "I have no carnal knowledge of a man, so no opinion on that. A bond exists between the two of you as it does with my mother and Arthur. Many lifetimes have only made that stronger."

"Do you think Elen will accept us eventually?"

"Elen is another matter. I think she belongs with us, on Avallach."

He drew a sharp breath. "I didn't bring her here to consecrate her."

"She won't be held against her will or yours. The Goddess forces no one to Her ways. You should know that, being the son of Lady Niniane."

"Yes," Lancelot answered, "but Elen has always been strong-willed."

"Your mother thought Elen was an old soul."

Lancelot was puzzled a minute, then understanding dawned. "Was that what she meant the day before she died?"

Argante nodded. "It may be why Elen feels so passionately about everything. And who knows what may have transpired between her and Gwenhwyfar in another life?" She leaned forward and took Lancelot's hand in hers. "We need wise old souls to carry on our work. If Elen is one, that knowledge will emerge as she spends time with us." She sat back. "As she matures, she'll accept Gwenhwyfar, I think. I'll see to it."

"I can visit as often as I like? And she'll be allowed to tell me the truth about wanting to stay?"

"For certes."

He sighed then stood. "I'd like to say goodbye before I leave."

Argante shook her head. "You already have, Lancelot. Let her begin her life with us now."

"Wehha is reinforcing his troops as well?" Lancelot asked Custennin. He'd stopped at Camelot on his way back from Avallach. Seated at the table in the map room, they examined a chart of the troop buildup.

The king nodded. "He has no Saracen bringing in horses, though. Still, I'd like to call Arthur's cohort back."

"Leaving Judwal without Camelot's protection would make a tempting invitation to Childebert."

Custennin looked slightly annoyed. "The purpose was for them to train Léon's men and keep Arthur from having to reveal his identity. How long does it take?"

"All I'm saying," Lancelot replied, "is that Childebert claimed Burgundia nearly a year ago. He may well be looking around for more land to seize. You know how important it is to keep Armorica free. Certes, Benoic will support Judwal."

"Your first duty is to Arthur, to Britain. You must hold the north." Custennin narrowed his eyes thoughtfully. "Tell me more about this cavalry trainer that Ida's hired. He is Saracen?"

Before Lancelot could do so, the gatekeeper warned of approaching riders. "Three!" he shouted.

Custennin and Lancelot waited in the bailey as Peredur, Galahad, and Dindrane rode through the gate. Time momentarily stopped and Lancelot wondered if Morgan le Fey was playing a trick on him. The girl could have been young Gwenhwyfar from the breeches and shirt she wore to the wild, reddish hair. He watched in surprise as his son helped her down from the palfrey and was even more amazed that Galahad kept his hand under her elbow as they walked over.

"We've found the Grail!" Peredur carried the wrapped bundle inside and placed it on the table. The cup seemed simple enough, a thing of graceful beauty. Although it lacked the radiance of light that had originally flowed from it in his mother's cave, Lancelot felt a quiet, calm power emanate from it.

"There was this serving maid," Peredur said, "who was really the Grail Maiden. She brought the cup—"

Lancelot was startled. "You saw her?"

Peredur furrowed his brows. "Yes. No. I'm not sure. She seemed real then faded away."

Custennin turned the Grail over in his hands, weighing it. "These runes are ancient." He fingered the ornate carving at the base. "The gold is thick on the brim." He held it up. "It's worth a good price; that should impress anyone I treaty with."

"Pelles asked us to give you a message, my lord," Galahad said.

The king looked up. "What is it?"

"The cup shouldn't be used for personal gain or its power will turn against the user."

"The king represents the land; how then can I not use it rightly?" Custennin looked annoyed.

"The Grail serves those who are pure at heart," Dindrane spoke carefully. "I fear a king has to make too many harsh decisions—sometimes cruel decisions—to be pure."

Custennin stopped admiring the cup to stare at the girl. "Who are you?"

"This is Dindrane, Peredur's sister." Galahad stepped closer to her and Lancelot could've sworn his son appeared ready to defend her at all cost.

"And Pelles' niece. I've come to ask a favor of you." She boldly stared back at him.

Custennin blinked at her directness. "What would that be, my lady?" He looked over the way she was dressed and accented the last word sarcastically.

Although she paid no mind, Galahad frowned. She looked at the king steadily. "That you allow Peredur and Galahad to be the Grail's keepers."

The corner of Lancelot's mouth quirked up and he stifled a grin. Custennin had little use for women, other than for bedding and only then if they didn't talk much. This young woman reminded him more and more of the early days at Camelot. Gwenhwyfar had always spoken her mind; it was one of the things he loved about her. He glanced at his son. From the way he acted, Dindrane had some effect on him. The smile started again.

Custennin kept his voice neutral. "You think I'm unworthy?"

Careful, Dindrane. Lancelot sat straighter. *Do not anger him.*

"You are most worthy. You are our sovereign," she answered correctly and Lancelot breathed a sigh of relief. "For certes, you would be the one to use it when negotiating."

"Then why should I allow someone else to possess it?"

"They would hold it in trust for you," Dindrane replied simply. "No one can actually own the Grail. It is a holy thing."

Lancelot groaned inwardly as he recognized the challenge to Custennin's authority and he knew Galahad and Peredur had too, for both paled. "If I might speak, my lord," he said.

Custennin's brown eyes glinted as he looked at Lancelot. "What?"

"If you let it be known you have the Grail, you'll need a means to protect it against theft."

"And if I don't? If I kept it hidden safely myself?"

"What good would that serve? If the Saxons don't think we revere it, they won't respect the ritual of drinking from it at treaty."

Custennin considered. "What do you propose? That Galahad and Peredur ride around with it?"

"No. Build a shrine for it, a place where it may be viewed. And post guards around the clock."

"Won't having it on public display invite more thieves?"

Lancelot shrugged. "The Grail will have to be protected, regardless. Setting it up as an example of Britain's supremacy—brought back under your rule—will give the people something to believe in. If faith is strong enough, the Grail will accomplish its mission."

Custennin brightened. "Arthur had Excalibur; I'll have the Grail."

"Something like that," Lancelot answered, remembering how the Grail had shifted him to the land of Faerie. *Faith and Faerie brought Gwenhwyfar home. Gwen...* Something worried the edges of his mind and he felt suddenly restless. *I must get back.*

"Very well," Custennin finally said. "We'll build this monument and I'll choose the most trustworthy of our men." He turned to Galahad and Peredur. "You will be in charge of the shifts. As Arthur had his Fellowship of the Round Table; your men will be called the Defenders of the Grail."

Lancelot said his goodbyes quickly at Camelot, for the uneasiness he'd felt the day before hadn't subsided. He motioned for Galahad to follow him to the stables. "I wanted to talk privately." He placed the saddle blanket on his horse. "I don't much like Custennin's ambition; his ego has grown since Arthur left. Your lady may be right."

Galahad colored. "I have no lady. Dindrane is but a friend."

Lancelot raised an eyebrow. "Well. Try and convince Custennin to choose the defenders soon. Train them as I trained you. No mercy until they've given their best and then continue to push."

His son smiled. "I hated you for that."

"Has it ever saved your life?" He adjusted the bridle's chinstrap, allowing for another finger of room. "You've got good leadership traits, Galahad. Use them."

"I've never wanted power or control," Galahad answered

"That's why men will follow you. Lead by example, as Arthur did." Lancelot tightened the cinch on the saddle before mounting. "And take care of your lady."

"I told you. She's a friend. Peredur's sister."

"Hmm." Lancelot leaned down from the saddle to look into his son's face. "Gwenhwyfar is a friend, too. Bedwyr's sister. And you see how that turned out." He straightened and grinned. "Don't look so horrified. There are fates worse than loving a woman...and one of those is never having loved at all."

Galahad's face was a mixture of emotion. "Mayhap, you're right. Say hello to the queen for me."

Lancelot nodded. Anxiety gnawed at him and he put his horse to a swift canter toward Joyous Garde.

~ Chapter 15—The Abduction ~

One morning, a fortnight after the fugitives had arrived, Morgana bolted the door to her room and lit the brazier. Even though it was summer, she could claim a chill this far north, if anyone questioned her.

She opened several pouches of dried herbs and added pinches to the glowing coals. Flames of blue, red and yellow leapt up. She held up her hands, guiding the flames' intensity. She had no intention of setting the place on fire; she just wanted to see who Lancelot's wife really was.

She began breathing deeply, inhaling the scents of felonwort, datura, and fly agaric. The flames swayed before her eyes, shifting shape, taking form...

What was this? Medraut talking to Ywaine and Gant in the tack room.

"Is Lancelot a wealthy man?" Medraut spoke in his Saracen accent.

"I'd say so," Ywaine answered. "In addition to Joyous Garde, he's a prince of Benoic."

Medraut studied the men. "Do you suppose he'd be willing to pay gold if his wife were...to become lost and someone rescued her?"

The men appeared puzzled. "She knows these lands well, why would she get lost?" Ywaine placed a saddle on a rack and a smile began to spread across his face. "Are we speaking of ransom?"

"A harsh word." Medraut looked from one to the other. "But yes, I'm a mercenary; I'd like to own my own land. I'm sure the two of you could make use of such funds, as well."

"We could."

Medraut continued in his affected, silken accent. "Gold from Lancelot—who had you flogged and turned out—would be doubly rewarding, no?" When they nodded, he went on. "Tell me the queen's daily habits. How can we best approach?"

Ywaine grinned. "That's easy. Each Wednesday, she and Lancelot ride to the peasants' hovels to check on their welfare."

"With an escort?" Medraut asked.

Ywaine shook his head. "No need. Lancelot trained all the serfs and villagers to bear arms. A bandit would stand a better chance against the devil himself than on those roads."

Medraut nodded. "She'll have some sort of escort, though, if Lancelot is not there. I have two trusted friends amidst the Saxons here, Thordor and Colgra. Neither will inform Ida of our intentions.Between the five of us, we should be able to overcome any opposition." He eyed them speculatively. "Are you ready?"

Gant looked tentative. "What will happen to his wife?"

"No harm, rest assured," Medraut answered. "An abandoned sheep herder's cottage is tucked into the hills, not far from one of their villages. I discovered it because my horse threw a shoe and I was looking for shelter for the night. I stumbled onto it accidentally. It's covered in vines and hidden from the road by boulders. We can keep her there."

"She'll be released?" Gant seemed to want reassurance.

"I swear I'll not harm her." A strange light glinted in Medraut's eyes. "One of my boats is always waiting at the quay. Once we get our ransom, we can be away in minutes."

The flames died down and Morgana blinked. This was unexpected. Medraut abducting Gwenhwyfar? Morgana sighed. She'd have to let him finally have his way with that blasted woman. It seemed the only way to cure his obsession. *And then, when I find where the cottage is, it'll be my turn to visit the queen.*

"A wonderful morning for a ride." Gwenhwyfar shifted her weight in the saddle and inhaled deeply of the fresh air. Morning dew had barely dried before they set out. She liked to visit the homes before the women had to concentrate on the noon meal. The smell of clover was sweet and the sun just beginning to warm. Lancelot had been gone three weeks and would be home in a few days. All was right in the world.

"Aye." Landinus, the older of her escorts, seemed eager to hold a conversation with her. He'd been the one to bring news of Elaine's pregnancy so many years ago. Gwenhwyfar knew he was especially proud Lupin had chosen him for her escort this morning. "Tis nothing better than a bright summer morning..." His words were muted by the pounding of hooves, seemingly coming from two directions at once.

Both escorts drew their swords, Landinus facing forward with Gwenhwyfar. The other guard, Karden, spun his horse to face the rear, keeping her in the middle.

She recognized Gant a split second before his sword swung home to pierce Landinus' side. He grunted and stoically backcut with his own weapon, catching Gant on the shoulder, the cut going deep. On the other side a Saxon exchanged blows with Karden. One Saxon already lay dead on the road.

She pulled the dagger from her boot, although she knew she couldn't do any damage against a broadsword. Gwenhwyfar turned her horse, trying to keep the mare between her escorts, both of whom were wounded now, but still in their saddles. Blood was spurting everywhere. She saw Ywaine riding at her. She reached over to pull the short lance out of its pocket on Karden's saddle. He threw her a startled glance, but was too busy engaging Gant's sword to protest.

Lancelot had made her practice with the lance and she hoped she had the strength to withstand the shock of impact. The quintain nearly unseated her in the lists. Now she couched the lance under her arm, its diagonal direction allowing part of the weight to rest on the pommel. She had the element of surprise since Ywaine wasn't expecting her to leave the safety of her escort and charge.

The lance nicked the edge of his shield and she raised it and pushed under the arm along the side of the hauberk, finding the skin only protected by leather. The shaft went in, wrenching her shoulder, but she gave a cry of victory when he rolled off his horse's crupper and lay still on the ground.

Thank God for Lancelot's insistence to always carry the short lance!

A Saxon swung his ax and Landinus dropped from his horse and lay motionless. Gwenhwyfar cried to him and started to dismount.

"Stay in your saddle, my lady!" Karden screamed. "Ride! I'll hold here. Go! Get help!"

Blindly, she kicked her horse to the gallop, only to hear hoof beats behind her. There should be no one. Three of the ambushers were dead or wounded. She braved a quick glance behind her to see the flowing robes and headdress of the Saracen. She urged her mare on, but the palfrey was smaller than the Saracen's horse and not used to running flat out for long periods of time. Gwenhwyfar could feel her slowing, even as the sound behind her got louder.

The man rode alongside, reaching for her reins and she slashed his arm with her dagger. He yelped and she felt a searing flash of pain through her shoulder as he yanked her arm back. Then her hand went numb. The dagger fell to the ground and the man had her horse's reins, which he looped over his pommel. Briefly, she thought of jumping and rolling, but there was no place to go. *He's going to have to stop soon. My mare is blown. I'll jump then.*

He seemed to read her thoughts for he slowed to a trot, loosened the rope belt from his robe and twirled it over her head; it settled on her chest and he pulled it taut, securing her arms to her sides. He pulled a sack from his saddlebag and threw it over her head, blinding her.

"Let me go!" her muffled voice cried. "I can't breathe!"

"It's not much longer." The voice answered and sounded vaguely familiar, although somewhat Frankish-accented.

Gwenhwyfar forced herself to slow her breathing to save what oxygen was left inside the bag. The horses were walking slowly now, but she had no sense of equilibrium. She clutched the horse tightly with her knees to keep from falling.

Finally, they stopped. She heard him dismount then he dragged her from the saddle. He held her tightly, nudging her in front of him. She heard a door open and she was pushed into a room. From the smell of fresh rushes, it was clean.

She was lifted and laid on something soft. She felt her captor hovering over her. "Remove the hood, please. I can't breathe." Although near tears, she determined not to show fear.

"In a moment." His hand touched the shirt over her breast and she pulled away and gasped. "Did you like that?" The hand moved to the other one, kneading it.

She tried to squirm further away from him. He laughed. *Mary, Mother of Jesu, help me with this. Lancelot can't save me this time.*

She heard the sound of a horse approach and her captive swore. He left her and she could hear voices outside. Too soon, the man returned.

"Damn, my love, I've got to go and take care of a small problem. Rest assured, though, you'll not be able to leave here."

Gwenhwyfar nearly fainted, for she recognized the voice. *Medraut*.

He removed the hood and bent down. "You're finally mine." He tried to kiss her, but she turned her head away. He smiled.

He watched her face. "No one will rescue you this time, my lady. Even the great Lancelot will never know. When I return, I'll finish what I started then we'll be gone by the time he gets back."

"Gone?"

"Yes." He smiled happily now, his eyes beginning to glaze with madness. "I have a ship waiting. Tomorrow, we sail to Gaul."

"I don't want to go to Gaul." Gwenhwyfar tried to remain calm.

"Ah, Gwenhwyfar." He sighed contentedly. "We'll get married in Gaul. I'll make you my wife and take care of you."

Gwenhwyfar held back the hysteria rising in her throat. "Medraut. I'm already married. I can't go with you."

He looked annoyed. "I can make you forget Lancelot."

The hysteria nearly bubbled over. "You cannot."

Medraut stopped smiling. "We shall see about that." He crushed her lips and forced his tongue inside her mouth.

Gwenhwyfar tried to bite him, but he backhanded her, causing a fiery sting that immediately welted. She moaned in agony, but frightened, she lay still.

"Tell me you love me. Tell me how much you want me," Medraut whispered in her ear.

"I don't!"

"Say it!" He slapped her again.

Oh, the pain...dear Jesu! She gritted her teeth then another knife-sharp pain pierced through her as his hands mercilessly squeezed her arms, forcing her to lay still. "I...want...you." She grunted out the words.

He grinned diabolically. "And you will have me just as soon as I can get rid of the problem waiting for me outside. I'll let you think about all the ways I want you to please me when I return. You'll do everything to me that you've done with that fey bastard. You'll kiss me like you do him. You'll spread your legs for me like you do him. You'll suck me like you do him.

How can I reason with a madman? He would tear me apart. Holy Mary, Mother of God...

Gwenhwyfar fought the revulsion she felt. It took all her strength to sound calm. "You said once you loved me, Medraut."

"I do. With all my heart. I want to make you happy."

She pushed down the hysteria. Surely if she gave in to it, she'd be dead. She tried to sound soothing. "You don't force someone you love to do things they don't want to do."

"Like what?" He looked honestly puzzled, then his eyes glossed over again.

"Like this." She tilted her head to the restraints. "Untie me, Medraut, and let me go."

He laughed again, and started to unlace his trews. Loud banging on the door stopped him.

"Are we going to take that ransom note or not?" a man yelled.

Medraut cursed and got off the bed. He leaned over her, sanity seemingly restored. "The door will be bolted from the outside. I'm leaving now, but I'll be back tomorrow. Before we go to the boat, we'll have another try at this little game. Once you're my wife, I'll expect your full cooperation."

When the bolt slid through, she curled into a ball, weeping softly, thankful to be alone. She had until tomorrow to escape or kill herself, for she would not let Medraut rape her. Ever.

"Gwenhwyfar." A woman's voice, soft and gentle. She struggled against the semi-consciousness of sleep, vaguely aware someone was in the room. A faint glow began to shimmer at the foot of the bed. A golden-haired maiden, dressed in white samite, emerged from the light.

"Who are you?" she rubbed her eyes, sure she was dreaming.

"I am Astrala, the Grail Maiden, sent to give you strength."

"Can you get me out of here?"

"No." She raised her hands and fashioned a fathom goblet out of the air. "Touch the Grail; it will grant your mind numbness if he returns. But you must not kill yourself. Lancelot will come."

"I won't let Medraut violate me!" Gwenhwyfar sat up and touched the cup.

The air was suddenly scented with frankincense and myrrh and Gwenhwyfar felt the healing effect wash over her, calming her. The maiden seemed to recede into the light. "Wait! Don't go! Please, help me!"

Even as the image faded, she heard the maiden whisper, "You will have strength; the Grail will be with you."

Lancelot arrived home to see the bailey bustling with preparations of war. Armored men mounted their horses, filing into formation.

"What has happened?" he asked as Lupin rode up to him. "Ida?"

His seneschal took a deep breath. "Gwenhwyfar has been abducted."

"WHAT?" Lancelot felt the blood drain from his face. "Who...why...?"

"The Saracen Ida keeps. She went to visit the villagers. Karden and Landinus were her escorts. When they didn't arrive back yesterday afternoon, we went looking for them. They'd been ambushed and badly wounded."

Lancelot's face set. "Where are they?"

"In the infirmary. Sedated."

When Lancelot started to dismount, Lupin added, "You'll not get more information from them than I already know."

Lancelot accepted a fresh horse from the groom. "Did they not keep my wife between them?"

"They tried. Apparently, Karden was fending off two of the attackers and told Gwenhwyfar to ride for help. He didn't see the Saracen until it was too late."

"Damnation! I'll have Ida's head for this, even if it means war." Lancelot swung his horse around and moved to the head of the line. One entire cohort. Five hundred men were ready. With a curt signal, he led them out.

He tried to collect his thoughts as they rode. *Why would Ida want to break the treaty? What reason could he have for taking Gwenhwyfar hostage?* It made no sense. He assumed the mercenary was acting on Ida's orders, then a thought chilled him. *What if the man is acting independently? If he is, what are his motives?* Hostage-taking was one thing; they were generally treated well, as Cynric had been. But if this abduction were of a personal nature... He urged his horse to a faster gallop.

Lupin caught up with him. "We can't keep this pace, Captain. It's near a half-day's ride to Ida's holding."

Lancelot was possessed. "She may not be a hostage, Lupin. I have to find her."

"I know, but we have to be prepared for Ida's men. This could be a trap; they may be waiting for us. We can't do that with winded horses."

He rode on at the fast pace for another half-mile before he finally slowed to a trot. "She was nearly raped once before by Saxons. I must get to her." He prayed they weren't too late.

"All the more reason we must be ready to fight," Lupin said logically.

Lancelot nodded. "We'll rest the horses in another hour or so."

The hills became steeper and as they approached an area lined with boulders, Lancelot stopped his men. "If Ida's men await us, this would be a good place for an ambush." He sent two of his scouts ahead, one riding to the east and the other to the west. "Rest while you can," he told the other men, but stayed mounted himself.

Lancelot watched the rider who took the western path pick his way carefully through the rocky terrain, keeping an eye on the forest line farther up the slope. Clearing the area, he signaled to the waiting army and they swarmed forward. Lancelot glanced at a vine-covered shack, tucked behind the boulder. It looked deserted, certainly no place for an ambush.

"I swear I don't know what you're talking about." Ida looked Lancelot directly in the eye, not wavering. "Your men are welcome to search."

"We're already doing that." Once Lancelot determined no army was ready, he'd sent search parties out. Now he glared at Ida.

"Where is the Saracen?"

"I don't know," Ida answered. "I haven't seen him in a day or two. But that's not unusual. He trains men in the camps north of here."

"He was seen on my lands. My soldiers didn't die in his raid," Lancelot answered.

"Did they know who he was?" Ida asked.

"Certes," Lancelot answered, wondering how one couldn't distinguish a traditionally dressed Saracen from normal soldiers. "He has my wife. I either find him, or your lands—and life—are forfeit for harboring him."

Ida paled beneath his tan. "His mother is here. She might know where he is."

"His mother?" Lancelot was nonplused. "I've heard nothing of an Eastern woman living hereabouts."

Ida shook his head. "She's not, nor is he. They both chose disguises." He hesitated. "I thought you said you knew who he was."

"What need does a mercenary have..." Lancelot's voice trailed off as an icy vein of suspicion flowed through him. "You thought I knew? Who are they?"

Ida looked uneasily at the soldiers behind Lancelot, all of whom had their hands on their hilts. He swallowed hard. "Relatives of your late king. Morgana and Medraut."

Lancelot spun around, but his men were already spreading out to search. He turned back to Ida. "Why would you harbor them?"

"They came seeking sanction. Childebert wanted to know if Arthur were really alive. Medraut offered to train my men for cavalry."

"So you could attack me?" Lancelot asked.

"No! I hold with the treaty I signed," Ida said hastily. "And I'll renew that pledge now. Raising arms against you was never my intent." He was jabbering. "You can't blame a man for wanting a good defense can you?"

Lancelot didn't answer. "Go on."

"That's all." Ida spread his hands. "I should've let them go sooner, but the woman could be persuasive." He arched an eyebrow and smiled.

"I'm aware of how that bitch uses men," Lancelot snorted. "You can be glad she didn't try to drug you; it's a favorite technique of hers."

Ida began to reply, but Lancelot's men returned. "There's no sign of either of them," Lupin said.

"Where could they have gone?" he looked at Ida.

"Mayhap hiding in the northern camps or they could be trying to get to Wehha for sanction or they could take the ship he always has ready."

Lancelot's face hardened. "Three different directions. I'll have to split my soldiers. Very good strategy if you're hiding them."

"I swear I'm not." Ida began to sweat as the soldiers once again reached for their weapons.

"Good," Lancelot replied. "You're my hostage now." He gave the command for his men to seize the fort and they moved quickly, two of them remaining with swords drawn on Ida. "Until I find Gwenhwyfar, you remain my prisoner."

"You dim-witted fool!" Morgana hissed as the oarsmen stroked away from the shore. "If I hadn't overheard the reason Lancelot brought an entire cohort north, we'd both be prisoners or dead by now."

Medraut stared defiantly at the receding shore. "What if Gwenhwyfar dies, Mother? Have you thought of that? If they don't find her, she'll starve. You should have let me go back for her."

She slapped him soundly. "I hope she does. It'll save me the trouble of killing her. She's been a source of trouble for me since Arthur met her."

He rubbed his cheek to relieve the sting. "If she dies, Lancelot will hunt us down wherever we are. Do you think Childebert will appreciate that?"

"You leave Childebert to me." But Morgana was shaken. *I'll create a diversion. Tell him Ida's troops are strengthened, Wehha is ready to move west; the time is right to move westward toward Benoic. That'll draw Lancelot off of us.* "Mayhap I should have left you for Lancelot. You've done nothing but destroy my carefully laid plans because you're besotted with that slut."

"Don't call her that." Medraut clenched his fists.

Morgana glared at him. "I'll call her whatever I wish. Get out of my sight. I need to think."

For the rest of the journey she planned her strategy. By the time they set ashore in Burgundia, Morgana was confident she could handle the Frankish king.

Lancelot's northern outriders returned two days later to Ida's holding. "They aren't in any of the camps. No one's seen two women of any description."

The second batch of outriders returned later the same day. Hesitant to speak, one of the soldiers finally said, "Morgana and Medraut are aboard the ship. They were seen leaving the same day we arrived."

"What of Gwenhwyfar?" Lancelot asked, not sure whether to be relieved or not.

The second man shook his head. "No sign of her at all. The men on the wharf were positive. Just a small black-haired woman and a bearded man."

Lancelot paced. "They've left Gwenhwyfar somewhere. We have to find her and quickly. It's been…" He looked at his men, knowing what they were thinking. "She can't be dead. I'd know." None would look him in the eye.

He went to the room where Ida was being held and told him the news. "If you value your life, tell me where Medraut might have taken her."

Ida shook his head. "I swear I don't know." He thought. "Four days ago, the two Saxons were killed and one of my men disappeared, but a fourth one survived. He was wounded badly and lies in the infirmary." He spread his hands apologetically. "I hadn't connected the two incidents. He told me they were ambushed by bandits."

Lancelot turned on his heel and was gone before Ida finished speaking. At the infirmary, he burst through the doors, nearly knocking an orderly to the floor. He stomped to the wounded man's bed. "Did you try to abduct a woman four days ago?"

The man feebly raised an arm to protect himself. "No one was supposed to know."

Lancelot forced his voice to be level. "Where is she?"

The man's eyes widened. "Moham took her." His voice trailed away, as the effort cost him.

"I know. Moham has disappeared. He didn't take her with him. Where is she?"

The man closed his eyes and Lancelot struggled not to throttle him. Slowly, he opened them. "He mentioned a shack, covered in vines—" He broke off.

"Where?" Lancelot asked desperately.

"By boulders. A road goes through them…"

Lancelot remembered the spot. He ran out, calling to his men as he raced to the stables. He waited for no one, but gave his horse his head as they thundered out the gate.

Gwenhwyfar looked at the abrasions on her wrists and felt the bruises on her arms and legs. *I was a fool to fight him. In the end, he'll win.* She closed her eyes, hoping to be rid of the horror, but the near rape hung suspended in her mind. At least, she'd managed to loosen her restraints quickly enough.

Medraut hadn't returned since that first awful night. She'd been glad the next day as she nursed her sore breasts and cleansed herself with the pitcher of water on the table. Now, she wished she'd saved that water to drink.

She hadn't been overly concerned the second day. She thought he was probably punishing her. Arthur once explained that a strategy of withholding food from prisoners made them appreciate their captors when they were eventually fed. Repeated often enough, the reality of being totally powerless turned into an obsession of loyalty to the one who held them captive. Brainwashing, Arthur called it and said he never resorted to such tactics. Medraut was devious enough to use it.

But this was the fourth day and her strength was ebbing. Thankfully, the Grail Maiden returned each night to keep the nightmares and anxiety at bay, or mayhap, Gwenhwyfar just dreamed her. She'd slipped in and out of consciousness for the past day or possibly two days. Time was becoming muddled, as it had in the land of Faerie. Even dreamed of Morgan le Fey and Cernunnos; both of them watching her sadly from the pool. *Can you save me from this hell? Ah, there had been no pain in Faerie.* She'd reached for them, but even as she did, the image faded and she was alone again.

She heard the pounding of horse's hooves, but she didn't stir. She'd heard a whole lot of them several days ago and had called out, but no one came. This was probably Medraut. *He'll feed me and then he'll expect...* She pulled her torn shirt closer and lay down, hugging her knees to her chest, her back to the door.

She didn't move when the bolt was thrown or when she heard the boots step into the room.

"Gwen!" Lancelot covered the distance in three steps and swept her up in his arms.

"You're alive!" He held her tightly.

She remained limp, her eyes tightly closed. "Medraut, I need food first..."

Lancelot leaned away from her and gently touched the bruises and the swollen face and lips. "It's me, Gwen. Lancelot. You're safe now."

She opened her eyes. "Lancelot? How...?" She slipped off toward semi-consciousness.

He shook her gently. "Wake up. You're delirious." He pulled the waterskin strap from his shoulder. "Here. Drink." He dribbled some water onto her lips, then a little more as her mouth opened. Her hands grabbed the skin. "Careful. Go slow." Lancelot supported the back of her head with his other hand. "You're safe now. I have rations in the saddlebags."

Slowly, her eyes focused, seeing him for the first time. "How did you find me? I was afraid Medraut would come back."

"Let me feed you first." His eyes took in her torn clothes and the abrasions on her wrists. His fists clenched. Silently, he went out and got the food.

She ate ravenously while he told her what had transpired. "So," he finished, “Medraut has escaped again, but I’ll find him. I’ll avenge you. You have my geis.”

Gwenhwyfar’s face remained impassive and she made no reply.

Lancelot looked at her anxiously. “Are you all right? I see the bruises, but...”

She started to cry. “He kissed me and made me tell him that I wanted him. I tried to resist saying that...but he hit me and I gave in. I’m such a coward. Dear God, I feel so filthy and not worthy of you—”

Lancelot gathered her close. “Shhhh. It’s over.”

She rubbed her eyes and sat up. “I just want a hot bath—it’s been so long—and to sleep in my own bed tonight.”

He steadied her. “I’ll hold you all night.”

Lancelot carried her outside and lifted her into the saddle, mounting behind her. He wrapped his arms around her and she settled back against him without another word.

By Mithras! What had Medraut done to Gwen?

~ Chapter 16—Exposed ~

Custennin began building the shrine for the Grail shortly after Lancelot left for Joyous Garde. Galahad and Peredur busied themselves finding worthy Defenders while Dindrane helped interview candidates.

"You'll be looking for warrior skills to defend the Grail; I'll be listening for what they don't say," she'd told the two the first day. "Their hearts must be devoted to this task."

Galahad and Dindrane stood going over a list of possible applicants. Galahad sensed Peredur watching somewhat jealously, but it didn't stop him from brushing his hand against Dindrane's every chance he got.

Dindrane looked up. "Peredur. Are you going to help us with this or not?"

He went over and sat, but appeared absentminded. Dindrane leaned across Galahad to point out a name to him. Galahad, pleased with her closeness, started to smile. Abruptly, Peredur stood.

"What is it?" Dindrane asked.

He shook his head. "The two of you can finish this. I have something to do that can wait no longer."

"What's more important than protecting the Grail?" Galahad asked.

"Love, mayhap," Peredur answered. "Lohengrin is twelve now. I once promised Blanchefleur I would come for her when the Grail was found."

"You went to her before." Dindrane searched his face. "She's married, Peredur. What do you hope to accomplish?"

"She was forced to marry Clamadeu. She doesn't love him," he said stubbornly.

Galahad sat back. "Her husband is formidable and no friend of Custennin. Do you want to start a war? Just now when we can have peace?"

"The Grail is supposed to grant peace." Peredur began to get angry. "Let's put it to the test. I'm going to collect my son and the woman who should be my wife." He turned and stomped out the door, leaving Galahad staring after him in amazement.

"He's a fool. He'll get himself killed!" Dindrane put her hand on Galahad's arm. "You've got to stop him."

"He's a grown man, Dindrane. What can I do?"

Her green eyes were bright with unshed tears. "Please, Galahad. He's your friend and my brother."

How can I refuse her? Suddenly, he knew how Peredur felt. He'd ride into an entire cohort single-handedly for Dindrane. *She's so beautiful.* He took a sharp breath. *So this is how love happens.* He didn't know whether to be giddy with joy or absolutely terrified. For the first time in his life, he wished Lancelot were there. To calm the rising hysteria, if nothing else.

"Galahad. Please."

With a small sigh, he nodded and rose. "I'll try."

Dindrane stood and gave him a hug. "Thank you!"

For a minute he pressed her to him, then stepped back quickly, nearly tripping as he hurried to the door in search of Peredur.

Galahad persuaded Peredur to wait until the shrine was finished before going to Beaurepaire. Now, three months later, they stood at attention as the ceremony for installing the Grail was about to begin. He glanced at his friend, hoping the ceremony would be impressive enough to cause Peredur to stay, although he couldn't blame him for wanting Blanchefleur. Every time he looked at Dindrane, happiness flooded him.

The shrine stood behind the Great Hall, near the old chapel that had once been given to the Roman's Minerva, but Ygraine had converted it into a Christian chapel and it later reverted back to the Goddess when used by Nimue. Custennin had invited all the warlords: Bredei, Cuneglasus, Keidyaw, Vortiporius, even Cormant. Usually, an uneasy tension existed among them, but they had all drunk from the Grail. Today, jovial laughter prevailed instead of frowns. Galahad gave a fervent prayer of thanks for the Grail's power. The Grail would bring a deeper allegiance from each.

Bishop Dubricius came from Caerleon to perform the Mass and recite the newly created office of the Defenders of the Grail. As each carefully selected man knelt and swore his oath to protect the Grail with his life, Galahad stole a glance toward his father across the bailey.

Lancelot stood stoically, the features of his face immobile, his dark eyes inscrutable. Beside him, Gwenhwyfar looked pale and drawn, her hair braided neatly and her eyes flat and opaque. Never had Galahad known Gwenhwyfar to look so listless, as though the spark of life had left her and only the shell of her body remained alive.

As the commemoration wore on and the heat of the day increased, she swayed on her feet and Lancelot put out a hand to steady her. Ever so slightly, she shied away from him. Galahad blinked, not sure he'd really seen her do that. A subtle expression of offense passed over his father's face then was gone. He wondered what had taken place at Joyous Garde.

The bishop intoned the benediction and the crowd began to disassemble, the guards for the first duty taking their places in front of the shrine. Later, at Matins, Galahad and Peredur would return to the shrine with Argante. She wished to add her own protective blessing over the cup.

"The first real test will be tomorrow at council," Peredur said. "I heard Custennin tell Bedwyr they're going to discuss how best to convince Wehha not to move west. I've never known one of Custennin's councils to go well."

"They'll drink from the Grail first," Galahad reflected. "But it's too bad Ryons and Guinglain can't be here. They're both level-headed enough to calm the hot bloods like Bridei and Vortiporius."

"Well, your father and Bedwyr will be able to convince Cormant and Cuneglasus of the need to stay united."

Galahad sighed. “I hope so, but I don’t think my father’s mind is on these talks either. Haven’t you noticed something’s wrong?”

“Yes.” Peredur pointed to where Lancelot and Gwenhwyfar stood in the shade of Great Hall. “Even now, look how serious they are.”

As they watched, Gwenhwyfar gazed up at Lancelot wide-eyed, and shook her head quickly. A look of impatience crossed Lancelot’s face and he took her arm and turned her toward the door. Although she didn’t resist, it was clear Lancelot and Gwenhwyfar, whatever their conversation, weren’t in accord. Peredur looked at Galahad inquiringly.

“You see what I mean?” Galahad asked.

Lancelot brought Gwenhwyfar to Argante’s chambers in the old chapel. “Please, Gwen, let the Goddess heal you. Argante can help.”

“I’ve told you, Lancelot, no one can help me.” She pulled away and ran crying from the room.

“What can I do, Lancelot?” Argante asked as they followed Gwen outside and watched her disappear into the walled herbal garden she used to love.

He looked at her helplessly. “I want you to get her to talk. She’s been this way since that blackguard bastard almost raped her. I can’t convince her that wasn’t her fault.”

Argante’s brow furrowed. “Why would she think that?”

“She doesn’t think she fought hard enough, even though she was bruised and swollen and had been badly handled. Bel’s fires! She was tethered, helpless. Gwen’s a fighter, but I think something happened to her mind as well. For four days she was helpless...lived without knowing when he’d return or what he’d do. She had no weapon to use against him. I think...I think in her mind she already felt raped even though he never actually did so.” He clenched his fists. “I thank the Goddess she lived. If I could only convince her to accept me...” He stopped and looked away.

Argante laid her cool hand on his arm. “Does she refuse you then?”

Lancelot turned back to her, feeling a mixture of sorrow and pity. “I don’t know if she would or not. I don’t have the courage to try.”

She gave a faint sigh. “I am pledged to celibacy. I know not what passes between a husband and wife. Gwenhwyfar is a Christian, though. Don’t the priests preach of duty to a husband?”

He winced. “That’s what I’m afraid of. That out of duty, she’d appease me. But it’s her love I want and I no longer feel that.”

“Love doesn’t die, Lancelot. Mayhap the Grail can heal her. I’ll ask for that tonight when I do my blessing.”

Lancelot brightened. “She said the Grail Maiden visited her each night; she was the reason Gwen didn’t kill herself.”

Argante raised an eyebrow and took one of Lancelot’s hands in hers. “Show her love and patience, Lancelot; it’s all you can do now. I believe the Grail will heal her.”

Even though Argante had dismissed the guards that evening, Galahad noted they’d retreated only past earshot and remained watching alertly from that distance. They’d probably not wanted to anger the Lady of the Lake, nor could they disobey the king’s commands. Peredur joined him.

Argante walked around the shrine, placing Galahad's shield on the north side and Myrddin's staff along the east side. She laid Peredur's Sword of Truth on the south side. Lastly, she took a cup and filled it with water she'd brought from the sacred spring of Avallach, setting it in front of the door, with its expensive glass window, that faced west, the direction to the Otherworld.

Galahad had frowned at the pagan influence. Peredur had reminded him the Grail was to serve all people. Argante indicated to Peredur and Galahad where they should sit and retrieved her candle. Once it was lit, she closed the circle she'd cast and called the quarters for the items which she'd so carefully placed. As she began the Blessing Ritual in the ancient tongue, moonlight washed over the dome of the shrine, reflecting off the glass, causing an illusion of light within. No. It wasn't an illusion. The light grew brighter, spilling out of the window, flooding the courtyard with the brightness of day.

Slowly, Galahad became aware of a low-pitched humming coming from neither of his companions. The sound grew, rising melodically into a pleasant, drawn-out sound of one syllable, repeated slowly, over and over. The vibration enveloped him, touching and becoming one with his soul. His mind soared overhead, looking downward at the luminescent light flowing through the pane. The Grail was sending forth the light and the sound and for one, sweet moment of eternity, he knew sheer bliss.

Argante's voice, or at least he thought it was her voice, came gently across the still air. "Send your love to Gwenhwyfar, that she may be healed."

The candle extinguished itself suddenly and Galahad felt the coolness of the night air, dim now with the silver swept moonlight. Beside him, Peredur sat transfixed.

"That sound... Lighter and sweeter than any bird," Peredur breathed finally.

"The sound of heaven," Galahad said worshipfully.

Argante smiled gently. "The riddle that I gave you has been completed. The Grail has accepted my prayer."

The next morning, Lancelot approached the warlords at council. "I'm only asking for a company—one hundred men—from each of you." Standing, Lancelot brought his fist down on the Round Table. "That number won't hurt any of your individual defenses, but combined will give me enough men to convince Childebert to surrender Medraut."

"If he shelters him," Custennin said. "You have no proof of that."

Lancelot glared at him. "Medraut and Morgana were seen leaving on the ship bound for Gaul. Where else would they go? No doubt, that bitch warms his bed like she did Ida's." He looked at the other men. "We would make a statement to Gaul; if Childebert dares to advance on Léon and Benoic, he'll face Britain's forces as well."

Custennin shook his head. "So far, those have been only rumors. Arthur keeps us informed. We have adversaries much closer to Camelot." He looked around as the warlords all nodded approval. "You have your own lands to defend. You've said you don't like the forces Ida's built."

"Exactly," Lancelot answered. "That's why I can't take my own cohorts and go. Joyous Garde would be open to attack. But I could spare a company if I had additions from the rest of you." He glanced around the room again, but the men weren't eager to meet his eyes. Drinking from the Grail had finally united them, but at the wrong time for him.

Cuneglasus, who'd fought with Agricola and Lancelot at Cam's Landing, finally spoke. "No one here denies you have the right to avenge the queen. Your wife," he corrected himself. "For certes, all of us would be glad to see Medraut dead. We all lost good men and comrades because of him." He looked steadily at Lancelot. "We can't risk war with Gaul until we have safety here."

A guard, appearing in the doorway, interrupted Lancelot's reply. The warlords all turned and Custennin asked, "What is it?"

The man looked both excited and frightened. "A messenger, sire, from Armel."

Everyone fell silent as Custennin told the guard to admit the messenger, but he hovered. "Is there more?" Custennin asked.

"Yes. A lady accompanies him."

He arched an eyebrow. "Why would Armel send a woman here?"

The woman's voice answered him. "Childebert has begun his advance westward toward Léon."

As one, each man turned at the sound of that soft voice, exuding power. Nimue stood in the doorway.

"Go with Nimue, Gwen. Please. You'll be safe on the Isle." Lancelot had finished his packing early one morning a few days later and now stood in front of where Gwenhwyfar sat on the lounge in their chamber. She was still in a simple nightdress, hair undone, and he restrained the urge to gather her in his arms.

"Elen is there. She'll not be glad to see me," she spoke in a monotone.

"The more reason to go." Lancelot knelt before her. "The two of you need time together. Mayhap, if I'm not there..."

She shrugged. "Custennin has offered to let me stay here. I should be quite safe at Camelot."

Lancelot's troops, as many as he dared pull from Joyous Garde, had arrived the day before and would be departing the next day. The warlords of the south had rallied immediately and already left. Keidyaw, whose lands were close to Lancelot's, and Bedwyr's men from Cameliard had been designated to stay behind to guard the Wall and keep an eye on Ida's movements. Custennin had left less than half of his troops at Camelot.

He sat beside her. "I would feel better if you were on Avallach." Even though Custennin had left a loyal man in charge, Lancelot did not want to take any chances on Gwenhwyfar's wellbeing. At fifty, Gwenhwyfar was still an attractive woman, the years in Faerie hadn't aged her, and she'd once been queen. A tempting combination for any man and Lancelot had caught several of them watching her more than once.

She suddenly took his hand and squeezed it. "You're afraid someone will hurt me again, aren't you?"

"Yes." He breathed a sigh of relief and put his other hand over hers. "Will you go to the Isle?"

She smiled faintly. "It's the least I can do, I suppose. I haven't been much of a wife to you for months now."

"Don't blame yourself. We've been over that. I'm happy with you."

She looked past him, her eyes on some distant point as though deep in thought. Finally, she gave herself a little shake and turned back to him. "Arthur always said a wife should send her husband off to war happy. I don't want you to leave like this. Like how it has been between us."

He looked into her eyes. "What do you mean?"

"I...you may make love to me, if you wish," she answered softly.

He felt a spark of hope kindle and quickly die. "If I wish? What about you, Gwen? I'll not force myself on you."

"Dear Lancelot." She brushed aside the stubborn strands of hair that always fell forward on his face. "I don't know that I can feel anything anymore. I'm so frightened when I remember what almost happened. But I won't deny you; you're my husband."

His eyes smoldered. "You have no duty to perform with me."

She met his gaze. "I know that. I'm being honest; this is all I have to offer."

He searched her face and then released her hand, sighing. "No. I'll not cause you more pain. I appreciate your intention, but I'll not have you pretending, just so I can leave knowing I've bedded you." Lancelot started to rise, but Gwenhwyfar clutched his hand. Surprised, he looked down.

"Please." Her green eyes brightened with unshed tears and her voice trembled. "Please. I don't think I can ask again. Take this moment."

He hesitated and she stood in front of him. Her voice had more spirit than he'd heard in months, fringed with a tinge of anger. "Use those skills your mother's courtesans taught you." Her voice rose, approaching hysteria. "Help me to stop hating myself. Make me a complete woman again. Make me want you, Lancelot."

A sound came from him, something between a whimper and a growl as he stepped closer. He traced her cheek and jaw lightly with his fingertips as his arm went loosely around her waist. He felt her stiffen. *By Mithras! My wife is afraid of me! My Gwen, so free and uninhibited... freezes at my touch.* He almost gave in to despair; how was he going to have her enjoy this?

"Gwen," Lancelot said quietly, "I love you. You know I won't hurt you."

Her eyes were wide and as green as a forest's shadows. "I'm scared, Lancelot."

"Of what?" He brushed kisses across her forehead and laid his cheek against hers and stroked her back soothingly and was rewarded by feeling some of the tension released. Tentatively, her arms went around his neck.

"I don't know," Gwenhwyfar answered. "Since it...almost happened, I've had no desire."

He felt the wetness of her tears as she buried her face in his shoulder and almost breathed a sigh of relief. Almost. At least she didn't despise him. Lancelot leaned back a bit and brought her chin up with one hand and began to kiss the saltiness from her face. She trembled, but didn't pull back. He nibbled her ear gently and moved on to the nape of her neck. Gwenhwyfar always liked having her neck nuzzled...and yes, there was that subtle shudder.

He gave her throat a series of butterfly kisses and then brushed his lips against hers.

There was no response, but no resistance either. He kissed her softly, applying no pressure, and then again and yet again. First the upper lip, then the lower, and again, a full kiss, still light, not asking for entrance.

Gwenhwyfar sighed and felt herself begin to relax. Slowly, she began to return his kisses, wondering when the pressure would increase, but he made no demands. Instead, he nibbled at her ear and throat and neck again, his arms still loose about her, the stroking of her back gentle. Lancelot stepped back and lowered her arms. He lifted one of her hands and began kissing the palm slowly, the soft pressure of his lips sending an unexpected quiver throughout her. When his tongue, supple and warm, traced circles, she gave an involuntary gasp. He continued sensually up the inside of her arm and mouthed her armpit, causing yet another sharp intake of breath. Very, very lightly, his lips barely grazed a nipple through the thin material of the gown and then he brought her into his embrace again, his lips tender and easy upon hers.

He traced the outline of her lips with the tip of his tongue and was rewarded with a soft moan. She parted her lips slightly and he began a slow, easy exploration of her mouth, teasing her tongue with his, withdrawing to merely kiss her again, moving to butterfly kiss the rest of her face and then her earlobe and throat again before returning to her mouth. This time, she initiated the tongue tasting and he let one of his hands move slowly up her ribcage to the swell of her breast. Whether out of instinct or desire, she moved slightly and he found himself cupping the whole breast. Lightly, he rubbed his thumb across the nipple and it responded to him. *Ah, yes, Gwen. Feel the passion. Let yourself be a woman.*

He lifted her then and laid her on the bed and stretched out beside her, his hand sliding over her ribcage and stomach and abdomen and back to the breast again. He undid the laces to the flimsy gown and stroked her bare flesh. *By the gods, I was afraid I'd never do this again.* Gwenhwyfar had her eyes closed, but the beginning of a little smile curved on her lips.

Lancelot let his fingertips trail lightly the length of her body and back before he teased the nipples, flicking them lightly with his thumb, kneading the breasts softly, suckling gently. He let his fingers drift lazily to her thighs and she offered no resistance when he parted them. Dipping a finger, finding the pleasant wetness beginning to form, he caressed and massaged and kneaded until she groaned softly.

She lifted her hips and then ground them into the mattress, her back arching.

He applied more pressure and she gasped and her eyes flew open.

Lancelot was propped up on one elbow, watching her, his other hand still creating a delightful diversion.

Gwenhwyfar smiled at him. "How are you going to ravage me with all your clothes still on?"

"Do you want to be ravaged?" Lancelot returned her smile.

"I do now. With you." She pulled his head down for a demanding kiss and reached a hand down to fondle what felt like a rod of iron. "Now will you get out of those clothes?"

Lancelot grinned. “Your request is my pleasure, my lady.”

Arthur was waiting with Ector and Lionel at Benoic when Lancelot and his men rode in. Lancelot’s hair had begun to silver at the temples since he’d last seen him, but he dismounted, still as agile at fifty-four as he’d been years ago. Instinctively, Arthur stood a little taller. Today was not a day he wanted to remind himself that he was well past sixty; he had a battle to fight.

“How is Gwenhwyfar?”

A dreadful expression crossed Lancelot’s face and Arthur’s mouth set in a hard line when Lancelot explained the abduction and near rape.

“I’d hoped Medraut had reformed somewhat. We heard nothing of his returning to the area.”

“That will change,” Lancelot answered. “I think he’s gone back to Childebert.”

“You think he marches against Léon and Benoic?” Ector asked as he joined them.

“He hates me, Brother. He always has. He’ll lead the Franks if it means he could take Benoic.”

Ector frowned. “Is he a disciplined warrior?”

“Yes,” Arthur answered grimly. “Lancelot trained him. But he’s more than that. He’s a strategist and an opportunist and...and evil. Witch’s spawn. Incest is a vile deed; he is my penance for that sin.”

“You paid that penance at Cam’s Landing, Arthur, with far too many lives,” Lancelot spoke softly. “Pray we can stop him now.” He turned back to Ector. “Where is Childebert’s army?”

“Just east of Rennes,” Ector replied. “Custennin’s men joined with ours and are holding the line. Tomorrow, we’ll march to reinforce what’s already there.”

“One other thing helping us,” Lionel added, “is that Childebert’s men are falling sick. We’ve discovered some corpses as we advanced near Rennes. No battle wounds, just black blotches on the skin that had festered and burst open. Swollen lumps in the necks and armpits. No one had an appetite when we found the first one.”

“Nimue calls it a plague and she warned us to burn the bodies. A stinking business in itself,” Arthur said, “but our men have remained healthy.”

“Is that why you sent her back?” Lancelot asked.

Arthur nodded. “That and I fear for her safety here. Your mother’s cave is too isolated and I wouldn’t be able to protect her if I’m fighting elsewhere.”

“Was she successful in raising the Old Ways?”

“No, Lance.” Arthur was pensive. “I think your mother knew the Old Religion was dead here. Christianity is heralded, nearly to the point of fanaticism. Nimue was even threatened on one occasion when she tried to talk to the people.”

“I’m sorry to hear that,” Lancelot said, “both for herself and for you. When this war is over, why don’t you come back to Britain? Judwal has proved himself a strong ruler and, thanks to the Grail, Custennin has been able to hold the warlords together.”

"And I'm old enough to be put out to pasture?" Arthur smiled.

"I didn't mean that," Lancelot said quickly. "You deserve to be close to the people you love."

Arthur's level gaze faltered slightly. *Nimue. Gwenhwyfar. The two women he loved and couldn't see again since he knew returning to Britain was something he couldn't do.* "That might create problems, Lance."

"Mayhap, but think on it."

Arthur nodded. "First, though, we must send Childebert packing."

They met with Custennin late the next day. Childebert had taken the fort at Rennes and the Breton army had besieged it. Each morning the usual sallies and retreats occurred. The big onager hurled rocks at the stone wall and parts had crumbled, but they hadn't been able to get close enough, without great risk, to use the scaling ladders.

"Does Childebert lead the charges?" Lancelot asked.

Custennin shook his head. "His nephew, Theudebert, is in charge here. My suspicion is that Childebert is still mustering more troops."

"Reinforcements?" Arthur turned to Lancelot. "Your men have arrived just in time, it appears."

Lancelot nodded. As usual, he felt edgy before the battle. "We'll meet them before they gain the fort. Until then, we wait."

The wait wasn't long. Only three days had passed before the out-posted scouts returned. "They come!" one shouted as he slid from his tired, nearly blown horse. "A good two cohorts, mayhap more."

"How far away?" Custennin signaled his captains.

"Less than three miles."

"That gives us less than an hour." Lancelot began organizing his men, only to stop as the gates of the fort opened and the first sally of the day began. "Damnation!" he swore as Custennin's men turned back to fight. "A perfect diversion. They must know how close Childebert is."

Arthur nodded and pointed. "The dust no doubt."

Custennin nodded curtly to Arthur to take command of the cavalry while he addressed the fort. They now formed a solid line to meet the charge, Arthur in his old spot in the center, Lancelot to his right.

"It's been a long time since we've fought together," Lancelot said as he adjusted the lance in its leather cup. "Pray it isn't our last."

Arthur glanced at him. "You used to say you wanted to die with your armor on."

Lancelot had time for a quick grin before the enemy appeared over the last hill behind the fort. They slowed to a stop when they saw Arthur's men waiting then quickly fell into formation.

"At least their horses will be tired," Lancelot said. "If they're smart, they'll try to get us to charge first, up the hill." No sooner were his words out, than Childebert raised his arm and brought it down and their line came down the hill at a canter.

"Not so clever, then," Arthur replied. "His father, Clovis, would have waited." Then he gave his own signal to move and they joined forces.

The battle raged for most of the day. Theudebert's men had poured out of the fort to join Childebert's and the air rang with the clashing of swords and shields, horses stomping, the thud of horseflesh against horseflesh and men shouting. Although Childebert's army outnumbered the Bretons, the additional cavalry from Britain were better trained, and slowly the Gauls were forced to retreat to the fort for protection. The foot soldiers prepared to use the battering ram, under protection of the Roman tortoise shield-wall. The petty kings had fought well, in accord with Custennin's command. The Grail's power shone through.

Lancelot had been watching one particular fighter all day. The man was vicious, clearly taking pleasure in hacking off heads and disemboweling fallen men. War meant killing, but it could be done without such malice. Although the warrior's visor was down, Lancelot had no doubts.

"That's him," he said to Arthur as the skirmishes moved away from them. "Medraut."

Arthur sighed. "I know. I've been watching him, too. He obviously doesn't know you and I are here."

"That will change." Lancelot raised his visor.

"Wait." Arthur laid a hand on his arm. "I gave my oath to the Grail Maiden that I would forgive him. I cannot fight."

"I wouldn't expect you to, Arthur. He's your son, even if his mother is demon sent. But I must avenge what he tried to do to Gwenhwyfar."

Arthur nodded slowly.

"Medraut!" Lancelot's voice carried over the clashes.

The soldier turned in his saddle. For a moment, he was still as a statue, then pushed his visor up. He stared; then, a diabolical smile spread across his face as he urged his mount closer.

"Lancelot," he said sardonically. "What brings you here?"

He ignored the sarcasm. "Name your weapon, Medraut."

He laughed. "I'm finally going to be able to kill you. But first, did Gwenhwyfar tell you how good I kiss?"

Lancelot gripped his reins and forced himself to remain still. "Name your weapon. I won't give you another chance for a choice."

"I kiss better than you. Gwenhwyfar said so. Unfortunately, urgent business prevented me giving her what she wanted then, but I'm sure she would've thought I did everything better than you." Medraut continued to goad him, ignoring the question. "When I finish with you, I'll go back to Britain and take her for my wife."

Arthur raised his visor then. "If anything happens to Lancelot, I'll take care of Gwenhwyfar."

Medraut was stunned into silence. "Fa...you're supposed to be dead."

"Not yet," Arthur replied.

Medraut's face changed and he sneered at Lancelot. "Now I see why you challenged me. I'll have to fight the both of you."

"No," Lancelot replied. "You're all mine. Prepare your lance. We joust."

"You'd like that advantage, wouldn't you?" Medraut snapped. "The whole world knows your name is because of your skill with the lance."

"Are you refusing a challenge, Medraut?" Arthur asked in the silken tone that was so dangerous. "I never thought you for a coward."

Fury burned in the man's face. Without answering, Medraut wheeled his horse to take position some paces away. He pulled his lance from its pocket and kicked his horse to full gallop.

"Fool," Lancelot said under his breath as he readied his lance properly and cantered. His shield came up to deflect the blow.

Medraut laughed as he thrust his lance and found himself lifted from the saddle, Lancelot's weapon catching him low and behind his shield. He hit the ground hard, the breath gone from him. When he finally sat up, Lancelot stood waiting for him, sword drawn.

He pushed himself to his feet, wary now, putting distance between them as his hand went to his hilt. Lancelot eyed him calmly.

They circled, each watching the other's face. Lancelot feinted right, but Medraut didn't take the bait. "You've trained me better than that, Lancelot." He lunged and thrust then, only to find his blade engaged. He pressed hard and quickly disengaged and retreated. Lancelot advanced with a head cut, and Medraut parried. They engaged again and broke apart. The fight continued well over an hour.

Lancelot felt himself tiring and cursed inwardly that age could be the deciding factor in this battle. *But Medraut's blows are not as strong as they were either and his cuts are slower*. He willed strength to his arm and lunged again.

Medraut sidestepped. Then, Lancelot suddenly feinted to his left. Medraut, anticipating, cut left, but Lancelot completed the step and dealt Medraut a blow to his wrist, numbing it and sending the sword flying. Quickly, he leaned down, but Lancelot's fist connected to his jaw, sending him sprawling. In another minute, the tip of the sword was at Medraut's throat.

"The double feint, Medraut, remember? You've never anticipated that one." Lancelot's sword pricked the skin of his throat. A thin line of blood appeared.

"If you kill me, Lancelot, you kill a king's son."

"For which the king will thank me, since he's sworn an oath not to." The sword point moved downward toward his heart. Medraut squirmed, only to find the point once again at his throat. "Move and you die now." Lancelot paused, thinking. "Then again, mayhap I'll show mercy and just keep you from ever raping anyone." The sword moved quickly to lift the codpiece protecting the vulnerable area. "You can choose life, Medraut."

Real fear showed in the man's face. "You wouldn't castrate me."

"No?" Lancelot smiled, but his eyes were cold. "I've done it before; only Aelle asked me to kill the men first."

"Men?"

"Two of them." The point of Lancelot's sword poked through the trews and nicked the nether skin. Medraut blanched. "Saxon mercenaries. They also TRIED to rape Gwenhwyfar." He moved the sword a little, watching the bastard pale. "Shall I drive this home and let you live?"

"No. Yes. Stop." Medraut whimpered. "Let me live. I will make amends..."

"You choose life?"

Medraut hesitated, rivulets of sweat running down his face. "Yes. Let me live."

Lancelot looked down at him in disgust. "You coward," he said softly, "a man would choose death." He plunged the sword down through the testicles, pinning Medraut to the ground. Ignoring the hideous scream, he turned and walked away.

He saw Arthur raise his arm and the dagger flashed in the sunlight, before it began to spin. He dropped and rolled. The dagger hit the ground near him. He closed his eyes and lay still. *I cannot fight Arthur. If he wants to kill me for what I did, so be it.*

Slowly, he became aware the screaming had stopped. Opening his eyes, he saw Arthur kneeling beside him, tears streaking the dirt on his face. "I thought you wanted to kill me."

Arthur merely shook his head and pointed. Lancelot sat up and turned to see the thrown dagger stuck in the middle of Medraut's chest, the sword on the ground. He looked back at Arthur. "What happened?"

"He had a dagger hidden. How he had the strength to throw it, I don't know, but he did. At your back while you walked away."

"You killed your son."

"You saved my life when you first came to me," Arthur answered and stood up. "I think we're even now." Wearily, he walked to his horse and mounted. "I doubt that I can look at you without thinking of what I did." He gave a Roman salute. "You'll not be seeing me again."

Lancelot sat on the ground and wept as Arthur rode away.

Morgana knew the moment it happened. A searing pain cut through her chest, leaving her weak and empty. She'd been having nightmares in which Medraut was fighting a battle he couldn't win.

Six weeks later, when Childebert's tattered and plague-diseased troops arrived back in Paris, she waited for him in his council chamber. "How did he die?"

Childebert removed his cloak and tossed it on the table. He didn't look surprised that she knew. "In battle."

She eyed him steadily. "Nobly? As a soldier?"

"For certes," he lied. "We gave him a soldier's burial."

"Who killed him?"

He swallowed hard. "Lancelot wounded him."

Morgana's black eyes glittered. "So Lancelot did follow us." She took a deep breath. "Was his the death wound?"

"No." Childebert finally looked at her. "Another man who fought with Lancelot. They'd been side-by-side all day, moving as one unit, each protecting the other. If I'd had the time, I would've admired their strategy."

"Who was the man?" Morgana leaned forward.

"That was the strange thing," he answered slowly. "He looked like the emissary who came to me years ago, when Judwal was still a boy. Called himself Armel."

Morgana's eyes narrowed. "Is Armel a native Breton? From Léon or Benoic?"

"No. From Britain. He admitted to fighting with King Arthur once, but he had no more wish to do battle he said." Childebert shook his head. "I had no idea the man was so strong a warrior. It was the two of them who literally drove our men back into the fort. Only Medraut stayed outside the walls."

She sat back with a slight smile. "So my son faced the two men he hated most in the world alone."

Childebert looked bewildered. "The two men he hated? Impossible. He wouldn't even know Armel."

"Ah, but he would, I think." For a moment, her eyes glazed as she recalled memories. She turned to him. "Most men know your emissary as Arthur, the king."

He stared at her. "Arthur is long dead."

Morgana gave a short laugh. "He wanted us to think so. But only one pair fights as you've described." She became serious. "Is he still with Lancelot?"

"He disappeared after Medraut's death." He paused. "Lancelot fought with his kinsmen after that."

"Lancelot's still in Benoic?"

"Yes," he answered hesitantly.

"What is it?" Morgana asked.

"He wants me to give you into his custody."

She eyed him warily. "And your decision?"

"I will not deliver you to him." He looked miserable. "But you cannot stay here any longer. Something has happened to Britain's army to unify it. We were forced to retreat. I won't risk war with all of Armorica while my army is so diminished."

Morgana patted his hand before she stood. "I'll go to Lancelot, but not now. On my own terms." *Oh, yes, Lancelot; you'll see me again. I'll take from you what you took from me. The person you cherish most, and the person Arthur does, too. Gwenhwyfar. You'll both finally pay the price for loving her...and feel the pain from her horrible death.*

~ *Chapter 17—Bedlam* ~

Gwenhwyfar sat in her favorite spot in the apple orchard on Avallach. The few times she'd come to the Isle, she'd been in need of healing. This visit was no different.

The sweet smell of ripe apples lingered in the still, warm air. Overhead, the brilliant blue sky featured tufts of cotton floating lazily along.

"I like the orchard, too." Elen drew her knees to her chin and wrapped her arms around them. "It's so peaceful here."

Gwenhwyfar smiled. *At least Lancelot will be glad to know that in the two months I've been here, Elen has begun to accept me.* "You like everything about Avallach," she said. "I've never gotten used to it."

Elen studied a cloud. "Since being here, I've changed my mind about a lot of things. Argante doesn't make me study Latin. Instead, she's given me lessons in harping and herbals and taught me how to see inside myself. I've almost mastered the art of being still." She pointed to her head.

"What is the purpose of that?" Gwenhwyfar asked, amused because Elen was an active child.

She looked at Gwenhwyfar seriously. "If I can still my mind, knowledge will come. Already, I see pictures sometimes."

Gwenhwyfar frowned. "Are you talking about what Nimue calls the Sight?"

Elen shrugged. "Mayhap. Argante is going to let me try scrying soon."

"Have you been to the Sacred Pool?" she asked.

"Not yet. I can't do that until I'm an Initiate."

Gwenhwyfar was surprised. "Is that what you want, Elen? To stay here? Become a priestess?"

"I think so." She plucked a blade of grass and ran it between two fingers, making it emit a soft whistle.

"But you're so young, not quite four and ten. You don't want to get married?"

Elen wrinkled her nose. "I don't think I'd want to be like you and my father."

Gwenhwyfar kept her tone light, teasing. "And what have your father and I done that is so bad? I think we have a good marriage. We're happy."

"I know," Elen admitted, "and I was jealous at first, but I don't think I could do what you do."

"What are you talking about?" Gwenhwyfar asked in bewilderment.

"Well, I...you won't get mad if I tell you?" Elen asked tentatively.

Gwenhwyfar looked at Lancelot's daughter, a bit warily. "I promise. I won't get angry. Did you do something you shouldn't have been doing?"

She shook her head. "No. One night I got up for some water and I heard some horrible noises. Like someone was hurt. Grunting and moaning. They were coming from your room."

"I think I'm beginning to see," Gwenhwyfar said.

Elen hung her head. "I shouldn't have opened the door. Your room is private, but I thought someone was hurt. I saw my father on top of you and you were both moving like the dogs do in the springtime."

Gwenhwyfar held up a hand, trying hard not to laugh. "I'm sorry you saw that, Elen," she managed to say gravely. "And, at your age, I might have thought the same thing. In fact, I did. I married Arthur when I was barely seven and ten and I was scared of him." She smiled then. "But when you're a little older, you'll meet someone who'll change your mind. If men and women didn't enjoy doing what you saw, there'd be nobody here."

Elen wrinkled her forehead, thinking. She was about to ask another question, but Nimue appeared at the end of the orchard.

"A messenger arrived a few minutes ago, Gwenhwyfar, with bad news. Ida has taken Joyous Garde, and Wehha marches toward Camelot!"

Landinus met Gwenhwyfar in Nimue's chambers. "Keidyaw's men were supposed to reinforce the three hundred Lancelot left behind. But they wanted to get their crops in first. Ida lost no time in laying siege."

"But Ida's army is about a thousand men," she answered, puzzled. "Joyous Garde always has stores for several months. Why couldn't you hold?"

Landinus looked embarrassed. "Unbeknown to us, Saxons were amassing further north. Dozens of keelboats had landed."

"Where were your scouts?" Gwenhwyfar demanded and started to pace. "God's grace! Lancelot always kept the shore well patrolled."

"Dead. Ambushed. So were Keidyaw's men when they finally came. They weren't expecting trouble and walked right into it."

"So you were forced to surrender?"

He hung his head and his face turned a deep red. "Yes, my lady. I'm ashamed to say it."

"Lancelot must return." She changed direction and paced in front of the white hart tapestry. "We must send word to him." She paused suddenly. "Did Lupin survive?" She thought of the strong, loyal man who'd always held Joyous Garde for Lancelot. The man who'd never judged them.

Landinus nodded. "Lupin offered himself hostage for the soldiers' releases." He lifted his head. "You should be proud to know, most of the soldiers did not flee. Ida holds them all now."

"Fie!" Gwenhwyfar exclaimed in distress. "It would have been better if they had and regrouped elsewhere. Lancelot would have more men to fight with."

"They did not want to appear cowards, my lady."

Gwenhwyfar sighed. "I know. Lancelot would not have thought them that. Still, it gives us more men inside. Lancelot will fight."

"Mayhap," Landinus continued cautiously, "but when the Captain returns, the troops must stop Wehha first. Gryflet's scouts from Camelot say keelboats are arriving in Anglia as well. Custennin will demand the south be secured before the north."

She stared at him. "This sounds like a well thought out three-prong invasion. Childebert lures Briton troops to Armorica and Ida moves south just as Wehha moves west." How she wished Lancelot or Arthur were here. War strategies were their field of expertise. Arthur. She looked at Nimue and wondered if they could get him to return. Abruptly, she dismissed Landinus. "You look dead on your feet. Get something to eat and some rest. We'll talk more later."

He flashed a grateful look and was gone. Once alone with Nimue, she said, "If only Arthur would come with them and lead the men. Wehha would retreat. Mayhap, Arthur could even get Wehha to share the Grail!"

From her chair, Nimue watched her. "Arthur will not return to Britain while you and Lancelot live."

Surprised, Gwenhwyfar stopped. "Is that a Sighting, Nimue?"

The priestess smiled a little. "No. Arthur exiled himself for you because you saved his life on Avalon. The pain would be too great."

"He loves you."

"Yes. That has been so since Argante was born, but he never lost his love for you. You will always be his wife."

"Arthur said I'd been declared dead; the marriage vows dissolved."

Nimue leaned forward. "Partially true. Now you are very much alive and for practical purposes, Arthur is dead, or at least, has disappeared. Why do you suppose he has taken an assumed name and stays in Léon?"

Gwenhwyfar's face paled as realization began to take hold. "He said to live in peace as an emissary and to strengthen Judwal's rule."

"Again, partially true." Nimue's eyes were as clear as the sea on a calm, summer day, but her voice distant. "He has always known you loved Lancelot more than him." She held up a hand as Gwenhwyfar started to protest. "It matters not, now. If Arthur returned, alive and well, you'd still be his wife. There was no divorce, no papal dispensation. Arthur, by law, would still be high king. You and Lancelot would be tried for treason."

Gwenhwyfar's eyes narrowed. "Come, Nimue. Morgana tried that once before. Arthur would not permit it."

Nimue inclined her head. "Even though he's abdicated, he's a living king. You have committed a crime against Britain."

"Still, Arthur would not allow..." Her mind spun. *Not again!*

"Gwenhwyfar. The man in power is Custennin. His hold on Arthur's men has always been tenacious. Cormant still yearns for the high kingship. Custennin cannot afford to show mercy in a suit of treason." The crystalline eyes pierced her. "Do you understand now why Arthur cannot return? He loves you and Lancelot too much to jeopardize your lives."

Gwenhwyfar sank into the chair silently and buried her hands in her face. "Arthur could save Britain. I stand between him and that. Why must I bear the burden for loving two strong men?"

Nimue laid her small hand on Gwenhwyfar's shoulder. "Much is asked of queens. You cannot revoke your queenship merely by saying so," she answered gently, "any more than Arthur's granting Custennin the crown makes Arthur less a king."

"What must I do?" Gwenhwyfar looked up.

"Give up Lancelot."

Gwenhwyfar shook her head. "That I will not do again."

Lancelot received the news of Joyous Garde shortly after Childebert's defeat. He'd begun to issue orders for his cohort's immediate return when Custennin stayed him.

"The damage has been done, Lancelot. I must secure Armorica before we return. Taking only your cohort will cost many lives and it will weaken our efforts here. Wait until the whole army can move."

"But my men will be expecting me."

"Your men are either already dead or captured. If they're alive, they are kept as hostages and won't be harmed." Custennin's hard brown eyes looked into Lancelot's smoky ones. "Think like the soldier you are. Your daughter and Gwenhwyfar are safe."

Thank the Goddess I sent Augusta with Gwenhwyfar. Lancelot didn't think he could bear the thought of what Saxon men would do before they killed either of them. "Lupin..."

Custennin cut him off. "Lupin is a warrior, your right hand man. He will do what he needs to do." He tilted his head. "Besides, there's a loose end here. Don't you want to take Morgana into custody?"

Lancelot's mouth set in a grim line. "Childebert won't relinquish her unless we march behind him and storm Paris."

"She is a liability to him. Why would he want to keep her?"

Lancelot gave a short laugh that sounded more like a bark. "The bitch lures men to bed; no doubt she warms his as well."

"The woman must be near seventy, man. How attractive can she be?"

"How she looks is not the point. The herbs she slips into their wine will make them ready to rut with a sow, the need is so strong."

"Are you speaking from experience, Lancelot?" Custennin looked almost amused.

Lancelot gave him a look that would have shriveled most men. "Elaine contrived with her. It is how I was forced into marriage."

Custennin stared at him a moment longer, then looked away. "We'll bide our time with Morgana. She's no Helen that I'll risk more men storming Paris. Sooner or later, she'll surface."

"This is madness," Galahad said to Gryflet as he followed him to the bailey where the men were mounted. "Let's offer to treaty with Wehha."

"Custennin already offered that. Wehha pretended to be thinking it over. This must be his answer."

"The Grail is supposed to bring peace," Galahad protested.

"Then I'll leave you and Peredur to protect it; I'll need the Defenders. My job is to protect Camelot." Gryflet sounded impatient. "Ida has already invaded your father's lands. Keidyaw lost nearly half his men in the Saxon slaughter. Bedwyr is just barely holding the line in the north. I'll not let this opportunist think he can trample on Camelot just because Custennin isn't here. Even the Grail cannot force peace on those who don't want it. We join Cormant to stop Wehha." He turned away, shouting orders.

"The message that arrived yesterday from Vortiporius warned of uprising in the west as well," Galahad argued to Peredur as they stood with Dindrane in the swirling dust watching the army move out. "If the Scotti grow restless with their share of Demetia, this will be the opportune time to strike."

"Beaurepaire lies between here and Demetia," Peredur interrupted. "If Clamadeu needs to defend himself while Gryflet leads our men east, Blanchefleur would be in danger. I wish I'd never let you persuade me to stay here."

Dindrane gave him a withered glance. "More likely, Clamadeu would fight with the Scotti, not against them. He's no friend of Camelot."

Peredur glanced at Galahad worriedly. "I should've gone to get her."

"You'll start a war for sure if you do." Galahad felt the pressure of Dindrane's hand, squeezing his fingers. He looked down to find her appealing to him silently. He sighed. "How do you know she hasn't reconciled to the marriage? Maybe she's even happy?"

Peredur gave them both a triumphant look as he pulled the leather cord from around his neck, revealing a small pouch that had been tucked inside his shirt. "Because she sent me this." Carefully, he opened it and withdrew a lock of brown hair.

Galahad looked at it incredulously. "How...when did you get that?"

"While I was training the Defenders, I kept thinking about her. I finally sent a messenger to Gornemant. Her uncle was to find out how things were at Beaurepaire. I just got this a few days ago. Gornemant invited Clamadeu to return with him to Gohort. Family business." He replaced the hair and tucked the pouch away. "This was her response."

"What will you do?" Galahad asked.

"I'm going to get her," Peredur answered. "Once Gryflet leaves, I'll slip off. One man, dressed not as a soldier, can travel inconspicuously.

"You won't be safe bringing her back here," Dindrane said. "Galahad is right; it will incite war."

"Then we'll sail for Armorica. Bors keeps his ships ready at Portus Adurni."

Galahad put a hand on his shoulder. "I cannot stand watch day and night. You would leave the Grail unguarded?"

Peredur hesitated for a moment. "Hide it until the troops are back."

"The cup is meant to be used," Galahad retorted, "or it should be returned to God."

"The Isle might be the best place for it."

"No. The Christos' cup belongs to the Christians. Joseph of Arimathea brought it to Britain from the Holy Land. If it goes anywhere, it goes there."

"Then do it," Peredur responded. "But wait for me to return. Blanchefleur and I will travel with you. It matters not where we go."

"Are you both mad?" Dindrane glared from one to the other. "Britain needs you and the Grail. Wehha may be willing to treaty once Gryflet gives him a good trouncing. You can't just disappear with the Grail. Custennin will be furious. You won't be able to step foot on Britain's soil again."

Peredur thrust his chin forward. "I want to raise my own son. Blanchefleur and I deserve happiness. You have it with Galahad."

Her face softened momentarily then she turned to Galahad. "Your father will think you a coward for running away."

A muscle twitched in Galahad's jaw. "What else can I do? I am sworn. The Grail must be protected."

"Then I'll help you protect it. I can handle a sword." Dindrane's voice went soft and low. "Do neither of you think a woman capable?"

Galahad smiled. "For certes, but we've had four armed men guarding the Grail on four hour shifts. Now, there would be only you and me."

She wasn't appeased. "The guardians were to ensure no pilgrim or stranger would try to steal it. Camelot's gates will be locked until Gryflet returns. There'll be no visitors. You and I can do this. I'll even cut my hair short, so I'll appear as a man in armor." When he didn't answer, she studied his face. "Do you not value my service, Galahad?"

He looked over her head at Peredur, knowing he'd lost the battle. He took a deep breath. "I value you, Dindrane. As you wish, then. The Grail and I will stay."

She threw her arms around him and he laid his head against the soft fragrance of her hair wondering how this woman could have so much influence over him.

Seated in the dining hall at Beaurepaire, Peredur studied his son. Lohengrin was three and ten and tall for his age with his father's brown hair and eyes, but with a confidence Peredur had never possessed.

Blanchefleur was making a big fuss over the extravagance of dinner and Peredur hoped, but didn't believe, it was what she normally did. He didn't want to attract any unusual attention.

"The king has sent me throughout Cambria to renew the allegiances of the lesser kings." Peredur spoke loud enough for the seneschal to hear. "I'd hoped to meet your husband. A pity he's away."

"Yes," Blanchefleur said, a twinkle in her blue eyes that belied the tone of her voice. "My uncle had need of his services again."

Peredur asked gravely, "We can be assured that he'll defend against the Scotti should they move eastward?" He was aware of the servants hovering.

"May I talk?" Lohengrin asked politely, his warm brown eyes serious. "We cannot speak for my father. His mind changes with his moods."

"Lohengrin," Blanchefleur admonished. "Remember your place." Discreetly, she tilted her head toward the immobile waiter standing at the serving board.

He lowered his voice. "I don't think my father would move against you himself. But there is strength in numbers."

"Your father's a formidable fighter," Peredur said. "Do you think he wishes to be independent of Custennin's reign?"

The boy glanced around. "I cannot say. But my mother and I are loyal to the king. Please tell him that when he returns."

"Would you like the opportunity to tell him yourself?" Peredur asked quietly, fully aware of the need to be discreet.

Lohengrin's eyes shone and he nodded. "When?"

"Just follow your mother's instructions." Then he changed the subject, raising his voice, making the conversation sound natural. *After tonight, my son, we will be a family.*

Galahad watched as Peredur's small party pounded down the Roman road to Camelot's gates the third day. He'd half-hoped Peredur would ride on to Portus Adurni.

"You're Galahad?" Lohengrin asked eagerly as he slid off his horse and looked up at him with awe. "Lancelot's son?"

Galahad grimaced, still not caring for the comparison, but the youth was already moving on. "The Grail is here? Can I see it?"

He pointed the way and the boy grabbed his mother's hand to take her with him, but Peredur stopped him. "Let me introduce your mother first." He turned to Galahad. "This is Blanchefleur; now can you see why I had to go?"

Galahad bowed slightly. "You're very beautiful, my lady."

She blushed. Peredur quickly kissed her before Lohengrin grabbed her hand again. The two men watched them walk toward the shrine.

"How far behind are they?" Galahad motioned for the guard to lock the gates. Already, he had men posted on the battlements.

Peredur shrugged. "They may not be. Conveniently, Clamadeu had been called away by Gornemant. I told the seneschal that Custennin ordered the lord's women and children to the safety of the fort at Caerleon because the Scotti had begun to move."

Galahad raised an eyebrow. "He believed that?"

Peredur grinned. "He did when I produced written authorization from Custennin. I told him I'd delivered the same message to the other holdings."

Galahad shook his head unbelievingly. "You're still the fool, Peredur, even more so for forging the king's seal. I don't even want to know how you got it. When Clamadeu returns, he'll be in pursuit."

"Gornemant promised to keep him three days. Once he realizes Blanchefleur is gone, he'll stop at Caerleon first," Peredur said confidently. "We'll be gone by tomorrow. Bors has the boat ready. You won't even have to admit we were here. There'll be no war."

Clamadeu attacked the next morning mere hours after Peredur, Blanchefleur and Lohengrin had left.

"How could he have gotten word so early?" one of the younger men asked as he pulled on his armor and reached for his swordbelt.

"The man is no fool," Galahad muttered as he put on his gauntlets. "No doubt he saw through the ruse of being needed at Gornemant's again and returned right after Peredur left."

"But he was supposed to stop at Caerleon first!"

Galahad signaled the gates to be opened. Their cavalry could best Clamadeu's infantry and the few horsemen he had. Better to fight the battle outside, away from the fort than let Clamadeu lay siege to it. He turned in his saddle to wave to Dindrane.

She was lightly armored, standing with another soldier at the door of the shrine. "We'll be waiting for you," she called.

On impulse, he turned and trotted to her, leaning down from the saddle to draw her up for a kiss. "I think Peredur's besottedness has spilled over on me. I love you and am ready to consummate this. Will you marry me tomorrow?"

Dindrane wrapped her arms more tightly about his neck, her toes barely touching the ground. "Yes, Galahad. I've waited so long to hear you say that." She clung to him and deepened their kiss. Reluctantly, he set her on the ground. "I'll be back." She nodded and watched him ride through the gates.

They cantered in pairs down the road to the open field where Clamadeu's troops formed. Gryflet had taken most of the men with him, leaving seventy horsemen.

"I offer to treaty; come share the Grail," Galahad called. "Peredur is not here."

"You harbored him," Clamadeu shouted back.

"He acted on his own. Without leave." Galahad tried once more to reason with him. "There is no need to fight!"

His effort was ignored. "Where is he?"

"Gone. Across the sea. Please, come partake of the Grail. It will allow you to forgive and understand."

Clamadeu snorted. "That's right. You wanted to be a priest. I have no desire to forgive. I want my wife back!"

"She's not here," Galahad repeated. "There's nothing I can do."

Silence followed and then Clamadeu raised his hand. Galahad's men positioned their lances. Clamadeu dropped his hand and his men cantered forward, looking like so many children's rocking horses, set in slow motion, the metal tips of the lances catching the rays of the sun, sending golden flashes through the air.

What Galahad hadn't expected to see were the hundreds of Scotti that emerged on foot from the trees behind them. He gasped involuntarily. Gryflet had left him in charge, expecting no trouble. Even though Lancelot had drilled battle strategy into him, the few times he'd seen battle, another more experienced man was beside him. He'd not anticipated more than Clamadeu's small army. They were now vastly outnumbered.

Then, he had no more time to think. The horses were engaged, the sound of the heavy lances hitting shields and the thumps of bodies hitting the ground taking all other thoughts from him. He concentrated on the man aiming for him, keeping his shield up, adjusting the lance slightly.

The man was lifted from his saddle and Galahad wheeled his horse, preparing for a second charge. Only then was he aware of the body of foot soldiers streaming toward the fort. He hoped enough bowmen were on the battlements to hold them then he was in the middle of the fighting again.

His arm seemed to move of its own accord, slashing on either side of his horse. Blood spurting from the first man's throat, nearly made him vomit. The pain from a cut to his thigh cleared his head. He sliced savagely with his sword, knocking the shield from the soldier; the point of his blade caught the man's soft middle under the hauberk. In a moment, he was impaled, the unbalanced weight nearly pulling Galahad from the saddle. He jerked his weapon back and the man fell, his entrails spreading over the ground. Briefly, Galahad thought he might be sick, then a spear whizzed by his head and he wheeled the horse and plummeted on.

Lances broke and men fought with swords, many of them unhorsed, as the battle wore on. Nascien's shield was strongly built and protected

Galahad from the worst blows. Eventually, the field thinned; more bodies lay on the ground than were standing. Clamadeu appeared suddenly in front of Galahad, his horse's hooves dancing.

"We can call a truce," Galahad offered from his saddle. "Enough men have died! Let's drink from the Grail."

"If my wife and her paramour are not here, you'll answer in his place," Clamadeu snarled back, ignoring the offer.

"I don't want to kill you, Clamadeu. We have no quarrel."

"Are you sure you're Lancelot's son?" Clamadeu taunted Galahad. "Lancelot wouldn't hesitate to fight. You want to grovel in front of a cup."

Galahad had had one too many comparisons with his father. His eyes shot bolts of lightning. "A duel then. The lance?"

Clamadeu looked surprised then laughed. "So, there is some of the Breton devil's blood in you. I accept your challenge."

Fighting now stopped as men formed lines on either side of the pair, creating an informal lists. Someone handed each a lance.

Afterward, Galahad had no recollection of riding forward, of the lance finding its mark and driving under the shield and armor and unhorsing the man. When he refocused, he realized men were cheering then he saw what he'd done. So this was battle frenzy. He didn't like it. He looked down at the bloodied body, still breathing. "Take him to the infirmary," he said tiredly. "This battle is over."

He turned back to the fort, which was eerily silent, as he rode in. *Some Scottis have gotten through, but they're all dead or captured. Why aren't the men celebrating?* He dismounted, wondering why men turned their head away from him. *Am I that bloodied?*

He pulled off his helmet and walked around the corner to the shrine and stopped. The world spun dizzily and the helmet slipped from his nerveless fingers. Slowly, he sank to his knees.

Dindrane lay on the ground, her blood drained from the slit in her throat, the soil a deep maroon around her. Her hand still clenched the Grail that lay at her side.

Galahad crawled to her, cradling the wobbly head in his hands.

"We have the culprit, my lord." One of the archers rested a hand on his shoulder.

He looked up blankly. "What?"

"We have the man," the young soldier stammered, "the one who did this to her."

Slowly, his eyes focused on the warrior. "Bring him to me."

They dragged the Scotti, kicking and screaming, to him. Galahad said nothing, but seemed to grow in stature. The soldiers who had gathered around began to shrink back for Galahad suddenly had become his father.

"Why would you kill a woman?" His voice was cold, hard.

The man whimpered. "I didn't know she was a woman. The armor..."

"No?" Galahad moved deliberately closer, menacing in his slowness. "Why were you back here? Weren't there enough men to fight in the bailey?"

"Yes. No. I was told to find...the Grail." The man stammered so badly he could barely be understood.

"Why?" Galahad's voice was flinty, every muscle tensed.

"Clamadeu thought...ransom..."

"To return Blanchefleur and Lohengrin."

"Yes. Yes. Please forgive me...I would not have killed a woman."

"It is not in my power to forgive," Galahad answered. "Only God can do that." He stooped to pick up the Grail, his fingers lingering slightly on Dindrane's hardening hand. "Take a look at it, soldier." He pulled his sword from its scabbard and held the tip of it to the man's throat.

The man pressed back against his captors, trying to avoid the tip. Instinctively, they pushed him forward, impaling him on the weapon. He gave a strangled gasp and blood spurted from his mouth. He sagged to the ground, dangling on the sword Galahad still held.

Like a man returning to consciousness, Galahad slowly released the sword. "I have murdered a defenseless man."

"No, my lord." One of the soldiers who held the man stepped up. "We thrust him upon your sword unwittingly."

"It was an accident," the other said.

Galahad ignored them and looked at the Grail he still held. "This cup would have brought peace. I have tainted it because I've shed blood." He wiped at his eyes with a bruised hand. "Dindrane. I have betrayed you; I wasn't true to the Grail."

The small crowd remained silent. He looked them over, then returned to study the Grail. "I will remove it from Camelot," he finally said. "It can no longer serve its purpose."

"Where will you take it, my lord?" The young man he'd talked to before they'd ridden out was beside him now.

Galahad looked at him. "It must be returned from whence it came. The Holy Land. I will find a temple for it there where God's grace may again claim it. Ride now, to Portus Adurni and tell Bors to hold his ship."

The soldier nodded and went to collect a fresh horse. Galahad looked at the rest of the group. "Leave me. In the morning, we will bury her."

They dispersed quickly and he sank down, cradling Dindrane's body, weeping quietly. *Forgive me, Father, for I have sinned. I have failed to be worthy of the Grail. It's my fault Dindrane is dead. I don't deserve Your mercy, but please, Lord, let me take the Grail to its rightful home.* He wept and prayed throughout the night. When dawn broke, he finally laid her gently on the ground. It was then he noticed something protruding from behind her swordbelt.

It was a soft leather belt, made to be worn with a tunic. He looked at it closely. Interwoven with the supple leather were strands of silken, auburn hair.

He held it in his hands until someone came for him and gently lifted him away.

~ Chapter 18—The Last Grail Keeper ~

"Lancelot!" Gwenhwyfar ran into Nimue's chambers and flung her arms around his neck. "Thank God you're safe!" *How good it feels in your arms again, feeling your strength!* "Six months is too long to be gone!"

He held her tightly then sniffed appreciatively. "I've always loved the scent of your hair."

She laughed delightedly. "Even if it's streaked with grey?"

"Like mine isn't?"

"Oh, Lancelot, in our minds, we think we're still young." She was stopped with his kiss and contentedly immersed herself in it.

He stepped back and gave her his lopsided grin. "Tonight I'll show you what an old man can do."

She reached for him again, sliding her arms around his neck and was interrupted by a polite cough from the doorway.

They both turned to find Nimue and Elen. Gwenhwyfar felt Lancelot's quick intake of breath and squeezed his shoulder comfortingly.

"Elen. How are you?" He looked at Gwenhwyfar and back to his daughter.

She caught the look and smiled, the dimple showing. "Everything is fine, Da. I've made my peace with Gwenhwyfar."

He breathed a sigh of relief. "I'm glad to hear that. Will you come with us to Camelot? I'm afraid I have no other home to offer at the moment." His voice trailed off.

Gwenhwyfar put her hand on his arm. "Let's not talk of that now. I'm just so glad you're here; we can sleep outside for all I care!"

Elen looked directly at her father. "You might as well know now. I've decided to stay on Avallach. Argante will make me her acolyte once I'm initiated."

Lancelot turned to Nimue. "She's so young. Should she not have some experience in the world before this kind of decision is made?"

Nimue rested a hand on Elen's shoulder. "The Goddess chose me when I was her age. Is it such a bad thing, Lancelot?'

"Not bad." He turned to Elen. "Do you not wish for a husband and children? I know several men whose sons would be happy for your hand in marriage."

Elen shook her head. "I've talked of this with Gwenhwyfar. I never think about boys." She held his gaze. "I don't think I could ever feel what I just saw with you."

He smiled. "That will come..."

"If it does," Nimue answered him, "she always has the right to choose; even as priestess she may celebrate Beltane and Samhain. Let her tarry with us awhile longer. I have some other news you need to hear."

Lancelot looked wary. "Do I need to sit?"

Nimue hesitated. "Mayhap. About a week ago, troops moved past here from the west. There was a battle at Camelot."

"From the west? Scotti?"

She nodded. "Yes, but they were lead by Clamadeu."

Lancelot frowned. "We have no quarrel with Beaurepaire. What reason would he have to attack?"

"Apparently, Peredur abducted his wife and son. I've not been able to find out much more."

Gwenhwyfar said softly, "I remember Galahad telling me Peredur had a lady." She turned to Nimue. "Have you not talked with anyone who was there?"

"As soon as Gryflet returned home, he locked the gates at Camelot."

"He won't even admit the Lady of the Lake?" Lancelot asked in surprise.

"He sent word no one enters or leaves until Custennin returns. I've scryed at the Sacred Pool, but the water remains still." Nimue hesitated then said softly, "I believe the Grail has left us."

"I've never known a man to be a bigger fool than Peredur. But Galahad? He went with him and took the Grail?" Lancelot was nonplussed at this last piece of information, still trying to reconcile what Galahad had done. He and Gwenhwyfar were sitting with Custennin in the small map room next to the council chamber.

"Apparently, he felt it had been defiled by Dindrane's murder," Custennin explained with a grimace. "He blamed himself and felt his penance was to take it back to Sarras. The priests, for certes, are thinking to make a pilgrimage out of it."

"You know how strictly devout Galahad has always been," Gwen said softly. "Too bad he's not more like you, Lancelot."

Custennin raised an eyebrow at Lancelot. "For what it's worth, he would have made you proud from all accounts. The bards are already creating a song about the battle and how he led it."

Lancelot felt a flicker of a smile. *At least my son didn't back down.*

Custennin continued, "However, the Grail, whatever one believes about it, was a king's property and a great political tool for me. It succeeded in uniting the warlords, something I hadn't been able to do. Gryflet managed to halt Wehha; now would've been the perfect time to treat with him." He sighed. "I have no choice now, but to ban both Galahad and Peredur to permanent exile."

"And if they return?" Lancelot asked.

"If they return," Custennin said flatly, "they will be publicly executed: Peredur for inciting a war and Galahad with theft of a royal treasure."

Gwenhwyfar gasped. "Isn't that a little harsh?"

"Yes, it is." Custennin stood and looked at Lancelot. "You know the penalty. If you wish to receive your son, you will have to do it on Benoic's soil, not Britain's."

"Are you asking me to leave?" Lancelot was also on his feet.

"Not at all." Custennin stood his ground. "You're still the best captain I have and your men are hard. I can't even afford to march to Joyous Garde with unrest both to the east and west of here."

"My own cohort will fight."

Custennin shook his head. "I have need of your men here. Wehha wasn't defeated, only halted. Without the Grail's influence, he'll move as soon as he has enough trained troops. If Clamadeu could muster that band of Scottis, you can be sure more are ready and eager for the land."

"You want us to stay at Camelot then?" Gwenhwyfar asked.

Custennin glanced at her, then to Lancelot. He replied formally, "I extend that invitation to you. You may have your choice of rooms, even the one you had as queen, since I've no use for it." He turned to Lancelot. "Arthur's room sits vacant as well; I use a room downstairs."

"That's an offer I'll decline," Lancelot answered. "I have no desire to take Arthur's room."

Custennin raised an eyebrow and glanced at Gwenhwyfar, but left the topic alone. "Choose another then. Take the day to settle in. I'll expect you at Prime on the parade grounds. We've work to do."

They chose a room at the far end of the upper hall, away from Arthur's old quarters. For most of the day, Gwenhwyfar puttered, sorting through the remains of her personal things that had been packed after Cam's Landing. Lancelot watched, with amusement at times, but then she would catch him with a glazed look and know he was thinking of Galahad.

Returning from the evening meal, they found a small fire in the brazier, warming the room with its colors of red and yellow, while the lamp by the bed glowed softly, lending a golden light to the corners. The bed had been turned down, the feather down plumped and two wine goblets stood on the small table, a wineskin beside them.

"At least Custennin shows good hospitality," Gwenhwyfar said.

Lancelot laughed and pulled her to him. "The servants remember you were their queen, Gwen. They will treat you as such."

She laid her head against his shoulder contentedly. "Do you think Custennin will object?"

"Why should he? He never married. His seneschal can never replace Cai. He should be glad to have someone take charge of the Hall."

"He doesn't much like me, you know."

"Custennin has little use for any woman, save to satisfy an urge now and then."

She snuggled a little closer, a hand maneuvering its way across his shoulders and caressing his throat. "What kind of urge are you talking about, Lancelot?" she asked in a husky voice.

"Minx," he answered. "I'll have to show you. Would you like to undress me?"

Gwenhwyfar slipped his shirt off, letting her fingers slide down his chest and his still taut belly until she reached the laces on his trews. With a smile, she pressed against him, letting her body slide down the length of his until she was on her knees before him. She tugged off his boots and he groaned as her fingers played lightly with the leather strings, undoing the trews and sliding them down.

Lancelot lay back with her on the bed and unfastened the bodice of her dinner gown and folded it back, exposing her breasts. He leaned over, his tongue encircling one nipple, teasing her. She shuddered in delight and let her hand trail to the silkiness of his nether hair.

"Why are you naked and I'm not?" she giggled girlishly.

"I'm working on it." Lancelot grinned and inched the gown down slowly, shifting himself lower so his mouth could follow the exposed, naked skin. He kissed the inside of her thigh, and she began to writhe as the velvet softness of his tongue lapped at the nectar her body offered.

"You never were able to lie still with this," Lancelot's hands slid to her hips to hold her in position.

"It's torment to lie still and you know it," Gwenhwyfar gasped.

He raised his head. "Do you want me to stop?"

She thrashed her head from side to side since she was pressed firmly to the bed. "God, no. Don't stop. Please don't stop." She groaned as he dipped his head and suckled her nub. She rode high on the crest of passion, wave after undulating wave coursing through her. Finally, she could bear no more. "Come to me, Lancelot."

He took his time, kissing his way across her stomach, letting his hands lightly roam her ribs, his mouth suckling her breast, brushing her lips lightly. He teased her with gentle probes, his hardness entering and withdrawing slowly until she was moaning in both agony and ecstasy.

Finally, when Gwenhwyfar thought she could bear no more, he gave a forceful thrust and she felt him fill her and butt against her inner wall. They moved together, in natural rhythm, suspended in time.

Later, when they lay exhausted, Lancelot's arm around Gwenhwyfar, her head resting on his shoulder, he murmured, "Galahad came so close to experiencing this. I could accept his exile if Dindrane had lived to be with him."

"At least he let his heart soften enough to know love." Gwenhwyfar raised up to look at him.

He adjusted her more comfortably across his stomach and wrapped his arms loosely about her. "Yes, I think he did that. She reminded me so much of you."

"Mayhap he will find someone else. He's still young."

Lancelot shook his head. "When a man actually gives his heart, there can be no other. Such magic doesn't happen twice."

"Don't tell me you and Arthur were both faithful to me," Gwenhwyfar said impishly. "Arthur was away too much and you were gone for years. I assume there were other women. Probably attractive ones."

He grinned lazily. "Are you prying for information?"

She slapped at him playfully. "Tell me. You're being mean."

"I'm being courtly." He grabbed her hands.

"I have no need for courtiers!" She was giggling now as he tickled her.

He gathered her close and rolled over with her. "Arthur and I deserved the reputations we had, at least, until we met you."

"Are you being courtly again?" She ran her fingers through his hair.

"I'm being truthful." He tapped the tip of her nose. "My point is Arthur and I genuinely liked pleasuring women. Galahad never trusted women to begin with. I'm afraid he'll see this tragedy as one more reason to close upon himself."

"Mayhap not. He found the Grail once he'd learned tolerance. And the Grail itself has accomplished the one thing Arthur always wanted. It has united Britain. We are once again, the Isle of the Mighty." She paused. "Galahad learned to love and in the end, he fought as you would." She took Lancelot's face in her hands. "Is he that different from you?"

Lancelot kissed the palm of one hand. "I tried to be honest and I never lied to Arthur, but always, you were between us. And we both knew we could do nothing about it. Galahad is what I was not. Pure of heart."

In the days following Dindrane's death and the long passage over the channel, past Gibraltar and through the length of the jeweled sea, Galahad sat near death, not caring whether he ate, drank, slept or bathed. Blanchefleur kept his thigh wound clean. Lohengrin finally broke through his melancholy.

"You have an important job to do when we get to Sarras."

"I do?" Galahad looked at him vacantly. "What is that?"

"You must find a resting place for the Grail."

"Your father can do that, Lohengrin. Leave me be."

The boy was stubborn and didn't move. Finally, Galahad opened his eyes. "Why are you still here?"

"Only a man pure of heart may handle the Grail," Lohengrin said, "Every child in Britain has heard the story."

Galahad sighed. "Your father is as pure a man as I know. A fool at times, but he's done no harm he could avoid. He's the one who hasn't shed innocent blood."

Lohengrin shook his head. "He had me."

"That's no sin. He loves your mother."

"When you and my father were on your quest, I heard rumors," Lohengrin persisted. "People said you didn't even look at women."

Galahad cocked an eyebrow. "I didn't know the world was interested in my private life."

"Oh, yes," Lohengrin said earnestly. "When you passed by our village, the girls were all atwitter. Clamadeu laughed about it."

"Say no more," Galahad begged. "It's no longer important."

"What I mean is you honored Dindrane; that's what my mother said."

Galahad felt as though a knife had been pushed through his stomach. He nearly groaned aloud with the pain of memory. "I did that." *Now I wish I'd been more like my father. To have loved her just one time...*

"So," the boy said triumphantly, "you did not lay with her."

Galahad gave him a penetrating look. "How is it you know so much for a three and ten-year-old?"

Lohengrin blushed. "I lost my...I became a man last summer."

Galahad stared at him. "You bedded a girl?"

His grin widened. "She was older than me." His face suddenly became serious. "My mother doesn't know. You won't tell her, will you?"

"Dear God," Galahad said, "you should be Lancelot's son, not I."

The boy looked pleased at the comparison then puzzled. Galahad grimaced. "Never mind. The fact is I loved Dindrane, I respected her and I honored her. Now go away and don't ask me about her again."

"But," Lohengrin said doggedly, "this is important. My mother told my father that because you didn't bed her..."—he stopped at Galahad's glare then finished hurriedly—"that's what makes you pure. You're the only one who'll be able to find the Grail its rightful home."

Galahad gazed after him as he scurried off. *Was there a meaning to Dindrane's death, after all? I would, for certes, have married her the next day.*

Slowly, his depression lifted as he pondered his fate.

Peredur watched Galahad waste away. He was nearly eaten alive with guilt; if he hadn't gone for Blanchefleur, Dindrane would be alive. Galahad couldn't forgive himself for letting her stand duty, but it was Peredur's fault she had to. He didn't know how to convey that to Galahad; he shared his grief, but Galahad was not speaking to him.

And yet, the truth—the horrible, awful devastating truth—was that when he looked at Blanchefleur and his son, he knew he'd do it over again.

He knelt on the deck, nearly tripping a sailor coming aft to adjust the rigging, and put his head against the rail. Even though he'd not shed blood, his sister's death was on his hands, not Galahad's. *Please, Great Mother. I'm not worthy to be a servant of the Grail any longer, but please, let Galahad feel its power once more and be healed.*

Near the end of the voyage, Blanchefleur managed to get both Peredur and Galahad together in her cabin.

"I know you both feel responsible for Dindrane's death, but it is my fault." She held up a hand as Peredur started to protest. "I should have refused to go with you. I should have honored my marriage vows regardless of how I felt. Gwenhwyfar had the strength to do it; I didn't." She touched Peredur's face and reached for Galahad's hand. "Love drives a man and it drives a woman. Is it more powerful than honor? I don't know." She sighed. "We can't undo Time." She reached under the bunk and brought the Grail forward. "I asked Lohengrin to get this from your cabin, Galahad. We can drink to Dindrane's bravery and her noble death."

She poured wine into the chalice and handed it to Galahad. "Drink. In remembrance. Dindrane would want you to be healed."

Galahad's hand shook and his eyes filled with unshed tears. He took the cup. Its warmth coursed up his arm and rolled over his body. He sipped the wine and felt it soothe his mind like a soft blanket of down on a cold, bitter night. He handed the cup to Peredur. "Here, brother."

When they'd drained the chalice, they set it down in the middle of them. It emitted a hum, the same one syllable drawing itself out for eternity, enveloping them in the warmth of unconditional love that surpasses all explanation.

Slowly, Galahad realized his work with the Grail wasn't over.

When they arrived in Sarras and requested an audience with the king, they were unpleasantly surprised. The Grail legend had originated in the Holy Land and even though Saracens as well as Jews and pagans who didn't accept the Christian faith inhabited the area, the Grail was valuable to the followers of Jesu. King Estorause was not a Christian, but he knew political clout when he saw it.

While they were eating and being entertained, the king's men had surrounded them. Since they were unarmed, they were easily taken and led to the dungeons. Peredur begged for Blanchefleur's safety.

"We are not barbarians," Estorause replied. "Your wife and son are free to leave. If she stays, there is domestic work to be had in my employ or she can join the world's oldest profession."

Peredur struggled against his captors to no avail. "Only barbarians would force a woman into sexual slavery."

The guard raised a hand to strike him, but Estorause stayed him. "She'll not be forced; some women just find that line of work easier." He shrugged. "It'll be up to her. The boy I can make use of in other ways."

Lohengrin gave them a long, terrified look as they were led away.

Estorause turned back to his prisoners and contentedly stroked the Grail. "This will make me the greatest king in the world."

"We'll find them," Galahad rubbed his wrists where the irons had held him. He blinked against the bright sunlight of the street. They'd not been outside for nearly six months.

"Why do you suppose Estorause freed us?" Peredur shielded his eyes with his hand and squinted.

"The king is dying," Galahad answered, "or so the guards say. His seer told him releasing us might save him. The Grail has brought him nothing but bad luck."

"Our luck hasn't been too good either," Peredur muttered.

Galahad glanced at him. "We're alive." *Although there was a time when I didn't want to be.*

"I don't even know where to begin looking." Peredur wiped a fine line of sweat from his forehead.

Before Galahad could respond, one of the king's personal protectors approached. He bowed low. "My lord would like to see you before you leave."

Ushered into the domed palace, the man said apologetically, "Please follow me. The king no longer leaves his bed."

They were led through cool passages, fragrant with the scent of exotic flowers that grew in the open courtyards. The attending servant rose and gestured them to the bed.

Estorause's dark skin contrasted with the whiteness of his bed linens, but his dark eyes were still sharp. The Grail stood on the bedtable.

"Take the damnable cup with you when you go," he said weakly. "It has caused me to be on my deathbed. I want nothing more to do with it."

Peredur quickly retrieved the cup and handed it to Galahad. "Where are my wife and son?"

The king groaned. "She sought shelter in one of the Christian houses. You'll not have trouble finding her."

"Which one?" Peredur leaned over the bed to hear the words, but the frail man had slipped into unconsciousness. Peredur turned to the man who'd brought them in. "Can you help me?"

The man shifted uncomfortably. "At this time of day, she'll be in the town square where she always is."

"Why?" Galahad asked. "Surely she isn't in stocks?"

"No." The guard stepped back. "Come outside."

He waited until they were alone at the palace gate and then looked carefully around. "The square is that way." He pointed and lowered his voice. "I'm a clandestine Christian. Those of us who serve the pagans must be careful not to say it."

"Why is this important?" Peredur was obviously impatient to be off.

"Because," the man continued, "your wife has rallied the Christians. Many of us have kept the fact hidden. She has preached the legend of the Grail to all who will listen. Now that the king lies near death, the people of this city will have to choose a new leader." His eyes shifted toward Galahad. "We've heard of King Arthur, for certes. She says you're the son of his closest friend, and the only man destined to serve the Grail. That even the maiden who was to be your wife sacrificed herself to your cause."

The old pain seared afresh and Galahad started to protest, but an odd look from Peredur silenced him.

"We have the numbers to elect you the next king, my lord," the servant whispered then quickly stepped back through the gate and slid the bolt home.

"Now I see why my father had no wish to be king in Benoic," Galahad said to Peredur a year later as he looked at the line of penitents lined up to plead their causes. "I don't know how Arthur endured it." He sighed. "But when the Grail was returned, I agreed to serve."

"You've been good with it. Each month," Peredur said, "they come to stand before the Grail, asking forgiveness or to be healed. Pentecost gives the common people a chance for redress, to have wrongs corrected as only a king can do. And you're a Christian king, Galahad, known to be merciful."

"The Jews and pagans don't think so," Galahad answered. "The Jews want moneychangers back in the temples, even though Jesu threw them out. The pagans want their sacrifices reinstated. I'll do neither and there are those that hate me for it."

"Some didn't care for Arthur, either," Peredur answered. "All greedy men, not caring for the good of Britain."

"Greed applies here, too. Do you know how often I turn down bribes? How often I feel threatened?"

"Are you in fear of your life? We'll double the guard." Peredur looked concerned as he surveyed the crowd.

Galahad shook his head. "I'm more in fear for my immortal soul. The bribers and politicians are wearing me down. If I give in, I'll lose myself." He looked back at the line of people and sighed. "We may as well begin."

For the rest of the day, he heard petitions, with Peredur sitting beside him. They'd just finished settling the last dispute when one more man appeared. Galahad sank back in his chair.

The man's eyes shifted right and left as he shuffled toward the dais.

He fidgeted nervously with a fringe of his tunic.

"You have nothing to fear here," Galahad said. "Have you a request?"

The man glanced furtively around, then pulled a piece of parchment from his pocket. He handed it, not to Galahad, but to Peredur.

Peredur glanced at Galahad as he opened it. A strangled sound emerged from his throat as his hand went limp, the paper floating from it.

Galahad caught it before it reached the floor. The messenger's face had paled as Galahad read the ransom note.

"What is the meaning of this?" he asked angrily. "Return Blanchefleur and Lohengrin at once and there'll be no penalty."

"I don't know where they are. I was paid to deliver that." Eyes huge, he held up a coin shakily. "See?"

Galahad signaled for the guards. "This man is a prisoner until I get answers. Give him bread and water, but nothing else." He turned to Peredur as the messenger was lead away. "The abductors won't sail away with her as they threaten. She is more valuable to them here."

Peredur's eyes were glazed. "The note says they'll be sold to Mongolian traders. They only keep women for one kind of slavery...and they...cut the boys so they never grow to be men."

"Stop." Galahad grabbed Peredur's arm. "Don't imagine the worst. I tell you, they're both still here. The note wants me to abdicate or appoint one of the pagans my chief advisor."

"You can do neither," Peredur said dully.

"I'll agree to meet at the appointed time." Galahad looked back at the note. "If I allow this advisor, I don't have to follow his opinions. Once we have your wife and son back, I'll get rid of him."

"Do you hear yourself scheming?" Peredur asked. "This past year, your reputation has been built on truth and honesty, not deception."

Galahad stared at Peredur then turned his attention to the Grail, standing on its pedestal before him. The metal looked tarnished in the light. *Strange, it had been so bright moments ago.* He sighed, knowing the Grail reflected the abandonment of his own soul.

Galahad held his steely composure while he listened to plans for yet another shrine to be erected. "Haven't you done enough?" he asked the man who'd been appointed his chief advisor.

The man, Saran, smiled, showing even, white teeth against a dark, golden skin. "Your friend wishes to have his wife and son with him, no?"

"You've been at this eight months now and we've had no word other than one letter. I think it's reasonable to expect more than that." Galahad slid the plans for the shrine across the table.

"We've already agreed our blood sacrifices won't take place in front of you, my king. That was a large compromise on our part."

Galahad bit his tongue. Arguing was useless. "When will Lady Blanchefleur and Lohengrin be returned?"

"When we have dedicated this shrine, we will comply." The infidel calculated. "A full moon rises in three nights. At—Matins, I think you call it—we'll have our service. We'll need the Grail."

Galahad glared at him. "No. I've told you before. The holy relic will not be part of your wicked ways."

Saran regarded him. "How do you know our ways are wicked? Do you not have the old earth worshippers in Britain?"

"We have the priestesses who worship the Goddess," he admitted.

"Ah, that is another thing. I'm speaking of the ways before your Druids came. When the earth demanded blood to produce."

"That has been banned since the time of the Romans."

"A part of my job, before I came to you, was to locate the old covens. You have them in Britain; I have been there."

"Impossible."

"Oh?" Saran smirked. "There was one at King Arthur's court."

"Whom?"

"Your king's sister, Morgana."

Galahad stared. "I did not know her; but I heard she was evil."

"Is, not was. She lives." Saran shrugged. "Use whatever word you like; we will need the Grail."

Galahad tossed restlessly. He must have dozed, for when he opened his eyes, the room was awash with a soft shimmer of golden light. The familiar scent of apple blossoms and tangy salt air reminded him of home and he knew, somehow, the Grail Maiden had come.

"I have failed you," Galahad whispered.

"No," the voice came back, soft and vibrant.

"I brought the Grail to the Holy Land to be reunited with the Christos," Galahad went on, "and now they will defile it."

"Never that." Her image began to appear, translucent in its filmy white dress, the golden hair swaying against her bosom.

"I should have left it in Britain. "

"Don't worry; I'll make arrangements for its safety. The cup is mine to protect." She paused, then continued softly. "The fault is not yours. Bigotry will cause fighting to continue in this region for another five and ten hundred years. I will return the Grail when a world leader emerges who can establish peace once again."

Galahad moaned in misery. "I have failed as king. Saran has taken over. I've broken faith with myself, jeopardized my own standards."

"Your life's lessons have been tolerance and humility." Her voice rang like tiny silver bells. "Have you learned them?"

"Tolerance, yes. Father taught me that...or maybe it was Dindrane's love." Galahad tried to sit up, but was held back with gentle, yet firm pressure. "Humility claims me for what I've done and allowed here in Sarras. I'm neither fit to be king nor to live."

The Grail Maiden looked at him with eyes of silver light. "You strived to remain pure in heart. You have earned the right to choose the hour of your death." She held out a preternaturally pale hand. "Would you like to come with me now to a place where everyone shares the wonder of the Grail?" She smiled. "Because Dindrane gave her life protecting the Grail, she's become one of us. She waits for you, Galahad."

He felt relief wash over him, as pure, unconditional love filled him. There was hope. Redemption. Unconditional love. A fellowship that understood the spiritual meaning of the Grail. Dindrane.

He reached out and took the hand of the Grail Maiden.

Peredur found him early the next morning, a smile on his dead face. The pedestal on which the Grail had stood was empty.

So the Grail has returned to its rightful place, after all, and you with it. He bid a silent farewell to Galahad. For a moment he wished he'd found the peace that showed on Galahad's face, but his duty wasn't done. He must find his wife and son.

As he left the room, he thought he heard the soft, harmonious chanting of voices softly rising and he wondered where the smell of apple blossoms came from. There were no apple trees in Sarras.

~ Chapter 19—Fate of Camelot ~

The elderly priest squinted as he looked at the holy sister who'd just arrived at the door of his hut beside the village church below Camelot. He'd just finished the burial rites for Clamadeu's men and was tired. Her face was ageless and with his blurred eyesight, he couldn't tell if she were young or old. The wimple and long dress concealed everything else.

"You ask to take residence here?" he asked.

Morgana nodded, her nearly black eyes cast demurely down. "Yes, Father. I'm newly returned to this country and have no convent. I'm learned in the healing arts."

The priest extended a hand in blessing and grunted at the pain in trying to move his stiff fingers. The nun looked up.

"I can prepare a tea of chamomile, rosemary, and eucalyptus that will ease the swelling," she said.

"I'd like that." He gestured to a chair. "What's your name?"

"I'm called Anna. Allow me to fix your tea before I sit." Morgana bustled about, taking in the lack of creature comforts. The priest was an austere man; his opinion would be valued and trusted at Camelot. She smiled to herself before she turned to hand him the tea.

He sipped gratefully. "We have no other sisters in the village. One who's also a healer would be of tremendous help. The medics are all gone with the armies."

"There is no old crone who practices?"

"We had such a woman; she died last year." The priest sniffed disdainfully. "There are those on the Isle of Avallach, but I do everything I can to discourage my flock from seeking the pagans."

Morgana nodded encouragingly. "It's our Christian duty to bring all to the light of the Lord."

"Ah, you understand." He peered at her again. "It'll be good to have someone of the Faith to talk to! Tell me where you've served."

"Recently, in the court of the Christian king, Childebert. Before that, I lived north of the Wall, trying to establish the Church's goodwill among the more civilized Saxons."

He looked at her admiringly. "A most godly thing to do. You'll be much blessed for such deeds. You're a devout woman who can help the village women in ways I cannot."

Morgana smiled, watching the effects of the tiny speck of woodruff she'd added to the drink. *A few more moments and he'll go into trance; I can subject his will to mine.* "Is the tea of comfort to you, Father?"

"Ah, yes," he drained the cup and flexed his hand. "I've not been able to move like this for many moons."

"Good. I'll prepare it for you daily. Of course, if I'm allowed to stay?" She folded her hands in her lap submissively.

"Certes!" The priest spread his arms expansively, the effects of the hypnotic taking hold. "The old woman's hut stands vacant just across the square. You may use it; I know the village women will seek your help. Some of them are near birthing."

"I'm skilled in childbirthing. There's much that can be done to ease the pain at such times."

The old man nodded. "I'm glad to hear it. Some of them suffer so, and I'm but a poor priest..." His voice drifted off and his eyes glazed. "The medics are all men." He sank back slowly in his chair.

Morgana sat and leaned over him. "Listen to the sound of my voice..."

The next day an old woman, ill with congestion and coughing, was the first to seek her help. Morgana mixed a tincture of goldenseal and elderflower with honey syrup. The next, a middle-aged woman with a rash was given a poultice of felonwort and mandrake root. The third required an infusion of birch and oak bark to stop the bleeding from a small cut.

And so it went. By the end of the first week the villagers accepted her; warm oatcakes and honeycomb awaited on her doorstep in the mornings, soft cheese and freshly baked barley bread arrived in the afternoons. If someone had gone hunting, cooked meat would be sent. The priest thanked God nightly for sending her.

If anyone heard strange squeaking from a corner of her room, no one mentioned it. She made certain no one was near her door when she lifted the cloth from the wire cage to feed the rats she'd brought from Gaul.

Over the next year, Anna's reputation grew. Her herbs worked on blocking the pain of childbearing as well as stopping the flow of excessive blood afterward so the village lost no women to that cause. Children had fewer fevers, the elderly less joint pain. The priest took to thanking God publicly for her each Sunday.

Morgana practiced another form of the art, also. Samhain fell shortly after she arrived and she returned to the place deep within the forest she'd discovered so many years ago. The black art rituals and ancient earth worship were still performed in secret. Through the use of her knowledge, she'd kept her skin smooth and soft and, although her hair had turned white, her black eyes and pale, ivory skin only enhanced the color. She danced naked before the fires, her body still enticing enough, under the film of illusion, to be taken and shared by the men who were without women. It was from these unknown men and casual sexual acts that Morgana drew her real power, as she always had.

Returning to her hut, dressed again as a nun, she found a young girl cowering behind a thicket of dogwood.

"Please, Sister. Help me."

Morgana bent down. "Young girls should not be out on a night like this."

"I know." The girl pulled at her torn dress, trying to cover herself. "I was late getting home; the sun had set..." She began to cry.

"Someone raped you?"

The girl snuffled. "Yes. It hurt so badly. I'm bleeding."

"Do you know who?"

The girl began crying again. "The smith's boy, Lore."

Morgana had covertly watched the smith's bare-chested, well-muscled shoulders and arms. She'd seen the boy, a strapping lad of five or six and ten, with promise to become larger than his father. He was a bully.

"Come, child. I have something to make the pain go away." She led the girl gently back to her hut and fixed an infusion of motherswort and hops. "What's your name? Won't your father be out looking for you?"

"Mary." Although she'd stopped crying, she still held her stomach. "My father's away hunting. My mother's dead. I had strict orders to be inside by sunset." She bent over, moaning a little. "What will happen to me? Will I have a child? My father will beat me for it."

Morgana added a drop of henbane and turned to Mary. "Here. Drink this. The pain will stop. And no, there'll be no child."

Mary's eyes widened. "You know that?"

"I know which herbs to use to prevent it," she said crisply. "If you have friends who find themselves in the same situation, have them see me. But it must remain our secret."

The girl was silent, the sedative effect taking hold. Morgana thought she'd fallen asleep, but then she spoke.

"I do have a friend, older than me. She has a suitor in the next village. He's asked for her hand, I mean, so I guess it's all right."

Morgana studied her. "She's lain with him and is with child?"

Mary looked at the floor. "Yes. Her parents don't know yet."

"Bring her to me." She paused. "Are there more girls with this problem?"

She shrugged. "I hear them talk and giggle of boys, but I think they're too scared to do anything."

An idea formed in the back of Morgana's mind. "As a healer, I could teach a group of girls about my art. The skill would enhance your prospects of finding husbands." A tingle started in her belly. "I could give special instruction to the girls who already have suitors." *Voyeurism is almost as good as participation; the men in the forest will be pleased with the induction of young girls...*

"You're so kind, Sister." Mary said worshipfully.

Morgana smiled. "I'll be glad to be of service."

Morgana had been tending to her rats carefully. Before Childebert had gone to Rennes, Constantinople traders had visited Paris. Filthy from the road, they'd been sent to the barracks to quarter. Shortly after they left, the soldiers who became ill suffered from numerous flea bites before taking any other symptoms. That soldiers in Childebert's army should harbor a disease was no surprise; the quarters were crowded, they bathed seldom and the stables were infected with rats and dogs, both carried fleas. Beggars who appeared daily at Childebert's gate slept in rat-infested allies by night. But when Morgana heard of the dark plague that had hit the Byzantine Empire, her heightened skills of observation led her to believe the rats spread the disease. Now, she was ready to test her theory.

"I find I must make a trip of some days," she told the old priest the morning before she left.

"Where will you be going?" he asked.

"East," she lied, "to the Saxon line. I have an old acquaintance there." *I'll go north, and reside in a convent while I find if my idea is right. When the plague comes to Camelot, I'll not be blamed.*

And so Morgana brought the Justinian Plague of the continent across the channel to Britain.

"I'm telling you," Cormant banged a fist on the table, "Wehha is amassing troops daily. Anglia is bursting at its borders."

Custennin looked mildly displeased. "I'm having enough trouble with the Scotti. You've been saying that for nearly a year now. Yet, Wehha has made no move. Mayhap, he remembers he was held back with but a part of Briton's forces."

"He'll move on Corinium first," Cormant replied, "and if Ida sweeps in behind him, we'll need every man." He glanced at Lancelot. "Since we haven't recovered Joyous Garde, Ida thinks he's invincible."

Lancelot winced. Custennin had refused to let him go north, since several cohorts had to be sent to assist Cuneglasus and Vortiporius in the west. Lupin and the rest of his men had finally been released when Ida realized there'd be no retaliation. They'd joined Bedwyr at Cameliard, but Lancelot knew they'd be ready once he could return. He sighed. "What would you have us do, Cormant? Strike first?"

He shook his head. "Get more men. Recall those in Armorica."

"They keep Childebert in check," Custennin said.

"Then, look south. Cynric holds his father's lands; if the Anglicans move through, his people will be threatened, too. This is a different breed of Saxon."

Lancelot nodded. "They're from the far north where the sun shines at midnight for part of the year. Cerdic's people came from past Gaul. Cynric's blood is also mixed."

"But will he fight with us?" Cormant asked.

"He'll not let his lands be taken. I'll ride south and talk with him." He stood, a little stiffly from too much sitting. "Since Bors has ports-of-call now past Gibraltar, mayhap someone in Portus Adurni will have news of Galahad."

Morgana returned quietly to the village below Camelot. News of the plague in the north had spread and when the townspeople learned she'd returned, many came to her in fright.

"I know nothing about it," she told them. "I've been east. Is it the same sickness that killed men in Gaul and beyond Rome?"

"Aye." One of the village hoopers stepped forward. "I was in Armorica with Custennin. We saw the same with Frankish troops. It spread even faster when we laid siege and their men were enclosed in the fort."

Morgana nodded solemnly. *Yes, when breathing becomes labored and the dying cough for air, those nearby get infected.* "I shall study this disease. Pray God, it doesn't touch us here."

When the townspeople had gone, she prepared the concoction she'd learned many years ago kept her healthy. She sipped it slowly as she walked to the corner of the room and lifted the cloth covering the cage. "My lovely rats," she crooned, "you'll be the death of Gwenhwyfar."

"Damnation!" Custennin muttered as the exhausted rider brought news that Wehha's army had taken Corinium. "Ten thousand men?"

Lancelot listened grimly. "Cormant tried to warn us."

The soldier said wearily, "Wehha appeared in battle formation two mornings ago, but he didn't show us his real numbers."

"And?" Custennin was giving orders to his captains and only half-listening, but Lancelot was intent, eyes narrowed.

"His army was small. Less than a thousand. Cormant almost laughed." The rider shook his head unbelievingly. "We rode out; once we were engaged, men sprang from everywhere."

Lancelot nodded. "Old strategy. Cerdic used it years ago to destroy Natanlaod at Nettley Marsh. Has Cormant surrendered?"

"Cormant is dead, my lord."

Custennin swung around at that. "Dead? How many more men did you lose?"

The man gulped. "More than half and most of the rest are wounded."

"By Mithras! If no one is opposing them, they'll reach Camelot by tomorrow." He looked pensive. "We're outnumbered three to one, with part of our men in Armorica and some in the west." He sighed and looked at the rider. "Better get some rest. By dawn, no doubt, you'll see battle."

The rider hesitated and Custennin paused on his way to the door. "Is there something else?"

The soldier's face blanched, he swallowed hard. "Yes, my lord. Ida is behind him."

On the third day of battle, the first of Custennin's men fell ill. A week later, the man was dead and several more had become infected.

"Plague," Lancelot said to Gwenhwyfar as they watched the funeral pyre. "Childebert's men fell to it, but we were lucky in Benoic. I thought we'd be safe here."

"What has caused it?" she asked as she thought of the swollen glands so many of the soldiers had developed.

Lancelot shrugged. "The medics seem to think it starts by some type of bite, but there seems to be a secondary form that invades the lungs."

"How do we tend the sick? They've been placed in a makeshift quarantine infirmary at the far wall of the fort."

"Their clothing's been burned. The medics take care to boil any utensils they use. They don't touch them unless they have to; they wash with lye soap."

Gwenhwyfar sighed. "It seems so little comfort, when the men cry and groan so."

Lancelot put his arm around her shoulders. "Once the delirium sets in, I don't think they feel pain any longer. It kills quickly."

She leaned against him, an arm around his waist. "Will we be safe?"

"I hope so, Gwen. I wish I could send for Nimue or Argante, but they'd never make it through the Saxon fortifications. They're camped everywhere."

"I've heard there's a healer in the village," she said. "Some of our servants have gone to her; they swear she works miracles."

"Is that the nun the old priest keeps raving about?"

"Yes. Apparently, she has no Order of her own. Shall I send for her?"

One of the captains hailed him. He kissed her forehead and stepped away. "Not yet. If we lose our medics, mayhap. I have no trust of a nun wandering alone."

The fighting continued and so did the plague. Word came that the villagers were ill as well, although for some strange reason, the disease appeared not to affect the Saxons.

"Why don't those yellow-haired devils fall?" Custennin muttered after they'd lost a second medic. "The plague will defeat us before reinforcements arrive."

"I wouldn't count on anyone arriving soon," Lancelot said. "Word of this illness has spread. No commander will want to lead his men into it."

"They're my men!" the king shouted. "They'll follow orders."

"If they can," Lancelot answered quietly. "The Scottis haven't surrendered that I heard. If Vortiporius turns toward us, he'll have the Scotti on his flank."

"Cuneglasus will come."

"He's an eye to keep on the Scotti as well, Custennin."

"Keidyaw and Bedwyr should be falling in behind Ida."

Lancelot nodded. "True. Do you think our messenger got through to the boats? Ector will send Guinglain and Ryons' men."

"I pray so," he replied, tiredly walking to the door. He turned with his hand on the latch. "Lancelot, we need Arthur. Do you think he'll come?"

Lancelot bowed his head and remained silent. Gwenhwyfar had told him the reason Arthur could not.

The small nun stood alone at the gate to Camelot, holding a large basket. "Word has reached us your medics have taken ill," she said to the guard. "I've brought herbs I've used in the village."

The man on the battlement conferred with someone and the gate swung open enough to permit her entry, then quickly locked again.

"The Saxons celebrated with too much of their mead last night." She smiled at the soldiers and brought the glamour of illusion down so she would appear younger. "Their camp will be quiet for a while."

"How is it the village hasn't been burned?" one asked as they escorted her to the infirmary.

The sister shrugged delicately. "They have use of the village services: the smith, the cooper, the baker." *My group of young girls pacifies the officers. Ida and Wehha share me. Why would they burn my village*?

At the doorway the young men backed away, clearly not wanting to get close to the sick. "These medicines I carry prevent the illness. I'll give you some." They looked skeptical as she unfolded a wax cloth in which lay blue mold. "A pinch of this will help." Still, they hesitated until she took some herself.

She spent nearly an hour with the medics, visiting the sick, passing out harmless herbals, laying a cool hand on feverish foreheads. But when she took a small cloth from her basket and wiped the spittle from a dying man, even the medics were shocked.

"Here." One of them handed her the lye soap. "Wash your hands immediately and toss the cloth into the fire."

"Such precautions are good," she said gently, "but the Lord keeps me safe. I have no fear." She dropped the soiled cloth unto the last of the herbs in the basket. "I must be going now."

Outside, she found a secluded corner where she quickly wound the cloth around the remaining herbs, making a small bouquet. This she quickly wrapped in a larger, silken scarf. As she approached the gate, she asked the young guard for a favor.

"The lady of the fort: is she not the former queen, Gwenhwyfar?"

"She is."

"I hear she is very gracious. Would she accept a gift from a humble sister?"

"Certes. Would you care to meet her?" The soldier started to hail a servant, but the nun stopped him.

"Oh, no. I wouldn't know how to speak in her presence. Just...give her this from me. Tell her the herbs will keep her well."

He promised to see to it. "God bless you, my son," Morgana said.

Lancelot sat with Gwenhwyfar in front of the hearth of the Great Hall where a low flame kindled. *This has always been one of her favorite spots in all of Camelot; she brought huge, stuffed chairs here when she first came to marry Arthur.* He handed her a cup of wine as the servant announced the arrival of the guard.

"For me?" Gwenhwyfar took the silken cloth and unwrapped it as the soldier explained.

"Why did she come?" Lancelot asked, "Did someone send for her?"

"I don't think so, my lord. She said she heard our medics were ill. She spent quite some time with them, passing out these herbs."

Gwenhwyfar unwrapped the cloth. "It's sticky," she said. "One of these herbs must have a sap."

Lancelot took the whole thing from her and laid it on the table. "You say she gave the men these to chew on?"

"Yes." The soldier looked startled. "Why?"

He shook his head. "Nothing. I'm just wary. We'll see if there are any harmful effects on the men before we touch these again, though."

Gwenhwyfar protested, "Lancelot, surely a nun would not..."

He brought her hand to his lips. "Gwen, I've been drugged too many times to trust someone I don't know and haven't seen."

"You take such good care of me." Lightly, Gwenhwyfar traced his lips with her finger.

"Hmm," he said and dismissed both the servant and the guard with a glance. "Come here, then."

Just a week later, in the early evening, Gwenhwyfar shivered and leaned forward to prod the fire. "Is it cold in here to you?"

"No," Lancelot took the poker from her and turned the log. "It's actually warm this autumn night. I'm wondering why you want a fire. Are you all right?"

"Certes. I'm just cold." She hugged herself.

Lancelot put his hand to her cheek. "Your skin is hot. You have a fever."

"I'm fine. It's just a sore throat."

"I don't know. A few days ago, you complained about a headache. Yesterday you said your knees hurt." A worried expression crossed his face.

She laughed. "Lancelot, I'm getting old."

He remained serious. "I want one of the medics to look at you."

"Silly. They have enough to do. I don't think the herbs the sister left last week did any good. The men are still sick. I'm just tired; let's go to bed."

Lancelot lay awake, holding Gwenhwyfar, not liking the way she shook. She'd break into a sweat, only to shiver and shake. By morning, his fears were confirmed.

"Her neck has swelled some," the medic said as Lancelot hovered over him in their room. The man sighed and looked up. "Plague."

"No." Lancelot paced. "How can that be? She's been nowhere near the infirmary. I've hardly let her out of the Hall; we've had no visitors..." He stopped, recalling the nun. *But we didn't see her.*

"I'm sorry." The medic rose and gathered his equipment. "A few of the men have recovered. I'll pray for her."

As he left, Custennin came to the doorway. He was silent for some time, watching Lancelot holding Gwenhwyfar to him. "She'll have to be moved. The bedclothes burned. I can have someone fix up the old chapel; it's near the infirmary. The medics can see to her there."

Lancelot turned cold, dark eyes on him. "I'm taking care of her myself. If only the Grail had not disappeared when Galahad died..."

"But it has. Lohengrin told us the story when he returned." Custennin answered then sighed when Lancelot remained quiet. "We're engaged in war, even though at the moment, Wehha has ceased fire. But I know it's not done; I need you commanding your men. The medics can care for her better than you can."

"I won't leave her. I'll see her through this." He held Gwenhwyfar tighter as she clung to him.

"I understand," Custennin said, clearly impatient, "but you must be disinfected then keep a distance."

"No, Lancelot. Don't let them..." Gwenhwyfar broke into tears, then choked, coughing. She breathed shallowly. "Please..."

"I won't let you go, Gwen. Don't worry." Lancelot stroked her back gently and glared back at Custennin. "She's my wife; I'll take care of her."

Custennin sighed again. "Your way, then. I'll see to the chapel."

"No." Gwenhwyfar looked up, her eyes bright with fever. "I want to go to the old cottage by the circle of stones."

Lancelot was startled. "Are you delirious? Why there?"

"It's where you first made love to me, Lancelot. Remember that day? We were so young."

"Certes, I remember. You're still young and beautiful."

"Now you're the one who's delirious," Gwen said weakly. "But I want to go. If I'm going to die, I want to be with you, in the place where we conceived our son, Llacheu."

"We did that in..." he stopped. "Mayhap, the stones could heal you."

Custennin stared at him. "That place is four miles from here and unprotected. Do you propose to ask the Saxons' permission to go there?"

Lancelot narrowed his eyes. "I might. Ida is camped past the village. I will treat with him; if Gwenhwyfar and I can use the cottage, unharmed, when she is well, I'll be his hostage."

"That's desertion, Lancelot!"

"The circle of stones may heal her. I must go." He kissed Gwenhwyfar and laid her back against the pillows, bringing the covers up. "I'll be back. Tonight, we'll be at the cottage. One way or another."

"You're going to let Lancelot have safe passage?" Morgana was incredulous.

"Safe passage into the heart of our army." Ida grinned. "Gwenhwyfar has the plague; how long do you think she'll last? Lancelot seems immune to it; he'll make a fine hostage. I'll be able to have free claim to Joyous Garde. Custennin will have to agree to it."

Morgana sniffed. "Are you winning this war or is he?"

Ida looked hurt. "Camelot cannot be taken in a month or two. We can outlast them. Especially since we don't have to worry about reinforcements from Armorica."

"You're sure?"

"Two messengers tried to slip through. Both are dead." He smiled again. "We'll wait."

Lancelot got Gwenhwyfar settled on the bed and sank in the chair beside it, exhausted. He felt a tightness in his chest and rubbed his aching arms. *I grow old, too, if I can't carry Gwen.* He got up and bolted the door, although there was no need. Two of Ida's men were posted outside.

In the morning, angry red lesions had appeared on Gwenhwyfar's body. Lancelot knew they'd turn dark in two or three days and give the black-bluish cast to the skin. He prayed as he strained to carry Gwen up the small hill to the circle of stones. *Please, Mother, Goddess of us all, let her get well; I'll send her to the Isle when I'm hostage. Make her yours. Please, let her live.*

He placed her on the pad of blankets on the altar stone and knelt, spending most of the morning in prayer. Ida's guards watched him from outside the circle, superstitiously not wanting to enter. They'd eventually lost interest and were now engaged in a game of dice.

By the time Lancelot staggered back with her, he was running a fever, too, although he hoped it was from exertion.

"Here." He lifted a spoon of warm porridge the cooks had sent for her. "You must eat."

Dutifully, she opened her mouth and swallowed a few mouthfuls painfully. "Your hand shakes."

"I'm tired." Lancelot answered. "Treating with Ida was not pleasant."

He continued to feed her until she pushed his hand away. "Why don't we get some rest?"

When she awoke later that afternoon, Gwenhwyfar said she felt well enough to walk outside, but when she opened the door, she saw the guards and turned to Lancelot. "We're hostage here?"

"I am. As soon as you're recovered, you'll go to Avallach."

"I'm not leaving you. If Ida holds you hostage, he holds me." She itched at one of the lesions. "Will these go away? I must look awful."

Lancelot smiled wanly. "I told you once, you'd be beautiful when the crone's shadow is on you. We haven't reached that point yet." He grimaced as he stretched his arms, then shivered.

Gwenhwyfar grasped his hand, terrified. "Lancelot...are you sick?" She felt his face. "You're fevered. Dear God, we both have the plague!"

They'd been at the cottage five days. Two nights before, when Ida had sent food, the guards had cautiously pushed it inside the door, seen their condition and fled. No one bothered to send another guard.

"Arthur. Can you forgive me?" In her delirium, Gwenhwyfar grabbed his hand.

"You're forgiven." He made no attempt to identify himself. She wouldn't understand and he was too weak to try.

We're dying. He prayed she'd be first, so she wouldn't have to witness his death, but then she wouldn't know...he shook his head. *My mind is going*. Lancelot drifted in and out of consciousness. *Gwenhwyfar, in the doorway in a yellow gown, the first time he'd seen her...the ride back to Camelot, already in love with her, knowing she'd be Arthur's wife. Their first kiss on the battlement the night of Arthur's Kingmaking. The first time she'd told him she loved him, standing in front of the hearth of the Great Hall. The treacherous betrayal by Elaine, followed the next day with Gwenhwyfar, right here in this cottage...their son, miscarried. The afternoon at Cynric's hidden place: how she'd loved the mirror above the bed...then, much later, the plot of Medraut that had nearly cost her life followed by the trial and rescue. And yes! The two glorious years at Joyous Garde before Arthur reclaimed her. And these last five years...*

"Lancelot."

He opened his eyes slowly, seeing a glistening essence hovering in the air. The Queen of Faerie danced in the mist above him. "Are you ready?"

"What...why are you here?" His voice was barely a whisper.

"To take you home, for certes!" Morgan le Fey giggled. "You are fey, you know. You belong to us."

"Us?" *I must be totally mad.* Then the antlered head of Cernunnos appeared behind her, his bronze hands encircling her waist. Lancelot blinked. "You, too?"

The hazel eyes were luminous. "You're being given a choice. Soon Rhiannon will escort your soul to the Otherworld where you can re-enter the pattern of reincarnation, or you can come with us and live in the land of Faerie."

"Time can stand still, Lancelot. You'll be young forever." Morgan twirled in the air. "How old do you think I am?"

"Not now." Cernunnos' voice was sharp as he stopped her. "We don't have much time. Gwenhwyfar will be dead in minutes."

Lancelot pressed his head with his hands. *Am I dreaming this or am I already dead?* "Gwenhwyfar can come with me?"

The demi-god smiled and his eyes glittered. "For certes, we want both of you."

Lancelot struggled to sit. Gwenhwyfar was so still, he thought it might already be too late. Gently, he shook her and called her name.

She opened her eyes and he saw the last seconds of lucidity that sometimes occurs on the battlefield just before a wounded soldier takes his last breath. "Lancelot."

"Do you want to live with me forever?"

She looked puzzled. "I'm dying. I love you." Her eyes started to glaze as the death rattle began.

Lancelot leaned to kiss her. "I love you, Gwen. We'll be together. My life, my wife. For eternity."

"Yes, Lancelot. Together. My love. My soul." Gwenhwyfar released her last breath and lay limp in his arms.

He gathered her spirit to him and as they floated free of their bodies, he heard the horses gallop up and a woman screamed. From an increasingly hazy mist, he saw the door fly open and a Saxon with a heavy mace crushed the side of his mortal skull, but he felt nothing.

They were in the land of Faerie, the skies blue, the sun warm. Birds sang joyfully in the trees and the scent of meadow flowers filled the air. Elfins, mannikins, faeries, and even the gnomes were waiting to greet them. The unicorn bobbed his head shyly from inside the tree line.

Lancelot took Gwenhwyfar's hand, young and smooth again. She reached up to brush back his hair, dark with no silver streaks.

"For eternity," he said as their lips met in a timeless kiss.

Cynric's forces had harried Wehha's army for nearly a week. The unexpected rout from the south had driven Wehha back to Anglia. Caewlin had pushed Ida's men north, just as Bedwyr's army, with Lupin and the remnants of Joyous Garde, met up with him. Peace once more reigned at Camelot.

They'd just finished fending off a group of deserting marauders and Cynric sat his horse now, on the road near the circle of stones. He looked up at the blue menhirs, glistening silver in the sun. It was a place he'd never visited. Today, something seemed to draw him to it.

He tethered his horse in the copse of hazel trees and walked up the hill. The wind rustled the leaves softly and water from the nearby Cam gurgled contentedly as it flowed past the stones. Birds had begun their songs again. He took a deep breath. *Strange, only hours ago, they'd fought near here.*

He noticed the clothing first. A nun's black habit and white wimple. Turning away from the circle, he made his way down and saw a foot protruding from a small thicket of gorse.

Drawing his sword, he advanced carefully. Morgana lay on the other side, legs splayed, deep cuts across both naked breasts. Then he took a sharp breath when he saw what had been done. Only the hilt of a sword remained showing through the bloody mess between her thighs. *Medraut always said you liked pain, Morgana; did you push too far?*

He left her there and walked to the cottage. The door was ajar and again, he held the sword in front of him and entered.

The light was dim and, at first, he didn't recognize the pair on the bed. Blood from the man's head wound covered both of them. They lay intertwined, arms wrapped around each other.

Lancelot and Gwenhwyfar. They'd persevered: through her marriage to a king, his marriage of entrapment. They'd endured charges of treason, been branded traitors, accused of breaking the Fellowship of the Round Table council, blamed for the years when the land didn't prosper.

Yet, their bond had held strong. *Somehow, I don't think Arthur will mind how it ended.*

Cynric walked up the hill and entered the circle of stones to pray for the future of Britain.

~ *Epilogue* ~

The elderly man still carried himself well. He'd been a soldier once. He raked his hand through wispy strands of white hair and took a deep breath. Somewhat painfully, for there was stiffness in his arm now, he pulled the sword from the scabbard. As always, it felt light and balanced in his hand. He held it high and waited.

The smell of the salt marsh and apple blossoms filled his nostrils. Memories flowed through his mind. Would she come?

By the time he heard the coracle scrape against the sand, his arm trembled. His grey eyes watched unwaveringly as she stepped ashore.

"You're still beautiful," Arthur said. He didn't know how much the effort of the illusion had drained Nimue.

She inclined her head and demurred. "And you're still handsome, my lord king."

He shook his head. "King, no longer."

"King forever," she replied. "Astrala told me to expect you."

"Astrala?"

"The Grail Maiden," Nimue answered. "A handmaiden of the Goddess from beyond Time."

"Ah, yes. She came to me once in a vision with the Grail, long ago. Do you remember my telling you?"

Nimue nodded. "Astrala brought the Grail to Gwenhwyfar and kept her from killing herself. She used it to convince Lancelot of the need to forgive. She's not only protector of the Grail, but guardian of the Blood Royal, as well."

"The end of the bloodline, you mean," Arthur said sadly. "Galahad is dead. The Grail will not return to an earthly realm again."

Nimue inclined her head slightly. "But you forget, Arthur. His sister, Elen, still lives. She, too, carries the blood of both lines."

Arthur raised an eyebrow. "She will be the next keeper?"

"Astrala didn't say. The Grail will return when needed; if not in Elen's lifetime, mayhap in her child's lineage."

"Child? What child? She is a priestess here, is she not?"

Nimue looked amused. "Yes, but even priestesses can celebrate Beltane. Elen turned eigh and ten last year and she had to make her choice of which aspect of the Goddess to follow: Maiden, Mother, or Crone. She chose Mother. Now she has a daughter."

Arthur shook his head, still surprised. "Who was the father then? If only Lancelot were still alive!"

"He would approve," Nimue said softly, "for the father is Lohengrin. The Blood Royal runs through the babe's veins from both parents." Nimue laid her hand on Arthur's arm. "Speaking of Lancelot... Come, I will show you what you came to see."

They walked in silence to the Christian graveyard at Ynys Gutrin. Nimue pointed to the site. "I didn't think she'd want to buried on Avallach and I knew he'd want a pagan passing." A mischievous look crossed her face. "So, while Gwenhwyfar is in Christian ground, she sleeps in the sacred hallow of oak, facing south as is our custom."

"Lancelot lies with her?"

"Yes."

"Why is the grave yet unmarked, after all this time?" Arthur knelt and ran his fingers across the hard, packed dirt.

"They had the plague, Arthur. Had anyone but Cynric found them, they would've been burned. Not something Gwenhwyfar would've wanted, I think."

Arthur nodded and rose slowly. "Cynric brought them here?"

"Yes. His men had been chasing marauders near the stone circle. He found Morgana first."

"Morgana? What was she doing there?"

Nimue shrugged. "No one knows. Come to spy, I suppose, since they were under Ida's protection and she was his consort."

He raised an eyebrow. "Wasn't she a little old to be using that trick?"

"She kept herself young with magic and illusion, but now she's finally dead. It's over."

"Did Lancelot kill her?"

She shook her head. "Cynric didn't think so. Lancelot's skull had been bashed in and Morgana had been raped. Brutally."

Arthur was silent a moment. "What did Cynric do with her?"

"He left her there for Ida to find."

He sighed. "Had Morgana not hated me so much and taught Medraut to hate, things might have been different. So many lives lost at Cam's Landing..."

Nimue touched his arm. "Bedwyr still lives; the last man of your Round Table fellowship. He came shortly after this happened."

"I may visit him before I return."

"Why must you go?"

Arthur smiled and took her hand. "I have created a life for myself as Armel. Judwal listens to my counsel; Childebert keeps the treaty as long as I'm there. He looked down at the unmarked grave. "My life at Camelot and with Gwenhwyfar was over years ago. I loved her, but she was never meant to be mine."

"Yet, she helped the land prosper," Nimue said quietly.

"She was a queen. She did her duty." He grew thoughtful. "Mayhap, it would be best if the world thought it was I who lay here with her. Her honor would remain intact and not be tarnished."

"But you live, Arthur. What will become of you?"

"I will be free to become Armel." He hesitated but a second. "Do it, Nimue. Have a leaden cross made, one that will withstand the centuries. Inscribe the words, "Here lies King Arthur with his queen, Gwenhwyfar."

People will know then that I accepted her, that she was a rightful queen, and not the cause of the destruction of the Fellowship of the Round Table."

"Morgana destroyed the Round Table with her charges of treason against Gwenhwyfar and Lancelot. You were the only one who understood their love was predestined."

"Myrddin knew," Arthur said. "He warned me she'd be the fate of Camelot if I married her. We had a big argument over it."

"It was your moira to marry her, as it was hers to bond to Lancelot." Nimue added, "Just as it has been mine to love you."

Hope sprang into Arthur's eyes. "Is there a chance for us? Would you be willing to return with me? To Léon?"

"I've tried that. The Old Ways are no longer welcomed there."

"But you'd come with me as my wife." Arthur grinned suddenly. "Would that be so difficult?"

"For certes, not!" Nimue laughed through the tears that glistened on her cheeks. "But I cannot stop being who I am."

Arthur studied her face then unbuckled the protected scabbard that held Excalibur. He knelt before her and held the sword out. "Then, as Lady of the Lake, I return to you what was once given. As Armel, I'll no longer have need of it."

She stared at him. "You think you can change that much?"

He looked at her solemnly. "It's a turn in the road, another path. Let Argante be the Lady. Come with me, Nimue."

Gently, she took the weapon from him. "Excalibur will remain on Avallach until it is needed again." She let her hand stroke the scabbard. "If you can change this much, then so can I. Go and visit Bedwyr. When you return, I'll be ready."

He drew her to him for an extended kiss. When he stepped back, he was grinning again. "I'd better get going then, the sooner I can be back."

She answered with a smile and they walked back to his horse. He mounted, a little more slowly but still with the skill of a warrior. He leaned down to caress her face. "Together, Nimue. For the years we have left. I'll finally be happy before I fade from this earth and from history."

Nimue kissed his hand. "That you will never do."

He raised an eyebrow. "A new age is coming; we won't be able to keep the Saxons at bay forever. But we had Camelot. For a fleeting, glorious moment in Time, we had peace."

Nimue's eyes glazed and she turned inward. Watching her, Arthur heard the Goddess speak.

"Though the Darkness comes, Camelot will live on. No matter how many myths about you and Gwenhwyfar and Lancelot are embellished in the future, an element of truth will ring true. Throughout the ages, you will become a legend. Arthur, King of Britain, shall never be forgotten."

The End and the Beginning

Author's Afterword

From the time I was a small child envisioning a beautiful princess riding a splendid horse on her way to meet a king, through teaching Mallory, Tennyson and T.H. White to high school sophomores, and finally to doing serious research on the non-fictional aspect of the Matter of Britain, I have always loved the Arthurian Legends. Did the main characters actually exist?

LANCELOT:

In researching the Arthurian legends, controversy has arisen over whether or not Lancelot really existed. Some scholars say that the French, namely Crétien de Troyes in *Prose Lancelot*, invented him.

Dr. Norma Lorre Goodrich, in her book *King Arthur*, offers another explanation. Geoffrey of Monmouth mentions a King Anguselus of Albania, who was equal in status to Arthur and attended his coronation. As Dr. Goodrich explains, the name "Anguselus" was Latin and when Crétien translated it into Old French, it lost its middle syllable and the consonant group "gu" dropped out, leaving the word "An+sel+o" ("o" or "ot" being the masculine ending of the name in French). This gives us the name "Anselot" or, as Crétien referred to him, "the Anselot." She believes the "L" came from a copying error with the use of the article "l" in front of the word Anselot, thus becoming Lancelot.

Another interesting theory regarding Lancelot's existence comes from P.F.J. Turner in his work, *The Real King Arthur: A History of Post Roman Britain*, Volume II.

He speculates that "Lancelot" is derived from "lancea," the Latin word for lance and that the Roman soldier who carried a lance would be called a "lancearius" or in today's English be termed "the Lancer." According to Mr. Turner, the Lancer was a member of the family of Dubnovalus Lothicus (King Lot of Bernicia). Mordred also was a member of this family and his mother was Anna (Arthur's sister). Mr. Turner concludes that the noble knight known as Lancelot was really none other than Mordred, the man we've come to think of as villain. This theory is strengthened by the fact that in some annuls of history Gwenhwyfar is depicted as having willingly plotted with Mordred to seek the throne.

Equally intriguing is a concept advanced by Knight Templar Laurence Gardner in *Bloodline of the Holy Grail*. Lancelot del Arcs was the son of the Britanny king, Ban of Benoic with his consort, Viviane II del Arcs of Burgundian Avallon. Her younger sister was Ygerna, mother of Arthur. Lancelot's grandfather was King Lancelot I and his great-grandfather, the bard Taliesin. It is through his maternal great-grandmother, Viviane I, that his lineage may be traced through the Sicambrian Franks and the Fisher Kings to Josephes, son of Jesus and Mary the Magdalen.

Mr. Chris Barber and Mr. David Pykitt, in their book, *Journey to Avalon*, cite Lancelot to be based on the person of Llwch Wyddel, also known as Lllwch Llawinawg, Lord of the Lakes. He was slain by Arthur in Ireland shortly before Arthur joined in the battle of Camlann.

GWENHWYFAR:

Dr. Norma Lorre Goodrich, in *Guinevere*, depicts Gwenhwyfar as a Pictish queen, born in Stirling, Scotland, whose function was to serve as both judge and priestess. As such, she would remain virginal and Lancelot would serve as both her acolyte and her champion, protecting her from the following taboos: A high-priestess must shed no blood; must not touch base metals; the parts of her body which were anointed at her coronation may not be touched; and her hair must not be cut.

Mr. P.F.J. Turner also places Gwenhwyfar near Scotland at Carlisle. Her father was a Roman Magister Militum for Arthur and the marriage of a very young Gwenhwyfar to a much older Arthur was arranged for political reasons.

Mr. Gardner mentions Gwen de Bretagne (of Brittany) whose father was Leo de Grance. She married Arthur, but bore him no children.

Mr. Barber and Mr. Pykitt believe Gwenhwyfar's father to have been a French count named Gwythyr, whose principality of Léon, Brittany, Gwenhwyfar inherits.

Perhaps the most provocative theory of all comes from Ms. Laurel Phelan, a past-life regression therapist, who claims in *Guinevere* to have been Gwenhwyfar in another incarnation. She, too, places Gwenhwyfar's birth in Scotland, in Northumbria. However, as the book ends, she visits Glastonbury and feels that Gwenhwyfar does lie buried there, which supports the hypothesis below.

ARTHUR:

Dr. Goodrich investigated Arthur's military career, including the twelve battles that end with Badon Hill and the halt of Saxon advances for twenty years. She places his major fort/home at Carlisle, which is in keeping with the whereabouts of Gwenhwyfar and Lancelot. After 542 AD nothing is heard about Arthur, so she theorizes that this is when he died, after the battle of Camlann.

Mr. Turner gives an explanation as to Arthur's title and rank, particularly regarding the term, "Uther Pendragon" who was not Arthur's father at all. The term "Uthr" meant "terrible" (as in awe-inspiring) and "Pen" meant chief. The Dragon standard was a common one for Roman war leaders. Mr. Turner states that Arthur began his career as a young military officer under the leadership of Cadwy, who was in charge of the large fort called Cadwy's Bury (Cadbury). As Arthur gained experience, he rode with Aurelius, the *Regissimus Britanniarum*, and helped defeat the Saxons. He was appointed to the highest officer rank of *Magister Militum* which was the Roman equivalent of "Uthr Pendragon." Eventually, he became the Imperator Britanniarum.

Mr. Gardner establishes Arthur as the Scottish son of King Aedàn mac Gabràn of Dalraida. Arthur's bloodline also follows the Grail family, descending from Joseph of Arimathea's daughter Anna and her husband, Brân the Blessed. Joseph of Arimathea was the blood brother of Jesus of Nazareth according to Mr. Gardner.

However, Mr. Barber and Mr. Pykitt make a valid claim that King Arthur did recover from Camlann, but due either to age or injuries, retired to Brittany where he chose to serve God for the rest of his life. He became known to the Bretons as St. Armel. Even today, the feast of St. Armel is celebrated on August 16 and a statue of him can be seen inside the church of *St. Armel-des-Boschaux* in the district called *Ille et Vilaine.*

The character of Arthur in *Fate of Camelot* is purely fictional and in no manner represents the life of the saint. However, I believe a real King Arthur did exist...and mayhap, he was St. Armel.

In 1191, in an old burial ground south of the Lady Chapel, the monks of Glastonbury Abbey unearthed a dug out oak coffin containing the remains of two skeletons. The one was of a tall man whose skull bore marks of a severe blow; the other was the lighter bones of a woman.

A leaden cross was found on top of the grave. The Latin inscription HIC JACET SEPULTUS INCLITUS REX ARTHURIUS CUM WENNEVERIA UXORE SUA SECUNA IN INSULA AVALLONIA translates as, "Here lies buried the renowned King Arthur with Guinevere, his second wife, in the Isle of Avalon." (Barber, Pykitt)

Was it really Arthur who was buried there? Or could it have been Lancelot?

About the Author

An avid reader of anything medieval, Cynthia Breeding has taught the traditional Arthurian legends to high school sophomores for fifteen years. She owns more than three hundred books, fictional and non-fictional, on the subject. More information on Arthur, Gwenhwyfar and Lancelot is available on her website, listed below.

She lives on the bay in Corpus Christi, Texas, with her Bichon Frise, Nicki, and enjoys sailing and horseback riding on the beach.

Readers can reach her snail-mail at: 3636 S. Alameda, B-116, Corpus Christi, Texas 78411 or on her website: www.cynthiabreeding.com.

Now Available:

Historicals:

Dawn Thompson
Rape of the Soul
Cindy Breeding
Fate of Camelot
Ashley Kath-Bilsky
The Sense of Honor
Isabel Mere
Almost Taken
Isabel Mere
Almost Guilty
Leanne Burroughs
Highland Wishes
Leanne Burroughs
Her Highland Rogue
Chris Holmes
Blood on the Tartan
Jean Harrington
The Barefoot Queen
Brynn Chapman
Bride of Blackbeard
Diane Davis White
Moon of the Falling Leaves
Molly Zenk
Chasing Byron
Katherine Deauxville
The Crystal Heart
Cynthia Owens
In Sunshine or In Shadow
Jannine Corti Petska
Rebel Heart
Phyllis Campbell
Pretend I'm Yours

Non-Fiction/ Writer's Resource:
Rebecca Andrews
The Millennium Phrase Book

Mystery/Comedic:
Katherine Deauxville
Southern Fried Trouble

Action/Suspense:
Eric Fullilove
The Zero Day Event

Romantic Suspense:
Candace Gold
A Heated Romance

Fate of Camelot

Jo Webnar
Saving Tampa

Contemporary: *Jean Adams*
Beats a Wild Heart

Young Adult: *R.R. Smythe*
Into the Woods
Anne Kimberly
Dark Well of Decision

Anthologies: *Deborah MacGillivray*
Cat O'Nine Tales
MacGillivray/Andrews/Chai/
Farr/Frank/White
Love on a Harley
Archer/Bell/Bowen/Gold/
Howell/Ivey/Roland
No Law Against Love 2
Young/Ivey/Chai
Brides of the West
Jacquie Rogers
Faery Special Romances
Holiday Romance Anthology
Christmas Wishes
Holiday Romance Anthology
Holiday in the Heart
Romance Anthology
No Law Against Love
Romance Anthology
Blue Moon Magic
Romance Anthology
Blue Moon Enchantment
Romance Anthology
Recipe for Love
MacGillivray/Burroughs/
Blizzard/Bowen/Peters
Love Under the Mistletoe
MacGillivray/Burroughs/Andrews/
Bell/Hatton/Howell/Mere
Romance Upon A Midnight Clear

Upcoming

Children's Illustrated: *Lance Martin*
The Little Hermit
John Nieman & Karen Laurence
The Amazing Rabbitini

Cynthia Breeding

Young Adult: *Amber Dawn Bell*
Cave of Terror –
Chronicles of a Vampire Gymnast
Contemporary: *Jacquie Rogers*
Down Home Ever Lovin' Mule Blues
Action/Suspense: *Chris Holmes*
The Mosquito Tapes
Romantic Suspense: *Ann Merritt*
A Cry From the Cold
Historicals: *Linda Bilodeau*
The Wineseekers
Judith Leigh
When the Vow Breaks
Freddie Currie
The Changing Wind
Sandra Cox
The Sundial
Anne Holman
The Master of Strathgian
Jeanmarie Hamilton
Seduction
Jean Adams
Eternal Hearts
Jennifer Linforth
Madrigal
Judith Leigh
Joshua's Faith
Judith Leigh
A Father's Hope
Jean Harrington
In the Lion's Mouth
Cynthia Breeding
Prelude to Camelot
Isabel Mere
Almost Silenced
Dawn Thompson
Counterfeit Lady
Dawn Thompson
Renegade Rider
Dawn Thompson
Drake's Lair
Dawn Thompson
Odin's Daughter
Dawn Thompson
Children of the Wind

Fate of Camelot

Katherine Deauxville
Enraptured
Katherine Deauxville
Eyes of Love
Anthologies: *Breeding/Bowen/Hatton/Howell/*
Ivey/Nutt/Scott
Second Time Around
Breeding/Ahlers/Bowen/Hatton
Dance of Manners
Romance Anthology
The Way to a Man's Heart
Burroughs/Blizzard/Howell/Van Arsdall
The Miracle of Love
Inspirational Romance Anthology
Faith, Hope and Love
Burroughs/Bell/Blizzard/Howell/Leigh
Flames of Gold
Holiday Romance Anthology
Love and Silver Bells
Burroughs/Andrews/Bell
A Pirate's Treasure
MacGillivray/Breeding/
Wildes/MacGillivray/Breeding/
Young/Burroughs
Castle of Dreams
Burroughs/Bowen/Houseman
Dance en L'Aire
WW II Romance Anthology
Love and Glory
Judith Leigh/Cheryl Norman
Romance on Route 66
Young/Ivey/Chai
Grooms of the West
MacGillivray/Breeding/Rogers
Love On A Dead Man's Chest
Romantic Suspense Anthology
Masquerade
Romance Anthology
Love Divided
Romance Anthology
Mardi Gras Fever
Romantic Suspense Anthology
Foreboding Senses
Paranormal Romance Anthology
After the Sun Goes Down

Cynthia Breeding

Flynn/MacGillivray/Breeding/Rogers
Romancing the Dragon

Cleora Comer
Just DeEtta
Don Brookes
With Silence and Tears
Katherine Shaw
Love Thy Neighbor
Kemberlee Shortland
A Piece of My Heart

Check our website frequently for future releases.

www.highlandpress.org

Praise for Highland Press Books!

THE CRYSTAL HEART by Katherine Deauxville brims with ribald humor and authentic historical detail. Enjoy!

~ Virginia Henley, NY Times bestselling author

* * *

THE SENSE OF HONOR - Ashley Kath-Bilsky has written an historical romance of the highest caliber. This reviewer was fesseled to the pages, fell in love with the hero and was cheering for the heroine all the way through. The plot is exciting and moves along at a good pace. The characters are multi-dimensional and the secondary characters bring life to the story. Sexual tension rages through this story and Ms. Kath-Bilsky gives her readers a breath-taking romance. The love scenes are sensual and very romantic. This reviewer was very pleased with how the author handled all the secrets. Sometimes it can be very frustrating for the reader when secrets keep tearing the main characters apart, but in this case, those secrets seem to bring them more together and both characters reacted very maturely when the secrets finally came to light. This reviewer is hoping that this very talented author will have another book out very soon.

~ Valerie, Love Romances

* * *

HIGHLAND WISHES by Leanne Burroughs. This reviewer found that this book was a wonderful story set in a time when tension was high between England and Scotland. The storyline is a fast-paced tale with much detail to specific areas of history. The reader can feel this author's love for Scotland and its many wonderful heroes.

This reviewer was easily captivated by the story and was enthralled by it until the end. The reader will laugh and cry as you read this wonderful story. The reader feels all the pain, torment and disillusionment felt by both main characters, but also the joy and love they felt. Ms. Burroughs has crafted a well-researched story that gives a glimpse into Scotland during a time when there was upheaval and war for independence. This reviewer is anxiously awaiting her next novel in this series and commends her for a wonderful job done.

~Dawn Roberto, Love Romances

* * *

I adore this Scottish historical romance! ***BLOOD ON THE TARTAN*** by Chris Holmes has more history than some historical romances—but never dry history in this book! Readers will find themselves completely immersed in the scene, the history and the characters. Chris Holmes creates a multi-dimensional theme of justice in his depiction of all the nuances and forces at work from the laird down to the land tenants. This intricate historical detail emanates from the story itself, heightening the suspense and the reader's understanding of the history in a vivid manner as if it were current and present. The extra historical detail just makes their life stories more memorable and lasting because the emotions were grounded in events. The ending is quite special and bridges links with Catherine's mother's story as well as opening up this romance to an expansive view of Scottish history and ancestry. ***Blood On The Tartan*** is a must read for romance and historical fiction lovers of Scottish heritage.

~Merri, Merrimon Reviews

* * *

I can't say enough good things about Ms. Zenk's writing. ***CHASING BYRON*** by Molly Zenk is a page turner of a book not only because of the engaging characters but also by the lovely prose. In fact, I read the entire thing in one day. Reading this book was a jolly fun time all through the eyes of Miss Woodhouse, yet also one that touches the heart. It was an experience I would definitely repeat. I'm almost jealous of Ms. Zenk. She must have had a glorious time penning this story. As this is her debut novel, I hope we will be delighted with more stories from this talented author in the future.

~Orange Blossom, Long and Short Reviews

***

MOON OF THE FALLING LEAVES is an incredible read. The characters are not only believable but the blending in of how Swift Eagle shows Jessica and her children the acts of survival is remarkably done. The months of travel indeed shows hardships each much endure. Diane Davis White pens a poignant tale that really grabbed this reader. She tells a descriptive story of discipline, trust and love in a time where hatred and prejudice abounded among many. This rich tale offers vivid imagery of the beautiful scenery and landscape, and brings in the tribal customs of each person, as Jessica and Swift Eagle search their heart.

Fate of Camelot

~Cherokee, Reviewer for Coffee Time Romance

***

Jean Harrington's ***THE BAREFOOT QUEEN*** is a superb historical with a lushly painted setting. I adored Grace for her courage and the cleverness with which she sets out to make Owen see her love for him. The bond between Grace and Owen is tenderly portrayed and their love had me rooting for them right up until the last page. Ms. Harrington's ***The Barefoot Queen*** is a treasure in the historical romance genre you'll want to read for yourself! Five Star Pick of the Week!!!

~ Crave More Romance

* * *

IN SUNSHINE OR IN SHADOW by Cynthia Owens - If you adore the stormy heroes of 'Wuthering Heights' and 'Jane Eyre' (and who doesn't?) you'll be entranced by Owens' passionate story of Ireland after the Great Famine, and David Burke - a man from America with a hidden past and a secret name. Only one woman, the fiery, luscious Siobhan, can unlock the bonds that imprison him. Highly recommended for those who love classic romance and an action-packed story.

~ Best Selling Author, Maggie Davis,
AKA Katherine Deauxville

* * *

ALMOST TAKEN by Isabel Mere is a very passionate historical romance that takes the reader on an exciting adventure. The compelling characters of Deran Morissey, the Earl of Atherton, and Ava Fychon, a young woman from Wales, find themselves drawn together as they search for her missing siblings.

Readers will watch in interest as they fall in love and overcome obstacles. They will thrill in the passion and hope that they find happiness together. This is a very sensual romance that wins the heart of the readers.

This is a creative and fast moving storyline that will enthrall readers. The character's personalities will fascinate readers and win their concern. Ava, who is highly spirited and stubborn, will win the respect of the readers for her courage and determination. Deran, who is rumored in the beginning to be an ice king, not caring about anyone, will prove how wrong people's perceptions can be. ***Almost Taken*** by Isabel Mere is an emotionally moving historical romance that I highly recommend to the readers.

~ Anita, The Romance Studio

* * *

Leanne Burroughs easily will captivate the reader with intricate details, a mystery that ensnares the reader and characters that will touch their hearts. By the end of the first chapter, this reviewer was enthralled with ***HER HIGHLAND ROGUE*** and was rooting for Duncan and Catherine to admit their love. Laughter, tears and love shine through this wonderful novel. This reviewer was amazed at Ms. Burroughs' depth and perception in this storyline. Her wonderful way with words plays itself through each page like a lyrical note and will captivate the reader till the very end. The only drawback was this reviewer wanted to know more of the secondary characters and the back story of other characters. All in all, read ***Her Highland Rogue*** and be transported to a time that is full of mystery and promise of a future. This reviewer is highly recommending this book for those who enjoy an engrossing Scottish tale full of humor, love and laughter.

~Dawn Roberto, Love Romances

* * *

PRETEND I'M YOURS by Phyllis Campbell is an exceptional masterpiece. This lovely story is so rich in detail and personalities that it just leaps out and grabs hold of the reader. From the moment I started reading about Mercedes and Katherine, I was spellbound. Ms. Campbell carries the reader into a mirage of mystery with deceit, betrayal of the worst kind, and a passionate love revolving around the sisters, that makes this a whirlwind page-turner. Mercedes and William are astonishing characters that ignite the pages and allows the reader to experience all their deepening sensations. There were moments I could share in with their breathtaking romance, almost feeling the butterflies of love they emitted. This extraordinary read had me mesmerized with its ambiance, its characters and its remarkable twists and turns, making it one recommended read in my book.

~ Linda L., Fallen Angel Reviews

* * *

REBEL HEART by Jannine Corti Petska - Ms. Petska does an excellent job of all aspects of sharing this book with us. Ms. Petska used a myriad of emotions to tell this story and the reader (me) quickly becomes entranced in the ways Courtney's stubborn attitude works to her advantage in surviving this disastrous beginning to her new life. Ms. Petska's writings demand attention; she draws the reader to quickly become involved in this passionate story. This is a wonderful rendition of a different type which is a welcome addition to the historical romance genre. I believe that you will enjoy this story; I know I did!

~ Brenda Talley, The Romance Studio

***

SOUTHERN FRIED TROUBLE - Katherine Deauxville is at the top of her form with mayhem, sizzle and murder.

~ Nan Ryan, NY Times bestselling author

* * *

INTO THE WOODS by R.R. Smythe - This Young Adult Fantasy will send chills down your spine. I, as the reader, followed Callum and witnessed everything he and his friends went through as they attempted to decipher the messages. At the same time, I watched Callum's mother, Ellsbeth, as she walked through the Netherwood. Each time Callum deciphered one of the four messages, some villagers awakened. Through the eyes of Ellsbeth, I saw the other sleepers wander, make mistakes, and be released from the Netherwood, leaving Ellsbeth alone. There is one thread left dangling, but do not fret. This IS a stand alone book. But that thread gives me hope that another book about the Netherwoods may someday come to pass. Excellent reading for any age of fantasy fans!

~ Detra Fitch, Huntress Reviews

* * *

CAT O'NINE TALES by Deborah MacGillivray. Enchanting tales from the most wicked, award-winning author today. Spellbinding! A treat for all.

~ Detra Fitch, The Huntress Reviews

* * *

BRIDES OF THE WEST by Michèle Ann Young, Kimberly Ivey, and Billie Warren Chai - All three of the stories in this wonderful anthology are based on women who gambled their future in blindly accepting complete strangers for husbands. It was a different era when a woman must have a husband to survive and all three of these phenomenal authors wrote exceptional stories featuring fascinating and gutsy heroines and the men who loved them. For an engrossing read with splendid original stories I highly encourage reader's to pick up a copy of this marvelous anthology.

~ Marilyn Rondeau, Reviewers International Organization

* * *

FAERY SPECIAL ROMANCES **- Brilliantly magical!** Ms. Rogers' special brand of humor and imagination will have you believing in faeries from page one. Absolutely enchanting!

~ Dawn Thompson, Award Winning Author

* * *

Christmas is a magical time and twelve talented authors answer the question of what happens when ***CHRISTMAS WISHES*** come true in this incredible anthology.

Christmas Wishes shows just how phenomenal a themed anthology can be. Each of these highly skilled authors brings a slightly different perspective to the Christmas theme to create a book that is sure to leave readers satisfied. What a joy to read such splendid stories! This reviewer looks forward to more anthologies by Highland Press as the quality is simply astonishing.

~ Debbie, CK2S Kwips and Kritiques

* * *

RECIPE FOR LOVE - I don't think the reader will find a better compilation of mouth watering short romantic love stories than in ***Recipe for Love***! This is a highly recommended volume–perfect for beaches, doctor's offices, or anywhere you've a few minutes to read.

~ Marilyn Rondeau, Reviewers International Organization

* * *

HOLIDAY IN THE HEART - Twelve stories that would put even Scrooge into the Christmas spirit. It does not matter what *type* of romance genre you prefer. This book has a little bit of everything. The stories are set in the U.S.A. and Europe. Some take place in the past, some in the present, and one story takes place in both! I strongly suggest that you put on something comfortable, brew up something hot (tea, coffee or cocoa will do), light up a fire, settle down somewhere quiet and begin reading this anthology.

~ Detra Fitch, Huntress Reviews

* * *

BLUE MOON MAGIC is an enchanting collection of short stories. Each author wrote with the same theme in mind, but each story has its own uniqueness. You should have no problem finding a tale to suit your mood. ***Blue Moon Magic*** offers historicals, contemporaries, time travel, paranormal, and futuristic narratives to tempt your heart.

Legend says that if you wish with all your heart upon the rare blue moon, your wishes were sure to come true. Each of the heroines discovers this magical fact. True love is out there if you just believe in it. In some of the stories, love happens in the most unusual ways. Angels may help, ancient spells may be broken, anything can happen. Even vampires will find their perfect mate with the power of the blue moon. Not every heroine believes they are wishing for love, some are just looking for answers to their problems or nagging questions. Fate seems to think the solution is finding the one who makes their heart sing.

Blue Moon Magic is a perfect read for late at night or even during your commute to work. The short yet sweet stories are a wonderful way to spend a few minutes. If you do not have the time to finish a full-length novel, but hate stopping in the middle of a loving tale, I highly recommend grabbing this book.

~ Kim Swiderski, Writers Unlimited Reviewer

* * *

Legend has it that a blue moon is enchanted. What happens when fifteen talented authors utilize this theme to create enthralling stories of love?

BLUE MOON ENCHANTMENT is a wonderful, themed anthology filled with phenomenal stories by fifteen extraordinarily talented authors. Readers will find a wide variety of time periods and styles showcased in this superb anthology. ***Blue Moon Enchantment*** is sure to offer a little bit of something for everyone!

~ Debbie, CK²S Kwips and Kritiques

* * *

NO LAW AGAINST LOVE - If you have ever found yourself rolling your eyes at some of the more stupid laws, then you are going to adore this novel. Over twenty-five stories fill up this anthology, each one dealing with at least one stupid or outdated law. Let me give you an example: In Florida, USA, there is a law that states 'If an elephant is left tied to a parking meter, the parking fee has to be paid just as it would for a vehicle.' In Great Britain, 'A license is required to keep a lunatic.' Yes, you read those correctly. No matter how many times you go back and reread them, the words will remain the same. Those two laws are still legal. The tales vary in time and place. Some take place in the present, in the past, in the USA, in England...in other words, there is something for everyone! Best yet, profits from the sales of this novel will go to breast cancer prevention.

A stellar anthology that had me laughing, sighing in pleasure, believing in magic, and left me begging for more! Will there be a second anthology someday? I sure hope so! This is one novel that will go directly to my 'Keeper' shelf, to be read over and over again. Very highly recommended!

~ Detra Fitch, Huntress Reviews

***

LOVE UNDER THE MISTLETOE is a fun anthology that infuses the beauty of the season with fun characters and unforgettable situations. This is one of those books that you can read year round and still derive great pleasure from each of the charming stories. A wonderful compilation of holiday stories. Perfect year round!

~ Chrissy Dionne, Romance Junkies

Cover by: Cheryl Alldredge

CPSIA information can be obtained at www.ICGtesting.com
Printed in the USA
BVOW040641200612

293191BV00001B/270/P

9 780981 557380